The Secret Cove in Croatia

Julie Caplin

A division of HarperCollins Publishers
www.harpercollins.co.uk

Harper*Impulse* an imprint of
HarperCollins*Publishers*
The News Building
1 London Bridge Street
London SE1 9GF

www.harpercollins.co.uk

This paperback edition 2019

First published in Great Britain in ebook format
by HarperCollins*Publishers* 2019

Copyright © Julie Caplin 2019

Julie Caplin asserts the moral right to
be identified as the author of this work

A catalogue record for this book
is available from the British Library

ISBN: 9780008323691

This novel is entirely a work of fiction.
The names, characters and incidents portrayed in it are
the work of the author's imagination. Any resemblance to
actual persons, living or dead, events or localities is
entirely coincidental.

Typeset in Minion by Palimpsest Book Production Ltd,
Falkirk, Stirlingshire

Printed and bound in Great Britain by
CPI Group (UK) Ltd, Croydon CR0 4YY

MIX
Paper from
responsible sources
FSC   FSC C007454
www.fsc.org

All rights reserved. No part of this publication may be
reproduced, stored in a retrieval system, or transmitted,
in any form or by any means, electronic, mechanical,
photocopying, recording or otherwise, without the prior
permission of the publishers.

For Gordana Sikora-Presecki who introduced
me to Croatia

... and sharing inspiring pictures when we
should have been working!

Chapter 1

Northumberland

Nick huddled into the collar of his coat, grateful for the thick tweed barrier protecting him from the brisk northerly wind that whipped around the lee of the craggy hillside. A wry smile touched his mouth at the sight of the two models shivering together like highly strung Arabian fillies.

Today the models were dressed in vibrant — Pucci style, he'd been informed, whatever that was — wool ponchos. Although, if anyone had asked his opinion, he'd have said it looked as if someone had run amok in a paint shop, but he was no fashion expert. The outfits were topped with dashing tam-o'-shanter hats, perched jauntily on their heads while striped woollen scarves, wrapped several times around their elegant long necks, flapped in the breeze like Himalayan prayer flags. The poor frozen models were as out of place as a pair of tropical birds as they waited for the photographer to line up the next shot.

1

Normally, at seven-thirty in the morning, he'd have the bleak moorland to himself, and if it hadn't been for the quelling looks his sisters-in-law had shot his twin brothers, Dan and Jonathon, over dinner last night, there might have been a few more people up here.

'Tara, stand on that rock in the shaft of sunshine,' directed the brusque photographer whose facial expression was well hidden behind dark bushy eyebrows and a fearsome, glossy black beard of biblical proportions, a stark contrast to his bald head.

Nick had to give her credit; the minute Tara moved into the unforgiving eye of the lens, she stopped shivering and threw a cool indifferent pose as if the freezing temperature was nothing. Her thin, haughty face stared out over the view, dispassionate and seemingly oblivious to the valley unfolding before her, the rich green grass softening the contours of the hillside and the sunshine dancing on the distant sea at the mouth of the valley five miles in the distance. Something twisted in his stomach at the sight of her standing on the outcrop of rocks, with one knee bent, a delicate, almost fey figure, with her flawless complexion and mane of golden hair burnished with red and gold threads picked out by the spring sunshine. She looked as if she might slip away into another realm at any moment. Then he told himself off for allowing the little kick of something to affect him and the odd desire to want to protect her from the cold. Compared to her, he was a steady, reliable carthorse hitched to unremitting destiny while she was like a delicate faerie creature, as unattainable and remote as the stars. She came from another world. A world a million miles away from this remote farm and the village community where he knew everyone and everyone knew him and had done since he was born. This was home. Always had been, always would be. His mouth twisted. Besides, if he weren't here, what else could he do? This was all he'd ever known or was likely to know.

'Nick, can you get one of the sheep into the foreground?' called a peremptory voice, waving a finger indicating where the animal was required.

'Sure,' he said, whistling to his border collie, Rex, not bothering to correct the photographer's assistant. He'd tried to explain several times yesterday but no one was interested in the difference between the sheep – actually ewes – and the lambs. They wanted the cute, photo-friendly lambs, which were now six weeks old and more photogenic than the just about to be sheared sheep, which looked scraggy and unkempt with their mud-encrusted, shaggy fleeces.

Since British Wool had approached him to photograph their brochure on Hadley land, offering to pay for his time, this job had proved one of the most . . . entertaining was probably the best word. Who knew that taking a few photographs was actually a full-scale production? Two vans had arrived two days ago, filled with several rails of clothes and enough photographic kit and caboodle to take pictures of the entire population of Bowden Rigg. These had been followed by three taxis from Carlisle station conveying a full entourage of four models, two stylists, two wardrobe ladies, the photographer, his assistant, a creative director, a PA and two clients from British Wool.

Rex rounded up one of the lambs, which skipped into shot baaing furiously, making the model smile winsomely. 'Oh, isn't he so cute?'

'He'd be a damn sight cuter if he stood still,' grumbled the photographer, peering through his lens.

Following a quick whistle and a few subtle commands, Rex nudged the skittish lamb back into place. Nick, impressed by her patience, watched as Tara tilted her head this way and that, angling her body to show off the garments. To his surprise, she turned her sleepy almond eyes his way, a sultry smile lifting the corners of her mouth as she stared rather blatantly at his.

'Yes, Tara. Yes, that look. Lovely. Lovely. Just tilt your head to the right, keep looking at Nick. Yeah, that's it. You want him bad. I'm loving it.'

A wicked glint lit the model's eyes and Nick felt himself blush to the very roots of his blond hair and a heated flush raced up his body. With a swallow, he resisted the urge to duck his head. Instead, he met her slightly mocking gaze with a quick lift of one eyebrow and some heat of his own. Country born and bred didn't mean that he was clueless. Nick Hadley, to his mother's despair, had yet to find the right woman, but that didn't mean he hadn't played the field.

Tara smirked in retaliation and then, in accordance with the photographer's next slew of commands, put her hands on her hips and threw her head back, once again distant and unattainable. Nick suddenly felt like a third wheel; he had a ton of stuff that he should be doing this morning instead of hanging around like . . . like a grubby schoolboy.

The photographer called out to Tara, 'OK, you're done for the moment.'

As Nick walked forward to chase the lamb back to the rest of the flock, Tara stepped forward to the edge of the rock. 'Catch me,' she said and launched herself into the air.

Surprised, Nick took a step forward and caught her easily in his arms. She weighed nothing and she crowed delightedly at his catch, as if he'd done something amazing, making him feel like every superhero rolled into one. Gently, he set her down on the ground, disentangling himself from her poncho and scarf. He gave her a smile. 'There you go, safe and sound.'

'You're all man,' she breathed and he almost wanted to laugh; it was such a clichéd line, but the knowing, suggestive look in her eyes stalled him.

'Last time I looked,' he said with easy confidence. Now it was her turn to blush. 'You're staying at The George Inn, in the village, I believe.'

She nodded. 'Quaint, but I've stayed in worse on location.'

'Dinner?' asked Nick.

5

'Are you asking me, or telling me?' Tara replied, her eyes coy, with a gentle smirk playing around her mouth.

'There's a very good restaurant at the local manor house. I could pick you up at seven-thirty.'

'Make it eight and you have a date,' returned Tara, with the air of someone who was used to having her own way.

Damn, it was after six. It had taken longer than he'd planned to finish today. Unfortunately, farming waited for no man and he'd had to catch up with those jobs that going out on the photoshoot had forced him to neglect.

The warm glow of the farmhouse kitchen, filled with the scent of sausages and Yorkshire pudding coming from the Aga, along with the comforting sound of chatter and laughter, embraced him – a hug of familiarity and simple pleasure. The huge pine table in the centre of the room was being laid by Gail, married to his eldest twin brother, Dan, and she looked up to give him a quick warm smile. He liked both of his sisters-in-law, although had yet to fathom how on earth either of the twins, Dan and Jonathon, had persuaded them that they would make suitable husbands. But then he'd grown up with them.

'Hey, Nick,' called Dan from where he stood in front of the dresser, rummaging through the assorted phone chargers and cables. 'Long day.'

He nodded.

At thirty-three, like his twin brothers and their wives, he still ate in his mother's kitchen, partly through sheer laziness but also because the warm, busy kitchen had been so much part of his life for so long. However, much as he loved them all, he was thankful for his own small cottage on the edge of the farm which afforded the necessary privacy for a bachelor, especially one whose mother was keen for him to settle down.

'Hey, Mum –' he turned to her '– I'm sorry. I've only just finished work but I'm going out tonight.'

'Excellent,' said Jonathon, eyeing up the toad-in-the-hole she was in the process of removing from the Aga. 'More sausages for me.'

'Are you sure you don't have time for a quick bite to eat? I'm literally serving up now. You can eat and run.' She grinned at him. 'I don't mind.'

'Or he could sod off down the pub and leave the sausages for us,' said Jonathon, dancing past his mother and pinching a piece of crisp Yorkshire pudding.

She gave his knuckles a sharp rap.

'Yeah, I vote for more sausages,' agreed Dan, backing up his twin. 'You can sod off to the pub.'

'There's plenty,' said Lynda Hadley, shaking her head with a tut. 'Honestly, boys, you'd think you'd been starved all your life. It'll take me two minutes to serve up and your father should be here any second.'

Bugger. He'd really hoped to make his excuses and make a quick getaway.

'No, seriously, Mum. I haven't got time. I haven't even washed up yet.'

Julie Caplin

'But when will you eat? You've been up since silly o'clock and I bet you only had sandwiches for lunch.'

'I'm eating out,' he said, edging towards the door.

Just then his father came in, tossing his car keys on the dresser on the side, scooping his wife up for a quick kiss. 'Evening. I've just been in the village. I hear you're eating at Bodenbroke Manor this evening, Nick.' He raised his eyebrows with a knowing twinkle in his eyes.

Nick held back the groan. *Thanks, Dad. Drop me in it, why don't you?*

'Bodenbroke Manor,' piped up Jonathon, settling against the back door, his arms folded and a mischievous smile playing on his face. 'Now that's fancy. A date, is it? Who's the lucky girl this week?' He frowned. 'I thought you'd finished with that posh, horsey bird.'

'Her name is Henrietta,' said Nick with a frown. 'And I'm not seeing her any more.'

'Didn't last long,' observed Gail with a sly smile.

Nick shrugged, edging ever closer to the door, hoping that Jonathon would move sooner rather than later. 'It was mutual.'

'When did you fix this up?' asked Dan, joining in the conversation, having found a charger to fit his phone and plugged it in. His face creased in sudden interest.

'Today,' said Nick. 'Look, if the inquisition can lay off, I need to shower and change.'

He was so close to the door and he actually had his hand on the doorknob when Dan suddenly crowed, 'It's

8

one of those London photo women, isn't it? You've been up on Starbridge Fell all day. You sly devil. You asked one of them out.'

Jonathon laughed and stepped back to block the door. 'What? And they said yes?'

Nick froze. 'Why shouldn't they?' he asked, regretting the sudden stiffness in his voice.

'Punching above your weight, aren't you?' teased Dan. 'Which one is it? One of the wardrobe ladies? The blonde one. What's her name . . . Georgina?'

Nick shook his head.

'What, the darker one?'

'Neither of them,' he said, trying to keep his expression pleasant.

'Well, who then?' asked Jonathon, screwing his face up in perplexed confusion. 'The stylist woman is married and so is the PA and Creative Director.'

'Bloody hell, you didn't pull a model, did you?' gasped Dan, pretending to reel back, bumping into a chair, which screeched across the tiled floor in protest.

Gail and Cath shook their heads in mutual mock despair at Dan's theatrics and then Gail said, with a naughty grin, 'And why not? Let's face it, he's the best-looking one out of all of you.'

Dan clutched his chest. 'I'm hurt, dear wife. I thought I was.'

'You're the best-looking of my husbands,' she teased, winking at Nick, who was grateful for the brief diversion in conversation. Sadly, Jonathon wasn't about to let it go.

'Seriously? Which one?'

Nick sighed, knowing if he were going to get out of here in time to wash and change, capitulation was the only solution. 'I'm going out with Tara. We got chatting. We fancied dinner together. For God's sake, it's not as if I'm going to ask her to bloody marry me or anything. She'll be gone by the end of the week. And I'll still be here.' His voice rose. Realising that he'd made a bit of a tit of himself, he grasped the door handle and yanked it open, leaving behind a collective gasp and a telling silence.

'Gosh, this place is really rather nice,' said Tara, taking in the expensive wallpaper, which reputedly cost over two hundred pounds a roll, the stylish furniture and the retro designed lighting. 'We could almost be in London,' she added in a conspiratorial whisper behind one hand.

Nick lifted his wine glass and took a sip. 'We're not all heathens up here, you know.'

'I think I can see that,' said Tara, giving his body a rather blatant once-over.

From the minute he'd picked her up from the George, she'd been flirtatious and forthright, which was a huge relief. If he were honest, as he was driving to collect her he'd had a sudden last-minute panic. What on earth was he going to talk to her about all evening?

He needn't have worried; as he'd helped hoist her tiny

frame into his truck, she'd murmured, 'Oh, this is very masculine,' as she'd settled herself into the seat. 'I don't think I know anyone who drives a truck,' she'd said, drifting her hands across the dashboard as he'd started the engine up. Within a few miles one hand had drifted to his thigh and he drove the rest of the way trying not to wriggle like an overexcited teenager.

She wore a floaty chiffon pantsuit thing with tiny straps that dipped so low it made it obvious she wasn't wearing a bra. Her legs in skyscraper heels, so high you surely needed a health and safety certificate to walk in them, looked endless and made his heart bump uncomfortably in his chest. She was the most gorgeous woman he'd ever laid eyes on. Her glorious hair was bundled in a big messy updo of some sort, with lots of tendrils curling around the white alabaster column of her throat.

For God's sake, get a grip, man – she's a flesh and blood woman, not a flaming Greek statue.

'How long have you been modelling?' he asked, forcing himself to make sensible conversation instead of staring at her like a lovesick puppy.

'For ten years.' She pulled a self-deprecating face. 'I'm old.'

'Don't be ridiculous.' He laughed. 'What, you're twenty-six, twenty-seven?'

'Twenty-seven,' she whispered, looking around the room, 'but don't tell anyone. That's quite old in this business. Although I'm ready to move on now. Do something a bit more meaningful, you know? I'd like to be an ambassador for something worthwhile. You know, saving the planet. Eradicating plastic. Something like that.'

'Sounds noble,' he teased.

For a moment her nostrils flared and he saw the tendons in her neck tense.

'I'm serious. I feel very passionate about some of the issues facing our planet. The amount of plastic in the sea is a terrible thing. It's a big issue. Animals are dying.' She fixed him with a rather intense stare.

'Sorry, I didn't mean to belittle your ambition. I was teasing. I'm used to brotherly banter.'

She dipped her head with gracious acquiescence. 'We have to save our planet.'

'You're right,' he concurred, realising that this was a big deal to her. 'Although I tend to get worked up about issues closer to home, I guess.' He gave a self-deprecating smile. 'Bit selfish, really. We're already seeing the effects of climate change on the seasons.' Last year's hot dry summer had had a major impact on the grasslands where the sheep grazed. 'So what will you do?'

She shrugged. 'I'll be an ambassador. You know, do photoshoots highlighting the issues. Be the face of a campaign. I'm just waiting for the right offer.'

Nick nodded, feeling a little out of his depth. He had no idea how these things worked. They lapsed into silence for a minute, until the waiter came to take their order.

'I'll have the medallion of beef,' said Tara before adding, to Nick's surprise, 'and can I have chips with it?'

'We do *pommes frites*,' said the waiter in a slightly stuffy accent, which made Nick want to laugh. They played five-a-side together on Thursdays and he was light years from stuffy.

'Perfect,' said Tara.

Nick grinned as soon as the waiter departed, taking his own order for confit of duck and seasonal vegetables. 'And there you've blown the preconception that models never eat anything but salad and carrot sticks.'

Tara tossed her hair over her shoulder. 'I have a fabulous metabolism. I can eat what I like.' She almost sounded defiant.

Nick smiled. 'That's good to hear as the food here is excellent.'

Tara nodded and picked at the tines of her fork, before rearranging her cutlery several times.

'So, do you have any brothers or sisters?' Nick asked to fill the silence.

She shook her head, pulling her mouth into a sad little moue. 'Just little old me. Mummy and Daddy had me very late in life. Poor Mummy nearly died, so Daddy put his foot down and said no more children. Mummy said that I was such a beautiful child, she was glad she couldn't have any more children because she couldn't bear risking having another child in case they were a disappointment.' Tara gave a tinkling laugh and tilted her head on one side, looking up at him. 'Isn't that the sweetest thing? Of course, utter nonsense. All parents think their babies are perfect.'

13

Nick laughed. 'You should speak to my mother. She doesn't have any illusions about her children, but then she had five of us.'

'Five! Good lord.' Tara's eyes widened dramatically and she put her hand on her stomach. 'Gosh. That's a lot. Your poor mother. That must have wrecked her figure.'

Nick's mother would have laughed her head off at that comment; she adored all of her children. He was sure she wouldn't have given it a second thought. 'I'm not sure she sees it like that.'

'Are they all as good-looking as you?' Tara slapped her hand over her mouth, as if the compliment had slipped out by accident. She lowered her eyes to the table.

Nick laughed, thinking of the conversation between his brother and sister-in-law as he'd left. 'I'm one of four brothers and one sister. I think we all agree that our little sister is the best-looking.'

'Oh,' said Tara, as if this was a very strange thing to say.

'So what do you do when you're not sheep farming?' she asked.

'It's not exactly a nine-to-five job,' said Nick, 'but when I can, I like to get away from the farm. My sister lives in Paris—'

'Oh, I adore Paris. I was there for the Paris Fashion Shows. I did a catwalk show for Dior this year. It's such a super city. When were you last there?'

They talked Paris, with Nick dredging up everything he

could possibly remember of his two visits there, until dinner arrived.

Tara certainly had a healthy appetite and scoffed down her food as if she were starving.

'You were hungry,' he said, looking at her clean plate as he finished the last of his food.

'I was in the fresh air all day,' snapped Tara, again sounding defensive.

'I had no idea modelling was such hard work,' said Nick. Clearly she wasn't used to the sort of banter he enjoyed with his family. He ought to remember she wasn't from a big family like his.

'It's not for everyone. I don't think people realise how hard it is. They just think we turn up and have our photos taken.'

The waiter appeared and took away their plates before returning with the dessert menu. 'Would you like anything else?' he asked.

'I shouldn't,' said Tara, perusing the menu, her tongue poking out rather adorably between her lips. 'Are you going to have anything?'

'I've not really got a sweet tooth.'

Her face fell.

'But we could share something, perhaps?' he suggested.

'Yes, the profiteroles. I adore them.'

Nick ordered dessert with two spoons, although he needn't have bothered because, although the dish was placed in front of him, as quick as a snake, Tara's hand would strike and snatch a spoonful of choux pastry and cream. She made regular moans of delight with each mouthful.

'I haven't had chocolate in ages. I'd forgotten how delicious it is. Such a sensual pleasure, don't you think?' She dipped her spoon in the last of the chocolate sauce and slowly licked the back of it with long slow strokes, all the while her eyes intent on Nick. She let out a breathy sigh. 'That silky richness on your tongue.' She ran her tongue up and down the handle of the spoon, her eyes dark and sultry with the sort of promise that had Nick shifting in his seat, very relieved that the tablecloth was covering things up.

When the waiter came to clear away the dessert dish, Nick was ready to decline coffee and take Tara straight back to the George. Given the suggestive signals she'd been sending him, he thought they were on the same page, but she rose from her seat, tossing her napkin on the table.

'Darling, could you order me an espresso? I just need to go to the ladies. Sort myself out.'

'OK,' he said, ordering himself a cappuccino and settling back in his seat, feeling his heated skin start to cool. He pulled out his phone, quickly checking his Facebook feed, smiling as he saw a post from his sister, Nina.

Chocolate Heaven was the caption underneath a picture of a perfect chocolate éclair and her fingers and thumbs just beyond it, shaped in a love heart.

God, how much would Tara enjoy one of those and what sort of state would he be in, watching her eat it?

Looks delish, sis, he posted quickly, scrolling through more of her pictures. Since going to Paris to run a patisserie and moving in with her boyfriend, Sebastian, who happened to be Nick's best friend, Nina had become the queen of éclairs and all things sugar. Perhaps he could take Tara there one day. He had a sneaking suspicion she might rather like it.

He commented on a few pictures, liked a few others and then realised a full fifteen minutes had elapsed. Where was Tara? Please don't say she'd done a runner. No, surely not. Despite his pre-date qualms, it had gone pretty well. She certainly seemed interested. Without being big-headed about it, he got on with women. Most dates he went on turned out well, more than well sometimes, although there had been the one time he'd been on a blind date with one of Gail's friends, who turned out to be best friends with one of his exes. That had been rather excruciating.

Just as he was seriously considering sending a search party up to the ladies, Tara reappeared, her eyes glittery and her face all smiles as she slipped back into her seat and took a sip of espresso as if there was nothing wrong.

Perhaps she'd had some female issue and she was too embarrassed to say anything.

'Ugh, this espresso is cold,' she said, pulling a face.

'Would you like me to get another?' said Nick equably,

not wanting to make her feel self-conscious by saying that she had been rather a long time.

'No, it's OK. It's quite late now and it will probably keep me awake.' She looked at her watch and then gave him a beautiful, sorrowful smile. 'You need to drop me back at the hotel. I'm afraid I need my beauty sleep. I can't turn up tomorrow with bags under my eyes.'

'Let me get the bill,' said Nick, wondering at what point the evening had suddenly petered out.

Chapter 2

London

Maddie gripped her knees together, her hands clasped over the kneecaps to stop them shaking, as Henry Compton-Barnes, complete with suede patches on the elbows of his jacket and a dicky bow, stared down at her work. It seemed to take forever before he finally looked up and spoke.

'Professor Gregory is a good friend of mine and you've come highly recommended. I shall therefore be completely honest with you.' His mouth pulled into a regretful line as if someone were tugging at strings attached to each end of his lips. 'Technically, you are very good. These are well executed. The detail, in fact, is brilliant.'

Despite the words, she knew there was a giant-sized 'but' headed her way.

'What I'm looking for in a painting . . . for this gallery . . .' He shook his head. 'These have no originality. No flair. They're missing that *je ne sais quoi*, the indefinable,

19

that makes a piece of art stand out. What I'm looking for is something that only the artist can conceive. When you look at their work, you know that only they could have painted it. I liken it to a singer, someone like, forgive me, I'm considerably older than you, but someone like Carly Simon, for example. You hear her voice and you know immediately it's her. Her voice, like a signature, is unique and that's what I'm looking for in a painting.

'These, I'm afraid, are good, very good, but I don't see your soul or any investment from you as an individual.

'Can I give you some advice, Maddie? Go somewhere new and different. Forget everything you've ever been taught or thought you knew – break the rules – experiment but, most of all, paint from the heart.'

Paint from the heart. Maddie rolled her eyes, picturing a Salvador Dali image of a red heart skewered by a giant paintbrush on a desert plain, with scarlet drops dripping from the brush onto the pale yellow sand. Paint from the heart. What the hell did that mean? Had anyone told Picasso to paint from the heart? Rodin? Van Gogh? Maddie winced. Not that she was anywhere close to emulating anyone in that league.

Sitting in Costa, she sipped at her coffee, regretting the impulse to drown her sorrows with a ridiculously expensive cappuccino.

'Dear God,' drawled an upper-class voice as someone

20

sat down behind her. 'What a chav. What was Henry thinking?'

'What? That girl that's just been in? I thought she was in fancy dress. You know, Toulouse-Lautrec.'

Maddie clutched the felt beret on her lap under the table.

'He was doing a friend a favour. He told me when he put the appointment in the diary.'

'Did he take her on? Surely not. God, the gallery would be going downhill fast.'

'Don't think so. By the look of her when she left, I think he sent her out with a flea in her ear. I could have told him when she turned up he was wasting his time. I mean, seriously, did you hear the way she spoke?'

The other girl let out a peal of laughter. 'Common as muck.'

'Shh, you can't say things like that now. It's not PC. I'm not sure you're even allowed to say chav any more.'

Both girls laughed with malicious superiority as Maddie flushed, feeling the heat in her cheeks. She probably looked like an overripe Christmas elf. Picking up her beret, she crammed it firmly onto her head and turned around. One of the girls looked up and at least had the grace to start, her mouth opening in a gasp.

'Thing about chavs,' said Maddie conversationally, 'is that they have no class, speak their minds and don't take crap from supercilious, stuck-up bitches like you two. Not all of us were born into money and, quite frankly, if that's how you talk about people, you need to go back to school and learn some manners. You should be ashamed of yourselves.'

Pleased with the way both girls sat there gawping like a pair of guppies, she sailed out of the coffee bar with her head held high.

Unfortunately, having the last word didn't change the fact that she had failed at her one and only shot at actually getting through the doors of a gallery in London and used up her only useful contact.

Maddie glared up at the departures board at Euston. Another two hours before her cheap fare train departed. Back to Birmingham and another conversation with her mum about another failed job interview. Maddie hadn't actually told anyone, apart from Professor Gregory, what she was really doing in London.

Sighing, she scrolled through her WhatsApp feed.

Urgent. Urgent. Urgent. Do you still need a job? It's temporary but it's in Europe and they're desperate. Call me. Nx

The message from her friend, Nina, made her smile. They'd met in Paris while Maddie was on her year of study abroad and, with so much in common, had quickly become firm friends. Both came from big families and, like Nina, Maddie was one of five, and while they missed being part of a community, they didn't necessarily miss the demands of their families.

The key word in the brief message was Europe. A siren call. Maddie longed to get as far away from home as possible. Since her time in France last year, she just didn't feel like she fitted in any more.

'OK, what's the deal?' she asked as Nina picked up the phone on the first ring. 'Where in Europe? And what? Grape-picking?'

'Something much classier.' Nina's voice bristled with that *ta-da* excitement. 'It's Croatia.'

'Did you just sneeze?'

'Very funny. No, seriously. Nick phoned Sebastian half an hour ago. He's going on this amazing holiday with his new girlfriend; a bunch of them are chartering a yacht . . . but the girl that was going to work on board as a hostess dropped out yesterday and they go in three days' time. All you have to do is a bit of cleaning and cooking. Basically looking after the guests. And there are only six of them.'

'I'm your girl,' said Maddie without hesitation, despite the fact that she'd never been on a boat in her life, unless you counted the pedalo in Tenerife that time. Thanks to a bit of tuition from Nina's chef boyfriend, Sebastian, she'd learned a lot in six months. Her cooking skills had come on loads, for someone whose repertoire once consisted of nothing more than shepherd's pie and Lancashire hotpot. Besides, didn't everyone on holiday live on salads and ice cream?

Nina squealed. 'Brilliant. You need to phone this Croatian guy. I'll WhatsApp his number. Oh, you're going to have such a great time. Two and a half weeks in Croatia! I'm quite jealous.'

Maddie squealed back. 'That's so cool. Thanks so much, Nina. And I can't wait to meet your brother. I feel like I know him already.'

Chapter 3

Croatia

'Whoa.' Maddie dropped her duffel bag on the quayside. Everyone who'd told her to expect conditions to be cramped, with no room to swing a goldfish, had not got the right memo. This boat was big. She yanked her phone out from her pocket and checked the name on the back of the boat with the details on her phone. Nope, this was definitely it – *Avanturista, Split.*

This was where she was spending the next couple of weeks? Well, hello, gorgeous boat and thank you very much. She did a little jig on the spot. In her natty outfit of blue striped Breton T-shirt and red Capri pants – well, she thought it was natty, although the Capri pants were an awful lot more tomatoey than she remembered when she'd bought them.

She took a quick picture of the boat and began typing a caption.

Nina, seriously, babe. Look at this boat! It's humungous. I love you. Thanks so much for getting me the gig. Now I'm doubly glad I paid attention to all those cooking lessons. Can you remember when we first met? I was the queen of nursery food and burnt cakes and now look at me. Can't wait to meet your bro. Maddie xxx

She would have been quite content to sit on the quayside in the glorious sunshine and gaze at the boat, but she figured she was here to work, even if it didn't feel like it. Since the coach from the airport had dropped her off at the busy ferry port she'd felt as if she was on holiday. The departures boards were full of the Jadrolinija line, with boats leaving for interesting-sounding places like Hvar, Jelsa, Stari Grad, Supetar, Bol, Milna, Dubrovnik, Korčula and Ancona. She grinned to herself. She wasn't in Birmingham any more.

Then she'd realised she was in completely the wrong place and had to walk all the way back to the other side of the bay to the marina, which wasn't quite the start for a shit-hot crew member but she hadn't minded the walk, not when the weather was like this and she was abroad.

Having been at home for a year after being in France, it was heaven to be back in the sunshine with all the sights and smells that told her she was a long way from the Midlands. She adored her family, she really did, but she also liked being away from them. Being in charge all the time was exhausting. Her sisters, two brothers and her mother were all so flipping disorganised. It was like herding cats all the time and it wasn't as if they were the least bit grateful. Theresa, the closest in age to her, had told her she was a bossy harpy and they'd been quite happy and had managed perfectly well when she was away in France. Which anyone with two eyes in their head could have pointed out was totally ridiculous, if they'd seen the state of the house when she'd got back. Brendan's shoe collection had tripled, Theresa could have opened her own beauty counter with the amount of make-up she'd stockpiled, a fair amount of which Maddie was sure had been shop-lifted, and they were all living on Chicken Pot Noodles, when it was far cheaper to cook proper meals.

Just then a man clutching several striped carrier bags appeared and, before she had chance to say anything, nipped nimbly from the quayside onto the boat.

'Hi,' she called. 'I'm Maddie. New crew member.'

Perfect white teeth framed by a bushy black beard curved into a piratical smile. 'Welcome aboard. I'm Ivan, the skipper. We spoke on the phone,' he said in heavily accented English as he mimed the action, as if reinforcing his words to make sure she understood.

Jumping the small distance onto the boat, she was immediately conscious of the unfamiliar bob of the boat on the water. She wasn't even going to think about seasickness.

'Nice to meet you.' He held out a tanned forearm, thick with dark hair, and shook her hand with a bone-crushing grip, which no doubt came from lots of sailory-type activities that Maddie couldn't begin to guess at. 'Come on, I'll show you around.'

Without looking back over his shoulder, Ivan pulled open a door and headed inside. She followed him below deck, down a few steps into a corridor which ran the full length of the boat. With solid, highly polished chestnut wood cladding the walls, floor and ceiling, it felt a little closed in and slightly claustrophobic but she was sure she'd get used to it.

'Cabins,' said Ivan, pointing to several doors leading off the corridor before taking her along through the boat to another short flight of stairs comprising no more than five steps. To the left there was a door, while a further flight of stairs led upwards and outside.

'Galley.' He indicated with his head as he led her into what she realised was the kitchen. She'd been warned by her brother Brendan's best friend, who apparently knew a thing or two about boats, having spent some time in Hull, that she should expect something like a caravan on the water. Having spent many a holiday at a caravan park in Filey on the North Yorkshire coast, she'd anticipated a couple of gas rings and a tiny fridge tucked under a counter, with minuscule cupboards built into every conceivable nook and cranny. This was a revelation, the sort of kitchen you'd find in one of those posh executive homes that were springing up on the outskirts of towns with gated railings around them. It even had a range with five gas burners and a fancy griddle plate.

Maddie's hopeful mental images of her preparing lots of salad and simply prepared meats went up in smoke. Holy moly, with this sort of set-up, was she expected to serve up Cordon Bleu standard food? Her cooking skills might have improved in recent years but they weren't going to be winning any Michelin stars any time soon. Thank goodness she was arty; she could do presentation over substance any day of the week, especially since Sebastian had taught her a few techniques to help hide her less than stellar skills.

'Wow.' She took a long, slow look around the kitchen.

'Nice, eh?' He dumped the bags and held out his hand. 'I picked up a few supplies for us before the guests arrive. After that you're on your own. In charge of cooking and food. What sort of charter experience do you have?'

Maddie winced but gave him a confident I've-got-this-covered grin. 'None, but I can cook, clean and I'm good with people. I'm a last-minute addition but don't worry, I'm a hard worker.'

'Better than the girl they had lined up then.' Ivan shook his head.

'When do the guests arrive?' asked Maddie, her curious gaze taking in the big stainless steel run of fridges and the marble-topped counter.

'Tomorrow. Plenty of time to get ready. I thought I'd have to get my grandma on board to help with the cooking and the serving. I'm grateful you could make it.'

Maddie gave him a brilliant smile. 'Excellent,' she said, making out she was far more confident than she was, but how hard could it be? She was going to be a glorified cook and chambermaid; as long as they didn't ask her to drive the boat, she'd be fine. 'This is all new –' she waved a hand at the kitchen '– but I'm a quick learner.' Her words were deliberately evasive.

'Most of it is easy . . .' He paused. 'But they didn't want to pay for any more crew, so you may need to help me from time to time.' He grinned. 'The sails, we don't use. It's mainly engine. But you'll have to learn how to drive the launch.'

'The launch? Great,' she said, as if she was asked to do this sort of thing all the time. That was the little boat that had been roped to the side of the big boat?

'Yes, with a trip like this, it's difficult to moor in some of the popular places, especially Hvar, so it's easier for us to drop anchor just outside and drive the guests in and out. A water taxi.' He shrugged. 'They call when they want picking up. And some celebrities like the privacy.'

'Ooh, celebrities?' Maddie's eyes widened and her dark curls bobbed as she shifted on the spot. 'Do you know who's going to be on board?'

Ivan threw back his head and laughed. 'Not until they get here. One year my friend had the big shock when

Beyoncé and Jay-Z turned up on the boat he was skippering.'

She whistled, not having given too much thought before about who might be on board.

'I do know they have lots of money. This boat costs over six thousand euros a day to charter.' His eyes narrowed with sudden authority. 'But I'm the skipper. I'm in charge. Me, I drive the boat, navigate. I'm the boss. You are the . . .' He frowned, his English failing him. 'What they want, you provide.' Although his eyes twinkled, she got the impression that what he'd just said was non-negotiable.

'So what about the quarters?' asked Maddie, wondering about sleeping arrangements and keen to see her own bunk.

'This gulet has eight cabins.'

'Gulet? I thought it was a yacht.'

'A gulet is just a type of yacht, usually two or three-masted, with several decks, typical of Turkey and Croatia. This has two masts.' Maddie nodded as if she had any idea what he was on about.

Ivan gave another one of his quick charming grins. 'This trip will be easy. Only six guests. The gulet sleeps many more.'

'Gosh, six people on this huge boat.'

Ivan rolled his eyes. 'Some people have money . . . Why they chartered a boat this big?' He shrugged. 'But it makes our lives easier. Especially yours. Not so many mouths to feed. Not so many rooms to clean. Not so many beds to make.'

'Easy-peasy,' said Maddie, thinking of home, with two brothers, two sisters and a mum who was disorganised at the best of times. Cooking, cleaning and tidying up after six people was the norm.

'There is a manual for crew.' He leaned down, opened a drawer and pulled out a royal blue ring binder with the charter company's logo on the front. 'Rules, regulations and guidance. The hours are variable . . .' He lifted his shoulders in a fatalistic shrug. 'You're supposed to get some time off, but one of us is on call all the time from breakfast until the guests go to bed. It depends on the people. Some like to stay on board, others like to explore and take day trips. Today we have peace and quiet. Tomorrow, it will be busy when they arrive. I'll show you to your quarters.' He glanced at the big chunky watch on his wrist. 'This evening I go home to Split. You like to come?'

Maddie unpacked her duffel quickly, a frisson of excitement running through her at the thought of being in sole charge of the boat. She must start calling it a gulet; that sounded far more professional.

Her cabin was on the upper deck, along with Ivan's cabin and two guest cabins and, she giggled to herself, she had her *own* bathroom. Talk about real luxury, even though she'd figured out it was possible to pee and shower at the same time. Waiting for her on the bed were a couple of freshly laundered pale blue T-shirts with the company logo on the front. Uniform of sorts, she guessed. She'd been told to bring navy shorts (which had been impossible to buy in the quick turnaround) and navy trousers (would leggings do?) to wear when she was on duty, which, from the sound of it, could be all the time. Although being out here in Croatia on this gorgeous yacht didn't feel the least bit like work. Well, not yet.

When she pulled shut her door, clutching the manual under her arm, she crossed to the rail to look out over the marina, tilting her face up to the sun. Not a cloud marred the sky and, at four o'clock in the afternoon, it was still very warm. This morning's grey skies in Birmingham seemed a world away and her cramped three-bedroom home would fit on this yacht five or six times over. Ivan might have described her cabin as small but, compared to sharing with her sister Theresa, and having her own bathroom, even with the shower and toilet combo, it was luxury.

A couple wandering along the nearby promenade skirting the marina paused, staring at the yacht. Maddie pretended not to see them and for a moment imagined she was a guest on the yacht and enjoyed their envious gaze. She couldn't begin to imagine what the man who'd chartered the boat did for a living to earn enough money to spend such an enormous sum renting this boat.

And this one wasn't even close to being one of the biggest in the marina, although it dwarfed its nearest neighbours. Over on the other side of the port were some seriously swanky boats. Ivan had pointed out Roman Abramovich's yacht, a sleek, sophisticated six-decked affair with so many satellites and gizmos on it that it looked more like a warship or a small cruise liner, and another not quite so large one that was reputed to have been chartered by Dua Lipa for the summer.

Beyond the marina was the town of Split, a collection of terracotta roofs huddled together in the narrow strip of land, bordered by a range of grey scree-covered rocky hills which rose steeply and ran in a sharp line parallel to the coast as far as the eye could see.

With a little skip of pure happiness Maddie dragged herself away from the view to explore the deck area. On this level, there was a small covered dining area at the rounded back end of the boat – there was probably some nautical term for it. Bow? Stern? She ran a hand over the bottles of a small, well-stocked bar tucked to one side. Beyond it, steps led up to the top deck, which she skipped up. Ooh, lovely. A collection of luxury wooden sun loungers with thick padded cushions in the now familiar navy blue were arranged around the small central deck, one of which she immediately decided had her name on it. Yes, a little G and T up here would be very nice.

Ivan had told her the guests couldn't check in before five-thirty tomorrow and he would meet them at the reception desk at the marina before bringing them to board the yacht. That gave her a one-off opportunity for some sunbathing before everyone arrived.

On the main deck, as well as the four cabins, there was an indoor lounge area with low-slung white leather seats, covered in expensive-looking blue and white cushions in an ikat print, and black marble-topped occasional tables which opened out to a shaded area with a big table. She crossed through the lounge and out to another deck and let out a low whistle – a Jacuzzi and plenty more sun loungers. A further flight of stairs took her down to the lower deck with six more cabins.

Having explored her little kingdom with utter delight, Maddie decided to treat herself to that G and T and to start reading the crew manual before heading into Split to meet Ivan who'd already gone to see his family. He'd circled a point on a tourist map for her and told her to ring him when she got there because she'd never find the family apartment.

Split was buzzing. Wandering along the crowded promenade, as she'd left herself plenty of time, she stopped to listen to a live band playing. They weren't in the first flush of youth, but played enthusiastic covers of the Rolling Stones, ZZ Top and Steve Harley, all of which Maddie recognised as favourites of her rock chick mum's. It was tempting to join in the dancing along with the hardened crowd at the very front but then Maddie could picture her mum, leather-jacketed and chain-smoking, who'd have been tapping her feet in time, no doubt head-banging to the music and flicking fag ash around her with careless laziness. Besides, she needed to find Ivan's house and didn't want to be late.

Maddie turned away and carried on walking along the busy promenade past the many restaurants, from which delicious smells spilled as waiters, trays held high, whizzed in and around tables with speedy efficiency. To her left, the sea sparkled in the low sunshine, an incredible blue that had her fingers itching to grab a paintbrush and capture the scene. She'd stowed her watercolour pencils and sketchbook in the drawer under her bed in the cabin in the hope she might get some days off, although from reading that manual it was looking less likely. Ahead of her, she could see the busy port, with queues of cars waiting to board and another stream of cars disembarking from a recent arrival. A large white ferry was chugging away out towards the islands that could be seen in the distance. This was the gateway to the Dalmatian islands and she couldn't wait to set sail and see them for herself.

Busy, busy, busy. And she loved it. There was a sense of life and vibrancy about the place. It had that European smell, the joie de vivre and the delicious warmth in the air. She'd missed living in Paris. Missed the cosmopolitan lifestyle. Now, here was her chance to live it again.

'Welcome, welcome, Ivan's friend. Come, come.'

Maddie, wide-eyed from leaving the thronging crowds of the narrow street and stepping into the cool quiet calm of the ancient apartment building, offered the bunch of flowers she'd bought in the market around the corner and stared curiously around at the stone-lintelled windows and the big archway over the door.

Ivan's apartment, at the top of worn stone steps, was in the middle of a wild warren of streets dating back to Roman times, lined with stone buildings within the boundary of Diocletian's Palace, which she'd glimpsed briefly on her way here. It was like stepping back in time.

Modern manners and the proffered bunch of flowers brought a torrent of smiles and Croatian from the prune-faced wiry lady who stood at the heavy wooden front door.

'This is my grandma, Vesna. She speaks a little English,' Ivan said.

'Hello,' said Maddie, smiling as the tiny woman studied her with dark raisin eyes before dragging her in through the door and closing it behind Maddie.

'And this is my wife, Zita.' A tall dark-haired woman appeared from the other room. Maddie guessed she was in her early forties although, with her flawless olive skin, it was difficult to tell.

'Thank you for having me,' said Maddie, feeling a little uncertain and worried that she was encroaching on family time.

'Company is always good,' said Zita with a broad smile, her dark brows lifting. 'You're very welcome. Both grandma and my mama are here today. They're very excited to meet you.'

'Really?' asked Maddie, frowning and glancing at Ivan in question.

Zita laughed. 'We love company and any excuse to celebrate together with some food. This is the Croatian way. We love our food and we love our family.'

'Gosh, your English is amazing.'

Zita tossed her heavy black-brown hair over her shoulder. She was a striking-looking woman with dark eyes and strong features and when she spoke her face danced with lively animation. 'I went to university in London, UCL. That's where I met Ivan. We worked there for some years and then came back to Split when our family was young and that's when Ivan bought the boat. He hires it to the charter company but skippers for them. I work at the airport, so I use my English. Every year the airport gets busier and busier.'

Maddie followed her through to the kitchen, a hive of bustling activity where diminutive Vesna and another, much taller, lady presided over two big pans like a pair of mad professors, throwing in seasoning and bay leaves from a large glass jar on the side. They were both talking away, shooting shy smiles towards Maddie and patting a little boy on the head every time he came within their reach, as he darted backwards and forwards through an archway to a long table with handfuls of cutlery clutched between his chubby fingers.

'This is my mother, Tonka, and that's Bartul, our son. He likes to be busy and help Nona Tonka. Both Nona and

Mama are very excited because Ivan said you wanted to learn about Croatian food.' Zita spoke a few rapid words of Croatian and Tonka turned round and responded, waving her hand towards the big steaming pan in front of her.

'She says she hopes you like fish. She wants to show you a traditional fish dish brujet.'

'Can you tell her that I'd like to learn, though I don't know much about fish?'

When Zita relayed this, Vesna looked horrified.

Zita translated again. 'She says, "But you live on an island".' They all laughed at that.

Vesna beckoned Maddie over as she grabbed a large plastic bottle and poured a generous glug of dark green liquid into a large frying pan.

'Is that olive oil?' asked Maddie, looking up at a shelf of assorted plastic bottles in varying sizes, all containing the same liquid.

'Yes.' Zita handed her the bottle. 'Smell.'

The distinctive fruity smell of olives hit her. 'Wow, that smells good. Fresh. Like . . . well, like real olives. You can almost imagine them being crushed.'

'Picked last October.' Zita tilted her head with a definite hint of pride. 'Here every family has their own piece of land with olive trees. We have a plot on Brač, up in the hills. In the autumn the whole family goes to the island for the week – everyone helps. And then the oil is pressed at a local co-operative. You must take a bottle back to the boat.'

'Thank you, that would be great,' said Maddie, thinking she'd save it to make a really good salad dressing.

'And you must have a glass of wine.' Zita pointed to a row of outsize glass jars tucked behind the archway.

'Wow,' said Maddie, eyeing the big jars of deep blackberry-coloured wine with their traditional wicker weave which looked fabulously rustic. 'What do you call those? And is the wine homemade as well?'

'In English you'd call them demijohns.' Zita laughed and shook her head. 'And yes, the wine is homemade but not by us, but there is a family connection of Ivan's – his cousin makes the wine.'

'Here, try.' Ivan thrust a thick glass goblet of the wine into her hand, having poured several from a jug on the side.

'I don't know much about wine,' said Maddie, gingerly tasting it.

'All you need to know is if you like it,' said Ivan, lifting his glass. 'Živilli.'

'Živilli,' said Zita.

'Mmm, that's good,' said Maddie.

Zita took a sip from her own glass. 'Dalmatian red wines are very good. We have many. The white is different and will often be served with water in the restaurants. The tourists get cross because they don't like it to be watered down. The red, I think, is the best.' She shrugged. 'Ivan and I, we prefer the red. You must take some wine back with you as well.'

Maddie was handed an apron and ushered over to the oven, where Tonka had begun to fry several pieces of different fish. Her impromptu cookery lesson featured lots of sign language and laughter as Tonka and Vesna attempted to teach her how to cook the dish. After that, to Maddie's surprise, they showed her how to make fresh pasta.

'I thought pasta was Italian,' she said to Zita.

'We're very close to Italy and our history is very intertwined. The Venetians ruled here for over three hundred years. We do eat lots of pasta although, when it is a main dish, it is made with meat and shellfish, not fish. We do add what we call rezanci, vermicelli in Italian, to some of the fish stews and my mother has her own special ingredient, which I know –' Zita's eyes twinkled with amusement '– she'll want to show you.'

Tonka was certainly an enthusiastic teacher, patting Maddie hard on the shoulder at regular intervals, while Vesna stood by and nodded approvingly.

'Mmm, that tastes amazing,' said Maddie when Tonka offered her a spoonful of brujet. The simplicity of the dish in terms of ingredients was belied by the fragrant, fresh flavours. 'I'm not sure mine will be this good,' she said, pulling faces and pointing to herself, to the amusement of Tonka, who patted her on the shoulder again and nodded in reassurance, while pointing to the fish and the herbs on the side.

'Mama says if you use good fresh fish from the market and lots of seasoning, you can't go wrong,' translated Zita.

Maddie smiled her thanks towards the older woman. 'That's what she thinks. But at least I know what fish to buy now.' Thanks to Zita, she had a page of copious notes and a list of fish to ask for at the market, as well as several recipes that Tonka had dictated, waving her wooden spoon at Zita, who'd painstakingly translated them all under Vesna's watchful eye. It was a real team effort.

Shaking her poor cramped hand, Zita looked up. 'Mama wants to show you her finishing touch. You're very honoured. Some of these recipes are closely guarded secrets and this one she's never given to me before.'

'Come, come,' said Vesna, pointing to the table as she started to ladle out the fish broth into wide soup bowls.

Maddie sat between Tonka and Zita and listened to the flow of Croatian around her, with Zita's occasional translations to keep her involved.

'Mama is talking about her neighbour, who she met in the market; she has trouble with her son. He started work on the top floor of his mother's house to turn it into an apartment for him and his wife, but he has stopped halfway through the work and there is water running down the walls.'

Tonka was shaking her head and said something else, with a dramatic roll of her eyes. Zita giggled. 'Apparently he's a plumber.'

'Oops,' said Maddie. 'I can see why he's not very popular.'

Zita translated and Tonka let out a delighted laugh.

'It's very common in Croatia for families to have big houses and the next generation moves into the top floor,' explained Zita.

'God, I'm glad that doesn't happen at home,' said Maddie with a slight shudder.

Despite the language barrier, Maddie couldn't remember an evening where she'd been made to feel so welcome. Without being unkind, she could have guaranteed that not one of her family would have been willing to try the fish or if they had they'd have stared at it with deep suspicion because fish came in batter with mushy peas and chips from the chippy.

'Is good, yes?' asked Vesna.

Maddie nodded. 'Very.' She patted her tummy in a Winnie-the-Pooh sort of motion that had everyone beaming. 'If anything I make turns out this good, I'll be very happy. Perhaps if I get stuck, Ivan can give me some help.'

Zita sniggered, translated for her mother and Ivan's grandmother and there was a very pregnant pause before all three women burst into uproarious laughter.

'That would be a no, then,' said Maddie, joining in the laughter as Ivan shook his head.

'I'm the captain of the boat.' He winked at her. 'I don't do the cooking.'

Chapter 4

This was heaven. The whole boat to herself and the pick of the sun loungers. Maddie sipped at her gin and tonic, stretching out, enjoying the feel of the sun on her skin. She'd earned these few precious hours of sunbathing. The crew manual had been absolutely invaluable, as had her visit to Ivan's house. She smiled at the thought of last night. She'd got it all sorted. Menu plans. Shopping lists. And, thanks to Zita, a complete selection of recommended markets and shops in all the different ports they were likely to visit. And first up, as soon as she got to a fish market, she would be making a fish broth.

Despite the delicious glasses of Ivan's family's red wine, which had slipped down rather well last night, she'd set her alarm for six and by eight-thirty this morning she'd checked all the cabins were clean, made sure every bathroom had fresh towels and planned today's and tomorrow's evening meal and lunch as well as early evening canapés, shorthand for olives, fresh anchovies and a plate of meat and cheese for the guests' arrival at five-thirty.

As she reached for her drink, tilting her book up against the sun to shade her face, she became aware of voices and the rumbling rhythmic thud of suitcases being pulled over the wooden planks of the jetty. Ignoring them, she turned another page of her book and sipped at her gin and tonic.

She'd read several more pages of her book and was starting to consider setting the alarm on her phone to have a little snooze when someone called out, 'Ahoy there, *Avanturista*. Anyone home?'

She froze, huddling rigid, back into her seat. Surely it couldn't be guests. Ivan had been quite specific. No one checks in before five-thirty. Looking anxiously from side to side, she worked out that no one could see her from the quayside.

'Hello, is anyone there?' called a second, female, voice.

Maddie sat tight. It was only three-thirty. It wasn't as if it was ten to five or anything. No one was supposed to be here and even if they'd made their way here by accident, this was far too early.

Unfortunately, it was impossible to relax now. Feeling resentful, she pressed herself back into the sun lounger, not even daring to use the straw in case she made an inadvertent noise. She listened, praying they might decide to turn around, but there was absolutely no sign of them shifting. Curiosity was also killing her. Who were the guests? She'd been wondering all day what they'd be like. There were no clues from the manifest as to whether the people were couples, family or a group of friends. Did she dare peep over the top and have a look? But she couldn't because what if they saw her? Then she'd have to explain that they weren't allowed on board and . . . well, she didn't think she'd be able to hold her own against posh people who were paying her wages.

Basically, she was stuck on the deck in a new bikini she'd bought on a whim and would never have worn in public. With big bones, Maddie was never going to be a size ten; she was a healthy twelve to fourteen and her stomach had never, and was never going to be, flat and, yes, she had muffin tops – double chocolate chip muffin tops. All bought and paid for.

Now she knew they were there it was impossible to concentrate on her book. She hardly dared breathe as she listened to the two people talking. She couldn't make out the words but one of them was getting quite irate and the other frustrated. Darn it and now she really wanted to pee. The more she tried not to think about it, the more she wanted to go. It was psychosomatic; she didn't need to go. Her bladder disagreed. Oh, why, oh, why hadn't she brought out her T-shirt to cover herself up? That would teach her for being so cocky at having sole run of the yacht.

Could she slide onto the floor and commando crawl her way across the deck to get to the stairs? The *Mission Impossible* tune unhelpfully played in her head. But then she'd have to slide down each step head first on her stomach. It was no good; she had to go to the loo. Gingerly, she lowered herself onto the wooden deck and, like a caterpillar, inched her way towards the stairs. How would Tom Cruise manage this? She regretted her initial decision to manoeuvre down the stairs on her stomach. Now she'd started, there wasn't enough room for her to stand back up again.

Thankful to reach the bottom, she kept herself pressed up against the stairs. If she could see the pile of matching, very flash luggage, could they see her? She stiffened and then stared. Lord, was it really Louis Vuitton? Having spent enough time in Paris, she knew that was seriously expensive stuff and just how many cases did they have between them? She didn't own that many clothes. Leaning forward just a touch, she held her breath, although why she did that she had no clue – did she think she was some sort of spy or something?

She could just see the tops of two people's heads. Neither were looking up, so she risked another peek. The taller man had sandy blond hair and, beside him, looking like a delicate waif, was a teeny, tiny petite woman with lots of blonde hair glistening with golden lights, wearing white jeans, which looked considerably more expensive than Maddie's Tesco numbers and a floaty silk top that had designer written all over it. From here, she couldn't tell if they were famous or not, but they were certainly wealthy.

But, wealth or not, this ship was not yet open for business, so they could sit tight. Hugging the walls, she inched her way along until she reached the next stairwell that would allow her to cross to the other side of the yacht, where there was no chance they could see her.

She was going to use one of the cabin bathrooms on the lower deck. Creeping along, she froze when she felt the boat dip slightly as if someone had jumped on board.

The cheeky bastards. Ivan had been quite clear. Check-in was five-thirty. And she'd planned her day so that she'd have this last hour uninterrupted to make the most of the sundeck. Who did these people think they were? Just because they had money it didn't mean that they could do what they liked.

She listened hard. No! Someone was winching down the gangplank.

Throwing back her shoulders, the pressing engagement to relieve her bladder forgotten, she marched along the corridor and mounted the short flight of stairs to the bow and flung open the wooden door, only then remembering she was in nothing more than a very small bikini.

'Excuse me,' she said, quickly taking in the scene.

The blond man turned guiltily, the gangplank now lowered into position onto the jetty.

'What do you think you're doing?'

His face flared red and he opened his mouth but, before he could say anything, an aristocratic drawl interrupted.

'We've been waiting ages. Didn't you hear us? Who are you?'

On six, maybe even seven-inch heels, the woman

marched across the gangplank with the ease of a mountain goat, a feat that had Maddie gawping in surprise, as well as at her sheer effrontery. Flipping heck, the woman was take-your-breath-away stunning. Maddie stared, unable to help herself – this was the sort of person you saw in magazines or in films. She had to be famous or something.

Just the sight of her and her imperious, entitled manner had Maddie's confidence leaking away with every second, horribly aware of her semi-nudity and less than perfect body.

'Well, don't just stand there. Are you going to let us in or not?'

Maddie clenched a fist behind her back. Remember, she told herself, paying customer. Remember the manual. It had been quite specific about the treatment of guests. Basically, suck up to them or else.

'I'm terribly sorry but check-in isn't until five-thirty. You're supposed to wait at the main reception and everyone is brought over by the skipper.'

'Well, what are you doing here?' The woman arched a scathing eyebrow.

'I . . . I'm one of the crew.'

'Oh.' In the one word, the woman managed to capture a wealth of disapproval and disdain.

'No one is supposed to come on board before check-in.'

'Well, we're here now and I am not trooping all the way back over there, not in this heat and not in these shoes.' She eyed Maddie's bikini with a sneering look, her eyebrows raising as if in surprise as she focused on the swell of flesh just above her hips. 'It's not as if you appear to be terribly busy at the moment.' The clear implication being that Maddie was just being lazy. She tossed her hair over her shoulder and held out her hand to the man, with mute, winsome appeal, who took it to help her over the last half metre of the gangplank, even though she'd been perfectly capable for the previous few metres.

Maddie swallowed. There'd been nothing in the manual about this.

Nick was feeling fed up and, if he were completely honest, slightly embarrassed at being caught out by someone on the boat. Since arriving at the airport Tara had been quite demanding, insisting that they got a taxi into Split in case she was recognised, and he still couldn't believe that she'd brought three suitcases with her. He'd brought one piece of hand luggage. Shorts, that was all you needed on holiday, although he still wasn't sure about the shorts Tara had persuaded him to buy or the cap-sleeved T-shirt. If his brothers had caught sight of them, he'd never have heard the end of it. The words *big girl's blouse* sprang to mind, but Tara seemed to like them and their shopping trip had gone much more smoothly once he'd acquiesced to her taste. After all, she worked in fashion, she knew what she was talking about and shopping was his least favourite thing.

Since they'd arrived in the baking heat at the marina

Tara had been quite piteous and he'd been really quite worried she might faint or something. But now they were here, what was the harm in going up on deck? It seemed entirely reasonable. They could just dump their luggage in the bow and at least have a cold drink or something. Surely Douglas, who had chartered the boat, could do the check-in stuff.

'Look, I don't make the rules, but the skipper made it quite clear,' said the girl in the bikini, looking red and flushed in the face. He frowned. They'd clearly interrupted her important work – sunbathing.

'Why don't you leave your luggage here and go back to the marina to wait to be checked-in properly?'

'Because, as Tara pointed out, we are here, we are hot, the boat has been paid for and we'd like to sit down somewhere cool and wait for the rest of our party,' said Nick firmly, deciding to take no nonsense. He wasn't at home now. This was Tara's world and he'd seen how her friends acted. Imperious and direct. That was how you got things done in this world. 'Is it going to inconvenience you hugely?' He gave a pointed look at her bikini, immediately regretting it when the girl glared at him, her face turning pink.

Now she was making him feel guilty. He couldn't bloody win. One thing he knew for sure was that his mum would not have been impressed with his behaviour. Refusing to meet the girl's eyes, he turned and stalked down the gangplank to collect Tara's luggage. At this very moment, he would have been happier in a pub on his own with a large pint of beer.

Tara swanned ahead and was already climbing the wooden stairs to the deck. As he wheeled one of her cases onto the gangway, she'd reached the rails and was waving down at him.

'Oh, this is lovely. Come up. Oh, you couldn't bring up my little case, could you?'

By the time he'd carried all the cases on board and went up to the first deck, taking with him Tara's small cabin bag, she had settled in the air-conditioned lounge and kicked off her shoes – quite literally, they were lying in the middle of the floor – stripped off her jeans and was lounging on a white leather sofa, all long tanned legs and a tiny pair of briefs.

Nick blinked at her, not sure where to look.

'Oh, darling, isn't it lovely to have nothing to do.' Peering up at her phone, held in one hand above her head to take a selfie, she stretched lazily. For a fleeting, disloyal second, when her white top rose to reveal a smooth flat stomach and the minuscule scrap of lace and silk masquerading as underwear, he wondered if she'd done it deliberately. His mouth went dry and he realised he was staring.

Peeling his eyes away from her endless legs, he turned and looked around at the boat, letting out a low whistle. 'This is rather nice.'

He was dying to take lots of pictures and post them onto the family WhatsApp group, but Tara seemed to take all this in her stride and he didn't want to look too keen and gauche in front of her.

With a careless shrug, she said, 'I guess,' and reached over to her tote bag to pull out one of the stack of glossy magazines she'd bought at the airport. 'I wonder what time the others will get here. Has that awful girl gone? Honestly, some people are such jobsworths.'

She opened her magazine and began flicking through the pages, tutting and shaking her head.

As she was clearly absorbed, he left the lounge area to step out into the warm air on the deck. With a quick grin, he took in the view of the hazy outline of the islands in the distance, lifting his head towards the pleasant balmy breeze. Standing with his legs slightly apart, his hands gliding with pleasure along the smooth surface of the glossy wooden rail, he enjoyed the slight bob and dip of the boat. He was really here. Nick Hadley, on board an expensive yacht with a stunning model girlfriend. Who'd have thought it?

Chapter 5

Now properly covered up, wearing her crew T-shirt and navy shorts, Maddie had taken herself off to the kitchen – sorry, galley – and was hacking a poor cucumber to death. If this pair of self-entitled dickheads were indicative of the guests, it was going to be a long trip.

She checked Tonka's recipe and grabbed an onion, peeling back the golden skin. Hopefully she wouldn't have to mix with the guests too much and they might not all be like Mr and Mrs We-know-we're-gorgeous-and-that-means-we-can-do-what-the-hell-we-like. Nina's brother, she consoled herself, wouldn't be like that. In fact she was hoping he'd be an ally. This pair were everything she'd feared about this trip. Maddie was looking forward to meeting Nick; at least he wouldn't have any airs and graces. You couldn't get more down to earth than a northerner and a farmer at that.

Chopping and slicing soothed her and she kept a close eye on the time. When she finally heard voices and the clatter of footsteps and cases, she knew the rest of the guests had arrived. That was her signal and she dashed out to lay the canapés on the table in the bow, as per instruction in her handy bible.

Hearing people start to assemble on deck, she tucked the ice bucket and champagne under one arm and picked up a tray of glass flutes, holding it, somewhat precariously, in one hand and headed out to meet the guests. The manual said champagne on the first day, although she was dying to bring out one of Ivan's demi-johns for a bit of Croatian authenticity.

As soon as she appeared on the deck, a woman with short bright red hair cut in a gamine pixie crop clapped her hands together. 'Oooh, bring on the champers. The holiday has begun. Can I help you with that?' She reached for the champagne bucket perched on the tray, carefully lifting it away from the six flutes.

'Thanks,' said Maddie, immediately warming to her and following her over to a table. 'So not all the guests are complete knobs then.'

The woman let out a loud belly laugh and to Maddie's horror she realised she'd said the words aloud.

'Oh, God, I'm so sorry. I didn't mean to say that.'

'Not a problem.' She winked at Maddie. 'I like people who say it like it is. I'm Siri. And no, I don't have the answer to everything.'

'Ah, everyone, this is Maddie,' announced Ivan, who now appeared to be wearing fancy dress.

Maddie bit back a laugh and looked down at her feet.

She could bet that Tonka and Vesna would love the dashing naval officer look with the white shirt complete with black and gold epaulettes, a white peaked hat and white trousers. She suspected Zita, with her wicked sense of humour and more pragmatic approach, would have a lot more to say.

'Hi everyone.' She looked around at the faces, deliberately avoiding the gruesome twosome, as she'd now dubbed them, who were on the far side of the table. Four other people had joined the party, two men and two women, and Maddie took a minute trying to work out the relationships between them all. They looked unlikely couples. Seated nearest her, on the ends of the benches, were the two men, one tall, dark and the sort of movie star handsome that could make you go weak at the knees. It was probably no accident that his blue linen shirt brought out the depth of his dark blue eyes. He sat with his long legs out, crossed at the ankle, leaning back in his chair with an arrogant confidence as if he owned the place. If it hadn't been for the fact that he was as dark as Nina, she might have thought he was the man that had chartered the boat, but he had to be Nick.

'Maddie is your hostess for the trip,' explained Ivan. 'She'll be looking after your cabins, serving breakfast and lunch and dinner, and on those nights we're not in moorings or too far from port, she'll take you in on the launch.'

'Hi, Maddie,' said the man she assumed was Nick, in a deep and very smooth voice, with a charming friendly smile. Of course he was being friendly; he knew she was

Nina's friend. Maddie's breath stalled in her chest as she turned to face him. Why hadn't Nina warned her? But then she guessed Nina probably didn't even notice and, if she was anything like Maddie, she thought of her brothers as nothing more than pains in the arse. Phew! Those eyes were amazing.

'Can I help you with that?' He took the bottle from her, his fingers brushing hers. Smooth. The corner of her mouth turned up; Nina's brother was full of surprises. He gave her a warm smile and then put out his other hand. 'Simon. Simon Beresford.'

'S-Simon.' Automatically she shook his hand, her brain whirling. 'Hi,' she said in a pathetic wheezy little voice.

She shot a look at the second guy, holding hands with the tall, slim woman next to him, who had a dark curtain of blue-black hair that hung in a perfect straight plumb line. So that was Nick. She remembered Nina saying he was going out with a model. With hair like that, the woman had to be a shampoo model at the very least. The thick lustrous locks glowed with health and vitality, which was a bit of a shame as they contrasted unfavourably with the thinning red-gold sandy hair of poor Nick, who was definitely on the losing side of the battle against baldness. Maddie pinched her lips to hide her surprise. Nick was no looker, although, despite his pudgy, pug-like face, there was something arresting about his hazel eyes which shone with bright enthusiasm as he looked round at everyone with eager beaver happiness.

58

In the meantime, Simon picked up the champagne bottle and with a deft twist undid the metal cage and removed the foil before removing the cork in a practised move which suggested he'd done it a time or two before. Not a drop was spilled and he handed the bottle to her with an easy smile.

'Thank you; you have had some practice, then.'

'Lots,' he said, managing to make the single word sound suggestive.

She grinned at him and filled the glasses one by one, handing them out to Simon, who passed them back around the table.

'Cheers everyone,' said Nick in an unexpectedly plummy voice, lifting his glass. 'To a *bon voyage*. May all who sail in this vessel have a jolly good time . . . and if you don't, I don't want to know.' He took an enthusiastic swig of his drink, beaming from ear to ear. 'Because this boat cost a ton of cash to hire, so anyone that doesn't enjoy themselves will have to walk the plank. Happy holidays.'

'Oh, Douglas,' scolded his girlfriend, pulling her hand away.

Douglas! Maddie blinked, completely confused, and realised she'd mouthed his name. If he was Douglas . . . No, no way. Maddie shot the man in the far corner a surprised look which, unfortunately, he happened to look up and catch at exactly the wrong moment. He lifted a sardonic eyebrow and she hastily looked away.

He was Nick! And by the look on his face, he knew

she'd realised who he was at that very minute. She shook her head slightly and he lifted his champagne glass in a mocking toast.

'You can be so crass sometimes.' Douglas's girlfriend was still scolding him.

'What?' he asked with a crestfallen expression.

'Nothing,' she said, pursing her lips and sipping at her champagne.

Simon and Siri lifted their glasses, repeating, 'Happy holidays.'

'Sorry, m'dear, I should have done proper introductions. I'm Douglas and,' he added rather proudly, 'I chartered the boat.'

'I think we all know that,' muttered his disgruntled girlfriend.

Ignoring her, he carried on making the introductions. 'This is my girlfriend, Cory.' The girl with the blue-black hair nodded politely, her eyes a little vacant as if she were miles away.

'And over there, that's Tara and Nick and this is Siri, my sort of cousin.' He shot her a warm smile.

Siri nodded, while Tara, who was now talking to Cory, didn't even look up and Nick stared with complete disinterest, away out across the sea.

'Lovely to meet you all,' said Maddie. 'I hope you have a great trip.'

'I'm sure we will,' said Douglas. 'I've just briefed Ivan on our course for the next two and a half weeks –' he tapped at one of the charts on the table '– and we're going to have an excellent time, island-hopping and partying.'

'I'm sure you're going to have a wonderful time. Now, would anyone like some canapés?'

'Lord, yes, I'm absolutely starving,' said Douglas. 'And what time is dinner? The girls will want to freshen up, if I know them.'

'What time would you like it?' asked Maddie.

'Cory, Tara, what time would suit you ladies?'

Tara frowned thoughtfully. 'Well, if I change for dinner, I'm not going to be ready before nine.'

'Me neither,' said Cory.

'Nine?' Nick looked ill at ease. Serves him right, thought Maddie; he deserved his picky girlfriend.

'Tara, darling,' drawled Simon. 'You don't need to stand on ceremony with us. Some of us are bloody starving. An airline lunch just doesn't cut it.'

'Nine is a little bit late,' said Douglas apologetically. 'And we barely ate a thing on the plane.'

'You had a sandwich and that packet of shortbread biscuits,' countered Cory, looking quite indignant.

'That is not proper sustenance,' announced Simon and Douglas gave him an obliging look.

What a bunch of hen-pecked wusses, thought Maddie.

'I'm always hungry,' announced Siri. 'Let's eat at seven-thirty.'

Thank goodness for someone decisive.

'Done,' said Douglas fervently.

Maddie beat a hasty retreat before anyone could change their mind.

'You don't mind, do you, Nicky darling?' asked Tara, laying a hand on his chest. 'But I really need my sleep, otherwise I get the most horrendous bags under my eyes. Poor Cory says that Douglas snores and keeps her awake half the night. Not, of course, that you would snore, but I just find it difficult to share a bed.'

'It's not a problem,' said Nick, taking her hand. 'Besides, I'm not sure I'd fit in a cabin with all your clothes.'

'Uh . . .' She rolled her eyes. 'Can you believe it? There's nowhere to hang anything. I don't know how I'm going to manage.' She looked at the slim gold watch on her wrist. 'It's so tiresome to have to eat so early. The Spanish know how to do it. When we were in Barcelona last year we never ate before ten.'

'Well, I for one am very grateful that we're not in Spain,' said Nick. 'I'm starving.'

'Lucky you have such a good metabolism.' She ran a suggestive hand down his chest. 'And such delicious abs,' she added with a naughty expression.

He lowered his head to kiss her, wrapping his arms round her. Touching her lips with his, he pulled her tiny frame closer, conscious as always that she was so delicate. For a second she kissed him back, with a little murmur, and he deepened the kiss, pushing his hands into her hair, stroking the back of her neck. She leaned into him, her hips grazing his thighs, which made his blood start to race.

'Mmm,' she said, and then pulled away, immediately smoothing her hair back into place. 'As the men have decreed an early dinner, I've hardly got any time to get ready.'

'Tara, you look perfect. You always do.' He pushed her glorious hair back and dropped a kiss on her shoulder. She squirmed, smiling up at him. 'Nicky, stop tempting me. I have to get ready.'

Knowing it was useless to argue – Tara redefined the word stubborn – he pushed back the ungallant thought that he hadn't actually ever managed to tempt her.

'OK, I'll see you at dinner.'

She pouted. 'Aren't you going to knock for me?'

He laughed. 'If you really want me to, but as my cabin is on the main deck we might as well meet at dinner.'

'All right then.' She turned and flounced into her room.

With a wry smile, Nick made his way up to his own cabin. There was no doubt that Tara knew her own mind. That was admirable, wasn't it?

Chapter 6

'Oof.' Maddie hit a broad wall of chest as she rounded the corner of the back – no, she must remember to call it the stern – of the boat as she headed out for an early morning trip to the bakery, Bobis, that Zita had recommended. She hadn't expected to see anyone at this ridiculous hour.

'Sorry. Oh, it's you.' Nick's voice sounded disapproving. She raised her gaze to meet narrowed blue eyes.

'What? You don't apologise to the help?' sniped Maddie. How disappointing to realise that *he* was Nina's brother.

'That's not what I meant.' He glared down at her and she glared back up at him. They were like two boxers in a ring, posturing before either threw the first punch. He stepped back with a snarky smile. 'After you,' he said, allowing her to go first down the gangplank.

She inclined her head with a brief nod and strode down the narrow corridor, clutching the wicker basket, the discovery of which, five minutes ago, had given her so much pleasure – she'd always wanted to go shopping with a proper basket. Now she wanted to use it to bash the irritating Nick over the head.

He fell into step with her as she hit the jetty. 'Where are you headed?'

'Into Split,' she replied, remembering that he was a guest and she owed him a modicum of politeness. At this hour she'd assumed all the guests were asleep.

'Is the centre far?' asked Nick, shading his eyes against the already brilliant sunshine and looking towards the town.

'Not too far, but a good twenty-minute walk,' she said.

'Presumably I've got time to see it, if you're going in. The boat won't leave without you.'

He stuck like unwanted glue beside her as they walked along the jetty. Unfortunately, from here there was only one route along the promenade.

'We're due to sail at nine-thirty. When everyone's had breakfast. I'm serving it at eight-thirty but I need to be back at eight.' She looked at her watch, which gave her a good two hours.

Nick let out a laugh. 'Good luck with that. Tara isn't an early riser and neither is Cory.'

'What? You know both of their sleeping habits?' asked Maddie. 'That's impressive.'

Nick pursed his lips. 'They share a flat. And models work long hours, lots of late nights.'

'Hmph,' snorted Maddie. 'Nice work if you can get it.'

'It's quite demanding,' said Nick.

66

'Yeah, I bet you really break into a sweat standing around looking gorgeous for a few hours.'

'And you would know?'

'Ouch,' said Maddie with a rueful laugh. 'He noticed I'm not a size zero.'

Nick stiffened, his mouth twisting. 'That's not what I meant and you know it.'

'What did you mean? I'm dying to know because from here it sounded pretty . . .' She deliberately left the sentence to trail, leaving him to fill in the blanks in any way he chose.

'I meant if you've ever been on a photoshoot, you'd realise that it is quite hard work.'

Maddie raised a sceptical eyebrow. 'No mate, hard work is when you break into a sweat, put in twelve-hour shifts, come home and your back is aching and you earn a pittance doing it.'

'Sounds like someone's got a bit of a chip on their shoulder. Is crewing hard work? Seems quite a nice gig to me. Didn't look as if you were working too hard yesterday when you couldn't be arsed to let us on board.'

'Like I told you, check-in was at five-thirty. Everyone else managed to get it right . . . or are you so important normal rules don't apply?'

His jaw clenched and Maddie was pleased to see that he looked mightily pissed off.

'Are you always this rude to guests?'

'No,' said Maddie cheerfully, swinging her basket as she strode along. 'Just you.'

67

Nick didn't have anything to say to that. They walked along in silence, Maddie smirking to herself. She could not believe this was Nina's brother. She'd been led to believe he was a nice, normal, down-to-earth bloke and, to be honest, she was a little bit disappointed. So much for her foolish imaginings that he might be a mate or even an ally on this trip. In those shorts, he looked, well, a bit of a dick, which he'd proved himself yesterday. Seriously, who wore shorts that tight, although they did wonders for his backside. If she didn't know better, in that get-up, she'd have assumed he was gay. And, judging from the second glance of the guy that had just walked by, she wasn't the only one.

'I think you've pulled,' she said, trying to keep her face straight.

'What?' Nick looked at her, puzzled.

'The guy that just passed us. Couldn't take his eyes off your arse.'

She laughed at the startled expression on his face as he shot a quick look over his shoulder and then laughed even more when the dark-haired guy grinned at Nick, revealing lots of perfect white even teeth.

'All the better to bite you with,' said Maddie, gurgling with laughter.

Nick's mouth was pinched shut in a straight line and he swivelled his head back so quickly it was a wonder he didn't crick his neck.

'Told you. I think it's the shorts.' She eyed the tight

fabric with the dodgy turn-ups. They didn't even look that comfortable.

'What's wrong with them?' he asked warily.

'Nothing, I guess, if you're a trainee gigolo or a bit of a fox.'

Nick blew out an annoyed breath. 'They're shorts.'

'They certainly are,' teased Maddie.

'You a fashion expert as well now?' he asked through gritted teeth.

'You're on holiday, not the catwalk. Time to relax and enjoy yourself. I'd have thought dressing for comfort was the most important thing.' Her lips twisted as she tried hard not to smile. In those shorts he might have difficulty fathering children in the future, although she'd be the last to deny that those muscular thighs, covered in crisp sandy gold hair, were pretty impressive and she was on the same page as the gay guy when it came to Nick's bum. Shame he was such an arse. 'You want to watch you don't cut your circulation off.'

'Is there any kind of filter with you?' asked Nick.

'No,' said Maddie matter-of-factly.

They continued in silence until they reached the palm tree lined promenade, the white stone pavement giving off a strong glare in the bright sunshine.

'It was pretty lively along here the other night,' said Maddie, feeling a little guilty that she'd given him such a hard time and that he'd seemed lost in brooding thought for the last five minutes. 'Are you headed anywhere particular?'

Nick shrugged. 'No, I just wanted to stretch my legs and see something of Split.' He gave a self-deprecating laugh. 'My brother and his wife are avid armchair travellers. If I don't take the chance to see the city while I'm here, I'll never hear the end of it. According to TripAdvisor and Dan and Gail, I need to see Diocletian's Palace, otherwise I might as well have not come.'

'Yeah, Ivan said it was worth seeing.'

'You've not seen it?'

'Only a tiny bit the other night and it was impressive,' she admitted, feeling she ought to try and see a bit more while she could. 'I might take a quick diversion once I've bought the fish from the market and found this bakery and picked up the pastries for breakfast.' She pulled out her phone and opened up the maps app, trying to work out which direction to head in. The bakery was one Zita had recommended. 'See you later.' Holding up her phone, she began to pace back the way they'd just come, then frowned and turned around. Bugger, the little blue dot kept heading in the wrong direction.

'Do you know where you're going?' asked Nick.

'Yes,' she said defensively, looking down at her screen. Oh, damn, she was going in the wrong direction again. Map reading, even with GPS, was not her forte. Her sense of direction was woeful.

'Why don't I come with you to the bakery and then we can both go to Diocletian's Palace? I'll help you find both. You don't even have to talk to me.'

She gave him a considering look. 'All right then. I might even let you select a couple of buns, if you're good.'

Nick laughed, his face lighting up. Bugger, he was a good-looking sod after all. Yesterday she'd been too pissed off to take it in properly. He took her phone from her hand and began to walk across the street to one of the small side streets.

'Buns.' He emphasized the northern 'u'. 'What happened to pastries? I bet you don't call them that in front of Nina.'

'God, no, Nina would scalp me.' She grinned at him as they walked along the narrow stone paved street. 'She's rather particular about her patisserie these days.'

'Yeah, she's done well.' He nodded, a proud smile tipping his lips.

'She certainly has. Her éclairs are to die for. You know they sell out by lunchtime every day?'

'No, I didn't.'

They smiled at each other.

'So how come you don't have such a strong northern accent? You sound quite posh for a sheep farmer.'

'Nina been filling you in?'

'Well, it stands to reason – if she grew up on a sheep farm, you must have done too. Don't worry, I wasn't asking about you.'

'Never thought for a minute you were. And, to answer your question. I got a scholarship to a local independent school. They were big on rugby and it just so happened

71

that all of us, Nina excepted, were pretty handy with a rugby ball.'

'Ah, that explains it. Public schoolboy.'

'And?'

'Nothing!'

'You do have a bit of a chip on your shoulder, don't you?'

'No,' said Maddie a shade too defensively. It was just that posh people . . . well, they made her feel stupid, clumsy and uneducated. On her History of Art degree course there'd been an awful lot of very wealthy people who'd grown up being taken to galleries and museums. It had taken her a lot of study and travel to catch up.

'Up here,' said Nick, indicating a street corner.

It was a good job Nick was with her, as her basket was quickly filled with delicious Croatian delicacies and she needed a second bag to carry the bread she'd stocked up on because they might not be mooring up again for a few days. Without asking, he took the bulging carrier bag from her.

They wound through tiny streets flanked by white stone buildings which were blinding in the sunlight.

'I had no idea it was like this,' exclaimed Maddie when they rounded a tiny corner and found themselves in what looked like a ruined Roman palace, with tall stone columns and windows high in the walls.

They wandered through a maze of tiny streets, munching

on a croissant each; neither of them had been able to resist the delicious smell in the bakery and had succumbed as soon as they'd left. The quiet lanes at this time of day were peaceful and shady with interesting little shops, sunken doorways and large stone flags. It was easy to imagine you'd slipped back in time until, turning a corner, they came to a big open square full of cafés and restaurants.

'Have we got time for a coffee?' asked Nick.

'A quick one, but, like you say, they can't sail without me and as you're a guest I can blame you if I'm late back.'

'Or we could grab a cab. It's quite a long walk back.'

'If you're paying,' said Maddie cheekily.

'I'm guessing I'm paying for the coffee too,' said Nick with a roll of his eyes.

'If you're offering.'

They chose one of the pavement cafés and sat outside. As it was still early the square was busy with tradespeople pushing trolleys loaded with boxes of fruit and vegetables, waiters laying up tables ready for the lunch crowd and a few eager tourists with sensible walking shoes and guidebooks, clearly anxious to make the most of the day.

'This is nice.' Maddie lifted her espresso and toasted Nick. 'Thanks.'

'No problem. You like espresso?'

'I acquired a taste for it in Paris.' It also, she liked to think, made her look more sophisticated but she wasn't about to admit that to Nick.

73

'What were you doing in Paris?'

'I was there on my year abroad, as part of my degree.' She still got a kick out of saying that. The first in her family to go to university.

She saw the quick flash of surprise cross his face. 'Yes, I'm quite old. Thirty. I was a mature student; I didn't go until I was twenty-six.'

'I sometimes think it's better to be a mature student; at least at that age you have a better idea about what you want to do. Rather than fall into the obvious.' His mouth flattened. 'What did you do?'

'History of Art.'

'Interesting. Did you enjoy it?'

'Yes, I bloody loved it. I've always liked art . . . I know, imagine – me, Maddie Wilcox from Selly Oak, wanting to study art.'

'Why shouldn't you?' asked Nick with a curious smile.

'Because it's not much bloody use to man nor beast, as my mum likes to remind me.' She pulled a face and mimicked her mother's strong Brummy accent. 'How you going to get a job with a Mickey Mouse subject like that? Not much call for History of Art down Tesco, love.'

'She has a point, I guess,' conceded Nick. 'But what do you want to do? I take it, by the last-minute nature of this job, crewing on a yacht is not your long-term career ambition.'

'Given I've not done a full proper day yet, who knows? But it certainly wasn't part of my plan.'

'Do you have a plan?' Nick's question sounded almost plaintive.

Maddie stared at the rooftops on the opposite side of the square, wondering what he'd say if she told him what she really, really wanted to do. He followed her gaze and they both stared at the line of the terracotta roof tiles creating a horizon against the pure blue of the sky.

'Not exactly. I know what I want to do, but . . .' She shrugged almost fatalistically. 'What about you? Did you go to university?'

'Yes –' he gave a short self-deprecating laugh '– Harper Adams. It's an agricultural college.'

'And what's wrong with that? It sounds eminently practical if you wanted to be a sheep farmer.'

'Who says I wanted to be a farmer?' said Nick, suddenly candid, his blue eyes holding hers, and she saw in them a mix of emotions: anger, sadness and confusion.

'Family expectation?'

'No, no, not at all,' said Nick hurriedly. 'It's in my blood. I enjoy it.'

Their eyes met and then slid away from each other and Maddie got the distinct feeling that perhaps Nick was being as circumspect with his true feelings as she was.

'Well, this has been nice, but unfortunately one of us has to get back to work and real life, otherwise I will turn into a pumpkin. Whereas you have got to get back for a life of decadence and leisure.'

A shadow crossed Nick's face. 'Yup, I guess so.' He peeled

some Croatian kuna from his wallet and laid the notes in the saucer with the bill. 'Back to real life.'

For someone who had nothing to do but laze around being looked after for the next few weeks, he looked remarkably ungrateful about it.

Chapter 7

A t exactly nine-thirty Ivan turned on the engines, taking his place at the wheel in the small cockpit area just off the lounge, and the yacht puttered its way out of the marina, heading for the open sea. The boat scythed through the waves, heading towards the green-covered islands in the distance as the sunlight sparkled on the water like silver sparklers.

First port of call was a cove just off a place called Sutivan on the island of Brač, where Ivan promised them the perfect spot for lunch and an afternoon of swimming and paddle-boarding.

Breakfast had been relatively quiet as neither Tara, Cory nor Simon emerged before they set sail. Maddie wasn't sure whether to be irritated or pleased; on the one hand it meant that there were plenty of pastries left over for the next day but, on the other, she'd had to hang on and hang on, leaving the breakfast things out in case they appeared. It also meant she had to tidy away while they were sailing, which was much harder as trying to balance in the small galley wasn't easy.

She managed to get quite a bit done, singing to herself in the galley, making sure everything was prepared for lunch. Cured meat, a couple of big salads and the fresh bread she'd bought that morning. When she went on deck to check if anyone wanted refreshments, Cory and Tara had now emerged, both looking immaculate in tiny bikinis and matching sarongs, which happened to co-ordinate with each other rather beautifully. Was that accident or design? wondered Maddie.

'Oh, cabin girl,' said Tara. 'Can't remember your name. Do you have any orange juice?'

Maddie smiled pleasantly. She'd just put everything away and was about to go and clean the cabins and make the beds.

'It's Maddie and yes, we do; would you like some?'

'Is it freshly squeezed?'

'Um,' said Maddie, putting on an apologetic face, 'no, I don't think it is.'

Tara sighed. 'Please don't tell me it's made from concentrate. I can't abide that.'

'I'm not really sure. It's a local make. So I'm guessing it probably is fresh.'

'Hmm, have you got any pomegranate juice?'

'No, I'm afraid not.'

'And I suppose it would be ridiculous to suppose you might have any coconut water.'

'Yes,' said Maddie.

'What, you have got some?'

'No, I meant . . . we haven't got any.'

Tara narrowed her eyes and under her suspicious scrutiny Maddie managed to keep her face impassive. 'Well, I suppose the orange juice will have to do.'

'Stop being a bitch, T,' drawled Simon. 'The poor girl's doing her best. It's not like there's a Harvey Nicks food store round the corner. The wrong orange juice is not going to spoil that beautiful figure of yours. Come and sit down and tell me all about that friend of yours that got booted off the set in Antibes last week.'

Tara's eyes suddenly gleamed, avid at the prospect of the opportunity to gossip.

Maddie headed back down the steps into the lounge area towards the galley as Tara called, 'No ice.'

'No pleases or thank yous either,' she muttered and then went pink as she realised that Douglas was sitting poring over one of the charts on the table, a pair of binoculars at his side.

He gave her a sly wink and a gentle smile before picking up the binoculars and peering out to the sea as if he hadn't heard a thing. At breakfast he'd been so excited about their departure, peppering Ivan with question after question, peering at the charts with him, boyish wonder lighting up his rounded face. Maddie thought if he was presented with his own captain's hat he'd be as pleased as Punch.

Cleaning cabins was her first port of call. Maddie grinned to herself. Port of call – see, she was right at home already.

Grabbing her bucket of supplies, she mounted the small flight of wooden steps leading to the main deck, where she found Siri sitting reading a book on one of the padded seats hugging the V shape of the bow of the boat.

'Hi, Maddie – isn't this fab?' Siri waved her hand at the view – the sunlight sparkling on the water, the choppy waves dancing up and down and the islands ahead of them shimmering with adventure and promise.

'It's a gorgeous day, that's for sure.'

'Will you get any time off to enjoy it?' she asked, looking at Maddie's bucket of cleaning supplies.

Maddie gave her a quick confiding grin. 'I thought I'd do these cabins first, so that I could be up on deck.'

'Ah, good plan. And what about later?'

'Probably not. It's dependent on what you lot get up to. When you're on board, I'm on duty.'

'No rest then, today,' said Siri, her eyebrows dancing with mischief.

'Not today, but it sounds blissful if you're a guest. Swimming and sunbathing in a secluded cove.'

'Don't worry,' said Siri, her voice dry. 'Cory and Tara are like a pair of toddlers; they'll get bored before too long. I bet you anything Cory will start nagging to go ashore for dinner. And Douglas will give in because he always does. Why do you think we've got this whacking great yacht, big enough for about twenty people, and there are just six of us?'

'He seems very nice,' ventured Maddie, intrigued by the

dynamics of the group and not willing to be drawn to comment. 'How do you all know each other?'

'Douglas is my sort of cousin.'

'Sort of cousin? I've never heard of one of those before.' She raised her eyebrows in a teasing grin.

'Our parents are best friends. Like the best of friends. Do everything together. Parties. Holidays. And we're both only children. I call his mum Aunty Margot. We're the same age, even though he acts as if he's ten years older, and we've been pretty much thrown together throughout our childhood and, yes, he is a lovely man, now. Bloody pain in the arse when he was fourteen.' She pulled a face. 'And at sixteen too, actually. But he got better. I quite like him now.' Her eyes crinkled. 'Ironically, now we're not stuck with each other, we actually voluntarily spend time together and he's one of my best friends.' For a second she looked a touch wistful as her gaze drifted out to sea and then she raised her head and said in a much more matter-of-fact way, 'Of course, now he's all grown up he's as rich as Croesus and . . .' her eyes darkened '. . . in love with Cory. And I bloody introduced them. I'm a fashion stylist –' she lowered her voice '– which is why Cory and Tara humour me. They know I could make them look crap on a photoshoot if I wanted to and we cross paths often enough for them to worry about it.' Her sudden smile was positively Machiavellian. 'Simon went to school with Douglas; they've been friends for ever and he knew Cory from his tennis days.'

'Am I supposed to know who he is?' whispered Maddie, looking over her shoulder.

Siri let out a deep, dirty laugh. 'Yes,' she said, widening her eyes in mischief.

'Oh, heck,' groaned Maddie. 'Epic fail. He is some sort of celeb?'

'He thinks he is.' She paused before adding in a kindlier tone, 'He used to play tennis – junior Wimbledon doubles finalist, twenty years ago. To be fair, he was pretty good, but he never quite made the grade after that.'

'That's a shame.'

'Don't feel too sorry for him; he seems to have built an entire career on it. And he's not exactly steeped in regret and misery.'

'Tara is Cory's best frenemy – whatever you do, don't get caught between the two of them. They're either joined at the hip or spitting like cats at each other, but it can change in an instant. Never side with one or the other of them.'

'And Nick?' asked Maddie casually.

'The new beefcake. Cute, isn't he?' Her eyes gleamed.

Maddie wrinkled her nose. 'Not my type.'

'Can't see him lasting long; he's not Tara's usual type. Her usual preference is for someone who can get her onto a red carpet, into a good party or is paparazzi friendly. Maybe this time it's something more.' She lifted her shoulders in an elegant shrug. 'He's certainly easy on the eye and not a complete idiot, although time will tell.' She laughed and waved her book at Maddie. 'And I am a cynical old harpy. Been in the business too long. Douglas is the best one of the lot of them. Not much to look at but the kindest heart.' Suddenly she lifted her chin, giving Maddie a quick sharp smile before she went back to her book.

Well, that was enlightening, thought Maddie, making her way to the first of the two guest cabins which were up on this deck, along with Ivan's and hers. She was intrigued to see how the six guests had spread themselves out among the cabins. As the boat danced through the waves, the wind whipped at her short curls, which had escaped the ponytail she could just scrape her hair into, making her wonder how Cory would keep her incredible hair under control. The first cabin she came to was empty. Given that there were eight cabins between six people, of which four were couples, that wasn't a big surprise.

The second showed a few sparse signs of occupation. A comb by the bedside table, a book and a phone charger. At the sight of the book, she paused. Someone after her own taste; she loved a good Dick Francis. This one was an ancient and battered copy. Then she smirked. A pair of salmon-pink shorts had been tossed onto the unmade side of the double bed. Pinching her lips, she folded the shorts and laid them neatly on the chest of drawers built into the bulkhead.

Then she frowned. It looked as if Nick was sleeping solo, not that it was anything to do with her. Quickly she remade the bed and gave the gleaming wood a quick once-over with a cloth. Everything had been cleverly designed to fit into the tiny room, the wardrobe built into an alcove, the bed tucked tight under the window and the bathroom a masterpiece in space saving. Nick was certainly clean and tidy and travelled light. Cleaning the bathroom took all of five minutes, wiping around a simple shaving kit, a small bottle of aftershave and the complimentary bottles of shower gel, shampoo and conditioner. She'd just finished in there when the door opened and she looked up to find a bare-chested Nick hovering uncomfortably on the threshold of the doorway.

'Oh, hi. Sorry, I . . . er . . . I just came up to get my sunglasses.'

'It's your room,' she said.

'Yes. I . . . er . . . didn't . . . um . . . expect maid service. I thought you'd have enough to do.' He stepped into the cabin and it immediately felt very small.

'I'm like Cinderella at sea,' quipped Maddie, desperately trying not to look at his broad muscled chest. Being in the same tiny room as a half-naked man suddenly felt rather intimate and she was noticing a lot more about Nick than she had done earlier. 'My work is never done. Would you like me to leave?' she asked, her voice over-bright. No wonder Tara fancied him.

'No, if I could just grab them from the bathroom, that would be cool.'

'No problem.' She moved to one side as he moved past her into the bathroom. 'I see you changed your shorts.'

*

Moving down to the lower deck, she found that Douglas and Cory had taken the master suite nestled in the bow of the boat. Simon and Siri had a cabin each. His had enough male grooming product to stock a branch of Boots and Siri's had a massive stack of books. And although it was quite untidy, with lots of bits of jewellery, scarves and shoes left lying around, all her clothes were put away.

Opening a few more doors, Maddie found Tara's room and very nearly slammed the door shut again.

'Holy shit!' she breathed, standing in the doorway. Surely nothing short of a tornado had swept through this room. Even her sister Theresa's side of the bedroom at home had never been this bad and on a scale of ten in the messy range Theresa punched well above her weight with an eleven plus.

'Where the hell do I start?' she asked herself, resorting to talking out loud because in some weird universe that seemed to help. Even Hercules would have turned tail at this task. Her initial flicker of panic was quickly doused by indignation. What an inconsiderate cow! Was Tara expecting someone to pick up after her?

Discarded clothes covered every inch of the bed, but when she turned to look at the wardrobe she realised every last hanger was full and dozens of pairs of shoes were spilling out of the bottom. Two wet bath towels had been abandoned on the floor.

No wonder Nick didn't want to share with her. Every available surface was strewn with stuff. There wasn't a spare inch to be seen on the dressing table top, which was covered with make-up: palettes of eyeshadow, a dozen lipsticks, most with their caps removed, at least ten eyeliner pencils and four different mascaras, while on the narrow shelf above the double bed were tubes of moisturizer, body lotion and a million vials and pots of things that Maddie had never even heard of. Midnight oil elixir, skin rejuvenation capsules, orchid oil, mattifying detox and oxygenating mister.

Gritting her teeth, she got to work. What were the chances of Tara appreciating everything being put in order? With the room done, she moved to the bathroom.

She was dismayed by the sight of once pristine white hand towels, dished out just yesterday, which were now make-up stained. The bathroom had been well used; the sink was filthy and the toilet . . . surprisingly, it looked as if Tara had tried to clean it, although she hadn't done a very good job. And then Maddie felt a little less self-righteous. It looked as if Tara had been sick. No wonder she hadn't eaten much last night at dinner. Or maybe she was seasick. It had been quite odd going to sleep the first night in the cabin, getting used to the bobbing motion of the boat. Maddie had brought a good supply of Stugeron seasickness tablets with her; perhaps she should offer one to the other woman. Maybe that was why she was so demanding this morning; she wasn't feeling well.

The hazy islands shimmering in the distance gradually morphed into green-clad hills rising out of the sea and while Maddie was laying the table for lunch, prolonging the task just to be on deck, she could feel the palpable air of excitement among the guests as they neared the island of Brač.

Everyone stood on the bow watching as Ivan guided the yacht into a quiet inlet just off the rocky coastline where the scrubby trees came right down to the water. The water glinted in the sunlight, a deep beautiful turquoise. It looked like paradise.

When Ivan dropped the anchor it was the signal for lunch and she brought up big platters of antipasti: cured meats, grilled peppers, artichokes, olives and local cheese, along with a selection of salads and some of the fresh bread she'd bought in the bakery this morning.

'Thanks, Maddie,' said Simon when he came to the table, where she waited for everyone to be seated. 'Looks delicious.'

Once they were seated, Maddie asked what everyone would like to drink.

'Well, I think we should celebrate our first day at sea with a lunchtime bottle of Prosecco,' said Douglas, putting his map down.

'Or we could have Bellinis,' said Cory with a definite hint of challenge in her voice.

Maddie didn't say anything, just waited for the consensus.

'I'll stick with Prosecco,' said Simon.

'I'm not fussy; I'll have whatever's going,' said Siri,

relaxing against the back of her chair like a contented cat. 'Drinking at lunchtime feels so decadent.'

'I'll have a Bellini,' said Tara.

'Would it be possible to have a beer?' asked Nick, almost apologetically.

'No problem,' said Maddie. 'One beer, one bottle of Prosecco and two Bellinis coming up.'

The serene, I've-got-this-smile lasted until she reached the galley. Fuck! What the hell was a Bellini? She dug out her phone, grateful she'd still got a couple of bars' worth of signal. Prosecco with peach puree! They had to be flipping kidding. Cory and Tara were having a laugh. Those two were clearly in a constant state of one-upmanship.

Who the flip kept peach puree as a store cupboard standby? Going through every cupboard, she learned there was Chinese five spice, Jasmine rice, baked beans and tahini paste but no peach puree.

She did, however, find a very dusty tin of peaches at the very back of one shelf. Pureed peach coming up.

Maddie one, Cory and Tara nil.

Nick stretched lazily on the sunbed, his muscles nicely aching after the afternoon's paddleboarding, enjoying the sun on his skin and the rhythmic bob of the boat on the water. The scent of pine and salt filled the air and as far as he could see the sky was pure, deep, glorious blue.

'Nicky darling, will you put some sun cream on my back?' asked Tara, unplugging her earphones and putting down the phone, to which she was addicted. She was lying on her front but had undone her bikini top and her bottoms, if they could be called that, covered nothing. It was officially the smallest bikini he'd ever seen in his life, not that he was complaining. That was one very pert bottom but he dreaded to think what his mother would have thought of the thong-style pants.

'Sure.' He rolled onto his side, sitting up and spraying the expensive suntan lotion onto her back and then rubbing it carefully into the nape of her neck, her shoulders and down her delicate spine.

'Mmm, ooh, that is nice,' murmured Tara, wriggling sinuously under his touch. 'Can you do my legs . . . and my bottom?' Nick swallowed and paused. She lifted her hips in quick invitation, turning her head and saying over her shoulder, 'Don't be shy.'

'Who said anything about being shy?' he countered. 'I'm just admiring the view.'

'Like what you see, do you?' she purred in a low sultry voice, giving him another sexy smile before dropping her head back onto her forearms to watch him with lazy half-closed eyes.

He sprayed the suntan lotion along the backs of her legs, massaging the fine spray into her calves, working his way up her slim thighs, conscious of her constant gaze. When he smoothed his hands over the perfect globes of her bottom, she murmured, 'Mmm,' lifting her hips and wriggling her bottom, squirming at his touch.

'I think I could get used to this,' she said in a throaty voice that had his senses humming.

'So could I.' He stroked her soft skin, the firm gorgeous flesh filling his hands as he pressed his palms over her bottom. There wasn't an inch of her that wasn't absolutely perfect and as he rubbed his hands in small insistent circles, desire tightened his groin. He let it build as he continued to massage her skin, before sliding his hands up her back to rub a gentle finger over the nape of her neck.

He lay down on his side on the edge of his sunbed, his head next to hers, and leaned forward to lay a soft kiss on her pretty pink lips. 'So beautiful,' he whispered and she smiled up at him.

He kissed her again, tracing his mouth over hers, and put an arm over her back to pull her closer, longing to feel her stunning body against his.

'Perhaps we should go back to one of the cabins for an afternoon nap,' he suggested.

Tara shifted and let out a long mournful sigh. 'Tempting, darling Nicky, but –' she patted his cheek '– it's imperative that I get an even tan. I need to do another half hour on my back and then half an hour on my front.'

'That's very precise,' he teased, slipping his fingers under her hairline and caressing her neck, before sliding his fingers down her back, skimming her skin with a gentle touch. 'Are you sure you can't be persuaded?'

Her pretty mouth tightened and for a brief second he

saw a flash of petulance on her face before she smiled, sincerity filling her rich dark eyes.

'Darling Nicky, you know how hard it is being a model. You have to be on it all the time. And I don't want Cory to be browner than me. We're both up for the same shoot when we get back and they want someone with a good all-over tan.'

'I'm sure a couple of hours won't make that much difference,' said Nick, nipping at her mouth with another gentle kiss as he put his arm around her shoulders, the sneaking thought batting at his mind that he was chasing an elusive butterfly.

'It will,' she said, her voice sharp as she shook him off. 'And I'd have to shower and I don't want to get my hair wet.' She reached for her earphones and plugged them back in, tucking her head between her arms, effectively shutting him out.

Nick rolled over onto his back, hot and horny, but at the same time mortification burned his cheeks; he'd never force himself on a woman. He knew what no meant, but Tara had somehow managed to make him feel like some kind of overeager fumbling schoolboy. Embarrassed, as much by the signs of his physical reaction as the worry that he'd come across as some kind of sex pest, he rearranged his swimming shorts, grateful that they were baggy. 'I think I'll go for another swim,' he said gruffly, not that she gave any sign of having heard him.

As he swung his legs over the side of the sunbed he

looked up to see Maddie at the top of the steps with a knowing smirk on her face. He flushed and glared at her.

'I was just coming to see if anyone wanted a drink.' Amusement brimmed in her eyes, suggesting she'd over-heard his thwarted attempt at seduction and thought it highly funny.

'No, thanks,' he snarled, his face burning as he walked past her down the stairs. For a moment it was tempting to push the dratted woman overboard. She always managed to catch him at the wrong moment.

As soon as he hit the water, the refreshing coolness calmed his bruised ego and he sliced into the waves in a determined crawl, wanting to put as much distance between him and the boat as possible. He focused on clean strokes, breathing and feeling the water stream over his body, working his muscles hard to burn up some of the antsy, edgy energy threatening to explode. Stroke, stroke, breathe, stroke, stroke, breathe.

When his shoulders started to burn he slowed and eased into a more leisurely breaststroke, taking the time to look around. Maddie was probably still laughing her head off. Why was it she had the ability to make him feel even more out of his depth than he already did? It always seemed as if she saw too much. He flipped on his back to gaze up at the sky and let out a long sigh. Tara confused him. She made him feel heavy-handed and gauche sometimes, but then there were other times, when she gave him that dazzling brilliant smile, that he felt he could conquer the world and fell armies for her. They came from such different worlds; there were bound to be teething problems but they could get through those, he could adapt. She was so beautiful; she was worth it, wasn't she?

He frowned; perhaps part of the problem was that he wasn't used to all this inactivity. At home, by this time he'd have already put in a full day's work, been for a run, walked several miles and put in some hard physical labour, shifting sacks of feed, building fences or wrangling sheep. Every day was different, although there was a constant reassuring cycle of familiarity. Looking up at the sky and the land in front of him, the dark green, the azure blue above and turquoise sea, he shook his head. How could he even think he was missing home when all this was on offer? He could hear his mother's amused voice telling him, 'You must have turnips for brains'. He smiled. He missed his family, that was for sure, but that was allowed, wasn't it? Knowing his place, the banter with his brothers, the unconditional love and the sense of community. Shaking his head, he rolled his eyes. Surely he wasn't homesick. He was a grown man, for goodness' sake, having the holiday of a lifetime. His brothers had been green with envy when he'd told them how amazing the boat was. How many other people were invited on a millionaire-style boat trip?

Come on, buck up, Nick, he told himself as he started to swim back to the boat. So your girlfriend didn't fancy a shag; it's not the end of the world.

'Hey, Nick,' called Siri, who was bobbing about on one of the ridiculous flamingo inflatables when he reached the boat again. 'We're going to get the jet ski out, fancy a go?'

'You bet,' he called back. Yeah, his brothers would be seriously envious when he told them about that.

Chapter 8

As they puttered towards the quayside, the engine humming and throbbing, Maddie wiped the breakfast table, rounding up all the dishes in record time, dashing backwards and forwards between the galley balancing as much in her hands as she could with each trip. Already in her head she was working out how quickly she could get the rooms cleaned and finished.

It was day three of the trip and just before breakfast was served this morning Ivan had weighed anchor and they'd left another of the pretty bays where they'd stayed the night and were now heading to their first port in the town of Bol on the other side of Brač. There was a distinct buzz of excitement among everyone as they neared land.

Over breakfast there'd been much debate on the plan of action for the day.

'We have to go to Zlatni Rat,' declared Tara.

'Yes, we absolutely must,' said Cory in immediate support.

'What the hell is that?' asked Siri. 'Sounds awful. Like

a rodent zoo or something. Doesn't sound like your kind of thing at all, Tara.'

'Don't be silly, Siri,' giggled Tara. 'It's a very famous beach. Voted one of the ten best in Europe. I need to get a picture of me there.'

'The third best beach in Europe,' added Cory. 'It looks divine.'

'It is a very fine beach,' interjected Ivan from his position at the wheel. 'One of the best in Croatia. You should definitely visit. You can take the snorkels and fins; the water is very clear. You can hire windsurfing boards. I would recommend you spend the whole day. There is an excellent promenade to the beach with plenty of bars and places for lunch.'

Tara clapped her hands. 'It sounds perfect. We have to go.'

Douglas gave one of his good-natured shrugs. 'I'm easy.'

'We know that, sweetie,' said Cory, her smile not quite meeting her eyes. Maddie narrowed her eyes; the girl didn't know how lucky she was. Douglas absolutely adored her and she wasn't always very kind to him.

'As long as I can be a complete slob, sounds good to me,' said Siri, stretching. 'Give me a good book, sunshine and the sea and I'm a happy bunny.'

'It's been a while since I did any windsurfing, but I wouldn't mind another shot,' said Simon, glancing at Nick. 'You ever done any?'

'A bit,' said Nick, with that bland look which Maddie

had quickly clocked was his defensive don't-give-too-much-away expression. Simon seemed determined to challenge him at every turn, almost as if he wanted to show him up in front of Tara.

'There is also a very good winery, Stina, just here on the quay.' Ivan pointed to a large square building over to the left. 'They produce some fine Croatian wines and in the evenings at five and six they do a very good tour and tasting for visitors. I could arrange for you to visit, perhaps before dinner.'

'That sounds like a very good idea,' said Douglas. 'We could stock up on some wine for the rest of the trip.' They'd already made inroads into Ivan's demi-john and Siri and Douglas were big fans.

'Let's hope they sell decent stuff, then,' said Simon, folding his arms. 'Sometimes the local stuff can be a bit earthy. No offence, Ivan, but I'm something of a wine connoisseur.'

Douglas wrinkled his nose. 'Yes, he is.'

'That's why you should listen to me. Remember the last time you got carried away. Bought that case of bloody Beaujolais Nouveau.'

'Oh, Lord, yes – still giving it away to the lower end clients.' Douglas rolled his eyes. 'Got a bit carried away at the chap's tasting. He assured me it was decent. Ruddy well should have been at the price.'

'You were done, mate. You know anything about wine, Nick?' asked Simon with deceptive casualness.

Nick shook his head. 'No, I'm more of a real ale man myself.'

'Yeah, I can see that,' said Simon before smoothly turning to Ivan. 'And where would you recommend we eat this evening? The captain always has the inside track on the best places.'

'There's a very good new restaurant a short walk from here, just up the hill. Would you like me to reserve a table for you?'

'That would be capital,' said Douglas. 'We'll do the wine tour, have a couple of drinks and then dinner at eight-thirty.'

'Excellent,' said Ivan. Before anyone had chance to agree or disagree, he walked off, pulling his phone out and climbing the stairs to the upper deck.

As soon as everyone had finished eating they all scurried away to their cabins to get ready for a trip to the beach and now Maddie was left to tidy up in silence, with the delicious prospect of the whole day to herself as soon as she'd done the cabins.

'You have the boat to yourself. A day off,' said Ivan, catching her in the galley. 'You're welcome.'

'Thank you.' She grinned back at him. 'Nicely done.'

He shrugged. 'Why not? They've not been here before. The restaurant is very good.' He grinned. 'It's run by an old friend of mine, who appreciates me sending custom his way.'

'Appreciates?'

Ivan rubbed his fingers together. 'It is an excellent restaurant. The guests have a fine meal. My friend gets their custom. I am rewarded. You have the night off from cooking. I have friends in Bol I like to catch up with. I'll stay the night with them . . .' He mimed having a drink. 'Everyone is happy. And you can be in charge.'

'Me?' she squeaked. 'Are you sure?'

'The guests will be out for most of the day. You have my mobile number. And I won't be far away.' He pointed to the hillside, where the houses ranged along the contours. 'My friends are just there.'

'OK.' She grinned, butterflies dancing in her stomach at all the options open to her. 'I'd better get finished in here.' She wasn't going to waste a single second. A whole day free.

Maddie was just about ready to scream. How long did it take to get ready for a trip to the flaming beach? She wasn't the only one; Siri was tapping her fingers on the rail by the gangplank, Simon was on the quayside pacing and Nick was sitting on a bollard, his face tipped up to the sun.

'I think we should just go without her,' said Siri. 'The day's a-wasting.'

Douglas and Cory were in the shop opposite and it looked as if Douglas was in the process of buying Cory a pretty cotton scarf and a straw hat.

'Nick, why don't you go and drag Tara out, like a good little caveman?' said Simon.

Nick's mouth tightened but his expression was hidden behind his sunglasses. 'She'll be ready in her own good time. Why don't you go on ahead? We'll catch up with you.'

Simon ignored his response and carried on pacing. While they'd been waiting Maddie had managed to slip in and clean all three of their rooms. She'd also mopped the deck where they'd had breakfast and the galley was now spotless.

At last Tara appeared. There was a collective gasp and one of the passing tourists walked straight into a bollard and a sharp slap from his wife. She stopped at the top of the steps in front of the gangplank to strike a pose, one hip angled out, so that the men could appreciate her full beauty.

Star Wars came to mind. Maddie stared at the scarlet bikini with its gold metal straps, reminiscent of Princess Leia's slave girl outfit, and the high-heeled matching sandals that accentuated the length of Tara's long slender legs. There was a resounding silence and then she clanked down the gangplank, which rather spoiled the effect.

'Planning on reducing the local adolescent population to gibbering wrecks?' asked Simon, a touch acidly.

Tara shot him a sneer and walked over to Nick, her hips swaying, and placed a proprietorial arm on his. Maddie tried hard not to smile at the stunned expression on his face. Actually, she decided, it was more shocked and horrified, not that she blamed him.

100

Luckily Tara wasn't watching Nick's reaction; she was too busy checking out who was looking her way.

'Are you going to be all right walking to the beach?' asked Nick in a strangled voice, looking down at her shoes. 'It's quite a long way. Haven't you got any flip-flops or anything?'

'Darling Nicky –' she reached up and kissed him on the cheek, rubbing her hand over his biceps '– I'm sure if I run into any trouble you could carry me.'

Easily charmed, thought Maddie crossly, as Nick's face creased into a doting smile. The man was a complete idiot.

'I could tuck you under one arm with no problem at all,' he said. 'Here, let me take that for you.' He reached for her enormous striped beach bag. 'Are you going to . . . have you got a cover-up or anything?'

'Darling, you are so cute. *Cuver up*.' She emphasised his northern vowels. 'I love it when you're all buttoned-up and northern. So prudish.'

Simon sniggered, while Siri tutted. 'For God's sake, Tara, put something on. You can't go parading through the streets looking like that. There's nothing prudish about it.'

'Bloody hell, Tara, that's some swimming cossie,' Douglas blurted out, bellowing across the road before coming to join them. Next to him, Cory in a white crocheted bikini top and tiny navy shorts turned puce.

'You're just attention-seeking,' continued Siri in a low voice, 'and trying to upstage Cory. Job done, so cover yourself up. Surely in that huge bag you've got something. What the hell have you got in there? We're going to the beach for the day, not on safari for a week.'

With ill grace, Tara yanked a sheer red chiffon tunic out of her bag, which still left little to the imagination but was a slight improvement.

Maddie heaved an enormous sigh of relief when they finally moved off and then began to giggle to herself. She was glad she wasn't joining the party.

An hour later, with her own beach bag of essentials, she set off, giving a cheery wave to the crew on the boat moored next door, who were still busy serving breakfast. She deliberately turned in the opposite direction to the one the others had taken this morning; she had no desire to bump into any of them. In fact if she saw Tara she'd have a hard job not to push her into the sea. Her room was back to being a pigsty and the wretched girl had been sick again and had tried to clean it up. Badly.

Bol, she decided, pulling down her sunglasses, was delightful. The buildings were all built from creamy white stone, with wooden shutters and the now familiar terracotta tiled roofs. Tall stone buildings lined the harbour area and she walked along the cobbles skirting the harbour's edge, where small boats bobbed gently and tables were laid for lunch. She followed the little stone path which wound its way around another smaller harbour area and then up some steps past a few buildings. At the top she rounded a corner and immediately below was a small pebbled beach edged by the deep aqua blue of the sea. She didn't think she'd ever seen a colour quite like it and it triggered that ache to paint, one that dogged her so often it almost hurt. However, she'd brought her sketchbook with her and today was a holiday, so she was going to indulge herself.

Skirting the restaurant commanding the main view of the beach, she skipped down a set of steps which led down through a small avenue of pine trees offering cool shade and hopped down from the stone wall onto the picturesque pebbled seafront. Maddie smiled. This was it, the perfect spot. The beach was no more than a few metres deep and some families had set up camp right at the water's edge, while others had spread themselves out on the wall.

Tramping across the small stones, which was hard work, she headed for a spot towards the other side of the beach near the sea and spread out her towel before stripping off. Yesterday she'd watched enviously as the others had swum and played in the sea. Now it was her turn. Picking her way barefoot was excruciatingly uncomfortable, although it didn't seem to bother the little children playing happily in the shallows. When she eased herself into the water she was thrilled to find that it was cool rather than cold.

She swam out to the boundary of the beach, where a rope and buoys created a safe area for swimming. There were quite a few boats shimmering in the hazy sunshine, a few as big as the *Avanturista*, gliding along in full sail, and lots of smaller speedboats zipping along, bouncing across the waves, the wash drifting into the shore.

Floating lazily on her back, she watched a group of Croatian children snorkelling, swimming and jumping from the rocks nearby. One of them emerged from the water, one hand held aloft, waving what looked like a small green rag, and began chasing another child, giggling as he waggled the green thing. Suddenly there was a spurt of water towards the second child, who ducked with a scream of laughter and the first child tossed away the makeshift water pistol.

Intrigued now, she watched as the other children began to dive below the surface, some of them finding more of what she guessed was some kind of sea creature.

'They are sea cucumbers,' said an elderly man swimming nearby, with a nod towards the children.

'Ah, I did wonder,' said Maddie with a smile.

The old man shook his head with an indulgent smile and swam off, giving the children a wave.

After a while the children grew bored with their game, or perhaps ran out of the poor creatures, and began a new game chasing each other in and out of the shallows.

This was the life, Maddie decided, looking back to the beach and the people enjoying the gorgeous day and the warm sea. If she could have the odd day off like this, then putting up with the likes of Tara and Cory was worth it.

Chapter 9

'**Y**ou're pretty good.'

Maddie jumped, dropping her pencil and clutching her sketchbook to her chest like some melodramatic miss in a period drama.

'Simon!' She looked up at him from her perch on the rocks at the far end of the beach, deliberately chosen to give her some privacy. 'What are you doing here?' She sounded accusatory but she'd thought this spot would be well away from prying eyes, especially any of the guests'. Tempering her tone, she added, 'I thought you'd be with the others.' She looked beyond him, praying they weren't with him. Thank goodness she'd pulled her T-shirt and shorts back on; she didn't want anyone seeing her in a bikini – her body did not hold up to comparison with a couple of models.

He gave her a wolfish grin before leaning down, picking up her pencil and handing it to her. Then, without invitation, confidently sure of his welcome, he sat down next to her.

'There's only so much a man can take. I needed a rest,' he said, lowering his voice in a confiding tone, tinged with amusement. So –' he nodded towards the book she was still protecting in her arms with possessive determination '– let's have a look.' Sudden predatory speculation gleamed in his eyes.

Maddie swallowed, realising with unexpected insight that if she denied him he'd see it as a challenge, one that he'd have to win, and that he'd read more than she wanted him to see into it.

'Oh, I thought I'd have a go at doing a bit of drawing.' She loosened her hold on the book, but left it lying propped up against her and looked out over the sea. 'It's so gorgeous here. I've never seen such clear sea or a colour like it. How was Zlatni Rat?'

Ignoring her pathetic attempt to divert him, Simon leaned forward and laid a lazy hand on the sketchbook and grinned at her, his dark blue eyes full of laughter as they met hers. 'Maddie, Maddie,' he said with mock reproach, 'what a fib.' His eyes holding hers, he gently took the book from her hands and laid it on his knees.

Gosh, they were such blue eyes. Her heart bumped uncomfortably in her chest as somehow his gaze moved from teasing to something a little more intense that made her breath catch in her throat. Simon Beresford was one of the most handsome men she'd ever seen. She felt herself flush and ducked her head.

Simon gave a low chuckle. 'So, what have we here?'

Maddie clenched one hand behind her leg, stiffening. Very few people had ever seen her sketches. She stared out at the distant island across the sea, her vision blurry.

Simon turned the book and whistled. 'This is good. Very good.' When he glanced up at her, the speculation was back as he narrowed his eyes. 'Having a go, my arse.' He nudged her with his elbow. 'I think someone's telling porky-pies.'

Blinking, she shrugged. 'I'm . . . It's just . . .'

'You've got some talent going on here, my lovely.' He laid a warm hand on her leg, just above the knee but not quite on her thigh. An ambiguous position that left her wondering, except he was looking at her lips. Then he jerked his gaze away as if he realised he shouldn't.

'I'm no expert, but I know enough to know this is pretty good. My uncle owns a couple of galleries. He's always said I've got an eye. If I hadn't gone into tennis, I probably would have gone into business with him.' With long elegant fingers he tapped the picture, before lifting the page. 'May I?'

Mute, Maddie nodded, even though she wanted to snatch it out of his hands.

She watched as he turned the pages, giving each one careful, silent consideration. A street scene of Paris, a run of terrace houses in Bourneville, the hallway of abandoned shoes at home, a detail of the window of Nina's patisserie, a wrought iron balcony from the Hôtel des Invalides, the clock at Musée d'Orsay.

The dryness in her throat almost hurt as she held her

breath while he pored over each image: pieces of her heart, beats of her life.

When he came to the first picture, done on the day she'd arrived in Paris for her year abroad, she gave a tremulous smile. She'd been so nervous, terrified and excited, but at the sight of the Arc de Triomphe she'd had to sit down and draw. That picture embodied all her hopes and dreams for the year, and what a year it had turned out to be. She'd met Nina and Marguerite and discovered a world away from the disorganised, narrow confines of the cramped house in Birmingham.

There was a whole world out there; she just needed to figure out where she belonged in it. Much as she loved her family, she wanted more.

Simon lifted his head, those blue eyes focused on her, and for a full minute he didn't say anything. She could feel the pulse in her neck thudding hard and wondered if he could see it.

'Have you ever shown these to anyone?' he asked, watching her carefully.

Before she had chance to answer, he said, 'I can tell you. These are incredible. You. Are. A. Very. Talented. Artist.'

'Really?' she breathed, a sudden whoosh in her stomach. 'You're not just saying that?'

He laughed. 'Maddie, Maddie, Maddie. Why would I do that?'

She gave him a shy smile. 'I don't know, but these are just for me.'

'You don't believe that, surely.'

She lifted her shoulders helplessly. 'People like me don't become artists.'

'Rubbish. Who told you that? I'll have words with them. Want me to duff them up for you?' He put up a pair of pretend fists and pulled a fierce face, which made Maddie laugh.

The thought of the elegant, immaculately attired Simon beating anyone up, even the two ice blondes from the London gallery, was ridiculous, although the sentiment was touching. 'I don't think anyone's ever offered to "duff" someone up for me before.' With her build, she was more likely to do the duffing-up for herself.

'Well, they should have,' said Simon, giving her another one of those warm looks, which made her feel unaccountably girly, which wasn't like her at all. 'Would you like to go for a drink? That place under the pines looks the perfect spot.' He'd already risen to his feet, holding out his hand to help her up.

Ignoring the natural instinct to say no, after all he was a guest, she found herself taking his hand and standing up.

'Cheers,' said Simon, lifting his elegant long-stemmed glass of white wine in a toast and swirling it in the glass before taking a careful sip. Maddie toasted him back, thinking that most men she knew drank pints, and then she remembered he was a wine expert.

The 'meh' face he pulled suggested the wine wasn't quite good enough but wasn't awful. He looked around at the wrought iron chairs with cream padded cushions arranged under the pine trees around little stone patios.

'This is a nice peaceful spot. God! Those girls this morning. Talk about exhausting. Halfway along the walk to the beach, which is a good bloody three kilometres, I might add, of course Tara started bellyaching about how far it was. And Cory couldn't resist having a pop at her about her shoes, jealous as a cat she was that Tara had upstaged her in her Johanna Ortiz number.'

When Maddie frowned, he added kindly, 'Johanna Ortiz is the hottest swimwear designer in town at the moment. Tara's bikini was this season's must-have. And Tara had already got two hundred likes on Instagram before we even left the yacht. Cory was livid.' He held up his iPhone, the latest model, Maddie noticed. Was she the only person on the boat who still had an iPhone 5?

'How did she manage that?'

'Why do you think it took her so long to get ready? Getting the right selfie for social media doesn't happen by accident. Tara lives for her Instagram account. Dear God, once we did get to the beach.' He rolled his eyes. 'Pebbles!' he declared in a falsetto, flapping his hands in mimicry. 'No one said it was a pebbly beach.' With a shake of his head, he took another sip of his wine, pulling another grimace of slight dissatisfaction. 'And then we had to wander around for half an hour deciding which sunbeds

110

were the best and away from the great unwashed. Cory insisted that Douglas pay for extra beds so that no one could be next to them. Then when the poor sod had paid a fortune for sunbeds, she and Tara decided they wanted to go and sit in one of the chi-chi bars in the pines. Which gave the rest of us a break. I was planning to do a bit of windsurfing but the kit wasn't up to much, although the he-man decided to have a go.'

'He-man?'

'Yeah, Tara's chum.' He glanced away at his phone, which had beeped on the table, but he didn't pick it up.

'What, Nick?'

'Yeah, poor deluded sap. He's barking up the wrong tree with Tara. Following her around like a lovesick puppy. She needs someone to bring under her control. Leading the poor fella by the nose.'

Maddie thought that was a bit harsh, but then she also thought Nick got what he deserved.

'And Douglas is no better. He ought to put Cory over his knee and give her a damn good spanking.'

'I don't think that's very PC these days,' giggled Maddie at the image he conjured up.

'She's a spoilt brat, milking him for every penny. I love Douglas like a brother, but he's got sod all sense when it comes to women.'

'He's very kind,' observed Maddie.

'Yeah, you think?' He raised a sceptical eyebrow, his eyes sliding right again when his phone beeped again.

'Yes.'

'You don't get to be that rich in the City without a ruthless streak. Come on, stands to reason.'

'I don't really know anything about the City. I don't even know what they do there.'

Simon laughed. 'You really are a little innocent abroad, aren't you? It's a den of vipers who are bloody good at gambling with other people's money, risking it and running to the wire. Investment, they call it. Douglas appears to be better than most at it. Just as well because he was bloody hopeless at everything at school. Think that's probably why they made him head boy. Consolation prize.'

'You were at school with him?'

'Yep. Top hats, prefects, the works.'

'Gosh,' said Maddie, not liking to ask which school they'd gone to but guessing that it must have been Eton or Harrow.

'Yeah, he's a decent fella.' Simon sighed and leaned back in his chair next to hers and lazily stroked her forearm, almost as if he were unaware of doing it.

For a while they sat in companionable silence, which was easy when the view through the needle-clad branches was so wonderful. From here she could see the beach, the sea and the hazy outline of Hvar over the water. A couple of children were playing at the water's edge. A laughing young man was towing a bikini-clad girl into the sea who was protesting and splashing him, all the while laughing back at him. A dad was wading through the lapping waves with a toddler squirming in his arms, her chubby hands leaning down to grab at the water, and there were several older people standing at waist height happily chatting in a neighbourly sort of way. Maddie narrowed her eyes, taking a mental photograph of the scene. The life, the fun, the warmth. Neighbours in the sea. That was what she'd call it.

'This is . . . very relaxing,' Simon said and she realised he'd been looking at her while she'd been daydreaming and people-watching, 'and, I tell you, a damn sight more enjoyable than this morning. You're so easy to talk to.' His face became serious as he studied her. 'You're . . . you're very restful.'

Maddie's pulse kicked but she scrunched up her face in denial. No one had ever called her restful; in fact her family complained that she was too full of beans and always on their case.

'And so much more interesting.'

'Ha! Now I know you're fibbing. Next to Cory and Tara I'm very dull. They lead exciting lives – going to parties, meeting famous people, travelling. They've got glamorous, sophisticated careers.'

'Oh, sweet Maddie, you have no idea what a refreshing change you are,' drawled Simon. 'That lifestyle is exciting for about five minutes and then you realise it's shallow and insubstantial. You know.' His intent look made her nod, even though she didn't know at all. Being beautiful, wealthy and going to lots of parties sounded like quite a lot of fun to her.

'I've reached a stage where I want more out of life. More fulfilling, deeper.' As his voice deepened, his little finger caressed the inside of her wrist, a barely-there thrilling touch.

She smiled nervously. Men like him never looked her way. No one had ever stroked her skin like this. How was she supposed to respond? Not like a rabbit in the head-lights, that was for sure, which was pretty much how she imagined she looked right now.

'Ah, Maddie, you're so gorgeous and you don't even realise it. You've no idea how attractive that is.'

'Me?' she squeaked.

'Genuine, natural. You look like a proper woman. With curves.' He dropped his gaze to her breasts which, unfor-tunately, thanks to her still damp bikini, were clearly visible through her wet T-shirt. 'Very sexy.'

She giggled and fumbled for her wine glass, almost knocking it over. 'I've got big boobs and big hips; that's not sexy.'

'*Au contraire*, I prefer to think of it as voluptuous and allow me to decide what is sexy.'

'This is very nice wine,' she said, taking a sip, wanting to hold the cold condensation-covered glass to her cheeks, which she could feel were burning.

'No, it's not, it's bloody shite. Stop changing the subject.' Simon smiled a knowing feral smile. If she tried to stand up now, her legs would probably give way.

'So, sexy Maddie, what are your plans for this evening while we're all out watching the Tara and Cory show?'

'I'm probably just going to stay on board the boat.' She gave him a quick relieved smile. 'Enjoying the peace and quiet.' In fact, she had it all planned. A few glasses of wine in the Jacuzzi, followed by a frozen pizza she'd found in the freezer so she didn't even have to cook, and she'd plug into her favourite comedy podcast with the boat all to herself – it sounded like heaven.

'Lucky you. Wish I could join you.'

'I'm sure you'll have a great time,' she said, shifting her legs, conscious of his approving gaze.

'The restaurant Ivan has recommended certainly looks good. I'm guessing one of his friends owns the place.'

'Oh!' said Maddie, immediately blushing. 'I'm not sure.'

'Liar! Does he get a kick-back? Commission on the side. Bound to. He's not stupid, that one. I've seen him, "handling" Douglas. Letting Douglas think the route is all his idea.' His phone beeped yet again and this time he rolled his eyes and reached for it and read the screen.

With an exaggerated sigh he put it down. 'I'm afraid I'm being summoned. My absence has been noted and poor Douglas needs reinforcements. I'm going to have to leave you lovely girl.'

He stood up with a regretful heavy sigh and, to her surprise, when she stood up he cupped her cheek and gave her another one of those soul-searching looks that made

Julie Caplin

her tingle all the way down to her toes. 'Perhaps I should leave dinner early and join you on deck for a starlit glass of wine tonight.' He kissed her on the cheek and sauntered off without a backward glance, leaving her ever so slightly breathless.

Chapter 10

The harbour came to life after dark, the lights in the nearby restaurants glowing, couples walking hand in hand, buggies pushed with small sleeping children and the latest ferry arriving with a new influx of visitors. A crescent moon shone high in the sky, its silver light a long glinting reflection dancing on the sea, and Maddie watched the waves rolling in to shore. Tucked away on the front deck, her feet dangling over the side with a glass of chilled white wine, she told herself, listening to the music and the sporadic bursts of laughter from a party on the boat two over, that she wasn't really feeling lonely or homesick, just a tad thoughtful.

She'd been on board earlier, having a doze in her cabin – also known as staying out of everyone's way – when she'd heard the others come back on board to change and get ready for dinner. As everyone but Nick were in the cabins below deck, the noise had quickly died down and all she could hear was him pottering about in the cabin next door to her. The walls were thinner than she'd realised before. Then the strains of familiar music. John Newman? She pricked up her ears. Yup, definitely John Newman. *Love Me Again.* Good to know, if nothing else, Nick had decent taste in music. And it was quite comforting to know there were other people about. Although she'd enjoyed the day to herself, she wasn't built for solitude.

And here she was on her own again, listening to everyone else having a good time. She'd be lying if she said she hadn't kept checking the time, wondering if Simon might get away from the others. She'd enjoyed her pizza, the dip in the Jacuzzi and having the boat to herself but now . . . it would have been quite nice to have someone to share the evening with. Deciding she was getting too maudlin, she hauled her legs in and went to sit at the table, picking up her Kindle, not entirely convinced that reading a thriller in the semi-darkness was her best idea, and had just started reading when she heard voices.

'Carry me, Nicky. Over the gangplank.' Tara's flirtatious giggles floated over the water. Bugger, not that sort of company. Anyone but those two, she thought.

She heard the sort of scuffles that suggested Nick had obliged, and then further muffled giggles and murmurs, from which she guessed there was a lot of kissing going on too. Yuk.

The two of them appeared on deck, Nick carrying Tara's tiny frame in his arms. She looked like some kind of fairy princess in a long multicoloured coat dress, the floaty sheer fabric billowing like gossamer wings over Nick's arms. Pretty as a picture and she knew it. Maddie couldn't help contrasting the image of herself in some poor sod's arms. They'd be buckling with the weight and staggering about. It made her smile. Strong as he was, Nick probably wouldn't be able to lift her.

They hadn't spotted her sitting in the shadows and she couldn't decide whether to make a deliberate noise to alert them or not.

Nick lowered Tara gently to the deck, sliding her down his body as if she was a fragile piece of china and then slid his hands down her back to cup her bottom.

'Mmm, oh, Nicky . . . Oh . . . Oh, Nicky, darling . . .' She'd wrapped her slender arms around his neck, her hand stroking his hair.

Maddie winced at Tara's breathy murmurs. She so did not want to be seeing this.

'Your cabin or mine?' asked Nick.

Tara unwound her arms and took a few steps. 'The others will be waiting for us. I said I was just going to get my wrap.'

'Tara –' Nick caressed her cheek '– I'm sure they won't mind if we don't go back.'

'But they'll wonder where we've got to. Why we haven't come back.'

'I don't think they'll worry,' he teased. 'They'll probably have a good idea.'

'Darling, we can't. I'll just get my wrap and we can go straight back. I won't be long.' With that, she darted away, down the stairs to the lower deck.

With a heavy sigh that made Maddie want to giggle, Nick turned and walked to the rails at the side of the yacht, gripping them with both hands.

Pinching her lips together, she reached for her glass of wine, slouching into her chair, hoping that he wouldn't realise she was there and, because she wasn't watching what she was doing, she chinked her glass against the wine bottle.

Nick whirled round. 'Who . . .? Oh, it's you!'

'Yup, it's me.'

'Get your kicks out of spying on people?' he asked bitterly.

'Not especially, but it was a bit difficult when the two of you were getting hot and heavy to say, *Excuse me, can you stop while I vacate the premises?*'

He pushed his hands in his pockets and turned away, walking back to the guard rail and then back again.

Maddie, refusing to leave, picked up her book and carried on reading, or at least tried to. Nick's brooding presence was distracting, especially the pacing. The minutes ticked by and she put her book down.

'Do you have to do that?'

'Do what?'

'That!' She wagged her finger from side to side.

'Oh.' Nick looked embarrassed. 'Didn't realise . . .' He

glanced at his watch and then towards the stairs, as if hoping Tara would emerge.

Maddie sighed. 'Would you like a drink? I suspect you'll be in for a long wait.'

He looked at his watch again and, while his expression gave nothing away, he shrugged. 'Might as well.'

She poured him a glass, the one she'd had ready just in case someone dropped by, and pushed it towards him.

'How was the restaurant?'

'Good. Expensive. Smart.' When he looked away, she studied his profile, silhouetted against the moonlit sea. No denying it, with that strong chiselled jawline, once broken nose and those broad shoulders, he packed a punch of masculinity.

'Not your cup of tea?'

'I didn't say that,' he muttered.

'You didn't need to.' She grinned.

'Take great delight in it, don't you?' he said, his mouth turning down at the corners.

'In what?' asked Maddie, her amusement dimming.

'Rubbing my nose in the fact that I don't belong.'

The bleak words made her pause. Guilt pinched at her. 'I didn't mean that. I was trying to . . . What I meant was . . .' She stumbled over the words, realising that he was right; she had been doing exactly that. 'Sorry,' she said in a quiet voice.

He didn't reply, instead pulling out his phone and giving all his attention to the screen.

Going back to her book, Maddie couldn't focus on the page, wishing instead she could take the words back. Why had she even said that? Was she trying to bring him back to her level? It felt petty and small.

'Do you think Tara's all right?' she asked after a while.

'I don't know. Do you think I should check on her?'

'Normally I'd say yes, but –' Maddie tried not to sound catty '– she does take quite a long time to get ready. Maybe she's changing into a new outfit or something.'

A rueful smile touched Nick's lips. 'I wondered why she had so many cases when we flew out; now I know.'

'She always looks amazing,' said Maddie in what she hoped was a conciliatory tone. She hadn't meant to hurt him earlier.

Nick nodded but he didn't meet her eyes. 'Maybe I'll give her another five minutes.'

With reluctance and only because he looked a bit lost, she put down her glass. 'Would you like me to check on her? I could always say I was bringing fresh towels or something.'

'Would you mind? She's probably fine, but just in case.'

'No problem.'

She went downstairs, nipping into the first empty cabin on the corridor and grabbing the set of clean towels from the bed to sacrifice to the task, thinking as her hands closed over the pristine softness, *You'd better be grateful for this, Nick flipping Hadley*.

She knocked gently on the door, just in case Tara had

gone to sleep or something. There was no answer but she could hear something and it didn't sound good. She knocked again and gently turned the handle. 'Tara . . .' she said in a soft voice as she pushed open the door. 'Tara, are you OK?'

But it was clear from the heave of her shoulders and the sudden flood of liquid that Tara was far from OK. Through the bathroom door, she could see Tara bent over the toilet seat, her hair twisted up in one hand, held away from her face as she vomited into the bowl.

Maddie hesitated, half of her wanting to give the poor girl privacy and the other half feeling a natural urge to comfort her, but then she decided Tara wouldn't thank her for the latter so she backed out, closing the door carefully behind her.

As it was unlikely Tara and Nick would be going out again, there was no hurry to go back up on deck, so she decided while she was down here she'd quickly turn down the beds in the nearby cabins.

She was just finishing and about to go and tell Nick that poor Tara was ill and unlikely to be going anywhere when she heard Tara's door slam. Making her way up to the deck, puzzled by the strong smell of mint and Black Opium, Tara's signature scent, she was amazed to see her in a brand-new outfit – different five-inch gladiator gold sandals and a halterneck dress which scooped so low you could almost see her bum-crack, which made Maddie want to giggle – bum-crack was not a word you'd associate with the glamorous model. There was absolutely no sign of any wrap to cover the expanse of bare back on show.

'Shall we go, darling?' she trilled, hooking her arm around Nick's neck.

'Are you sure? I thought something must be wrong, you were gone so long.'

'You men, always complaining about how long we take to get ready.' Tara rolled her eyes, put her hands on her hips and smiled prettily up at him. 'I'm worth it, aren't I?'

Maddie stared at her, noting the glittering eyes and high colour in her cheekbones. Most people when they were sick were pasty and green. If it had been Maddie, she'd have mascara down both cheeks and be feeling like hell. Tara looked bright and excited. Almost as if she'd been doing drugs or something. And then it clicked.

They'd come straight from dinner. Tara insisting they came back. The stained towels. The dirty toilet bowl. How sad.

'Sure you want to go back now?' asked Nick, making no move. 'The others have probably moved on.'

'They have. Cory texted me. There's a darling cocktail bar they're in now. Come on.' She tugged at his arm. 'It's still early.'

'Early?' Nick laughed and looked at his watch. 'Some of us would be thinking about going to bed at this time.'

'Darling, you are such a bumpkin sometimes. Seriously, no one goes to bed at this time.' She kissed him on the forehead. 'It's still early. Come on, we'll be late.'

124

Tara clearly operated on a different timescale to normal people.

It was the first time Maddie had seen the resigned expression on Nick's face as he heaved himself to his feet. He looked tired and she actually felt a bit sorry for him. And, although she didn't like Tara, she felt a bit sorry for her too.

'OK, then. Let's go party.'

As Tara's heels tapped across the gangplank, Maddie pulled out her phone, bringing up the Google search page, and typed in the word, *bulimia*.

Chapter 11

Nick picked his way out of the water, wincing as the pebbles bit into the soles of his feet. Compared to yesterday, when the famous horn-shaped beach had been absolutely packed, the place was deserted, but then at six-thirty in the morning it was hardly surprising. Despite the late night, his body clock still insisted on waking him at five-thirty.

His shoulders ached slightly from yesterday's windsurfing but it was worth it. Those years windsurfing on the windy reservoir at Kielder Water had paid off. He was still relishing wiping the smug smile off Beresford's face and his cocky assumption that someone like Nick had never windsurfed.

Gathering up his stuff, he packed it all into the backpack, ready to run back along the pine promenade, and took a few shots of the deserted beach, the view of the steep rocky hill, the town in the distance, and shared them on the Hadley Massive family Whatsapp group.

The beach this morning.

So jealous. Raining here. That was Gail.

What Billy no mates, where is everyone? asked Dan.

He's frightened everyone away, quipped Jonathon Looks lovely. I do hope you're having a wonderful time and enjoying yourself. Give our love to Tara.

Seeing the message from his mum, Nick pulled a face. He'd hoped this trip would give them a chance to spend more time together, but it felt as if Tara was as elusive as ever. She was a night owl, he was a lark. Perhaps today he could suggest that the two of them went out to lunch together, spend some quality time together, away from everyone else.

Pleased with this plan, he set off back to the yacht at a steady jog, the wind ruffling his short damp hair as he pounded along the pine-fringed walkway.

The harbour was a little busier when he slowed to a walk, breathing hard. It was still only just after seven. A few crew members were up and about on the yachts moored near the *Avanturista*, cleaning decks, laying tables for breakfast, polishing the wooden rails. Everyone looked very industrious. All with a job to do. He thought of the farm, the morning routine. Dad would be up doing the rounds with Rex, probably already up on Starbridge Fell. Nick looked at the closed, covered portholes of the yacht. No sign of life, and there wouldn't be for at least another hour and a half.

With a sigh he dropped to sit on one of the low walls, wondering whether to keep walking and explore, when he spotted Maddie lowering the gangplank, her wicker basket on her arm.

'Morning,' he called.

She jumped, startled. 'Nick . . .' She looked from the gangplank to him. 'I didn't know anyone was up.'

'Didn't want to wake anyone.'

'Fair enough.' She eyed his hair. 'You been for a swim?'

'Run and swim. Went down to Zlatni Rat. I took a few photos.'

'If you'd gone that way –' she tried to hide her smile and failed miserably as she pointed the opposite way '– there's a nice little beach only a short walk away.'

Why did she always make him feel like a complete idiot?

'I fancied a run but I'll know for next time. Where are you off to?'

'Market and butcher's.'

Both sounded more interesting than sitting on the yacht on his own.

'Mind if I tag along?'

'Going to buy me coffee again?'

'Isn't it your turn?'

'I'm just a poor deckhand.'

He rolled his eyes. 'All right then.'

'You can carry my basket again, if you like. You seem to like carrying heavy things.' Yeah, she was smirking again, looking at his biceps.

'I think Tara would be highly pissed off if she caught you referring to her as a heavy thing.'

'I've no idea what you mean.' Maddie walked past him and headed up the short sharp hill to his left.

Nick gave a strangled laugh and followed her.

The market was a mass of colour, with several stalls bursting with a rainbow array of fruit and vegetables. Baskets piled high with plump green grapes spilling over the edges were lined up next to bags of fresh figs, trays of nectarines, peaches and oranges and open carboard trays of the most brilliant scarlet tomatoes perfectly juxtaposed with the deep green of beans in a box next to them. Arranged on a shelf above were tall slim bottles of local olive oil and bunches of lavender. Croatian voices surrounded them, chatting, haggling as purchases were bundled into crisp brown paper bags.

Maddie darted forward. 'Gosh, look at those tomatoes; I've got to get some of those. And the watermelon. Do you like watermelon?'

Nick shrugged, coming to stand alongside her, eyeing the display of unwieldy-sized oval green striped watermelons which were enormous and the equally large slices that had been pre-cut. It wasn't something he had ever tried before but he wasn't going to admit it to Maddie. No doubt it would elicit another one of those smirky smiles she seemed to reserve just for him.

'It's OK,' he hedged, looking at the pink flesh dotted with dark pips, clueless as to its flavour.

'Yeah, I'm with you on that. Looks delicious but doesn't taste of much, apart from water.' She gave him a speculative glance. 'I bet Tara likes it. Probably low in calories.'

He laughed. 'She's got a pretty healthy appetite. I'm not sure she needs to watch the calories.'

Maddie narrowed her eyes, opened her mouth and then snapped it shut before turning away abruptly. He was surprised by her unusual circumspection. She hadn't held back before. It was clear that she had no time for Tara; they were the original chalk and cheese. You couldn't get two more different women.

There was silence as Maddie devoted herself to a careful and thorough perusal of the fruit under the watchful eye of a young Croatian woman who seemed to be manning about three different stalls at once.

He took advantage of her preoccupation to study her. She was only a few inches shorter than he was, but, despite being broader, with wide swimmer's shoulders and long limbs, she was all in proportion. She certainly wouldn't blow away in a strong gust of wind, he thought, staring at the baggy company T-shirt and unflattering knee-length cargo shorts, which looked suspiciously familiar. He gave her legs, already a light golden colour, the faint tan shown off to advantage by her white tennis shoes, a second look. They'd look good in short shorts. And where had that thought come from? He tried to wipe the image from his brain. He was not interested in seeing her in that way, he thought hurriedly as she turned to face him, feeling a little caught out.

'You OK?' asked Maddie.

'Yes, fine,' he said, his voice ever so slightly strangled. And then it clicked. 'Nice shorts.'

Stiffening, she frowned at him as if he were taking the piss, and then looked down at his and then laughed, sticking out a leg to compare her navy shorts with his sand-colour ones.

'FatFace?'

'I think so,' he said.

'I nicked mine from my brother.' With a swift move, she lifted her T-shirt to show the fabric bunched around her waist and cinched in with a sturdy leather belt. No wonder she looked a bit bulky around the middle.

'I'll make sure I don't leave any clothes lying around.'

'Don't worry, no one's going to want to borrow those shorts you had on the other day.'

He groaned. 'You're just never going to let that one go, are you?'

She thought for a minute and then her eyes twinkled. 'Nope.' She shook her head, her curls dancing with devilment. 'Now, some of us are here to work. Come on, I need to stock up on fruit as we're due to set sail tomorrow to another part of the island. To Pučišča – I think I'm saying that right.'

'Where the stone for Diocletian's Palace came from.' Nick grinned as her eyes widened.

'You're well informed. Swallow a guidebook? I avoid them. Rather discover things for myself. Makes it more of an adventure.'

'There is that,' conceded Nick, amused by her defiant attitude. 'I'm easy either way; it's my brother and sister-in-law who are the TripAdvisor addicts.'

'Ah yes, Dan and Gail.' She turned, cocking her head, the sun catching at the red lights in her curly dark hair, the corners of her mouth twitching in secretive amusement and mischievous triumph.

Nick stopped dead and turned to her, a little wrong-footed. 'I'd forgotten. You know Nina.'

'I know Nina.' Her wide mouth curved into a smile that filled her face. When Maddie smiled, she really smiled. In spite of himself, he laughed, until she added, with a sly wink, 'You should be grateful I didn't take a picture of you in those shorts and WhatsApp it to Nina. I bet you'd have got some stick on the Hadley Massive family group.'

'You're obsessed with them – sure you don't want to borrow them?'

'No, but I wish I'd got a picture now.'

He gave a theatrical shudder. 'That would have been mean.'

'Yeah, but funny.' She grinned at him.

133

'I can see why you're mates with Nina. Cruel and heartless.'

'I have brothers.' She gave an exaggerated long-suffering sigh. 'We learn to get our shots in when we can.'

'And I bet you give as good as you get,' said Nick, nudging her with his elbow.

With a wicked look, she nodded. 'Hell, yeah,' and they both burst out laughing.

He whipped out his phone. 'Come here.' Like she'd done earlier, he stuck his leg out next to hers and took a picture of their matching shorts. 'I'll WhatsApp this one to Nina.'

'Send her my love.'

'Mmm, I'm not so sure I should. What other gossip has she shared with you? Should I be worried?'

'Possibly, despite the fact she was so desperate to get away from you all, Nina talked about everyone a lot.'

'Did she?' Nick rubbed at his neck, wondering just what Nina had said about him. That was the problem with sisters; they knew all your secrets and the worst of your humiliations.

'Yeah, she seems to like you the best.' Maddie paused and then shot him a cheeky grin. 'Go figure.'

Unable to help himself, Nick nudged her with his arm, realising it was the second time he'd done it, but there was something comfortable and familiar about being with her. Maybe it was the easy banter which reminded him of home and his brothers and sister. 'We're the closest in age and we always got on pretty well. I'm not that bad, you know.'

'Hmm, you have your moments,' she said, her eyes sharpening. 'Perhaps I shouldn't judge you by the company you keep.' Her candid words brought him up short and irritation pricked him.

'Tara . . . she's complicated. You don't know her like I do.'

Maddie snorted. 'I would hope not.'

'You know what I meant. There's more to her than you realise. She's quite insecure in spite of the front she puts up.'

'Being insecure also doesn't give you licence to be a bitch,' said Maddie tartly.

'And being insecure doesn't make it right for you to bitch about other people.' As soon as he said the words, he realised he was being rude and unfair. He had no right to make such a personal comment about her. Tara was prone to make bitchy comments and he was being disingenuous to deny that.

'Who said anything about me being insecure?' Maddie whirled and put her hands on her hips, cocking her head, giving him an I'm-just-about-tolerating-you look. 'I'm just peachy in my own skin, don't you fret. I'm not defined by the lipstick I wear or how many Instagram followers I have. Forty-three, by the way, if you're interested.'

Nick burst out laughing. 'Forty-three – that's good. I've got ten and fifty per cent of them are family. I'm sorry. I was being rude.'

'Forgiven, and I was being a bitch about Tara. I'm sure

she has deep-seated issues which make her that way. Doesn't help if you're starving all the time.'

Nick blinked, not sure what she meant but smart enough to grasp an olive branch when it was being held out. 'Shall we change the subject?'

'Back to fruit. Help me out here. Grapes? Nectarines? Peaches? Bananas? Any preferences?'

And, just like that, it was over. No sulking, no brooding or pouting.

Together, they chose a fine selection and Nick took the basket from her as they headed through the market towards the butcher's.

'There's Ivan,' said Nick, pointing up ahead, seeing the captain walking ahead of them up through the narrow street.

'Where?' asked Maddie, somewhat unbelievably as the captain was only a few yards ahead.

'There, with the girl in the pink dress, walking along the front there.'

'Oh.'

'What's wrong?'

'I wasn't looking for a couple. They look pretty cosy for this time of the morning.'

'And is there something wrong with that?'

'Yes, he has a wife and child in Split,' said Maddie, shaking her head. 'I met them. His wife, Zita, is lovely.'

'Maybe she's a friend,' he suggested, eyeing the other man again.

'At this time of day?' asked Maddie with a touch of tartness in her voice.

'Well, we're out together at this time of day,' he replied reasonably.

She pulled a pitying face at him as if humouring his stupidity. 'Yeah, but you don't have your arm around me.'

'You have a point there.' And the completely unprompted thought popped into his head that it might be quite nice to have his arm around someone like Maddie instead of a tiny delicate little woman a fraction of his size that he spent half the time worrying he might break.

'I hope he doesn't see us,' said Maddie, slowing down.

'Why? It would be his problem rather than yours.'

'It's all right for you, but it would be awkward for me. He's sort of my boss. I'd rather not know what he gets up to when he's ashore.'

Seeing that Maddie was genuinely uncomfortable, he suggested they took a side street and the long way around to the butcher's situated in one of the narrow cobbled side streets.

'Wish me luck,' said Maddie, pushing open the door to the old-fashioned-looking shop. 'I'm clueless when it comes to buying meat. I only just managed fish and I'd had a lot of briefing from Ivan's family. But tonight's recipe is for grilled meat kebabs. So this could be interesting if they don't speak much English.'

Nick smiled but didn't say anything. Perhaps he could

show himself in a better light for once, he thought, as he followed her into the white tiled shop.

When they emerged ten minutes later, Maddie exclaimed, patting him on the arm, 'The coffee's on me. My hero! You just saved my bacon.' She laughed at her own pun. 'You knew what you were doing.'

'That would be on account of being a farmer,' he said gravely, with a twinkle in his eye as he took her shopping basket from her. 'Occasionally I have my uses.'

'Yeah, today you did good. My hero.' She linked her arm through his with cheerful friendliness, reminding him of his sister, Nina. 'Come on, there's a great coffee shop up here; I found it yesterday. It has an awesome view.'

Unable to resist her natural, easy familiarity, Nick allowed himself to be pulled along. If he were being completely honest with himself, her unselfconscious, cheery company made a refreshing change.

When they returned to the boat, Douglas was on deck, sitting studying something on the table, but there was no sign of anyone else.

'Morning, Maddie, Nick. Another gorgeous day,' he greeted them, looking up from his charts. 'Don't suppose you know when Ivan might be coming back?'

Maddie exchanged a quick look with Nick. 'No, I'm sorry, I don't. Why, is there a problem?'

'No, no,' said Douglas, but despite his denial there was a world-weary air about him.

'Shall I take this down to the kitchen for you?' asked Nick, his arms still full of her shopping.

'You mean the galley,' said Douglas, with nautical precision. 'Kitchen is a galley on board.'

'That would be great, thank you,' she said. 'Douglas, would you like coffee while I sort out breakfast?'

'That would be bloody marvellous.'

She gave him a curious glance but Douglas had ducked his head down and was studying his charts again. Worry and a touch of anxiety had replaced his usual affability and cheerful bonhomie. Something wasn't right. She wondered what could have happened overnight to upset him.

As she stowed the shopping, Nick prowled around the area, opening drawers and poking into cupboards.

'Do you want something?' she finally asked, hands on her hips, waiting for him to leave. 'I'm grateful for your help this morning but I do need to get on with some work now.'

'Do you want some help?' he asked, pulling open another drawer.

'No, I'm fine, thanks. Besides, you're a guest; you're not supposed to be down here.'

'Yeah, but I'm sure I could help, do something.'

'Thanks, Nick, but seriously, you shouldn't be down here.' Pushing past him, she started to load up a tray with crockery and cutlery.

'I could take that up for you.'

She turned and fixed him with a stern stare. 'Thank you but no thank you.'

He shrugged and sighed. 'Only trying to help.'

'Help is forbidden. It's in the crew manual rules. Thou shalt not let guests into the galley, so you're already breaking cardinal rule number one. What do you want, Nick?'

'Bacon butty?' he asked with boyish hopefulness.

She rolled her eyes. 'Aha, so that's why you're hanging around.'

'Busted.'

'Why didn't you say so?'

'Didn't want to make extra work for you, but I'm starving and the girls won't make an appearance for ages. I'll be ready for a second breakfast by then.'

'Poor baby,' she teased, patting his hand, before adding with a roll of her eyes, 'Just give me a minute. I'll just make Douglas's coffee and lay the table.' She reached for the large insulated cafetière.

'I could do it,' he said, giving her the full benefit of a plaintive, puppy dog look.

Damn, he looked . . . He looked too flipping handsome for his own good with those big blue eyes and the curve of his wide mouth. *All the better for kissing with.* No. Nick Hadley was not her type. And she certainly wasn't his. He clearly preferred flighty, high maintenance stick insects.

'You'll get me the sack,' she said briskly, skirting around him.

'It's OK, we can blackmail Ivan.'

An unwilling laugh burst out of her. Nick Hadley might not be her type but he made her laugh and this morning she'd enjoyed his company. 'Oh, go on then,' she said, handing him a frying pan and digging a pack of bacon out of the fridge before showing him how to fire up the gas burner.

'Don't burn the place down,' she admonished as she picked up the heavily laden tray to take it up to lay the breakfast table.

When she came back, Nick seemed to have made himself at home, slicing a loaf and happily shaking the pan of bacon.

'Want me to slice some extra bread for toast?' he asked.

'That would be great,' she said and, before she knew it, they were working companionably around each other in the small galley area.

Simon, Siri and Douglas were all on their third cup of coffee when Tara and Cory finally appeared. Nick had had no such compunction and had smuggled his bacon sandwich and a glass of orange juice up to the top deck with his Dick Francis book, where he enjoyed twenty minutes without anyone lecturing him about the perils of fat, gluten and additives.

Hearing their voices, he came down from the deck to join the breakfast table.

'Morning, Nicky darling,' said Tara, patting the seat next to her. He slid into the space, his awareness of how tiny she was heightened after spending time with Maddie. As always, she looked immaculate in another fancy bikini. This one was one-shouldered in a pale blue fabric with an extravagant diagonal orange ruffle that ran from left to right across her chest and was repeated on the bikini bottoms, which today were more like shorts.

'Morning. Did you sleep well?' His nose twitched at Tara's overpowering perfume but he dropped a kiss on her cheek.

'No, not at all. I'm . . . well . . .' she looked over at Cory, who was hanging onto Douglas's arm '. . . I'm a bit . . . We've had the most amazing news overnight. It's all over Instagram. You'll never guess what.' She paused, her eyes bright, and she waved her phone. 'William Randall.'

Across the table, Cory drew in a sharp exaggerated breath. 'Don't, Tara. Douglas says we can't go.' Her face crumpled as she clutched at her neck, a tragic expression filling her face before she turned to Douglas. 'I can't believe you. This could be . . . life-changing. It's William Randall.'

'Cory, my sweetheart, as soon as Ivan comes back then we can go but in the meantime we've got a perfectly nice day lined up.'

'But I don't want to go to some boring old winery.' Cory pushed her plate away, making it rattle against the cutlery. 'It's miles away and it will take forever to get there.'

'Don't fret, Cory, sweetheart, it will be fabulous. You will love it when we get there, you know you will.' Douglas patted her forearm. 'Besides, we can't go anywhere without a captain.'

'Well, that's just ridiculous. You're in charge. You chartered the boat. Get him back.'

Nick felt sorry for the poor sod. Cory reminded him of a bratty teenager, although, to be fair, even at her worst Nina had never been this bad.

'But I told him we'd be here until tomorrow,' said Douglas, chagrin written all over his face. 'We're not due to sail to Hvar for another three days. If I'd known . . .' He let the words trail off helplessly.

'Surely there's another way to get to Hvar,' said Tara, tossing her hair. 'It's only over there.' She flung out her arm, pointing towards the island just across the water.

'Tara, love,' interjected Simon with calm indolence, 'why would you want to leave the comfort of this rather fine yacht? You don't want to get a ferry with the great unwashed, do you?'

Tara shrugged, lifting her chin in disdain, but didn't say anything.

'Well, there's no point having a perfectly good boat if we can't even get to where we want to go. It's ridiculous. I don't know why you've let the captain go,' groused Cory.

'Because the world doesn't revolve around you,' snapped Siri, dropping her coffee cup on the table and glaring at Cory and then Tara. 'Some of us would like to go to the Senjkovic Winery. It's got a fantastic reputation and while we're on Brač it would be a shame not to visit. This holiday isn't just about what you want.' Disloyal as it was, Nick wanted to cheer. Siri seemed to be the only person who was prepared to stand up to her.

Cory ignored her and clutched Douglas's arm. 'But it's imperative we get to Hvar today,' she muttered through gritted teeth.

'What's so important about getting to Hvar today?' asked Nick in a low voice, slipping his arm around Tara, trying to cheer her up. Her fingers were gripping the edge of the table.

'Because,' she said urgently.

'Cory, love, William Randall is still going to be there tomorrow,' said Douglas.

'Yes, but . . .' said Cory.

'Give the poor guy a chance to settle in,' said Simon. 'He'll probably be jet-lagged if he's flown in from the States.'

Cory rocked in her seat, more than ever like a petulant teenager.

'Who is William Randall?' asked Nick, completely confused.

Tara turned huge incredulous eyes his way. 'William Randall. You don't know who William Randall is?'

The immediate, almost accusing silence made Nick want to squirm in his seat as if he were back at school. There was a collective rustle and then Cory gasped and Simon, of course, couldn't resist muttering nastily, 'Oh, dear God.'

Douglas turned a kindly smile his way, which only served to make Nick feel even smaller.

'William Randall is a film producer.' Simon's patronising tone rang out, clear and cutting. 'He's currently casting the next Marvel movie, as well as a new Charlie's Angels film, and it's whispered that he's cosying up to Barbara Broccoli.'

At Nick's blank face, Simon shook his head. 'Bond films?' he drawled in that superior way that rubbed Nick up the wrong way. 'You know Barbara Broccoli, successor to Cubby Broccoli, legendary Bond film producer?'

'Yes, I do know that,' said Nick, trying to hide his irritation at the up-his-own-arse prat.

'So you'll know that they're on the lookout for potential Bond girls and other roles,' sniped Simon.

'Shh,' squealed Tara, looking around anxiously at the other yachts moored next to them. 'Don't tell everyone.'

Chapter 12

'Lord, it's all kicking off up there.' Simon's lazy drawl startled Maddie, as did the dirty coffee cups in his hands. 'Where do you want these?'

She took them from him. 'Thanks. I'll just put them by the sink.'

'Can I just hide in here for a while?'

'No,' said Maddie with a quick glance at the door. Guests weren't supposed to come into the galley, although Nick hadn't taken much notice this morning.

'Maddie, take pity on me. Cory and Tara are like a pair of hysterical Chihuahuas, snapping at poor Douglas because he won't take them to Hvar now this minute.'

'Oh, dear. Why are they so desperate?'

Simon explained about William Randall, whom Maddie had never heard of.

'Tara's got her eye on being the next Bond girl and Cory can't decide whether to team up or scratch her eyes out.'

'Sounds fun,' said Maddie, starting to transfer all the dirty crockery to the counter by the sink.

'Want me to wash up for you?'

Maddie gave him a puzzled smile over her shoulder. 'No, it's fine.'

'I don't mind helping, you know,' he said, moving to stand next to her, leaning against the counter giving her a scorching look. 'Seems a shame to think of you as poor Cinders all on her own down here, slaving away.'

Blushing, she turned her head away and took a small step sideways, her legs almost brushing his as she pulled open a door. 'There's a dishwasher,' she said and lowered the door to the floor.

'Ah.' Simon smiled. 'Even so, I can stack a dishwasher.'

'Thanks, but . . . you really shouldn't be down here.'

Simon lifted an arm and put it across her body to cup her waist, his arms just brushing her breasts, so lightly that she couldn't tell if it was by design or accident.

'I shouldn't, should I? But no one's going to know if you don't tell them.' He winked and a hot flush raced across her skin. The teaspoon she was just about to put in the dishwasher fell out of her hand, rattling on the floor. When they both ducked to pick it up, Simon caught her forearms and drew her towards him.

She tried to pull away. 'I'm supposed to be working.'

'Why don't you forget about that for a moment?' he asked in a low voice, plucking the spoon from her hand and putting it down, while the other hand slid around her waist again, pulling her even closer. Under her fingers clutching his forearms, his shirt was crisp linen and he smelled expensive and well groomed. A light subtle after-shave teased her nose as she gazed at his smooth, clean shaven skin, unable to meet his eyes.

'Don't be shy, Maddie,' he whispered as his head dipped. 'Even though it is rather adorable.'

The caress of his words whipped her pulse into a high-speed canter. Bloody hell, Simon Beresford was going to kiss her.

The lips he slid over hers were smooth and practised and she was too bemused at first to do anything but stand there like a lemon. Simon Beresford was kissing her. Her, Maddie Wilcox. Her knees decided to have a funny turn and went all wobbly.

'Maddie, you are one gorgeous woman,' he murmured against her mouth as his hand stroked its way up her spine. As his mouth moulded over hers, she swallowed and tried to kiss him back but her lips were starstruck and seemed to have frozen. Not that it fazed Simon; his mouth pressed against hers, encouraging her to open up, and when she did, with a touch of diffidence – she was so out of her league here – his tongue slipped into her mouth and he deepened the kiss.

Caught up in the mechanics of not bumping his nose, worrying if her breath smelled and wondering if she was doing it right, she didn't hear the door open. When someone cleared their throat behind her, she jumped out of her skin.

Startled, she pulled away, her heart thudding fast, and turned to find Nick looking disapproving.

'Did you want something, Hadley?' asked Simon, raising a superior eyebrow. Maddie blushed so hot she thought her skin might sizzle.

'Just brought this down.' Nick strolled forward and dropped a bread basket on the central counter and left without another word.

'Oh, shit,' said Maddie, holding her hands up to her burning cheeks.

'It's cool,' said Simon. 'You don't need to worry about him, he's just an oik.'

Before Maddie could say anything, Simon looked at his watch. 'And I'm afraid my duties await. I can't leave poor Douglas to escort the hellcats by himself today. Poor chap needs some moral support. I must away and leave you.' He kissed her again, his hand lazily cupping her breast and squeezing it slightly. She stiffened at the unexpectedly familiar touch.

'But I'm glad you have a dishwasher. I'd hate to think of you slaving over a hot sink down here.' With that he sauntered off, stopping in the doorway to give her a quick wink.

Well. That was . . . Maddie held onto the counter. Unexpected and . . . She wasn't a prude by any stretch of the imagination, but clearly sophisticated people moved a lot faster than she was used to.

Waiting for the colour in her cheeks to subside, she quickly loaded up the dishwasher.

When she finally felt her equilibrium return, she ventured back on deck to find the whole party waiting for two taxis to take them to lunch at the winery.

Tara, standing on the top step where Maddie had to pass, was stabbing at the floor with one of her heels, her face scrunched in a mutinous scowl, while a few feet ahead Cory, leaning against the table with her arms firmly folded under her breasts, had her nose stuck up in the air, ignoring every word that Douglas attempted to address her way.

'I think this is a complete waste of time,' muttered Tara as Nick took her bag.

'Well, Siri wants to go and so does Douglas,' he said in a painful attempt at diplomacy.

'Well, they're being totally selfish. This could be my big break. I can't believe Douglas is being so difficult. This is his boat. He needs to find a new captain.'

'Tara, relax, you're on holiday. We'll get to Hvar in a few days. If this bloke has just arrived, he's not going anywhere yet.'

'Which just goes to show,' Tara sneered, 'you don't know Hollywood.'

'True,' Nick bit out tightly.

'They have personal jets, superyachts. They can leave at any minute.' She looked ready to cry. 'They go to the sort of parties where they meet someone who says, "Come on over to my island, my yacht, my villa", and then they're gone.' She clicked her fingers. 'Just like that. You wouldn't understand. How could you? Has anyone in your family ever moved away, left the village, let alone a party?'

Ouch, thought Maddie, but Nick's face was expressionless, apart from a certain tightness in his jaw. He turned away from Tara to gaze out to sea.

'I need to get to Hvar,' Tara said, her voice a long whine.

Maddie thought what she really needed was a good slap and that Nick needed a boot up the backside.

Chapter 13

Ivan scowled and jabbed at one of the charts with his thumb. Douglas pointed back, shaking his head.

The party had returned from the winery trip shortly after three and Ivan had boarded the boat not long after that with a chipper stride and a cheerful grin.

'Everything OK on the boat?' he'd asked, following her down to the galley, where she'd just begun to marinate the meat for this evening's kebabs.

'All fine with the boat,' she said, thinking that she was being honest enough. The guests wanting to change their plans wasn't her problem.

Ivan's affable smile had vanished about ten minutes later and he and Douglas had been sitting at the table pointing and prodding at the charts for the last hour. When Maddie ventured out of the galley, they were still at it. As she glanced over to them Ivan threw up his hands and shook his head, pointing at the chart. Douglas folded his arms, a recalcitrant set to his mouth.

Time to brave the lion's den. 'Can I get you a drink or anything?' she asked, feeling rather sorry for Douglas.

He looked up gratefully. 'I'd love a G and T, make it a double. Ivan?'

Ivan scowled. 'Scotch on the rocks.' Apparently it was all right for the captain to join the guests if he was invited.

When she returned with the drinks, she put them down, avoiding the charts.

'When we go to Hvar there will be no mooring,' said Ivan, looking worried. 'We have to moor out of the harbour. It can make shopping and catering difficult.' He looked up at Maddie, a frown lining his forehead. 'If we go to Hvar tomorrow, with this new plan you will spend over a week out of the harbour. Every time you want to do something you will have to take the launch into the town. Hvar is very busy; it could take more than half an hour each trip. Everything has been planned. Where to buy the food. When.'

Maddie widened her eyes and nodded.

'Maddie's a very capable young woman. I'm sure she'll be able to cope,' said Douglas, taking a hefty swig of his drink. 'If we weigh anchor outside Hvar, we've got the launch. You or Maddie can run us in and out.'

Ivan pinched his lips, but Maddie got the impression he was about to lay his trump card. 'There is one big problem. Staying in one place for this long when we are away from the harbour means we can't refuel or fill up the water tanks. Water may have to be rationed. If we run out of water, there will be no showers. No toilets.'

Douglas sighed. 'How often do the water tanks need filling up?'

'Normally we can go a few days . . . Your party. They use a lot.'

Douglas winced.

Maddie was guessing, from the way they got through towels, that Tara and Cory must shower at least twice a day, if not three times.

'And if we fill up today, how long will the water last?'

'A few days, not a week,' said Ivan. 'And there would be no guarantee I could get us a mooring in Hvar to fill up before we moved on to Korčula.'

'That would . . .' Douglas hesitated '. . . be bad. The girls are really keen to get to Hvar sooner rather than later.'

'We will visit very nice places,' said Ivan, beaming as they neared a compromise. 'And we can moor on the harbourside. Fill up the water tanks and . . .' His voice trailed off as Cory drifted towards them, coming to stand with her hand on Douglas's shoulder.

Douglas swallowed.

'Is it all settled? What time are we going to Hvar?' She gave Douglas one of her beautiful smiles, her blue-black hair draping across his chest as she bent to kiss him full on the mouth.

'Well, the thing is, my darling . . .' said Douglas, glancing at Ivan warily. 'It's not that simple.'

'What do you mean?' Cory's voice was shrill. 'This is a boat. That's water. Hvar is over there. We can see it. Why can't we go?'

'We can, sweetheart. It's just that it's not so straightforward. There are other things to think about. Refuelling. Water. You wouldn't want to have to go without –'

'Douglas, you promised. I can't believe you'd do this to me.' With a childish, 'Urrrgh,' she whirled around and stomped away, her lemon-yellow chiffon throw billowing behind her like a desert storm.

Douglas winced and drained his glass. 'That didn't go well.'

Ivan patted his arm. 'Sometimes it is good to show who is in charge. Be the boss.'

His words made Douglas square his shoulders. 'You're right. It's silly to make such a fuss about changing our schedule. We will stick to our original plan.'

If dinner was going to be much later, the kebabs were going to be tough and dry. Maddie looked at her watch again. It was eight o'clock, but Douglas had insisted that they wait for Cory and Tara who, as usual, were late.

She popped back up on deck, ostensibly to offer more drinks and see if anyone wanted more bread, and was relieved to see Tara making her way to the table. Thank God for that. Crossing to the table, she lifted the empty bread basket and caught Nick's eye.

He shrugged. 'I was hungry.'

'You'd better have left room for the lamb kebabs; you chose the meat.'

'I've always got room, don't worry.'

'Well, let's just hope they're not ruined,' she whispered back and was about to turn to head down to the galley when Tara's cutting tones stopped her.

'Seeing as how none of you are the least bit sympathetic, Cory and I are going to have dinner in my cabin – she's really upset. We'll have a girls' night. Watch a Netflix movie. You don't need to worry about us.' She lifted her long neck and looked haughtily down her nose at the assembled group before turning to Maddie. 'Send dinner to my cabin.

'Oh, and Douglas . . . Cory will be sleeping in my room tonight.' She shot him a triumphant smile.

Not once did she look at Nick throughout the whole exchange.

As she walked off, Simon began to snigger under his breath. 'So that's told you, Douglas. You're not getting any oats tonight.'

Siri started to laugh too, until she noticed that Douglas was actually looking a little stricken. 'Hey, don't fret, babe. She's just throwing a tantrum. She'll come round. It's about time you stood up to her for a change.'

'I know,' sighed Douglas.

'You really should,' added Simon. 'She treats you like shit sometimes.'

Siri nudged Simon sharply in the ribs but Douglas smiled forlornly at her. 'He's right. I'm a muppet.'

To Maddie's surprise, Siri leaned over and squeezed his hand. 'I wouldn't say that. You're just too kind-hearted and she takes shameless advantage of you. Maybe it would do you good to stand up to her this time. Let her have her tantrum. Ignore it.'

'Do you think?' he asked with a hopeful lift to his voice.

She patted his hand again, before saying firmly, 'Yes, I do.'

'You're the one that holds the purse strings,' chipped in Simon. Siri glared at him.

'You're right, old man.'

Maddie's heart went out at his quiet resignation and she felt a burst of irritation at Simon being unnecessarily cruel. It was obvious that Douglas genuinely loved Cory, or at least believed he did. Simon's callous words highlighted the underlying subtext: Cory loved Douglas's money rather than him.

During all this Nick's face was curiously impassive, as if he were a detached onlooker. When he caught her looking at him, he turned away and stared out over the moonlit sea.

The rest of dinner was a subdued affair and for the first time since they'd left the marina in Split everyone went to bed by ten o'clock, for which Maddie was rather grateful. After all the drama she felt exhausted, so an early night was most welcome. She left Ivan drinking a solitary whisky on the deck, looking rather pleased with himself.

Something woke Nick in the night – piercing whispers that bounced off the water. He lay listening for a moment and then heard the wheels of suitcases on cobbles. With a sigh he checked his watch – four in the morning and still dark. Some lucky person with a ferry to catch. For a foolish moment he was almost tempted to throw back the light duvet and shout, *Wait for me*. What the hell was he doing here?

Last night, well, to be honest, it had . . . shocked – maybe that was too strong – disturbed him was a better way of putting it. You didn't live in a family of seven, with assorted in-laws and a dozen cousins, without some drama but, no matter what the disagreements around the family kitchen table, there was always a degree of understanding or sympathy.

The previous evening's unpleasant comments, with their swirling undercurrents of nastiness, had left a slight churning in his stomach and a desire to put distance between himself and these people.

Ill at ease and with regret at coming on the holiday clouding his thoughts, he finally dropped back to sleep and thought nothing more of what had woken him until Simon stormed onto the deck halfway through breakfast the next morning, having been despatched to check whether Tara and Cory wanted any breakfast. Ivan was preparing for departure and waiting impatiently for Maddie to be released from galley duty to help with the fenders and undo the mooring lines. A couple of times Nick almost stood up to offer to help.

'Bloody stupid bitches,' seethed Simon, waving a sheet of paper.

'What?' asked Siri with a mouthful of toast.

Simon dropped the sheet of paper in front of Douglas, who'd been staring morosely into his coffee for the last half hour. 'They've only gone and run away to sea.'

Douglas's head shot up and he snatched at the piece of paper as Siri bobbed up and skirted around the table to read it over his shoulder.

His lip quivered and Nick genuinely thought he might cry. Siri patted him on the shoulder, her eyes wide in disbelief.

'What's happened?' he asked.

'Cory and Tara have gone to Hvar.'

The words didn't make any sense. 'When?'

'About four o'clock this morning,' said Maddie, quickly adding when several heads turned accusingly, 'I heard lots of whispering but I didn't think anything of it. I never dreamed . . .'

'How?'

'They must have taken a water taxi,' said Ivan. 'There is only the catamaran to Hvar and that doesn't leave until quarter to five.'

Nick shook his head, pulling out his phone, looking to see if there'd been a text from Tara. Not a word. He gritted his teeth.

'But that's mad,' said Siri. 'What are they going to do when they get there? Where will they stay?'

'You think a couple of airheads would have thought that far ahead?' snarled Simon. 'Spoiled bitches.'

'That is enough,' Douglas suddenly snapped and turned on Simon. 'Don't talk about Cory like that.' In one sharp movement he rose to his feet, heedless of the cup of coffee he'd upended, and stalked to where Ivan stood at the wheel in the cockpit area, his body language suddenly authoritative and grim determination stamped on his face. 'We're going to Hvar. Now. Start the engine.'

Ivan's eyes flashed momentarily but he nodded. Within minutes he barked a dozen orders at Maddie, who looked like a startled rabbit, not sure which way to run or which command to follow first.

'Let me help,' said Nick, jumping to his feet, needing to get away from the others and not caring what they thought. 'Want me to take the left-hand rope?'

'Line,' said Maddie as they scrambled away from the table, where Siri was frantically mopping up coffee. 'For some reason they're called lines. And it's starboard as we're at the stern of the boat.'

'Do you want me to help or not?' He glared at her. 'It's only because I'd rather be doing something than sitting, especially with an atmosphere like that.'

'Yeah, must be a bit odd. Your girlfriend doing a bunk and not telling you.'

Nick couldn't help himself and he snorted. 'Tell it how it is, why don't you?'

'Oh, God.' Maddie slapped a hand over her mouth. 'Did I just say that? I'm so sorry.'

'The tact instinct gave you a wide berth, didn't it?'

''Fraid so.'

'Don't worry. It's not as if you're telling me anything I didn't know. My girlfriend *has* done a bunk and it's bloody rude. Glad you're not pussyfooting around it. Now, come on, let's sort these *lines* out.'

'Thank you, I appreciate the help.' Her grateful heartfelt smile made him forget the tension gripping his shoulders.

With the lines secured, they jumped back on the yacht as Ivan began to steer out of the harbour, the engine's propeller churning up the water and leaving a small wake behind them.

Following Maddie's lead, Nick went to the port side (see, he was learning) and hauled in the fenders on that side, while Maddie took care of the others.

As he worked his way forward to the bow of the boat, he saw that Douglas was standing on the little walkway that protruded out over the water from the prow of the ship. Simon had followed him, but Nick was surprised when Douglas suddenly shook Simon's arm off with an angry expletive.

Good, thought Nick. Simon, he'd decided, was pure poison. A two-faced, back-stabbing little git. He hadn't liked him since he had met him. Always whispering in Douglas's ear, making comments about other people, when he was as much a hanger-on as Cory. He'd noticed Simon's wallet seemed to be missing in action on any occasion where drinks and food were being consumed. Douglas, generous to a fault, always picked up the tab, even though he'd paid for the boat charter. Nick had managed to get a round of drinks in the other night but Douglas had refused to let him pay for his and Tara's meals, either at lunch or dinner.

Simon walked off, leaving Douglas on his own. The man looked like he wanted some time alone so Nick carried on pulling the fenders into the boat, but when he looked up Douglas had come to stand next to him.

'What do you think I should do?' he asked miserably. 'Everyone else seems to want to chuck their two penn'orth in. Have you heard from Tara?'

'No,' said Nick shortly.

'I texted Cory. Told her we were on our way.' His mouth turned down. 'Course the little monkey asked me to text when we arrived and she'd let me know where to meet her. She knew I'd come after her. They're just sussing out places for lunch.'

'Fair enough.' Nick paused. 'You could always keep them waiting, though.'

'What do you mean?' Douglas frowned.

'Well, given this seemed quite an impetuous flight, it's fair to assume that they have nowhere to stay for the night. Although they took some luggage with them to make it look good.' He recalled the sound of wheels on cobbles in the wee small hours. 'Which means they're going to have to spend the day lugging their bags around with them, hanging around in bars and restaurants. They're soon going

163

to get bored. They're relying on being back on board tonight, but we could take our time. Make them sweat a bit. You know they're in Hvar. They're safe.'

A slow reluctant smile curved Douglas's face. 'You're a strategist. I like that. Think slow, plan long.'

'Something like that,' said Nick dryly.

'Yes, our trip could take longer than planned,' suggested Douglas, almost cherubic innocence supplanting the earlier misery etched on his face.

'And there's no mooring in Hvar.' Nick raised his hands, a who-knew?-style gesture. 'It's going to take a while to find a place to weigh anchor.'

'And then the launch is going to take a while to motor in.'

'And, by that time, it could be as late as ten o'clock at night.'

'Or even eleven.'

Nick laughed. 'You really want to make them suffer.'

Douglas winced. 'They have been rather naughty.'

'Douglas, they're not schoolchildren. They're two adult women, capricious, selfish and thoughtless. This yacht, this holiday – it's a real treat. You've paid a lot of money.' He held up his hand as Douglas started to demur. 'But not once have you said that to anyone. Not once have you made any of us feel beholden. You're a generous host. And I'm cross that the pair of them – I know Cory is your girlfriend – but that the two of them have so blatantly taken the piss out of your hospitality and generosity.

They're not just thoughtless, they're bloody self-entitled and, to be honest, it's really wound me up.'

Douglas shrugged, a pink tinge further deepening his normally rosy cheeks.

They stood side by side in silence before Douglas finally said, 'I think, Nick, that's a fucking brilliant idea. Don't suppose you play poker?'

'Only with my brothers. My second eldest, Jonathon, is a card shark.'

'I play with Siri; she's pretty sharp with a pack of cards too. Fancy a beer?'

Maddie climbed the stairs to the top deck with another three bottles of beer balanced on her tray, following the sound of raucous laughter.

Downstairs, on the main deck, Simon was sulking in the shade on his own, although Maddie wasn't sure why. He'd plugged in his earphones, put on his sunglasses and turned a sun lounger to face the sea. When she'd offered him a drink earlier he'd given her a curt, dismissive shake of his head, a clear reminder that she was just the hired help.

At the top of the steps she paused to take in the view and enjoy the smooth rolling motion of the boat as the wind teased her hair. The air felt fresh and sharp, rippling over her face, while the sun heated the skin on her arms and legs with a delicious glow. This was the life. The engine throbbed as the yacht skimmed across the open water towards Hvar and now that Ivan had resigned himself to the change in schedule he'd finally stopped stomping around doing his Blackbeard impersonation.

'Ah, there you are, Maddie,' called Douglas at the top of his voice, as if she'd been missing for hours instead of a scant five minutes. She laughed; he was absolutely steaming but Douglas was one of those delightful drunks, happy, avuncular and very chatty. It was the most relaxed she'd seen him since they'd embarked on the trip.

'Hello, Maddie,' called Siri, holding her cards up in front of her face so that only her mischievous dancing eyes could be seen.

The three of them had been playing cards for the last two hours, steadily drinking their way through the stock of lager.

'Who's winning?' she asked, dishing out the cold bottles of Karlovačko, the local Croatian beer.

'Nick!' screeched Siri in disgust, poking at her dwindling pile of matchsticks, pinched from the galley. 'Making out he's all innocent and clean-living. Huh!'

'Long, dark winters' nights.' He grinned, clumsily tapping his mini mountain of matchsticks.

'And I'm about to lose the shirt from my back,' said Douglas cheerfully, waving a solitary matchstick. 'Good job I'm not this bad in the City; Cory wouldn't want to know me then.'

There was a collective pause as all three of them looked at him. He took a long swallow of beer, blinking owlishly off into the distance over the sea. 'Mmm, that is good stuff, and don't all of you look at me like that. I'm not daft.' He borrowed Nick's northern vowels for a second. He kept his gaze turned away, his voice quieter. 'I know she's only with me for my money. Stands to reason. Gorgeous girl like that with a short, dumpy, ugly bloke like me. Not like you, Nick, handsome, athletic. No wonder Tara fancies you.'

Siri grabbed his hand. 'Douglas Spencer-Jones, don't you dare say that.' Her voice trembled with all the ferocity of a mama bear protecting her cub but her eyes softened as she looked at him. 'You're the kindest man I know.'

'I'm a bloody fool, that's what I am.' He waved his beer bottle. 'A bloody fool, but I love her.' His face crumpled in apology, oblivious to the sudden bleakness in Siri's eyes as her face became curiously expressionless.

And in that moment Maddie saw it. Siri was in love with Douglas.

She glanced at Nick, who winced and took a long swallow of beer, oblivious to Siri's unhappiness and clearly uncomfortable with Douglas's declaration.

'Anything else I can get you?' she asked.

'Sit down and have a beer with us.' Douglas suddenly rose to his feet. 'Can you play poker?'

'I'm afraid not,' said Maddie with a polite smile. 'And I need to prepare lunch.'

'You're a nice girl. Why can't I fall in love with a nice girl like you?' he asked with a mournful sigh.

Maddie looked helplessly at Siri, who rolled her eyes

and winked, the brief sign of her earlier emotion wiped away. 'She's far too good for you, Douglas. For one thing, she knows how to work hard and isn't some decorative, sponging layabout.'

'Harsh, Siri, harsh.'

'No, it's not,' she said, flinging herself back in her chair, crossing her ankles and taking a swig of beer. 'Admit it, Cory does bugger all. Fannying about on the occasional shoot. What? She's had two jobs this year. I don't know why you put up with it, not when you have a strong work ethic. We might have come from money but neither of us expected to have everything handed to us on a plate. I had to work like stink in my first job at *Vogue* to prove that I wasn't just the CEO's best friend's daughter. And Charles didn't give you an easy time when you started at Citibank, just because you were his godson or because you were at school with his son.'

Nick caught Maddie's eye and raised his eyebrows imperceptibly. She suppressed an answering smile.

'Siri, don't get yourself all worked up.' Douglas patted her hand. 'You don't understand. Cory's very insecure. She needs me . . . She just –'

'Takes advantage.' Siri's voice was flat.

'Now, now.' Douglas took her hand. 'You don't need to worry about me. It's my problem and I'm a big boy.'

'Big idiot, more like,' said Siri, a smile returning to her face as she squeezed his hand back. 'I just hate to see you get hurt.'

'Hmph,' said Douglas. 'I'll survive.' A sudden naughty grin broke out over his face. 'But there's no reason for me to be a pushover.' He glanced at Nick. 'Eh?'

Nick looked puzzled for a second and then his face cleared and he gave Douglas a nod.

'Maddie, dear, there'll just be four of us for dinner tonight.'

'Four? But aren't . . . but we'll be anchoring just outside Hvar in less than an hour.'

'Yes –' Douglas's eyes danced with a touch of gleeful naughtiness '– but Cory and Tara don't know that. We'll go and collect them when we're ready.' He looked at his watch. 'What do you think, Nick? About half ten, eleven?'

'Oh,' said Maddie, trying not to giggle. 'I get it.'

Siri sat up and raised her bottle in toast to Douglas. ''Bout time both of them realised that the world doesn't revolve around them. Go you, Douglas.'

Chapter 14

As they neared the island, rounding the south-eastern tip heading towards the town of Hvar, the number of sailboats proliferated and Ivan steered into an inlet which was already busy, with other boats anchored.

'This is a good place to stay,' explained Ivan. 'It's sheltered and not too far from the harbour, which is just along the shore. Although it is very busy already.' From a boat only a hundred metres away strains of music bounced across the water. 'It will take about twenty minutes in the launch. Have you ever driven a motorboat?'

'No,' said Maddie, a prickle of alarm running down her spine.

'Can you drive a car?'

'Er . . . well, sort of.'

Ivan cocked his head.

'Well, I passed my test but I've never driven since. Couldn't afford the insurance.'

'But you know how?'

She nodded.

'I will give you lessons this afternoon after lunch.'

'Why? Why can't you drive the launch?'

'Because we will be here for a few days. I am going to visit friends. You will have to run the guests in and out of harbour. And there is nowhere to moor, so it's like a taxi. You drop them off and then come back when they call. We'll go out in the launch after lunch.'

It was during lunch, as Maddie was serving a prawn salad, that the first plaintive text arrived from Cory.

When do you think you'll get here?

When Douglas read it out, Simon snatched the phone from his hands and with a look of malice glanced around the table. 'OK, what are we going to say? Make them stew or keep them on tenterhooks?'

Douglas made a half-hearted attempt to take back his phone. 'I'll just tell her we're on the way and will let her know ETA nearer the time.'

'Where's the fun in that?' Simon began to stab at the phone, saying word by word, 'No. Idea. Stopped for lunch. And a swim. Going to call in at nice-looking place for a drink. See you later.'

'I'd not bother answering,' said Siri. 'Definitely leave them to stew.'

Maddie noticed that Nick hadn't looked at his phone at all and wondered if he'd had any communication from

Tara. Despite the seeming laughter and jollity of the poker game upstairs, there was a definite set to his jaw.

'Just tell them we'll be there soon,' said Nick dispassionately. 'Whatever you tell them isn't going to be soon enough.'

'Haven't you heard from Tara, then?' asked Simon with mock sympathy.

'No,' said Nick, seemingly unmoved.

Maddie admired his apparent stoicism, or was it misguided loyalty?

'But she's not the best at remembering to charge her phone.'

'She's certainly been busy on Instagram this morning,' Simon drawled, giving Nick a taunting smile as he handed Douglas's phone back to him. 'Hvar looks rather stunning.'

'I'm not really on Instagram that much,' said Nick.

'No, I don't suppose there's much call for scenic shots of sheep.'

'Sheep?' asked Siri. 'Why would Nick want to post photos of sheep?'

Simon hooted with pretend laughter. 'Didn't you know? Tara let slip that our Nick here is a bona fide sheep farmer.'

'Someone has to be.' Nick shrugged, but the set of his jaw had firmed even more. 'Where do you think the wool for your fancy sweaters comes from? Dropped in little bundles from outer space?'

Simon flicked at the arms of the fine wool jumper

casually knotted over his shoulders and ignored Nick's comment.

'Nothing wrong with being a sheep farmer,' blustered Douglas, which in Maddie's view made things worse.

'No one said there was,' said Simon, the wry twist to his mouth suggesting the complete opposite.

Maddie sighed and retreated to the galley. Sometimes Simon could be such a bitch.

Almost as if he'd read her mind, he appeared not long after with the large glass jug she used to serve water. 'Thought I'd get a top-up.' He flashed a smile at her. She gave him a brief nod and renewed her efforts at cleaning up the prawn shells dotted over the counter top.

'Maddie, you're not cross with me, are you?'

'Why would I be?' She turned to face him, folding her arms and then quickly unfolded them because it looked as if she were keen to hear what he had to say.

'I can tell – your mouth turns down and goes a bit pouty.' He leaned forward and touched her lower lip. 'It's very sexy.'

She pulled back, rolling her eyes. 'Don't be silly –' she said batting at his hand, even though inside some small gullible bit of her sat up and took notice. She reached for the tap to soak her cloth.

He suddenly clutched his hands to his chest with mock alarm. 'Don't tell me you fancy Nick? And you're cross with me for being mean to him?'

'Now you're just being ridiculous. Of course I don't fancy

Nick.' She didn't even like Nick – well, not initially. He'd grown on her, a bit.

'If you must know, it makes me uncomfortable. Some of the things you say.'

'You're such a sweetheart. It's just banter. I don't mean any of it.'

She shrugged. 'Nothing to do with me.'

'But it is, if it's upsetting you.'

'Did I say I was upset?' she said quickly. 'Like I've said before, you're the guests. I'm just crew.'

'But you don't approve.'

'Simon . . .' She looked into his altogether too good-looking face, aware that his proximity was making her pulse misbehave and doing her best to hide her reaction to him. 'Why do you care? What are you doing down here?'

Simon sighed and held her steady gaze. 'Because you intrigue me. You make me feel . . . well, it sounds cheesy, but you make me want to try and be a better person. You're so honest and natural. It's so refreshing. I don't think I've ever met anyone like you. Come out to dinner with me?' He slipped his arms around her waist and nuzzled at her neck, stroking her arm, his fingers trailing up to the back of her neck.

'I can't,' she replied, pulling back, even though a frisson of excitement flashed through her and inside a little voice was crowing, He wants to go out to dinner with *you*!!!! This gorgeous, just-stepped-out-of-a-magazine, model handsome man wanted to take her, ordinary Maddie Wilcox, out to dinner.

'Course you can,' Simon breathed into her ear.

She squirmed. 'I really can't.'

'Why not?' he asked, his voice low and husky, his hands skimming the underside of her breasts. 'You have fantastic tits, you know. You really are driving me mad.'

Maddie swallowed as he pressed against her. 'Because I'm working and you're a guest.'

'You're telling me.' His fingers stroked her hairline at the nape of her neck, making it hard for her to think. His hands seemed to be everywhere. 'There's a rule that stops crew going out with guests? Bollocks. No one can stop anyone going out with anyone. And if there is a rule I'll take it to the Court of Human Rights.'

She let out a breathy, girly laugh that really wasn't like her. 'I'm still working,' she managed to get out, although his hot breath in her ear again was very distracting, as was the hand squeezing her breast making her feel a little uncomfortable.

'But you must get time off.'

She flinched as he ran a palm over her groin, whispering, 'Come on, lovely Maddie, you're running out of excuses.'

'I do get time off, but only when everyone leaves the boat.'

'Well, that's sorted. In fact, even better. We could have the boat to ourselves one night.'

His husky, hoarse suggestion brought a contradictory

pang of pleasure and anxiety. He was so sophisticated and worldly. Was he expecting her to sleep with him?

'The chances of that happening . . .' Maddie shook her head. 'Look, I need to get tidied up. And you really shouldn't be down here.' She pushed his roving hand away. God, she sounded so prissy and prudish, but he was moving way too fast for her.

Simon smiled and kissed her on the side of her mouth. 'I'm going, I'm going. And don't you fret. Leave it to me.'

'This button is the trim control.' Ivan tapped the button on the throttle with his thumb. 'You press it to bring the trim up.'

'You've lost me,' said Maddie, standing with her legs wide apart to counteract the bobbing of the boat in the light swell as Ivan showed her the controls, aware that up above on the yacht she had an audience for her first ever motorboat lesson.

'Let me show you. Sit over there.' He nodded towards the other tan leather seat in the bow of the launch and started the engine. 'This is the throttle; you push it forward to increase your speed. When you set off, just push it forward very, very slowly. Can you feel a slight drag?'

Maddie nodded although she couldn't tell any difference.

'That's because the engine is down in the water, the trim controls the engine angle. You trim up once you've moved off, to bring the engine higher out of the water, which optimises the angle of the boat. It pushes the stern down and the bow up, so you move through the water with less drag, so more fuel efficient and makes the boat goes faster.'

'Right, engine up, stern down, bow up.'

'Watch.' He speeded up and then pressed the button.

Immediately she could feel the difference; the engine speeded up and the ride was smoother.

'But if you trim up too much, this is what happens.'

As he held the button down the boat began to bounce up and down. 'See, we call it porpoising. Jumping up and down. Not good for the revs or fuel consumption. You see plenty of the young guys showing off, just shows they have no idea what they're doing. And it isn't safe for passengers. You don't want to lose one over the side.' He flashed her an evil grin. 'Well, it's best not to.'

He took her on a quick circuit of the bay and then out into the open sea, increasing the speed gradually until they were flying, Ivan standing at the wheel, his teeth white against his dark beard in a grin of pure delight. Maddie laughed as the wind whipped at her hair and pushed the wayward curls out of her mouth and eyes, feeling her heart race with exhilaration.

'This is great,' she called, looking back at the foamy white wake billowing behind them.

'Yeah,' he yelled above the noise of the engine. 'As long as the fuel's on the client. These babies burn through it. Keep an eye on the gauge when you're coming in and out. They sell fuel in the harbour.'

Circling, he turned the boat back towards the bay. 'Now it's your turn.'

Jumping up, her palms prickling at the thought of getting hold of the wheel, she settled into the driver's seat, pretty sure that probably wasn't the right terminology at that moment, not that she cared. Never in her life had she imagined driving a motorboat.

But before he was about to let her loose, Ivan went through the controls again with considerable patience and a thoroughness she had not expected.

'Always feel that you are in control of the boat. There are no medals for going fast. Don't ever forget the safety of your passengers or the other people around you.' He tapped the wheel to emphasise his words. 'There can be serious accidents with a motorboat. People can die.'

Maddie swallowed; this was quite a responsibility.

'Always check the water around you before you set off.' He slowly turned his head from left to right. 'Always. Even when you're leaving dock. Never go into a buoyed area where there are swimmers. Always make sure your passengers stay in their seats. Sometimes that is hard, especially if they are coming back from a happy night out.'

'OK.' She nodded carefully, praying she was going to remember everything.

'But it can be lots of fun. Just be safe as well. Now it's your turn.'

The engine had been idling as he talked her through

everything, but now she tentatively took hold of the steering wheel.

'That's it, ease forward on the throttle.' The boat began to move forward. 'Now pull the trim up.' She pressed the button slowly, feeling the change of the angle of the boat as the bow lifted up, and gradually pushed the throttle forward, feeling the boat picking up speed. Wary at first, her heart bumping, she held tightly to the wheel with one hand and the throttle with the other, her concentration fixed on the boat and the sound of the engine.

'Play with the trim, get a feel for it. Today the conditions are good, but don't be fooled by the weather we've had; we can get thunderstorms that appear from nowhere in the summer. If the water is choppy you want to trim down, get the boat flatter in the water as it'll be steadier.'

'God, I hope I remember all this,' said Maddie.

'The boat will tell you; you can feel the drag, the engine revs.'

For a while she played with the throttle and trim under Ivan's exceptionally patient guidance and then, like magic, something clicked; it all seemed to come together.

This sensation of the boat slicing through the waves, leaving the churning wake like a long white comet's tail, was just the best feeling in the world. She lifted her face up into the wind, feeling the cool bite of the spray of water on her skin and, charmed, watched the rainbow iridescence as the sun lit up the fine droplets. Feeling in control, she relaxed as the hot sun warmed her back, its bright rays glinting off the waves with lightning flashes of brilliance.

Ivan made her practice turning the wheel in a wide sweep before getting her to do S-bends, as he called them, turning the wheel left and then right, allowing her to get a feeling for the boat.

'What do you think?' he asked, sitting back in the other seat, putting his feet up on the front.

'Awesome,' said Maddie.

'Now faster,' he urged, once she'd got a real feel for the boat.

Flashing him a dazzling grin, she pushed the throttle forward, standing upright, feeling like a warrior princess at the head of an invincible army as they raced across this sea. She laughed out loud at the ridiculously fanciful notion, not something she was prone to at all. Clearly being on a luxury yacht was starting to turn her head.

'Woo-hoo,' she screamed into the wind. 'This is so much fun.' She grinned at him.

He fixed her with a stern look. 'But, whatever you do, you mustn't let any of the guests drive the launch. They can while I'm in the boat with them and I'll let them have a turn in the bay this afternoon. But you are insured because you are crew. They are not.'

'You're kidding,' laughed Maddie. 'No one's driving this except me.'

'When we go into Hvar later, I'll give you a few lessons about manoeuvring into dock.'

Maddie's face fell. 'Eek, that sounds hard.'

He laughed. 'Don't worry – as long as you go really slowly, it's easy. You took to this, no problem.'

As soon as they returned to the boat, the whole party, who had been watching from on deck, were keen to go out for a spin in the motorboat, with the exception of Siri, and Maddie left them to it, glad to come back to earth quietly by herself as they all climbed down into the launch. She watched as Simon was the first to take the wheel; he wasted no time in hitting maximum speed, with lots of showy turns. Boys and their toys, she thought, heading up to the top sun deck. She probably had a quick half hour to soak up some rays before they came back.

'Oh, hi,' she said, coming to a halt at the top of the steps.

Siri raised her head from her book. 'Hi, that looked fun.'

'It was. So much fun. You didn't fancy it?'

'With all that testosterone fighting for supremacy, no, thanks.'

'Yeah, I get that. Maybe you could ask Ivan to take you out another time. He's a very good teacher. Can I get you anything?'

'No, I'm good, thanks.'

Maddie turned to go down the stairs.

'You can stay . . . I won't tell anyone.'

Maddie smiled. 'Are you sure you don't mind? I was just going to have a quick lie-down.'

'Doesn't bother me. Although I tell you what does bother me . . . those shorts. Serious fashion crime.'

Maddie laughed, remembering the very first time she'd meet Nina. 'And I have Crocs.'

'No.' Horror crossed Siri's face. 'Please tell me it isn't true. Although I think they might be slightly more forgivable than the shorts.'

Tugging at the fabric, Maddie looked down at them. 'They're not that bad, are they?'

Siri shuddered. 'That would be an affirmative in every language under the sun. Seriously, do you even own a full-length mirror?' She rose. 'Take off your T-shirt.'

Startled, Maddie took a step back. She had a bikini on underneath but there was a determined glint in Siri's eye that worried her.

'Off,' said Siri, tipping her head to one side with a definite hint of challenge.

Slowly Maddie peeled off her T-shirt.

'Oh, dear God. A travesty. Those are men's shorts. No wonder you look like a pudding on legs. Fabulous legs, by the way.' She actually walked around Maddie as if she were a prize pig on show.

'Take them off.'

'What?'

An impromptu strip down to her bikini in public was not what she'd signed up for, but Siri was already plucking at the belt, pulling the buckle undone. As soon as the belt loosened, too soon for Maddie's comfort, Siri tugged them down and then took several paces back, her eyes running up and down Maddie's figure in professional assessment, while Maddie was desperate to grab her T-shirt and cover up again.

'Blood and thunder, woman. You have a gorgeous figure. I thought as much. Great shoulders as well, by the way. Seriously, with a figure like that, you can really wear clothes.'

Maddie turned scarlet.

'What the hell are you doing hiding it under those rags?'

'Gorgeous figure my arse.' Maddie turned her T-shirt the right way out. 'Is this a posh person's idea of having a laugh?'

Before she could pull it back on, Siri snatched it out of her hands.

'I'm not looking at your size, love. You are perfectly proportioned. Those shoulders, seriously, they are to die for. Hip-shoulder ratio is just divine and you have a waist and boobs.'

'Next you'll be telling me I could be a model,' replied Maddie with withering, embarrassed sarcasm.

Siri cackled. 'No. They make those sample clothes ridiculously small . . . keeps costs down, they don't use as much fabric. That's why teeny-weeny bundles of bones like Tara and Cory are models. But no one would think they have gorgeous figures. Too bony, no curves and more like boys.'

'Men seem to like them.'

'Yeah, that bit I've never figured out. Pretty faces but not a lot up top.' She gave Maddie's body another assessing look, which left Maddie desperate to put her T-shirt back on.

'You could look amazing, you know.'

'Yeah, with a million pound budget, I'm sure.'

'Hello, do you know who you're talking to? When the Oscar nominations are announced, my phone rings off the hook 24/7 for a week. It's not about the budget, I've got skills.'

'Wow.'

'Yeah, the A-listers have me on speed-dial. Why do you think Cory and Tara lay off their shit when they're talking to me?'

'I had noticed.' Maddie grinned. 'I thought you were the mob or something.'

'Or something in the fashion world.' Her answering smile was positively evil. 'But I'm also bloody good. Under these clothes I'm a dumpy little pear shape. You know Esther Macmillan?'

'No.'

'Up-and-coming rapper, with the shortest legs and biggest thighs you've ever seen. And so self-conscious about them, poor chick. Sweetest girl. By the time I'd finished with her, in her last photoshoot you'd never know.'

Maddie nodded not knowing what the heck to say.

'You need style advice, which is where I come in.'

Maddie felt herself weakening, having always been a bit clueless about clothes. On the odd occasions when she had tried, she'd ended up getting it so badly wrong she'd stopped bothering. Having lived in Paris for a while, where French women made being perfectly dressed an absolute art form, it had reinforced her own sense of inferiority. How nice would it be to feel confident in the way she looked for once?

'Your cabin, now.'

'What?'

'I'm going to go through your wardrobe. I've been itching to sort you out.'

Reality stepped in and gave Maddie a sharp kick up the backside. Come on, she wasn't Cinderella and Siri was not her fairy godmother, not with that sharp tongue. 'That's a kind offer, but you people forget that I'm working.' Besides, she was well acquainted with the phrase, *You can't make a silk purse out of a sow's ear.*

Siri raised an eyebrow, amused rather than insulted. 'It's more than kind; it's very generous. In the States I can charge a thousand bucks a half day for personal styling. Now, get a move on before the others come back.'

Chapter 15

'Would anyone like anything else to eat?' asked Maddie.

'No,' said Douglas a little bit too quickly.

'Actually, yes,' said Siri with a defiant lift of her head, knocking back the last of her white wine. She'd been drinking heavily throughout dinner. 'I'd like some cheese, please. And another glass of wine.'

'Cheese, please, Louise,' said Simon.

'I think we ought to get going, don't you?' said Douglas.

'What happened to keep them waiting until half ten?' asked Siri, her eyes flashing.

Douglas shoulders drooped. 'I . . . They . . .'

'They're a pair of spoilt bitches who did what they wanted to and now they can take the consequences. I really am sick of you pussyfooting around Cory all the time. You're worth ten of her.'

'And I'm sick of you slagging off my choices all the time. I love her and if she makes me happy what's that got to do with you?'

'But she doesn't make you happy.'

'She does.'

'Rubbish.' Siri's heated tones carried on the still night air. 'When was the last time you were at a party and you could let her out of your sight, confident that she wouldn't be chatting someone else up, confident that she wouldn't be chatting someone else up, confident that she wouldn't, confident that she wouldn't be chatting someone else up? Not watching her batting her eyelashes at some film producer or casting director?' There was a brief pause, almost as if she were balanced on the edge of the precipice, the split second before she went beyond the point of no return. 'Can you even be sure she's not slept with some of them?' she asked and then, like a car slamming on the brakes, she pulled up, her face suddenly ashen, realising what she'd said.

Douglas's head reared back as if she'd hit him, which Maddie thought she might as well have done.

'Sorry,' Siri gasped. 'Sorry, Douglas. I shouldn't have said that.'

'No,' said Douglas, getting up from the table, throwing down his napkin, 'you shouldn't.' He walked with slow defeat through to the lounge area, where Ivan sat in the cockpit chair. 'We'll leave straight after dinner, as soon as Maddie has cleared the table.' He walked out of the door at the front of the lounge out onto the bow.

Siri immediately burst into tears. 'I . . . I didn't mean to say that.'

'Well, you did,' said Simon. 'And it wasn't well done at all.'

'I . . . I know. It just makes me so mad. The way she

treats him. And now I've really upset him.' She clutched at her stomach, chewing at her lip.

'All you can do is apologise,' said Nick calmly. 'It will blow over. Sometimes what those closest to us say hurts the most. They feel they can be more brutally honest because it's a reflection of how much they care for us.'

When the launch pulled into the harbour area at ten-thirty that evening, Tara and Cory were perched on their cabin bags like a pair of disconsolate parrots.

Hvar twinkled in the darkness, the lights reflected in the harbour with a dramatic floodlit fort dominating the skyline of the town. Interesting-looking buildings in the now familiar white stone lined the big harbour, although, as Ivan had said, there was very little mooring for larger boats. Instead a central area was rammed with lots of motorboats, reminding Maddie of a car park on the last Saturday before Christmas, but Ivan guided the launch over to a less crowded area on the far side of the harbour near a little park area with palm trees and benches.

'Where have you been?' wailed Cory. 'We've been waiting for hours. And we didn't have any money because nowhere takes cards. Everything is in cash.'

This was something that Maddie had noted in Bol, although it explained why there were so many ATMs everywhere.

'Sorry,' said Douglas with determined cheerfulness,

hopping out of the launch onto the side, 'but we're here now. Who's for a drink?'

The atmosphere in the launch coming over had been a touch tense, to say the least.

'I fancy a cocktail,' said Siri in response, all breezy and isn't-this-fun, although Maddie could sense the slight hint of strain in her voice as she desperately tried to act as if everything was normal.

'A nice cold beer would be great,' said Nick with further fake encouragement.

To Maddie's mind they sounded hammy and insincere.

'A drink,' cried Cory, looking horrified and exchanging a look with Tara. 'But we've been waiting for you all day. We're exhausted.'

'I just want to go to bed,' said Tara wistfully, turning her big luminous eyes Nick's way. She straightened, pushing her glorious hair over her shoulder, and rushed up to him, flinging herself at him. 'Oh, Nicky darling, I've missed you.'

Nick pulled away, putting a little distance between them, and Tara's face fell for a brief second, before she looked at him. Slightly in awe, Maddie watched as Tara turned huge brown beseeching eyes on Nick, her mouth quivering, and wait, was there an added sheen of tears?

'I know, I've been very naughty.' She wound her graceful arms around him. 'I should have told you, but Cory was determined to come and I couldn't let her come all by herself.'

'And what – you couldn't text or phone?' Nick lifted his eyebrows.

'My battery ran out, and I knew you'd be cross.' The little girl coy smile coupled with the studied gesture when she smoothed his hair away from his forehead made Maddie feel a little sick. She'd never seen such a pathetic non-apology. In fact she hadn't even used the 's' word.

'It was a dreadfully naughty thing to do; I shouldn't have done it.' She looked beyond him. 'Where's the boat?'

'Apparently mooring is in short supply here, so we're anchored in one of the bays a little way out.' Nick's voice was still stiff but Tara seemed not to notice or was ignoring it. Maddie suspected the latter.

'Oh, that's a bit rubbish. It would have been fun to be over there.' She pointed to the busy promenade on the other side of the harbour. 'There are lots of big boats over on the other side. Honestly, you should see them. People drinking Cristal. Partying all day. It's just like St Tropez.'

'That, Tara darling, is your own fault,' said Simon. 'If you and Cory hadn't jumped the gun, we'd have moored up later in the week when we've got a slot.'

'Well, it was all a waste of time because, apparently, William Randall isn't even here yet and me and Cory have had the most boring day. And the water taxi cost us a fortune to get here.'

'Serves you right,' said Siri, ruthless as ever, although she shot Douglas a quick wary glance. 'Now, let's find somewhere to drink. Maddie and Ivan are coming with us.'

Cory's eyes shifted and she frowned, opening her mouth as if she might be about to say something.

'Yes,' agreed Douglas, looking round at everyone but Siri. 'Buying Ivan a drink is the least I can do after messing up his schedule.'

Cory shut her mouth with the quick snap of a Venus flytrap.

Ivan smiled, all charm again. 'It is no problem.' Maddie kept her face in the shadow. Not what he'd said at nine o'clock this morning. 'I know a very nice bar. Follow me.'

To the left of the harbour area there was a large stone-flagged piazza full of restaurants, their outdoor tables packed with people sitting enjoying the balmy evening air. At the far end of the square, more floodlights illuminated a beautiful five-storeyed bell tower adjoining a gable-fronted church. Hvar, Maddie decided, was very pretty.

They passed several little steep narrow alleyways where the tall stone buildings crowded each other and walked along white flagstones, so polished by years of footsteps that they were slippery underfoot. Plenty of smart and trendy bars and restaurants, along with interesting-looking boutiques, lined the narrow streets.

'Gosh, this place is lovely,' said Siri, falling into step next to Maddie. Despite her words, her tone sounded forced, as if she were trying to sound enthusiastic. 'And so different from Bol.'

'It's certainly much busier,' observed Maddie.

'And much smarter,' said Simon, touching Maddie. 'I think I'm going to like Hvar a lot.'

'And you're looking rather lovely this evening,' he whispered in her ear as Siri stopped to look at some jewellery in one of the windows.

'Thank you,' said Maddie, blushing, grateful for the loan of Siri's dress.

Siri had been quite ruthless in her assessment of Maddie's wardrobe and had confiscated quite a few items, including the Breton T-shirt and red trousers which she'd thought were so natty. As consolation, she'd pressed a couple of dresses upon Maddie, insisting that dresses were her new best friends.

This white shift dress was far shorter than she would normally have worn but as soon as she'd put it on she'd fallen in love with it, unable to believe her reflection in the mirror. Who was that tall, almost elegant woman? Even Nick had given her a look of admiration when she'd climbed into the launch at Douglas's clumsy compliment of, 'Gosh, don't you scrub up well?' Which had mercifully raised a laugh from all, scotched any feelings of being self-conscious and helped to defuse some of the tension in the air, although Douglas and Siri refused to even look at each other.

'A shame we can't ditch everyone,' he said, glancing around.

Maddie turned. At the bottom of the street, Tara and Nick were having a furious whispered conversation, although she'd clamped herself to his side like a baby koala to its mother. Ahead, Douglas and Cory were walking along behind Ivan, hand in hand.

'We can't leave Siri; she's really upset.'

'But if we were on our own, we could have a lot more fun,' he whispered, his hand skimming her thigh under the edge of her dress. She jumped, anxiously looking around, hoping no one had seen.

'Simon,' she hissed, feeling the colour rushing into her face.

He laughed. 'What do you expect? I can hardly keep my hands off you. That is one tantalising dress. You do have a cracking pair of pins.'

She stared at him, a horrible sense of anxiety burning in the pit of her stomach. He was being complimentary, wasn't he? He mixed with the beautiful people. But his words made her uncomfortable.

'Don't be daft,' she said, moving away from him, grateful to see that Siri had rejoined them.

'I am so coming back here tomorrow. There are some gorgeous shops and there were some serious signature necklaces in that window.' She looked at the simple neckline of Maddie's dress. 'That's another trick I need to teach you: jewellery and scarves. Accessorising, the friend of travelling light.'

'Maybe you should teach Cory and Tara,' said Simon. 'Not sure either of them have ever heard of travelling light.'

Siri didn't respond but her jaw tightened as if she were

holding back her usual acid observations and she fell back into step alongside Maddie.

Ivan led them to a bar, which spilled down several wide flat steps on the side of the street, the plush seating areas lit by flaming torches in wrought iron baskets suspended from the walls. It was already busy with tables full of empty glasses, groups of laughing people crowded into the woven seats.

'This is very nice,' said Cory graciously as she lowered herself into one of the seats, her arm stretched along the back, immediately looking at ease, as if she owned the place and taking up the lion's share of the corner seat.

'Mikail who owns the bar is an old friend of mine,' explained Ivan. 'This is one of the best bars in Hvar. Tom Cruise was here last year, Chris Hemsworth. Lots of famous people come here.'

'Good evening, everyone. What can I get you to drink?' asked a chirpy-voiced young girl with a slight Scandinavian accent and a gorgeous perfect white-toothed smile. Maddie almost laughed out loud as all of the men, without exception, sat up straighter at the sight of her swathe of pure white blonde hair that fell in waves to her bottom and the deep golden tan that set off her long lean body to perfection. Fresh-faced, she wore not a scrap of make-up and Maddie could almost see Tara and Cory's hackles rise.

'I'd like a Strawberry Daiquiri,' announced Tara.

'Where's that on the menu?' demanded Cory. 'I didn't see that.'

'There isn't one, but –' she turned to the girl with a sugary sweetness that was as fake as saccharine '– I'm sure you can do one.'

'*Ja*, it's not a problem. Eric, the barman, he's a professional mixologist. Nothing is too hard for him.' The Scandinavian girl gave her an infectious perky smile, oblivious to Tara's deliberate posturing.

'I'll have the same,' said Cory a touch sulkily, as if once again Tara had upstaged her.

Maddie had decided to keep her wits about her. 'I'll have a Coke, please.'

'Diet or regular?'

'Regular, please.'

'Ooh, no! You can't drink regular. Have you any idea how much sugar is in regular Coke?' squealed Cory.

'Clearly not,' muttered Tara, under-her-breath, shooting a disdainful glance at Maddie's middle.

A fierce red blush rolled over Maddie's cheeks but she managed to school her face so that she didn't react or even look at Tara.

'I'll have a cold beer,' said Nick quickly. 'What're you having, Siri?'

'A Pornstar Martini for me.'

'What's in that then?' he asked, trying to bring a smile to her face, which was missing its usual bright-eyed sparkiness. 'Not real porn stars, I'm assuming.'

'Oh, Nicky, you are silly. Everyone knows what's in a Pornstar. Gosh, I remember drinking it for the first time

196

in the LAB bar in Soho. That was the night that Madonna was in there. Remember, Cory?'

'Here you go.' The waitress doled out the drinks and Maddie admitted to a tiny bit of envy at the colourful exotic-looking cocktails in their glamorous-shaped glasses as she lifted her plain old Coke in the toast of cheers with everyone. Nick clinked her glass with his lager and winked as if he knew exactly what she was thinking.

'Mmm, I think the mixologist knows his flavours,' murmured Cory as she sipped at her bright pink concoction. 'Do you remember the Daiquiris we had in Antibes that time, T?'

Tara giggled. 'And Simon bet that up-and-coming pop star – what was his name? – that he couldn't drink three strawberry daiquiris.'

'I think you mean Bruno Mars, sweetie,' said Simon.

'Wasn't he a darling man?' Cory sighed.

'Although they weren't as good as the drinks in that bar in St Tro; do you remember, Douglas?' Tara leaned forward.

Douglas laughed. 'All the drinks in St Tropez were good; they had to be, they were bloody pricey and you girls insisted on drinking on the front. Double the cost.'

'Oh, Lord, that was a fun evening,' said Simon. 'Do you remember going on Jay-Z's yacht?'

Cory began to giggle. 'Yes, and remember Douglas calling him Mr Z all night. That was hilarious.'

'I didn't know the chap was famous. He was American,

he seemed jolly nice. We talked for a long time about investments. I thought he worked on Wall Street,' Douglas said with indignation although it was tinged with a touch of pride as he looked down at his phone. He straightened.

'I've had a text from Genevieve Ellingham!' He scrolled through his message. 'How jolly. They've invited us to lunch. The day after tomorrow. They've rented a place out here for the whole summer.'

'I adore Genevieve,' said Tara, turning shining eyes to Nick. 'Oh, you'll love her, she's so much fun.' And then she turned back to the conversation, her hands flapping enthusiastically. 'I can't wait to see her.'

'That'll be a blast. I've not seen Evie since Silverstone last year when Vettel won the Grand Prix and we all went back to their place,' chipped in Simon. 'Lewis was livid.'

Maddie leaned back, sipping her Coke, trying to remember if she'd ever met a famous person in her life. Hanging around the stage door after a JLS concert hoping to meet Marvin probably didn't count, even if he had signed her programme and smiled at her. Looking up, she caught Nick's eye and he winked and took a long swallow of his beer, his face completely impassive. She wondered if he was as unimpressed as she was by all the name-dropping. Surely Mr Z and Lewis and Genevieve Ellingham, whoever she was, all went to the loo in the same way and all breathed the same air. They were human beings, not some superior interplanetary species above everyone else.

'Oh, what fun. You'll have to wear the nice shorts,' said

Tara, digging Nick in the ribs, lifting her hand to his face and rubbing at his chin. 'You can't go the Ellinghams' looking like a scruff. In fact, I might take you for a haircut tomorrow.' She gave him a seductive look that made Maddie want to vomit. The woman was so fake.

'I can get my own haircut, thanks,' said Nick, dropping a kiss on Tara's cheek as if to soften the words.

'I know, sweetie.' She paused. 'Have you ever thought about having your chest waxed?'

Nick's eyes widened with definite *No! And not in this lifetime* horror and Maddie couldn't help sniggering.

'It doesn't hurt that much, darling.' Tara's tinkly laugh rang out.

'I'll take your word for it,' he replied, glaring as he caught Maddie's eye; her shoulders were shaking with laughter.

When the conversation had moved on she leaned over and whispered, 'Want me to share that with Nina?'

Chapter 16

'Wait.'

Maddie looked up at the middle deck. It was seven o'clock in the morning and she'd just stepped into the launch, not expecting anyone to be up and about yet. Last night had been a late one by the time they'd returned to the boat and a fair number of cocktails had been consumed, although, conscious she was still on duty, she'd stuck to Coke.

Simon's head disappeared and a second later he came down the steps onto the stern.

'Where are you off to at this ungodly hour, Cinders?' he asked, still trying to button up his linen shirt while clutching a pair of deck shoes under one arm. A fine set of abs were on show and a nicely muscled smooth chest. Everything about Simon seemed smooth. She wasn't sure she'd ever seen such a perfect body in the flesh. It had to take some work, although he didn't seem to have done much in the way of exercise while he'd been here. How did he keep up those perfectly sculpted muscles?

'I'm going to the bakery. I thought you all might appreciate some carbs for breakfast.' She smiled warily at him.

'Oh, Lord, yes, I do feel a bit delicate but not enough to stop me accompanying you.' He jumped down into the launch and Maddie felt a momentary flicker of irritation at his presumption. She'd been looking forward to a solitary trip into Hvar. Last night had been a little too much for her, with all the name-dropping and *my holiday was bigger and better than yours*. It must be exhausting keeping up with the Joneses.

As her shoulders sank there was another rock to the boat and she realised Nick had appeared and also jumped aboard.

'Can I cadge a lift into Hvar?' he asked. 'I want to get a haircut . . . unsupervised.'

'Yeah, sure. Why not?' said Maddie with an uncharitable shrug, although secretly she was quite glad to see him. Hopefully, in his presence, Simon would keep his hands to himself.

Nick went and sat in the seats at the back of the launch, leaving the seat next to Maddie free for Simon.

As the boat drew away from the yacht, Maddie eased up the trim, feeling the bow lift and enjoying the sensation of having mastered driving the motorboat. Simon's shirt flapped in the wind and he turned in the seat to face her, his eyes hidden behind his Ray-Ban sunglasses. It didn't take Einstein to realise that the unbuttoned shirt was a deliberate oversight and purely for her benefit.

'You can get dressed now, Simon,' she said dryly, facing the wind, not bothering to look at him.

'You spoil all my fun.' He laughed, pulling together the fabric, doing up the buttons and tucking his shirt into his shorts.

She was rather pleased with the way she docked, cutting the engine and allowing the boat to drift into the harbourside. Simon watched as she jumped out and quickly cast a line around one of the mooring posts, Nick still clambering forwards from the back of the boat.

'Feel free to join in,' she said from the side as Simon straightened up and got out of the boat just ahead of Nick.

'You were being so capable and efficient, I was enjoying watching. Independent women really turn me on.'

Nick rolled his eyes.

'You are so full of . . .' said Maddie, picking up her trusty basket.

'Language,' admonished Simon. 'So where are we headed, Little Red Riding Hood?'

'Ah . . .' she looked down at her scribbled note '. . . I'm not a hundred per cent sure, but it shouldn't be too hard to find.'

'I'll see you guys later,' said Nick, skirting around them. 'What time shall I meet you?'

'Back here in forty minutes?' suggested Maddie before adding, 'Think you'll get a chest wax in as well?'

Nick glared at her and turned on his heel and strode off.

Zita had recommended a place on Stjepana Papafave, which Maddie quickly realised was the big main square that they'd seen the previous evening. It took only a few minutes to load up her basket with burek, crescent rolls with cheese, little breadsticks and Croatian-style sausage rolls, as well as apricot croissant and jam doughnuts. According to her phone – how on earth had anyone ever managed before Google maps – there was a good-sized supermarket, up beyond the square past the bell tower near to the bus station.

Simon sauntered along with her in the early morning sunshine and Maddie was grateful for his silence as she let her artist's eye rove over the view. Compared to last night when the square had been buzzing with people, redolent with the scent of fish and cooked meat, this morning there was a quiet sleepy air to the town, reminding Maddie of its historic origins and how it might have looked in times gone by. Apart from the modern signage tacked onto the front of some of the buildings, the basic fabric looked untouched and unchanged. Her flip-flops slapped on the glossy white paving slabs as she walked back into the square, passing the beautiful carved bell tower with its arched windows on each storey. It felt as if the town had held fast to its history, an iron white stone grip, telling of its community and a solidarity beneath the surface.

She stared up to the top of the hill, the fort dominating

the skyline. Not one of the party last night had voiced any desire to climb up there. As soon as she had some free time, she'd do it. The views must be amazing.

'Right, where next?' asked Simon as she was studying one of the buildings by the harbour, wishing she had her sketchbook with her.

'Sorry?' She realised she was daydreaming.

'You've done shopping. Want to stop for a drink? Hair of the dog? Breakfast?'

'No, thanks, I'm OK. Besides, I have to get back to the *Avanturista*. People will want their breakfast. And we need to meet Nick in five minutes.'

'Oh, yes, good ole Neanderthal Nick.'

Maddie raised a careful eyebrow. 'Why don't you like him? What's he done to you?' She stopped to put down the awkward wicker basket for a quick rest before she transferred it to her other arm. Served her right for allowing herself to give into the impractical romance of the basket. In reality only pretty slight girls in novels and films fannied around with whimsical baskets and trugs. She should have stuck with a plain old carrier bag.

'I don't dislike him.' Simon sighed, a long-suffering, bored exhalation which Maddie found overly dramatic and more than a touch studied.

'But he has no place here. I don't know what Tara was thinking . . . well, I do. Thought a bit of Daniel Craig beefcake would make her look good. Putting the idea into people's heads.'

Maddie snorted with ill-disguised impatience. 'Nick doesn't look anything like Daniel Craig.'

'No, more Chris Hemsworth. Tara's not stupid. He's got the rough and rugged look. Sets the scene rather well.'

'I don't think so.'

'Come now, Maddie. Surely you can see Nick's appeal in a rough and ready way.'

'You make it sound as if he's just stepped off a council estate. I'm pretty sure his family own their own home.'

'What?' Simon drew his hand against his chest in camp shock. 'Don't tell me that they have their own inside toilet?'

'He lives in the north, not the post-apocalypse,' said Maddie in slightly frigid tones. What on earth would Simon make of her family's home? OK, so the outside toilet had long since been converted into a shed but it was not so long since a previous generation had made complete use of it.

'Maddie –' his voice took on a wheedling tone '– I'm only teasing.'

But it didn't feel like teasing and suddenly Maddie wasn't sure she liked Simon very much. He never seemed to have anything positive to say about anyone. And she'd noticed he could be like quicksilver, one minute cosying up to Tara and Cory, but the next, when they weren't around, quick to complain and moan about them.

Simon shrugged with nonchalance, adding, 'To be honest, he's not really important enough for me to care one way or the other about whether I like him or not. Tara will ditch him soon enough. Now, are you going to have a coffee with me or not?'

'I've already told you; we haven't got time.'

'Come on, Maddie, you know you want to really.' Simon tried to press a kiss on her neck but she pulled away.

'No, Simon. I don't.'

He rolled his eyes and despite the charming smile she could sense his irritation. 'All right then, we'll go back to the boat. You're no fun, you know.'

Swapping the basket, which had left marks on her arm, to the other arm, she ignored him and picked up her pace, heading to the little harbour area with a determined stride.

Simon sauntered along behind her, whistling as if he had all the time in the world.

She turned.

He flashed her a grin which she was sure he thought was charming, but she was too wound up by his unwillingness to see she had to get back to the boat.

'Are you being deliberately difficult?'

With a stupid, she-couldn't-possibly-really-be-mad-at-me smirk, he said, 'OK, we'll go back to the boat. Are you going to let me drive?'

'No,' she said shortly.

Simon laughed and slid his hand into her shorts pocket. 'Sure about that?' he asked, pulling out the ignition key.

'Simon, give those back.'

'Only if you let me drive the boat.'

'You're not allowed to.'

'Who's going to know? We can swap when we get to the bay.'

'I'll know and if anything happens we're not insured.'

'What is going to happen? It's hardly the *Titanic* and last I heard there were no known icebergs on the Dalmatian coast.'

He dangled the keys out of reach above her head when she made a grab for them. 'Careful, you don't want me to drop them in the sea, do you?'

Maddie could feel herself getting hotter. 'Simon, this isn't funny. Give me the keys back and stop mucking about.' She looked around, hoping to see Nick. At least he would talk some sense into Simon.

'Come on, gorgeous, stop being so strait-laced. No one is going to know. And you don't need to worry about the insurance. I can drive this thing fine. I've driven an F1 around Brands Hatch; I don't think a poky little engine is going to cause me any problems. I'm an experienced driver.'

With his eyebrows quirked in challenge, he got into the boat and went and stood behind the wheel, looking at her over his shoulder. 'You can cast off.'

Maddie put down her basket. 'Simon,' she ground out, folding her arms, making it clear she had no intention of getting into the boat, 'we've got to wait for Nick.'

After a small standoff, he walked lightly to the stern and held out a hand. 'Come on, get in.'

She jumped down into the boat and arranged her basket

in the back seat. They were still moored and there was no sign of Nick. When he got here, he could untie the line.

Simon got out of the boat onto the side. 'No sign of him.'

The next thing she knew, Simon had the line in his hand, had jumped into the boat, slotted the key in the ignition and turned on the engine and was pulling away from the harbourside.

'Simon! What are you doing?'

With a devilish grin, he increased the speed, making the boats around them dance up and down in the wash. 'Live a little, Maddie. Come on, let's have some fun.'

She turned back to look at the quayside, anxiously scanning along, looking for Nick.

'We can't leave him.'

'Course we can.'

'Simon –' she folded her arms '– turn around now. We need to go back.' She didn't want to leave Nick. It was wrong.

'Don't be such a bore. He's a big boy. Old enough and ugly enough to look after himself.'

'I'm not being a bore. You're being an arse.' And Nick wasn't old or ugly, he was . . . Something flipped in her stomach. Gorgeous in a rugged, masculine, action hero sort of way. Oh, heck, how come she'd only just noticed that now?

'Ooh, Maddie, I love it when you get all feisty. Aaaaarrrrse,' he repeated in a mocking Irish accent.

'For fuck's sake, Simon, will you stop and let me take over? You're not supposed to be driving. Slow down. Ivan's going to kill me.' She looked back over her shoulder towards the harbour, growing smaller with every second. Where was Nick? What was he going to think? She hated the thought that he'd assume she'd been party to this. Right now she'd far rather have Nick in the boat.

'Don't be silly, darling. I'm a guest. He's not going to say anything to me. Now, let's see what this baby can do.'

He was going so fast now that she couldn't stand up without hanging onto the seat. There was no way she could wrest control from him. Resigned to his idiocy, she sat in the other seat with her arms folded, refusing to acknowledge him even as he whooped and kept trying to catch her eye.

'Come on, Maddie, cheer up. This is fun. We're having fun.'

Another time in another pair of hands, she might have found zipping across the water exhilarating and enjoyable but a tight bud of anxiety had lodged under her breastbone and she clung to the sides of the seat, wondering what Ivan was going to say to her.

The motorboat raced past several big yachts moored in prime spots. They were in a different league to the *Avanturista*. Huge, many tiered superyachts like floating wedding cakes. Some were silent and still, sleeping off last night's party, as evidenced by the empty glass flutes, abandoned bottles of champagne and beer cans, strewn across the tables on the main deck, while others were hives of mini industry with crew members in smart uniforms buzzing about cleaning decks, polishing brass, having already, Maddie guessed, cleared up the previous evening's debris.

As they skirted one of the biggest gin palaces at anchor, they emerged directly in the path of another motorboat with three men on board. The other boat veered sharply away, narrowly missing their bow, making the boat rock violently in the sudden wall of water created by the wake.

'Oy,' yelled Simon. 'Watch where you're going!' But his words were carried away by the wind and drowned out by the whining pitch of the engine as it struggled to crest through the choppy water.

One of them gave a cheery no-harm-done sort of wave.

'Tossers,' muttered Simon.

'They didn't do it on purpose,' said Maddie. 'They may have had right of way.' Ivan had definitely mentioned some points of seafaring etiquette and in the rush of driving the boat she'd not paid any attention.

'Bastards,' said Simon as the boat veered around with a splashy turn, increasing the churning wake before zooming off, with one of the men giving another cheery wave. 'I'll show them.' He wrenched the throttle forward and the boat jerked forward, throwing Maddie back into her seat.

'Don't!' she cried, but Simon wasn't listening. The engine groaned and hiccoughed before dropping into a low growl as it settled into top speed. There was a grim hunger in the profile of Simon's face as he stood up, one hand gripping the wheel and the other holding the throttle down, his thumb pressed on the trim.

'Simon, slow down!' screamed Maddie as the bow tipped up, too high out of the water, while the engine was too low, but Simon, intent on hot pursuit, was so focused on the boat ahead that he didn't seem to notice the rollercoaster up and down bounce in the water, each smack down leaving Maddie's stomach in freefall.

There was a whoop from the other boat and it began to swerve in a flashy show – this driver knew what he was doing – as he sliced left and right. Simon pushed the boat faster and it bounced higher, hitting the choppy waves of the wake from the boat ahead. The boat rolled hard to the right, almost tipping over.

'Slow down!' Maddie screamed again, but it was too late; the boat rolled again as it hit the trough of the wake from the other vessel. Simon stumbled, letting go of the wheel. The boat swung wildly to the right. He grabbed at the wheel, caught it and then lost it again, sending the boat into another wild turn.

'Simon!' Maddie's voice was little more than a gasp as she hung on, trying to catch her breath as adrenaline punched its way through her system.

The boat rocked violently from side to side, each time the angle sharper. Maddie clung on, although it was difficult as her wet hands were finding it hard to grasp the smooth fibreglass edge. Simon managed to throw himself forward and take hold of the wheel. His haphazard grab sent the boat lurching in the opposite direction, banking hard as it hit the trough of the wake with an enormous bang. Maddie's precarious hold failed. The impact threw her out, smacking into the sea with a painful slap of water on skin. The white wall of the boat towered over her, filling her vision, coming closer, closer . . . Oh, God, it was going to . . . At the last second it sliced by, the chainsaw buzz of the propeller just shy of her head.

Before she could draw breath the wake closed over her head, swamping her, pushing her down. Everything was water. Pressing at her face. Filling her ears. Scouring her nose. Gulped into her mouth, the salt making her gag. She flailed, arms and legs thrashing, not sure which way was up or down. Tossed and spun like a washing machine and then, mercifully, the reprieve of cold fresh, air. She sucked in a desperate lungful of air, throwing her head back, trying to keep it out of the water as she splashed her arms and legs in a flight or fight automatic stay-afloat response as the waves rolled towards her, tossing her up and down. Her hair was plastered over her face and she swiped at it, while trying to swim with one arm. All she could see was the white froth and foam spewing behind the rocking boat, which was disappearing fast.

Gradually the roll of the waves settled and she trod water, gasping for breath, her heart pounding so hard she could almost feel the water pulsing around her. She was conscious of the weight of her clothes dragging at her, the sea sucking at her. Already her muscles, limp from shock, were failing her. From here the shore looked a very long way and with waves swelling up and around her she couldn't see the boat. Surely Simon would come back for her. God, what if he crashed the boat? What if he'd fallen out too? Had the occupants of the other boat seen what had happened? What if another boat came along and didn't see her? Her heart beat along with the rapidity of her starburst thoughts. Calm down, Maddie. Calm down.

She looked at the shoreline. Would Simon be able to see her? The waves and the swell meant she couldn't see him. Perhaps she could swim to one of the yachts moored near the shore. Get some help. But she wasn't the strongest swimmer. If only she'd insisted they waited for Nick. Where the hell was Simon? Ivan was going to kill her. If she survived. It suddenly struck her that she was alone in the sea and, with the exception of Simon and possibly the three men in the boat that was probably at least a mile away by now, no one knew she was here.

With no sign of Simon coming back for her she struck out for the shore, but swimming in the sea, when the water sucked and clawed at her heavy clothes, was hard work and it didn't feel as if she was making any progress. It had barely been five minutes and already her arms were too heavy.

The sound of a boat approaching made her heart pick up; she stopped swimming, hoping that someone would see her and not mow her down. The white hull of the boat grew closer. She waved her hand in the air, sinking briefly, with another rush of water up her nose.

The boat slowed and her limbs went limp with relief, ironically making things easier as her body floated on the surface.

'We've got you,' called an American voice. There was a splash and a life belt landed just a few feet in front of her. Gathering the last of her strength, she struck out towards it and, as soon as she'd grasped it with both hands, someone began pulling her in towards the boat. Hands grabbed at her and hauled her in and she slithered over the side and flopped onto the floor like a dazed fish.

The engine cut with an abrupt halt and the boat bobbed gently up and down.

'Here . . .' Someone wrapped a blanket around her, immediately shielding her from the brisk breeze which felt icy on her wet, chilled skin. 'You're OK now.' She shivered into the blanket, her teeth chattering so hard she couldn't speak.

The kind concerned eyes of a movie-star handsome, preppy, good-looking guy stared down at her. He wore the crisp white polo and pressed chinos uniform that denoted crew on one of the superyachts. He was also one of the three men in the speedboat that Simon had decided to take on.

'Th-tha-th-anks f-for r-rescuing m-m-m-me . . .' her teeth chattering, she said carefully, worried she might bite her tongue.

'No problem. You OK? No injuries? No bangs to the head?' He scanned her body, efficient and impassive. 'There's no blood, so that's a good sign. I've seen some nasty post propeller meet-ups and they're not pretty.'

She shook her head.

'Aaron, man, don't tell her about the babe who lost a leg. Not helping, dude.' A second equally handsome man in the same uniform came to join the first.

'Both legs still here,' Maddie managed.

'Cool. Wouldn't want to lose those.' Aaron grinned at her, flashing all-American hero teeth at her. She felt at a decided disadvantage. 'You're English.'

'All the way through,' she replied.

'Yes. Who's your friend?' He nodded out to sea.

'Not a friend. Guest. He wanted to drive.' Maddie shook her head. 'I let him. I'm not supposed to.'

'Mmm, can be tricky when the guests throw their weight around.'

'I heard that,' said a much louder and stronger American accent, with a rumbling laugh. An older man stepped into view. 'Except I'm the owner so I'm allowed to drive the boat.'

The two younger men grinned at him and one of them quipped, 'I hear you're allowed to do anything.'

The man clapped him on the back. 'And you're my voice of reason when I shouldn't.' He turned and crouched down in front of Maddie. 'You OK, honey? Took a nasty –' he pronounced it with two extra a's '– spill there.'

216

'I'm feeling a lot better now I'm on . . . not quite dry land – dry boat?'

He laughed. 'Out of the water.'

'Yes, that. Thank you for rescuing me.'

'Least we could do. Your pal has gone back to base. We gave him a little talk on the rules of the road.'

'My fault, I should've –'

'Honey, there's no need to apologise for an asshole. How're you feeling?'

'Soggy. Embarrassed. Knackered.'

'Knackered.' He mimicked her English accent with a delighted crow. 'Love it. I meant how are you feeling medically speaking?'

Maddie shrugged. 'I'll live.'

'You Brits crack me up with your understatement. Half the folks around here would be threatening to sue my ass off.'

'You rescued me.'

'With some folk that wouldn't measure. Your pal back there was all affronted at first. He wanted to get litigious at the get-out. Saying we cut him up. Max here quickly shut him down.'

'I'm fine.' She clutched her stomach, wincing, which rather ruined her nonchalant attempt to hide the fact she felt horribly sick with all the seawater she'd swallowed swilling around. 'Oh, God,' she moaned, suddenly going hot, that horrible aching jaw feeling signalling that she was going to throw up any second.

Aaron moved quickly, steering her body round so that her head was over the side. The contents of her stomach erupted with a godawful noise. She wanted to die of embarrassment. She heaved again and again. This was almost as bad as being in the sea. Her nose stung, her eyes watering as she hung her head, the bobbing of the boat making her feel even worse.

When she came back up, Max had a bottle of water in his hand held towards her and Aaron a tub of wet wipes. 'Wow, you're like a pair of efficiency superheroes or something,' she said, wondering what on earth made her blurt that out.

The older man laughed. 'I like that. Maybe I'll change the uniform. Capes. We could do capes.'

'Bill, with respect,' said Max, 'no capes. The chinos are just fine.'

'What he said,' added Aaron.

Bill lifted his shoulders and smiled at Maddie as she gratefully took a wet wipe and cleaned her mouth. 'You'd never guess I pay their wages.' Then he lowered his voice. 'They're good boys. Best crew I ever had, but don't tell 'em I said so.' He winked at her.

'I won't,' she said gravely, feeling a lot better now that she'd been sick. Her heart had stopped trying to beat its way out of her chest and the frightened panicky feelings had subsided. 'And I'm sorry about . . .' she inclined her head '. . . the side of the boat.'

'That's all right. I'm sure I can find someone to clean

it up. That's the really great thing about having crew.' He included both Max and Aaron in his grin.

'Talking of which –' she sat up straighter, clutching the blanket '– I ought to get back. I don't suppose you'd mind giving me a lift?'

'Not at all,' said Bill. 'But not until my doctor has checked you over, little lady.'

'Doctor?'

'Yes, one of those fellas in white coats.' His eyes twinkled in his tanned weathered face. 'Except she's a she.'

'We do have doctors in England,' she said repressively, pursing her lips but unable to hide her smile. 'But I feel fine. And I need to get back to work.'

'Not until my doc has given you the all-clear. Can you be sure you didn't bump your head?'

'Er . . . yes,' she said, not sounding sure at all because the whole of her left side hurt where she'd hit the water, especially her ear. 'Honestly, I'm OK.'

'We're taking you in for a check-up. One of the boys can run you back when the doc's given you the all-clear.'

'Honey – what is your name, by the way? – I'm paying that doc through the nose; she hasn't worked since we left New York. It'll do her good to reacquaint herself with a live one.'

'I'm Maddie.'

'And I'm Bill. And these two guys are Aaron and Max. Actually my wife's nephews but for some goddamn reason they insist on working.' Bill didn't look as if he minded;

in fact it was said with a touch of pride. 'And I can give you some ID if you're worried about boarding a boat with three strange Yanks.'

Maddie chewed at her lip. 'I guess I'm a bit naïve. I figured if you were kind enough to rescue me rather than leave me to drown, you probably were the good guys.'

Bill tipped his head to one side and nodded. 'You got a good point there, little lady.'

Chapter 17

Bill's boat was not a boat. It was a floating mansion, a palace, a small village.

Aaron helped her out of the boat and guided her up the steps, while her eyes bugged out on stalks at the sheer opulence. Oh, hell, her shoes were soaking and her clothes were sodden, dripping down her legs, leaving small puddles in her wake.

'Why don't you take a shower in one of the state rooms and I'll get my steward to rustle up some clothes for you?'

'That would be very kind, thank you.'

Bill beamed at her. 'Aren't you just the politest little thing?'

Maddie snorted. 'I think that's the first time anyone has ever called me little. Even when I was five I was on the big-boned side.'

'Healthy and happy; that's all you can ask for. You eaten?' He laughed at himself. 'Stupid question. You just brought it all back. Why don't you get yourself cleaned up and then come back on deck, join me for breakfast, after you've seen the doc?'

Before she could answer, not that she was going to turn down the offer of a hot shower, he'd walked off.

'Is he always like this?' asked Maddie, the room suddenly feeling emptier without his larger than life presence.

'Bill doesn't like to take no for an answer, but he's a good guy. A really good guy. Looks after me and Max and Mom real good. Dad cleaned her out and took off when we were small. He's looked after Mom ever since. That's why we try and work ... payback during the summer vacation. He's paying our college tuition so it only seems right.'

Well, that reassured her that she wasn't in any danger. Although, to be honest, she was so grateful for being rescued, any concerns about being sold into the white slave trade had been pushed to the back of her mind. Now she was safe and about to be warm and dry again, she did wonder how Simon was and glad she didn't have to talk to him. A flash of fury at his behaviour spiked but she took an even breath.

'Wow, you're really slumming it here!' said Maddie when Aaron opened the door to the stateroom.

He laughed. 'No expense spared. Neat, isn't it?'

'How many cabins do you have and are they all as big as this?'

'This is one of the bigger ones but it's nowhere near as big as the master; that's probably three times the size. And on board we've got twenty staterooms. Cinema, of course. Cocktail bar. Swimming pool. Sauna. Jacuzzi.'

Maddie nodded, swallowing, momentarily lost for words. 'That's a lot of boat.'

'That's superyacht for you.' With another smile, he nodded towards a door. 'Shower through there, plenty of towels. Shampoo, soap. Anything else you need?'

'Just a bag for my wet things. And I don't suppose you've got a bag of rice on board?' She unbuttoned the pocket of her cargo shorts and pulled out her phone. 'It's worth a try, I guess.'

'Aw, shoot. It got a pretty good dousing. I think ma'am, you're going to have to get a new one.'

'I think you're probably right,' she said with a disconsolate sigh.

'Why don't you . . . er . . .' he coloured '. . . change and throw out your wet stuff? The steward can probably rinse your panties and bikini top and get them dry and I'll leave some dry things on the bed. Take your time. Doc Cannon knows you're here. Think you can find your way back up?'

Maddie laughed. 'I think I'll manage.'

'Yeah, as long as you don't fall overboard.'

'Thank you.'

She slipped into the bathroom, stripped off quickly and with one hand threw out her bikini through the door.

'Thanks,' she yelled.

'No problem. Take your time.'

She heard the stateroom door shut and wrapped herself in one of the huge navy bath sheets with a row of pale blue embroidered flowers bounding the hem and stepped back into the room. Oh, heaven, it was super-fluffy.

Holy moly. Maddie looked around the room. She'd thought the *Avanturista* was posh; this was . . . extraordinary. Crisp white sheets on the bed, monogrammed with the name of the yacht. A plush carpet that threatened to swallow her feet.

Blimey, the bathroom was as big as her cabin back on the *Avanturista*. Just look at that bucket head shower and all the different shower heads on either side which just begged you to step right in. The row of expensive toiletries lined up on a smoky glass shelf lit by concealed lights above looked seriously exclusive and when she picked them up she discovered they were ESPA. She took a sniff of one of the bottles to find out just what bergamot, jasmine and a hint of cedarwood did smell like.

Grinning at herself in the mirror even though she looked like a bedraggled mongrel, she dived into the shower, which did a fabulous job of washing away the indignity and embarrassment of her dunk in the sea.

Using the lush toiletries, she emerged in a cloud of delicious scent, her wet hair feeling softer than it had ever done before. She wrapped the big bath sheet around her and scooped her hair up into another towel and wrapped it up turban-style. Of course, as soon as she opened the bathroom door, the towel slipped down over her eyes. As she tried to salvage it, she stepped forward blindly and . . .

'Aargh!' She jumped as two hands grasped her forearms.

Startled, she threw up her head, trying to see properly, and headbutted someone.

'Ow, Maddie!'

Yanking the towel off, she looked up to see Nick standing in front of her with his hand pressed to his nose.

'Nick!' She stared at him, blinking, as if to check it really was him. 'What are you doing here?'

'Making sure you were OK,' he muttered, rubbing at his nose.

'I meant, how did you get here?'

'After you abandoned me in Hvar –' he glared at her '– I grabbed a water taxi and saw what happened, but I was too far away.' He shook his head. 'I thought the launch was going to run you over. But then, before we could get any nearer, you got into a boat –' he rolled his eyes angrily '– with three fucking strangers. What were you thinking?'

'Seriously!' Maddie glared back at him. 'I was thinking thank God I don't have to swim to shore.'

'Very funny, but couldn't you have asked them to take you back to the *Avanturista*? When I saw them going off with you in the opposite direction . . . well what was I supposed to think?'

'That I was being sold into the white slave trade, of course,' replied Maddie, her eyes flashing at his ridiculous behaviour.

'A single girl with three men in a boat heading off to who knows where. You don't think I should have been worried?'

Now that her heart had stopped racing, she looked at his face. 'OK. You've got a . . .' It was then she noticed he'd had a haircut. Oh, boy, he'd had a haircut. For some stupid reason, her breath caught in her throat at the sight of him, almost as if in the space of an hour she'd forgotten what he looked like and now he was different. It suited him although, she told herself sternly, she preferred the longer, shaggier style. Now he was all chiselled cheeks and sharp jawline, that had been softened before. Suddenly he was too masculine, too good-looking . . . intimidating in a way he hadn't been before. Although, despite his golden tan, he looked a little pale.

'Are you OK?'

She realised she was staring at him while her heart seemed to be having a moment. Today he looked like he belonged to Tara and co's golden world and it made her feel a little sad for him.

'Just peachy, thanks.'

Injecting a bit of snark into her voice immediately made her feel a bit more . . . or a bit less, well, weird.

'I meant after the accident.'

'I know what you meant.'

'So what happened? I wasn't close enough to see.'

Her head shot up and she coloured under his intense, calculating scrutiny.

She felt an idiot for letting Simon take control of the boat. She should have stopped him.

'I fell out of the boat.'

'I saw that bit,' said Nick, going to sit down on the bed, making himself at home as if he had all the time in the world.

Maddie sighed. 'Simon . . . He decided he wanted to drive the boat.'

'And you let him?' Nick scowled. 'I take it it was his idea to leave the "dumb schmuck" behind.'

'No, I didn't let him!' Her snappy reply was indignant. What sort of person did he think she was? 'He snatched the keys from me. And then he wouldn't give them back. And when I thought he was prepared to sit and wait for you, he just fired up the engine and, before I knew it, drove off. I promise you I tried to stop him.'

Nick looked a little mollified but his mouth was still tight with displeasure. 'He was driving like a maniac.'

'Yes . . . and you don't think that I might have told him to slow down?'

'I'm not blaming you.'

'Thank you. Big of you.'

'Oh, for God's sake. You could have been killed.'

'I didn't know you cared,' she countered hotly and then screwed up her face in self-disgust at her own childishness.

'That's a bloody stupid thing to say. Of course I . . . well, no one likes to see anyone else come to harm.'

'I'm sorry.' She sucked in a weary breath and sat down abruptly on the bed, suddenly feeling exhausted and a little light-headed. She dropped her head into her hands as the enormity of what could have happened rolled over her. 'Oh, shit,' she said in a small voice.

'You OK?'

She didn't answer; there was a massive lump in her throat.

'Maddie?' She closed her eyes tighter, wanting to burrow into herself. Nick's warm arm draped across her shoulders and he pulled her into him.

She turned her head, grateful to nestle into his warm strong body, and felt the involuntary shudder of her shoulders as she bit back a sob. Oh, God, it could have been so much worse. Who knew what damage a propeller could do? Or if the hull had mown her down?

'Hey, it's OK. You're OK.'

She concentrated on the gentle soothing strokes on her arm.

'They want you to see their doctor, just in case.'

Maddie nodded and took a few deep breaths before raising her head to look up at him. All the air in her lungs evaporated. He was so close. She stared at his jawline, praying that he couldn't hear her heart bumping at a ridiculous rate in her chest. His chiselled bone structure was different to Simon's smooth even features. Nick's top lip was a slightly crooked bow, his day-old bristles glistened red-gold and there was a telltale bump on his nose. One eye crinkled more than the other when he smiled.

'Make sure you're all right,' he said, his voice raising in query as she stared at him, a little too stunned to speak.

The blue eyes flecked with tiny shards of grey studied her. 'You are OK? Not going into shock or anything?'

With a quick exhalation, she shook her head. 'No, I'm fine. A little shaken but I'm all right. I ought to get dressed. Americans, eh? Desperate for me to see a doctor. And they have their own doctor on board.'

'Yeah. Which reminds me, Max said he'd be back in ten minutes to take you up. I'll go wait outside while you get dressed.' He nodded to a new black bikini on the bed, still with the tags on, and a turquoise linen tunic and a pair of plain white flip-flops.

'Wow, that's impressive. All kitted out for kidnap,' said Maddie, fingering the pretty tunic.

'Only you would come out and say that,' Nick said with a smile.

'I guess rich people do things differently. They have brand-new spares of everything for every eventuality. I'll get dressed in the bathroom.' Reluctantly, she stood up and grabbed the new clothes. 'Be back in a second.'

'Hi there, you must be Maddie.' The doctor had very short, tidy, almost masculine black hair, run through with threads of unruly grey, and a small, neat build.

'You're English!' Maddie blurted out at the sound of her rather precise, clipped accent.

'Yes, but I retired to Florida and when my husband died Bill and Gloria decided they needed an onboard medic. That was a tough decision, not.'

'I bet,' said Maddie politely.

'I'm Dr Cannon, but you can call me Zoe. Bill doesn't believe in standing on any sort of ceremony. In fact if he calls you Mrs, Ms or Miss, it's not a good sign at all.'

'Oh.' Maddie pulled a face.

'He can sniff out a fraud in seconds and he doesn't like social climbers or sycophants. You look as if you've been offered five-star assistance. If you hadn't, you'd be wrapped in a blanket and I'd be seeing you in the motorboat. Bill prizes his privacy. You wouldn't have set one foot on one rung of the ladder of this vessel unless Bill wanted you to. I think your boyfriend got the third degree before they let him on board.' She pulled out a stethoscope from one of the drawers.

'Boyfriend?' Nick hadn't mentioned that one.

'The handsome blond. That's what he claimed he was.'

'Concerned friend is probably the best way of categorising him,' said Maddie, surprised by the hopeful little flutter of her heart.

The doctor nodded. 'Well, you seem quite chipper. Shall I take a look at you? Make sure there are no ill-effects.'

'Well, you're good to go; you can get back to your concerned friend and I can get back to my book and a little more sunbathing.' With an unexpected wink, she put away her stethoscope, closing the door with a flourish.

'Tough gig.'

Zoe laughed. 'I'll be lucky to see a patient with anything

more than sunburn or a wasp sting, not that I'm complaining but I do get a bit bored sometimes. Occasionally I miss my practice but I don't miss the stress or the rain. I'll never lack for Vitamin D in this job.'

Concerned Friend was waiting outside the door, leaning on the wooden rail, looking out over the bay which now looked as busy as a highway in rush hour.

Like a faithful guard dog, he immediately turned around and looked her over. 'Everything all right?' His eyes narrowed as he studied her face.

'Yes.' She reached forward and patted his arm, touched by his concern. 'I've got the medical all-clear. And she's not the sort of doctor that you'd mess with. No-nonsense. Very British.'

'Good.'

'You can stop worrying now.'

'I wasn't . . .' Nick looked a touch defensive and then his face softened. 'OK, I was.' He lifted his shoulders in question. 'What would I have told Nina?'

Maddie laughed and nudged him with her elbow. 'Yeah, because she's such an ogre.'

They found their way to the main deck where Bill was seated under a canopy with two phones on the table in front of him, along with a big A4 notebook and a fat fountain pen, and he was talking into a third phone. At their approach he nodded and held up his hand. 'Five minutes –' he mouthed '– help yourself.' He indicated a buffet table to the side with a flask of coffee, a water boiler and a wooden box filled with loose teas, with everything from the familiar Earl Grey, green and chamomile through to the exotic-sounding Rooibos, Black Dragon Pearl, Gyokuro and Jade Oolong.

Nick immediately perked up. 'I could murder a cup of tea and something to eat.'

'That's not like you,' teased Maddie.

He grinned at her. 'Growing boy.'

'Still? What at thirty . . .?'

'A gentleman never reveals his age,' said Nick in a ridiculous coy voice, winking at her, and then he pulled a face. 'Although, with all this food and lazing about, which I'm not used to, my shorts are getting a bit snug.' He tugged at the waistband of the familiar FatFace cargo shorts.

'I don't think that's your only problem with shorts.'

Nick looked interestingly defensive. 'Are you still going on about those shorts? What's wrong with them?'

She grinned at him. 'They're . . . short. And pink.'

He groaned.

'They're linen.'

'Yes, I'm aware of that.'

'They've got turn-ups.'

'And?'

'They're very camp.'

Nick shut his eyes, but not before she saw the slight grimace. 'Perhaps I'm in touch with my camp side.'

'There's in touch and there's feeling up,' retorted Maddie with a sudden smirk.

'Tara really wants me to wear them. These Ellinghams sound . . .' He held his hands out in question. 'Important. Rich. And they all know each other.'

'You'll be fine.' Maddie patted his hand, glad that it was his problem rather than hers. 'Remember they pee the same way as everyone else. Besides, you're rocking the camp Chris Hemsworth look nicely. *Everyone* is going to love you.'

'That's what I'm afraid of,' said Nick.

They both helped themselves to a glass of freshly squeezed orange juice and loitered together, unsure as to what to do as Bill was still on the phone. Just then one of the other phones rang and Bill snatched it up.

'George? I'm on the line with Grayson . . . Give me some good news . . . What? For Christ's sake, you are kidding me? Appendicitis, my ass. Well, that's just fucked up the whole week . . . Yeah . . . see what you can do.'

He returned to his original call, his shoulders slumped, pushing the other phone around the desk with one finger. 'Yeah, d'you catch that?' He sighed heavily. 'Benson is in hospital, burst appendix. Last night. I guess it's as good a reason as any to miss a flight. You and me both. Blows the schedule right out of the water. It's taken me weeks to pin Saunders down. We're going to have to go with what we've got. No, I know it's not ideal. I never wanted to leave it this close to the wire but George insisted we wait for Benson because he's the best.'

Taking their orange juice and not wanting to intrude on Bill's conversation, they wandered into the adjacent saloon and Maddie was immediately drawn to a painting hanging on the far wall.

Her eyes lit up. She moved to study the painting and then stopped dead in front of it. 'Oh,' she breathed.

'What?'

'This is . . . Oh, my God, it's real.' She'd thought it was a print at first but no, she could see the very fine brush strokes, the purity of the pastel colours and blurring of the lines between the abstract shapes.

'What is it?' whispered Nick but she'd spotted another equally heart-stopping painting on the other wall.

'Oh, my . . .' She reached out her fingers, wanting to touch but knowing it was sacrilege; instead she touched the frame with almost reverential awe.

'Like it?'

She was so lost in the painting she hadn't even heard Bill's approach.

'Love it. Dirk Smorenberg.' She nodded at the other one. 'And a Sonia Delaunay.'

Nick's mouth twitched and he gave her a discreet impressed nod.

Bill looked surprised. 'You know about art; not many people would know either of those.'

'I studied art history, lived in Paris for a while. I love the Art Deco period.'

'Do you now?'

234

Maddie nodded absently, tracing the lines and colours of the Smorenberg. 'Yes, sorry,' she apologised, realising she'd zoned out. 'These paintings are just . . .' She paused, adding a little dreamily, 'I'd love to have that much talent.'

'You got some? His eyebrows drew together, making him look like a cunning fox, and in that second Maddie could see sharp intelligence and got a fair inkling of how he might have amassed his wealth.

With a self-deprecating laugh she shrugged, slightly horrified that she'd volunteered that much.

'Would you like some breakfast?'

Nick's eyes gleamed and she laughed. 'My friend would. We missed breakfast.'

Bill turned around and patted Nick on the back. 'Man after my own heart. Breakfast is the best meal of the day. What do you fancy? Full English?'

Nick nodded. 'Never going to turn that down.'

Maddie rolled her eyes. 'Unfortunately, some of us are supposed to be working.' She glanced at Nick. 'I've got no way of contacting the boat to tell them what's happened. Although I guess Simon will tell them, but they're not going to know where I am, or you, Nick.'

'I didn't bring my phone,' he said. 'Sorry.'

'Well, mine is well and truly waterlogged.'

'Yeah, I heard your cell took a ducking,' Bill said as he led them up to another deck where a round table with white linen was laid for breakfast. There were even flowers on the table.

'Now, what do you guys fancy? Nick here is clearly a bacon, eggs and the works kinda guy but my chef does a mean Eggs Benedict and a neat smashed avocado with chilli and a *poached* –' he emphasised the word with a miserable attempt at an English accent '– egg.'

Maddie laughed. 'It's poached,' she corrected as she sat down. 'This is very nice. Suddenly that early morning dip is starting to look like a lucky break. It's not often I get breakfast . . .' She broke off with a peal of laughter. 'I've never had a breakfast like this.' Her hand swept out, encompassing the view.

'Me neither,' said Nick, sending a quick conspiratorial smile her way.

'Pretty spectacular, isn't it. And I praise God every morning that I am lucky enough to have all this. Never take it for granted.'

'Ah, Krish. Maddie, Nick, this is my steward, Krish. He is the king on board here.'

'Nice of you to say, sir,' said Krish, another one with a very proper English accent, although a naughty dimple in his dark-skinned cheek belied his stiffness. 'What can I get for you this morning?'

'Nick here will have full English. I'll have the Eggs Benedict. Maddie?'

'I'll have the same and I don't suppose Aaron mentioned to you about some rice? For my phone.'

'Rice?' Bill looked perplexed.

'To soak my phone in. It's worth a try, although I'm

not sure that this one is coming back from the dead.'

'Forget the rice,' said Bill, rising from the table and walking to the saloon bordering the deck.

Maddie sighed and squinted out at the sea. 'You're probably right but I need to try.' She was going to have to buy a new phone and she was only halfway through the contract on this one.

'Happens all the time on board. In the pool, over the side.' He came back holding out a box. 'Here you go.'

Maddie's eyes widened. 'I can't take that.'

'Why not? I've got plenty of 'em. All you have to do is pop your SIM card in.'

'But these cost a fortune.' It wasn't the latest iPhone but it was two generations up from hers. She shot a quick glance at Nick, as if asking him what she should do, but he shrugged. This was as alien to him as it was to her.

'I don't pay for 'em. I get given them.' He pushed the box across the table. 'That's what happens when you're rich. Ironic, you get given stuff when you already have stuff. Lots of stuff. Nobody gives poor people stuff.'

'That's true,' said Maddie. 'It still doesn't feel right, though.' Nick caught her eye, a glint of agreement in his, although he didn't say anything.

Bill laughed, a deep belly rumble. 'You're a real breath of fresh air, little lady.' Something pinged in Maddie's brain. Simon had said the same thing but somehow it had sounded calculating.

'Maybe you could do something for me?'

Her eyes flew to his face and she sensed Nick stiffen next to her.

'And not like that.' He tsked and shook his head. 'I'm a married man. Gloria would take a knife to the boys in seconds if she thought I'd been goofing around.'

Maddie pressed her lips together and Nick gave an outright laugh, although Bill looked deadly serious until his face relaxed into a grin. 'Can you draw? I got the impression you paint, do something arty? Am I right?'

'It's a . . . hobby.' Something about Bill – his shrewd gaze? – the fact that he was a stranger and after this their paths would probably never cross again made her add, 'I'd like it to be more but . . .' She lifted her shoulders.

'Yeah, you need the breaks.' Cool sharp eyes assessed her, pinning her with sudden intensity. 'But you gotta be hungry for it. Talent helps but grit, determination; that separates the players from the winners.'

Maddie looked down at her hands. The words, like darts, stabbed into her brain and hit the bullseye. Guilty colour flooded her face.

The experience at the art gallery in London had panned out as she'd expected. She'd almost gone in with that expectation. What those girls had said, she could have written the script for them. And since then she'd let that rejection and their attitude become a self-fulfilling prophecy. She hadn't even tried again. The answer blew up inside her. The truth scratched, an uncomfortable realisation. It had been easier to hide behind excuses than expose herself and her pictures to the possibility of more of the same.

'You can pay me for the phone.' Every bit of him seemed to have sharpened, all the smooth avuncular softness of him fined to a point, all business and focus. 'I need some drawings done. Storyboards. Benson, the guy who was supposed to be doing them for me. You probably heard. He's laid up with a bust appendix.'

'Storyboards?'

'Yeah, like a cartoon strip that tells a story. I'll tell you what I need. You draw it. Think you can do that? Nothing fancy. Stick men in proportion will do at a pinch.'

'I can draw,' said Maddie. 'And I've grit and determination. It's just been in hiding for a while.'

Since she'd come back from Paris.

'Great. As soon as we've had breakfast, we'll get started.'

Maddie pulled a face. 'And what about my job? How would you like it if one of your crew went AWOL? I need to get back.' No one would be doing her work for her. According to the clock on the deck it was mid-morning; presumably someone would have sorted breakfast out. But there were cabins to clean, lunch to prepare and possibly dinner to shop for.

'No problem. I'll send Max to cover for you and my chef can sort any food out. Next?'

With a laugh, Maddie said, 'Don't you think I ought to check with my boat?'

'I reckon, after Simon's behaviour this morning, the least

Douglas can do is give you the time off,' interjected Nick. She smiled gratefully at him and when he returned her smile Maddie's stomach did a weird little flip.

They stopped for coffee at half past one.

Maddie's hand ached as she put down her pencil. Bill had spread the completed sheets of A3 paper around the saloon and now he was wandering past each one, tilting his head, frowning and muttering. As soon as they'd got down to work, a very different man had emerged. Focused, driven and exacting. He spoke with sharp staccato demands, clear and concise instructions and no-nonsense observations.

Now she sat on the edge of her seat, tension gripping her shoulders, her mouth dry as she awaited his verdict. Every now and then he'd lean forward, as if checking a tiny detail, and then step back, narrowing his eyes.

Maddie felt wrung out but at the same time slightly exhilarated. It had taken a while to capture the style he was after at first but once she'd done that the rest was easy.

'You're real good, Maddie.' Bill held up the large sheet of A3 paper, a slow satisfied smile spreading over his face. 'Real good. This is exceptional work.'

Nick, who'd sat in the shade setting up her new phone for her and patiently waiting like a faithful Labrador, peered at the sketches, shooting Maddie a look filled with respect.

She shrugged, colouring quickly. 'Thank you, but you did most of the work.'

'Now you're just being modest.'

Her blush deepened. 'Well, you made it . . . so fascinating. You had a very clear vision. Is this how you see a film? In your head?'

'Yeah, I see it real clear, way before I start, but I gotta make other people see it the same way before they bankroll the project. But you, little lady, have got it down pat. This is really good work. Better than Benson, and do you know he charges a coupla hundred dollars an hour.'

'What do you do in England?' She'd already explained to him that this was her first and probably her last job as crew.

'Do?'

'For work?'

'I think they call it resting. I'm between jobs.'

'Jeez, please don't tell me you're an actress.'

Maddie burst out laughing. 'Not even close. I just finished my degree. I was a late starter. Mature student.' She lifted her head and looked Bill right in the eye. 'What I'd really like is to be an artist. But I need to earn money as well.'

'You should go for it. You can certainly draw.'

Maddie gave him a perfunctory smile. To be an artist you needed to be different. Proper artists went to art college but there was no way she could afford another three years of education. Two years into her History of Art degree, she'd realised that, much as she loved art, she wanted to create her own. But it could be a hobby and she'd have to be content with that.

'And you get up at five every morning?' asked Bill.

Nick nodded. 'Pretty much. There's always something to do.'

Maddie was tidying up the storyboard sketches, half listening to Bill skilfully drawing Nick out. It appeared he had a fascination for sheep farming and was asking Nick lots of intelligent questions which, to Maddie's surprise, Nick answered with real passion and enthusiasm. Whenever the subject had come up on the boat, Nick had seemed reluctant to talk about his life but, over the last hour, he'd told stories of rescuing sheep from the deep snowdrifts and lambing in the spring, describing a way of life in tune with the seasons. Maddie was charmed by this open, man-to-man discussion.

'Jeepers, Bill!' Max burst onto the deck, shaking his head. 'You owe me.'

Maddie bit her lip, trying to hide a smile. 'Sorry, I should have warned you.'

'What?' asked Bill.

Max caught Maddie's eye and shuddered. 'I have never seen a cabin that bad in my entire life. I coulda done with a Hazmat suit.'

'That chick sure has a lot of clothes,' said Max. 'And a shedload of blonde hair . . . shed being operative, man.' As he spoke he pulled a long golden strand from the sleeve of his polo shirt.

'Thanks for covering for me. I really appreciate it.'

'No sweat,' said Max with a good-natured grin, waving away her thanks. 'I always wanted to see one of those gulets. Nice inside. And Ivan was very hospitable, showed me all over.

'Hey, these are real good.' He came to stand in front of Maddie's work.

'Yeah, I'm thinking about keeping her. Sending you to take her place,' drawled Bill, with a mischievous wink at Maddie.

Max dropped to his knees, clasping his hands out in front of him. 'Please, God, no.'

Maddie laughed. 'You get used to it.'

'You are a better person than I am,' said Max. 'I'd never get used to that.'

'Talking of which. I do need to go back.'

'There's no hurry. Ivan says to tell you they're all going out for dinner. So you don't need to rush back.'

'Excellent,' said Bill. 'Time to finish this last one off and if you like you can have a swim on deck. Excuse me, I got calls to make. The States is open for business. Make yourself at home. If you need anything, just ask Max here.'

Bill left, scooping up his three phones, all of which had started ringing in the last hour and he'd ignored.

'What exactly does Bill do?' asked Nick, watching the retreating figure.

Max grinned. 'You really have no idea, do you. That's

Julie Caplin

why he likes you guys so much. Most people are hangers-on. Want something or are impressed by him.'

'Is he famous?' asked Nick.

'Oh God, should we know him?' Maddie cringed and looked at Nick.

'You'll have heard of the films he's worked on. He's a director and producer.' Max reeled off a list of films that not only had Maddie heard of; she'd seen several of them with her brother Brendan at the local multiplex. 'William Randall.'

Maddie looked at Nick and together they burst out laughing.

Chapter 18

Excitement shimmered in the air the next morning, that fraught, barely contained buzz like children about to go on a school trip. Everyone was looking forward to the novelty of spending some time with some new faces. Maddie had certainly enjoyed a day away from all the guests yesterday. Rather confusingly, Nick had moved into a new category, not quite guest and not quite friend. On Bill's boat they'd felt like friends and allies but as soon as they'd come back to the *Avanturista* they'd fallen into an uneasy silence, as if both knew that the lines had blurred but neither knew on which side they stood.

'Morning, Maddie, how are you feeling after your mishap?' asked Douglas, sporting smart light-weight cotton trousers and a Ralph Lauren short-sleeved shirt with its familiar polo logo on the pocket. With his Ray-Ban sunglasses tucked in his pocket, his thinning hair brushed and staying put for once, he looked every inch the successful City trader.

'Fine. It was just a bit of shock. The people who rescued

me were being ultra-cautious, which was very kind of them.'

'Least they could do, when they caused the accident,' snorted Douglas in a loud voice.

Next to him, Simon shifted in his seat. Maddie shot him a quick narrow-eyed glance.

'I'm not sure kind had a lot to do with it,' he said in response to Douglas's comment. 'Not when they cut across us like that.' He met her eyes with breathtaking guileless innocence.

That was the story he was telling, was it?

'You up to driving us into Hvar for lunchtime, Maddie? Get back on the horse and all that,' asked Douglas. 'Although I don't want to cause you any stress. Do say if you're not feeling up to it.'

'I think I'll be fine, thank you, Douglas,' she replied, refusing to look at Simon as she headed down to the galley to finish the last bit of tidying up after breakfast.

'Simon!' The sneak attack, bundling her into his cabin as she opened the door to clean it, startled her.

'Are you OK?'

'I'm fine, no thanks to you.' Her eyes flashed.

'I know, I know. I was a macho idiot. I nearly had heart failure when I saw you go over the side.'

'And that stopped you coming back for me?' Maddie thrust out her hip, wincing slightly at the movement, and planted both hands on her waist.

'I tried to . . . but the bozo twins on the boat caught up with me, gave me a proper lecture and insisted they'd get you and take you to their doctor.' Simon's hard done by expression didn't dent Maddie's anger.

'And what's this about them causing the accident?' she asked, her words quick and fast.

'Maddie, sweetheart. It was the only way I could cover up for the fact I was driving. I didn't want you to lose your job.'

'Big of you.'

'You're mad at me.' He put his arms around her, pressing his body closer than she was comfortable with. 'How can I make it up to you? I was an idiot. I apologise. Let me take you out to dinner.'

'No, thank you.' She pushed him off.

'You really are mad, aren't you?' Simon took a step back, a hint of wonder in his voice.

'Of course I'm mad.' What the hell was wrong with him?

'Sorry, I'm used to fake temper tantrums from Cory and Tara. I'm not used to real emotion. You look rather magnificent.'

'Don't talk bollocks. You drove like a maniac. Wouldn't listen when I told you to stop and now you're blaming someone else.'

'Doesn't sound great, does it?' Simon sucked in a breath. 'And you're not going to let me off the hook, are you? That's what I like about you. You've got integrity.' He leaned forward and stroked her cheek. 'I've never met a woman like you.' His voice dropped to an admiring husky whisper which sounded completely fake. 'You're incredible. Shall I go out there and tell them what an arse I was and that I caused the accident? Tell Ivan I insisted on driving the boat and that you tried to stop me.'

'You can save your breath,' she said, moving away from him to the other side of the bed on the pretext of straightening the sheets. 'It's done now. There's no point in stirring up trouble. No one needs to know that I wasn't driving the boat.'

'Forgive me?' His eyes danced in what she imagined he thought was a charming way. Actually, he looked like a conniving prat and those blue, blue eyes looked sly.

She rolled her eyes. 'Not sure I have much choice. Let's just agree not to mention it again.'

'Ah, Maddie. You're still mad at me.'

'Simon, I've neither the time nor the inclination to be mad at you.' She tried to brush past him, but he caught her arm. 'Let's just draw a line under it. Now, if you'll excuse me, I've work to do.'

Tara was actually in her cabin when Maddie walked in to clean it. She looked up from the mirror where she was applying her lipstick.

'Do you want me to come back later?' asked Maddie, drooping a little at the sight of the usual cyclone-has-just-swept-through destruction.

'No, you can carry on,' said Tara, barely sparing her a glance.

Maddie would normally start in the bedroom and collect up all the clothes from the bed to make it, but with Tara using the chair there was nowhere to put them, so she opted to start with the bathroom.

The rancid smell made her stomach turn. Tara had been sick again, and recently.

Maddie looked back through the bathroom door and in the same moment Tara looked into the mirror. Their eyes met in the reflection. Guilt and unexpected vulnerability tinged the other woman's expression.

Somehow, talking to Tara's reflection rather than face on seemed to make it easier.

'Tara . . . are you . . . OK? It just seems . . . well, you've been quite sick. I've got some seasickness tablets if you'd like them.'

Tara blushed. A full on ruddy, red-faced flush and a marked contrast to her usual delicate appearance.

'Or is it something else?' Maddie halted. 'I'm sorry. It's not my business but . . . are you OK?'

Tara's shoulders slumped a little and she closed her eyes as if in pain. For a moment Maddie was reminded of a small vulnerable child trying to hide.

'I'm OK,' she whispered, opening her eyes but looking down at the dressing table rather than in the mirror.

'There are people who can help, you know,' said Maddie gently, aware of the other woman's stillness.

Tara shuddered and then lifted her head, her eyes bleak in the mirror. 'Who?' she whispered. 'I don't know how to stop.'

'A doctor?' suggested Maddie.

Tara bit her lip. 'It's . . . it's . . .'

'Making that first step?' asked Maddie.

Tara nodded and was about to say something when Cory burst into the room, looking immaculate in a white playsuit.

'Tara, have you borrowed my Stella McCartney top? I can't find it anywhere.'

'No,' she said, lifting her head in haughty response. 'Have you asked the cabin girl if she's seen it? Maybe she moved it. At least you don't need to worry about her borrowing anything, not like that chambermaid at London Fashion Week.' Tara shot Maddie an unkind smile.

Maddie pursed her lips, ignored them both and turned back to cleaning the bathroom sink. So much for trying to help.

Chapter 19

Nick smoothed the fabric of his shorts, resisting the temptation to put his hands in his pockets, which apparently made him look like a schoolboy. He picked up his bottle of beer, his palm clammy despite the condensation on the side of the glass. The beer was window-dressing; he'd never felt less like drinking it as he stood on the magnificent balcony commanding an incredible view of the sea and a secluded bay below. It was only his second since they'd arrived two hours ago. For some reason his stomach was doing death-defying loop the loops. Foolish to be so nervous. Like Maddie said, all these people peed the same way.

A wry smile touched his lips. Lucky her, back on the boat, having it all to herself.

'Nicky darling, there you are. Come and be sociable.' Tara grabbed him by the arm and pulled him back into the thick of things on the terrace below. His stomach protested at the quick movement.

'Tara, sweetie. Not seen you in ages.' Air kisses. Lots of air kisses, thought Nick. What was it with air kisses?

'And who is this gorgeous creature?' an artful voice asked. The question came from a woman wearing a purple turban. Nick rearranged his face into what he hoped was a smile, all the while trying not to stare at the turban, which put him in mind of Aladdin. Her tanned liver-spotted hands almost dazzled him as she waved them in his face, the pudgy fingers puffed up around the rings on every finger. He'd never seen so many diamonds in one place.

'This is Nicky, my boyfriend. Nicky, this is Arabella Pennistone-Smythe.'

He swapped his beer to his other hand, about to shake her hand, but the woman swooped in with a waft of acidic perfume that made his eyes water and mwahed him on either cheek.

'And what do you do, gorgeous young man?' She fluttered lashes as thick as spider's legs at him, which he stared at with repellent fascination, imagining them walking off by themselves. 'Did I see you in last month's *Harper's Bazaar*?' Her coy smile held a touch of something cold and reptilian.

'He's a landowner,' said Tara a little too quickly. 'Owns vast swathes in Northumberland. Beautiful country.' He frowned at the unexpectedly plummy tone to her voice as well as at his newly inflated status. Vast swathes was somewhat of an exaggeration. 'Do you know it?'

'No,' brayed the woman. 'Know North Yorkshire well. The Cavendish estate. Part of the Devonshire's estates. They own Chatsworth as well. Although I've not been there since Debs died in 2014. Know the family, do you?'

'Course I do. I haven't seen Will for ages. Or Celina.'

'They're all fine. Did you know Hugo Heyward-Lonsdale's gone into property development?'

Nick had quickly realised that he didn't need to join in any of these conversations. As his stomach rolled again, he realised Tara was holding court for both of them. He could feel sweat beading on his forehead, even though they were standing under the shade of a big white sail suspended across half of the terrace. The buzz of the chatter around them receded momentarily and then came back louder than ever.

'Nicky darling.' Tara poked at him, her fingers pecking at his forearm with sharp jabs like a little bird. 'Are you listening?'

'Sorry.' It took him a good second or two to focus.

'Bella wanted to know what you think of the party.' Tara lowered her voice. 'We're thinking it's a bit trashy. I mean, Cristal champagne on tap is just showing off. They should be serving a vintage Dom Pérignon.'

Thankfully the opinionated Arabella beat him to an answer.

'Well, sweetie, far be it for me to say that, but Oscar Ellingham hasn't an ounce of taste. That's what happens when you marry new money. He refused to send the boys to Harrow.'

An unwelcome sensation gripped his jaw. His mouth

went dry and his stomach rose and rolled. Oh, God, he needed to find a bathroom.

Wiping his mouth and splashing cold water on his face made him feel a hell of a lot better. He still looked a little pale but hopefully whatever had upset his stomach was out. The throbbing headache was probably just tension. Straightening, he looked in the mirror. He'd do, even though the last thing he wanted to do was go back to the fray. There was a distinct newborn lamb wobbliness to his knees.

A pinch of homesickness plucked at his heart and he swallowed, thinking of the quiet calm of the fell, the occasional bleat of the lambs. He'd never felt further from home in his life. What was he doing here? He put his hand on the washbasin to steady himself as a wave of light-headedness swamped him.

Come on, Nick. You've been sick now. You'll be fine. Just feeling a bit sorry for yourself. Pull yourself together.

With slow careful steps he walked back out onto the terrace, looking around for a familiar face. There must have been upwards of a hundred people here. He sank into a chair in the shade with relief and from the secluded vantage point people-watched. Dan and Jonathon would have had a field day here, with their wry down-to-earth observations and his sisters-in-law, Gail and Cath, would have enjoyed themselves looking at all the different fashions on display.

When the buffet lunch was announced at three o'clock Nick's stomach was still being rebellious, so he stayed put.

'Hello you, good spot here. Mind if I join you?' asked Siri, balancing a plate on her knee with one hand and holding a fizz-filled flute in the other.

'No,' he said, his voice weak, wincing at the smell of smoked salmon wafting his way as she took a bite of a loaded canapé.

'You don't look so hot. Are you OK? Do you want something to eat?'

'I'm fine. Not hungry at the moment.' He was feeling a lot better for sitting in the shade. Perhaps he'd just had a touch too much sun.

'Quite some party.'

'Yeah.'

She gave him a kind smile. 'Not your type of thing.'

Nick tried to give a non-committal shrug.

'Not mine either. But I treat it as work. Networking. Which isn't great when you're supposed to be on holiday. And Douglas says he enjoys these things but he always ends up in an office somewhere on his phone.' Her mouth settled in a downward curve. 'I'm an idiot. I shouldn't have come.'

'To the party?' he asked, clutching his stomach as a sudden stab took his breath away.

'You OK?'

He nodded.

'I meant I shouldn't have come on the holiday. I thought I could cope.'

Nick dredged up a kind smile, ignoring the sudden eruptions in his bowel. 'Cope?'

'With being around Cory and Douglas.'

'If I were you . . .' he winced as another swirl of discomfort hit his stomach '. . . I'd hang on in there.'

'Really?' Siri's head shot up, her eyes full of hope.

'Sometimes it takes people a while to see what's right under their –' He lurched to his feet. ''Scuse me.'

Chapter 20

Maddie looked down at the makeshift easel she'd fashioned, her collection of watercolour pencils and paint tubes and her paintbrushes. Drawing for Bill had rekindled her desire to paint. While he'd been generous in his praise for her work, there'd been nothing artistic about it. She'd just drawn what he asked.

Aqua and turquoise, ultramarine and azure. The colours of the sea and sky were jewel-bright in the brilliant sunshine. The wind lapped at the water, cross currents rippling around the boat, the waves tipped with silver as the sun danced and teased the surface, twinkling like starlight. Maddie could hear the rhythmic chirrup of cicadas echoing across the bay and smell the scent of pine teasing the air from the scrub on the shore. She could paint this scene, reproducing it faithfully, but Henry Compton-Barnes from the London art gallery's words rang in her head. *When you look at their work, you know that only they could have painted it.* Any number of people could capture the same scene. What did she really want to say with her pictures? *Paint from the heart,* he'd said. Her mind went back to the day on the beach. The people on the beach, the chubby baby, the laughing girlfriend and the elderly neighbours.

Her heart leapt as she made the first stroke on the thick cartridge paper, the blue just right, brightening against the deeper wash. She could see it. The people on the beach, their characters unfolding in her head, some standing on the water's edge, others waist-deep and more bobbing out by the buoys. The beach on a Monday afternoon. There it was. The magic. She could feel it. A composition that wouldn't win prizes . . . but it was from the heart and now she understood what Henry had meant.

A gentle growl from her stomach reminded her it was well past lunchtime and probably closer to teatime. She stood up, stretching her legs, and looked at the two pictures drying beside her, weighted down with various books from the salon. They were a sort of homage to Beryl Cook, although no one was going to bite her hand off to put them in a gallery, but they might sell in a local shop, the sort of thing holiday-makers might pick up as a memento of their trip. She felt she'd put a piece of herself in them, her unique memories of the people, her own characterisation of them.

She was rather pleased with the second picture; it looked like the neighbourhood had gathered on the beach to chat and gossip. As she mentally ticked off the characters – the new mums, the middle-aged best friends, the lone swimmer, she stopped at one character. What? With her index finger she traced the figure, a sudden bump in her pulse. It had been a completely unconscious addition. She bit her lip. What was he doing in the picture?

Before she could give it too much thought the whiny buzz, a mosquito engine of a boat, caught her attention. All afternoon there'd been plenty of coming and going but this was a particularly persistent whine, getting closer all the time. Crossing to starboard, she looked over the side and spotted a small boat puttering in a direct line towards the *Avanturista* with a solitary passenger hunched over the side.

The driver hailed her and indicated with his thumb towards the passenger. Maddie hurried down to the stern, now recognising the clothes on the huddled figure. It was almost as if her ruddy subconscious had conjured him up again.

The little water taxi closed the distance quickly.

'Nick!' she called and he looked up, his face a pale green.

Somehow she helped haul him up the ladder and onto the deck, where he collapsed for a frightening moment at her feet.

'You look terrible,' she blurted out, fear fine-tuning the bluntness of her words. Bloodshot eyes squinted up at her while he dragged a hand through the sheen of sweat dotting his clammy forehead. The once smart clothes were now nothing more than a collection of creases, the white, wrinkled shirt suspiciously stained.

'Feel terrible,' he groaned and pulled himself to a sitting position, slumping against the wooden side.

He didn't smell too good either, but there was no hint of alcohol.

'Something you've eaten?'

He nodded.

'Come on, let's get you to your cabin. I think you need to get to bed.'

His eyes drooped in defeat. 'Feel awful.'

As she hooked her arms under his, helping him to his feet, he suddenly shook her off and lurched to the side, while a racking retch seized him and he promptly vomited down the side of the boat.

Limp and spent, he hung there gasping and groaning, his eyes closed.

Her own stomach clenched in sympathy, remembering the indignity of throwing up over the side of Bill's launch.

Steering poor Nick up to his cabin, clutching a bucket in one hand and trying to support him, was hard work and it was a relief when she shouldered her way through the cabin door. Propping him against the wall, she pulled back the sheets and ushered him gently onto the bed. He sat down with a thump, arms and legs limp, before flopping back, letting out a heartfelt groan and closed his eyes.

The green tinge colouring his skin worried her, as did the shallow breaths and the rapid rise and fall of his ribcage.

'Nick, I've put a bucket here for you. And there's a bottle

of fresh water here on the bedside. Can I get you anything else?'

With another groan, he made a tiny movement of his head which she took as a no. She stared down at him, feeling a little helpless. What should she do? There must be something. She couldn't just leave him.

She stepped forward and eased his shoes off. 'Do you want to take your dirty stuff off and I'll rinse it through for you?'

There was no response. Telling herself she'd seen him in swimming shorts before, she leaned forward to pull down the crumpled linen shorts. He moaned but lifted his hips slightly.

Grasping the waistband of his damp shorts, she wriggled them down, trying not to notice the feel of the crisp hair on his legs or the muscular thighs revealed. Up close and personal, Nick was all man. What was wrong with her? He was sick, for God's sake, and here she was eyeing him up. Briskly she pulled the shorts down past his knees, averting her eyes from his legs as she dumped the shorts on the floor with his dirty shoes.

Feeling braver now, she knelt on the bed to undo his crumpled shirt.

'Nick, you're going to have to help me here,' she said, touching him gently on the arm.

He opened one bleary eye and exhaled and then winced as if mere breathing hurt.

'Come on.' She took both his arms and hauled him up.

'Sorry,' he said huskily as she began to unbutton his shirt, his head drooping.

'It's OK. Once I've got this off, I'll leave you in peace and you can sleep.'

Obligingly like a child, he lifted each arm as she slid the shirt down to his wrists, her fingers gliding over his cool skin and the silky golden hairs on his forearms. She sucked in a breath. Nice chest. Broad, smooth, a smattering of hair dusting that little V between pecs. Yeah, proper pecs. And she could bet these did not come from gym workouts. Poldark, eat your heart out. She had a sudden vision of Nick bare-chested, tossing hay bales, and felt a little flushed.

Behave, she told herself. You're acting like some swoony teenager. You got over this sort of thing years ago.

She tossed the shirt aside and lifted his legs onto the bed, carefully pulling the sheet up to his chest. Despite the late afternoon heat, his skin felt cold and his arms were covered in goose bumps.

Tucked in, with the sunlight slanting over his face, he looked like a sleeping Norse warrior, golden and strong, weakened by illness. It made her feel unaccountably protective. She looked around to see if there was anything else she could realistically do to help him and pushed the bucket closer to the bedside, made sure the bottle of water was in reaching distance and scooped up the dirty clothes. She couldn't help looking at him, even though it felt wrong. Seeing him like this, vulnerable and lifeless, made her feel uneasy.

Of all the guests on the boat, he was the vital, strong, reliable one. Not just in physical strength but in terms of doing what was right and wrong. Him being like this made her feel vulnerable. The accident with Simon had made her mentally categorise who was safe, steady and reliable. Douglas was steady enough but being at the mercy of Cory's whims made him unreliable and she'd lost all respect for Simon. Siri would be good in a crisis but only if it suited her and, as for Tara and Cory, they were about as much use as an umbrella in a force nine gale.

With a heavy sigh she crept out of the cabin, heading for the iPad in the saloon to google 'what to do when someone has food poisoning'.

Nick threw up once more, waking briefly, and although his colour was somewhere between grey and green, his stomach pains had gone and his temperature was only a little high. Maddie felt a little more in control, having had a phone conversation with Bill's Dr Cannon, who insisted she call her Zoe, and surmised that it was most likely food poisoning and that he could be laid up for a couple of days. To Maddie's relief she gave her a list of instructions and the invitation to call any time, which made her feel a lot more confident about the role of nurse.

So much so that when Douglas called, asking for a pick-up, she asked if there was any way they could use a water taxi. She really didn't like to leave him. Of course Douglas didn't mind at all. And as soon as they disembarked he came straight up to see how Nick was doing, with Siri in tow. On the deck she could hear lots of laughter and squealing. Tara didn't appear to be rushing to check on Nick.

'Sleeping again, but he's out of it.' She wasn't sure he was even aware she'd been in his room or remembered her taking his clothes off.

'Poor guy, he didn't look good at the party.'

'What's all the excitement?' asked Maddie, hearing another gale of laughter.

'The Ellinghams have invited us all to go and stay at their villa for several days. I've spoken to Ivan, so there's a slight change of plan. We're going to move the boat to a new location tomorrow where it will be easier to refuel and fill up the water tanks. We're off to Stari Grad. Ivan assures me it's an excellent location and we can get taxis into Hvar. Then he'll come back to Hvar later in the week to pick us up. You're going to have the boat all to yourself.' Douglas beamed at her.

Maddie nodded with a pleasant smile, thinking of all the painting she could do.

Another high-pitched squeal from Tara on deck made Maddie raise an eyebrow. Douglas and Siri exchanged a look which she couldn't translate. 'Perhaps you can let Tara know Nick is really quite unwell.'

By ten o'clock, Maddie seethed. She'd served a light supper which Tara and Cory barely picked at, making her crosser for wasting the time, and she resented serving everyone while trying to keep an eye on Nick. Tara's complete disinterest in Nick's condition was astonishing and sheer pig-headedness stopped Maddie saying anything to her. If Tara wasn't interested, Maddie certainly wasn't going to volunteer any information.

Tara's only comment during dinner was to say that Nick had better be better by the time they headed to the Ellinghams' villa on the following day.

By the time Maddie cleaned up, everyone had retired to bed. She checked on Nick again. In the light of the bedside lamp, he still looked sweaty and clammy, tossing fitfully. Hesitating, she stood over him. Leaving him felt wrong. Deciding quickly, she ran up to the sun deck, removed the cushions from one of the sunbeds and then gathered up a blanket and pillow from her room to create a makeshift bed on the floor in his room. It seemed mean to abandon him when he was so far away from home. It took a while for her to fall asleep, starting each time he turned over and straining her ears with each movement, but eventually she fell into a light doze.

She awoke to a long low groan. Instantly she was on her feet, putting on the small side light. His hair was plastered to his head in sweat and his eyes squinty at the sudden light.

'Here, bucket,' she said, lifting the bucket just in time but, although he retched and heaved, there was nothing there. In the dim light he looked pitiful and Maddie's heart went out to him. She soaked the face cloth again in the bathroom and returned to sit on the side of the bed, where she gently wiped his face. He opened his eyes. 'Maddie?' he croaked.

'Yes.'

'That's nice, thanks.' He lifted his head, his eyes bleary and barely focused. 'What time is it?'

'It's about three o'clock.'

He nodded as if that was important and meant something.

'You've got a touch of food poisoning. I've spoken to Dr Cannon from Bill's boat. You just need to stay put.'

There was a ghost of a smile on his face. 'Not going anywhere.'

'Here, have a sip of water.' As he began to drink thirstily she pulled the bottle away, her fingers touching his, trying to soften her voice to mask her fear. She didn't want him to be sick again. 'Sip. I know you're going to be dehydrated. But little sips. It's better for your stomach.' Thank God for Dr Zoe Cannon; at least she sounded confident even if inside she was terrified.

'Yes, nurse.' That faint smile flitted across his face again. 'Can I clean my teeth? Mouth hideous.'

'Yes.' She stood up, watching as he swung his legs over the side of the bed, gingerly putting them on the floor. As he rose to stand, he wobbled and she gripped his arm.

'Want a hand?'

'No,' he muttered; she suspected if he'd had any energy at all it would have been more of a growl. He wobbled for a minute. He held out an arm like a tightrope walker trying to balance. 'I'm . . . fine,' he said, his voice hoarse like sandpaper on wood.

'No, you're not. For goodness' sake, stop being all manly and admit you need some help. I won't tell anyone if you don't.' She put an arm round him and tucked herself under his shoulder to support him. They made slow shuffling progress to the bathroom and from the tension in his body Maddie could tell he wasn't very happy about needing the support.

In the bathroom he leaned against the marble vanity unit, his head drooping. She skipped around him and loaded a ball of toothpaste onto his toothbrush.

He studied himself in the mirror.

'Yes, you look like shit, feel like shit, so why don't you give up, accept you're not well and take the help?' said Maddie with feeling, handing the toothbrush to him.

'Great bedside manner,' he muttered, jamming it into his mouth.

'You do know I'm not a real nurse.'

He closed his eyes and carried on cleaning his teeth.

'Better?'

'Much. And I think I can make it back on my own.'

She let him but hovered at his side and when he reached the side of the bed he collapsed into it.

'Want anything else?'

'Apart from to die.' He shivered and she pulled up the sheets and the thick blanket, which he'd pushed aside earlier, and tucked it around him.

'Thanks,' he said, resting his head against the pillows, then he frowned. 'Are you sleeping on the floor?'

'Yes,' muttered Maddie, a little embarrassed. 'It's only because I was worried about you being sick in your sleep. I don't have some weird watching-a-person-sleep fetish or anything.'

'Good to know. What I meant was that I feel bad you're sleeping on the floor.'

'Not as bad as me,' said Maddie, rubbing her hip.

'You don't . . . You don't have to . . . you know . . . stay.' He nodded towards the floor.

She raised an eyebrow.

'But I'm . . . really grateful. It's nice to know . . . you're there.' The concession cost him; she could see that. 'I feel bad that you're on the floor.'

'It's fine.' She wriggled, trying to ease the dull ache in her back. 'I'll sit in the chair for a while. I'm wide awake now anyway. I promise I won't watch you sleeping. Or take any dodgy photos and send them to Nina.'

His eyes were already drooping but he lifted them as if fighting it.

'Go back to sleep. I'm fine.'

With what looked like a final push, he opened his eyes again. 'Sleep. Here.' He pointed to the other side of the bed and as if the words had used up his last reserves of energy his eyes closed again and she could almost see him slide into sleep.

For a while she did watch him, examining his pale face, the dark circles under his eyes and the tousled hair as he lay motionless, lost in a deep sleep. When her own eyes started to droop she crawled onto the bed next to him and fell fast asleep.

Chapter 21

'What the hell?' demanded Tara, bursting into the room.

Maddie startled into wakefulness, struggled to find any words and then gradual realisation sank in. At some point Nick had turned to face her and his arm was now draped across her waist.

'Nick!' Tara's shrill tones were piercing, tempting Maddie to put her hands over her ears, which would have been childish but oh, so satisfying.

'Nick! What's she doing in bed with you?'

Poor Nick, who looked as pale as the pillows he was nestled into, struggled into consciousness, his blue eyes looking faded and red-rimmed as he exchanged a confused look with Maddie before he slowly withdrew his arm.

'Tara?'

'I asked you a question. What. Is. She. Doing. In. Here?'

Nick frowned and clutched his stomach, his eyes seeking out the bucket beside him.

'For goodness' sake, he's ill,' snapped Maddie, swinging

her legs over the side of the bed and standing up. 'He's been throwing up all night. Someone had to keep an eye on him.' She shot the irate model, who looked as glamorous as ever, a telling glare.

'Hmph.' Tara gave her a dismissive glance. 'Nicky darling, how are you feeling?'

'Alive,' mumbled Nick, hauling himself up, the sheets dropping to his waist, and flopping against the pillows.

'You look terrible.' She glanced around the room. 'You haven't started packing.'

'Packing?' Nick pushed at his hair, making it stick up in tufts as he blinked like a confused owl. He looked adorably rumpled and lost, making Maddie want to step between them, give him a hug and tell him not to worry. He didn't have to do anything.

'Yes. Packing. We're leaving the boat.'

'Leaving?' Nick parroted again. 'Is it sinking?'

Maddie put her hand over her face to hide her smile.

Tara glared at him. 'Sinking? Why would it be sinking?'

'You leave a sinking ship,' said Nick, his forehead creasing as if he were having trouble keeping up with the conversation.

'That's rats,' said Maddie, conjuring up an air of innocence.

Tara whirled round and shot her a sharp glare; any sharper and it would have skewered Maddie to the wall.

'Not permanently, silly.' Tara's girlish chiding tone made Maddie grit her teeth. 'Just for five days. I need a break from that poky little cabin and the bathroom is doing my head in. There's no room for anything.'

'Where to?' Nick seemed incapable of stringing a proper sentence together.

'Back to the Ellingham's. They've invited us all to stay. You need to pack. We're leaving as soon as Ivan has moved the boat to the new port place. This afternoon.'

'Tara,' interjected Maddie, 'Nick's not going anywhere. He's still not well.'

'Don't be ridiculous,' said Tara. 'He has to.' Her voice rose in pitch. She turned to Nick and collapsed with ridiculous drama on the edge of the bed, putting both her hands on his shoulders. They looked like tiny bird claws. 'You've got to come. I can't go without you.'

Nick tried to smile but it was a weak, half-hearted affair and when he opened his mouth to reassure the spoiled brat Maddie clenched her fists, imagining herself picking her up and dropping her overboard.

'I . . . I . . .' He winced, his hand rubbing at his stomach.

'He's really sick,' said Maddie, watching him closely, seeing the fine lines tightening in his cheek and the tendons sharpening in his neck.

'But you're better now, aren't you, Nicky? You were sick yesterday.'

He nodded.

'And he's still recovering.' Maddie didn't want to embarrass him but he couldn't even walk to the bathroom unaided.

Tara drew herself up with an imperious sneer. 'He's just been sick. Everyone's sick all the time.'

Maddie fixed her with a stern glare. 'No, everyone is not sick all the time. That,' she said with cutting emphasis, 'is not normal. Nick needs to stay in bed and rest.'

A faint blush stained Tara's cheeks. 'Nicky darling, you have to come.' She glared at Maddie. 'I think you can go now. Leave us alone.'

Maddie stood up, almost nose to nose with Tara. 'I've spoken to a doctor and Nick needs to rest and he shouldn't be up for forty-eight hours in case he's infectious.'

'Infectious?' Tara took a step backward.

'Yes, it could be viral.' Maddie sucked in one of those Granny-knows-all sort of breaths, like a boxer pulling his arm back to deliver the knockout blow. 'You wouldn't want to catch it, would you?'

It wasn't funny really but the speed at which Tara shot off and Maddie's smug expression made him laugh; actually it was more of a wheezy breath that hurt like hell. Some bulldozer seemed to have scoured out the inside of his stomach at some point. He couldn't remember the last time, if ever, that he'd felt so ruddy pathetic. Being ill was the pits.

'Thanks.' He winced, trying to drag himself back up the pillows. 'Can't decide if you're a nurse or a Rottweiler.'

'Here.'

Rottweiler, he decided at her exasperated tone.

'Let me.'

She pushed him out of the way to plump up the pillows, her cheek brushing his, and he smelled warmth and rosiness, a just-woken-up female scent that made him want to nuzzle in.

'There. Better?'

With a nod, he fell back.

'Do you think you'll be all right for a while? I need to go and sort breakfast out.'

'Of course. I'll be fine. Thanks for staying all night. That was . . .' It had been reassuring. 'Kind, especially when you've still got to work.'

She gave him a cheery grin, the brief burst of sunshine somehow making him feel a lot better. 'Ah, but the unexpected bonus is I've got the next week off.' Then she looked at him. 'Well, except for you.' Despite her blunt words, suppressed amusement tinged them.

'I'll keep out of your hair and you can pretend I'm not here.'

'I'm sure when you feel better in a day or two you can join everyone at the famous Ellinghams'.'

'Yeah,' he agreed without enthusiasm, quite sure that he didn't want to go back to that white mausoleum of a villa where everything was designed for style rather than comfort. Ice-white and just as cold.

'Do you want anything? To eat?'

'God, no,' he said with feeling. Maddie flashed him a warm, sympathetic look. 'My stomach is in full revolt.'

'OK.' She pursed her lips, studying him. 'I'll . . .' there was a pause, almost as if she were reluctant to leave him '. . . come and check on you later. You've got enough water; keep drinking it but small amounts.'

'Yes, nurse.'

As soon as she'd gone he closed his eyes, feeling inadequate and defeated. What wouldn't he give to be home right now, for his sister-in-law to smuggle one of the dogs over to his place for company? Oh, to be in his own bed, with the knowledge that the rest of the family were just across the courtyard and that Mum could appear at any moment with her chicken broth, which she'd been doling out as a family cure-all for as long as he could remember.

He blinked hard and wiped away at the sudden self-pitying dampness. Get a grip, Hadley. You've been ill, your system's under attack; you're just feeling under the weather.

He closed his eyes, let his mind wander. Unerringly, it kept going back home, picturing what everyone would be doing; Jonathon and Dan picking up some of his jobs on the farm with Dad, Mum baking a cake in the kitchen for one of her WI dos, the dogs keeping guard on the farm gate, and the sheep would be in the lower pastures, eating the short summer green grass. He could see the sun at its peak in the sky, slanting down over the steep sides of the fell, poking its way into the dark fissures of the crags cresting the skyline.

The boat's engine had changed pace, the soft throb becoming stronger and more determined. Through the porthole he could see the shoreline moving more quickly as they headed further out to sea. He would have liked to see where they were headed; this sensation of sailing off into the unknown was mildly disturbing. He'd lost his bearings.

He was attempting to read but had gone over the same paragraph three times without making any sense of it when his door opened and Tara appeared, fractious and crackling with furious energy. 'Nick.'

He fought the childish urge to duck under the covers and pretend he wasn't here and it was too late to pretend to be asleep, although she'd have probably shaken him awake anyway.

'Tara.'

She put her hands on her slim hips, tilting her head with an approving smile.

'Well, who's looking much better already?'

He blinked, his eyes gritty and sore. Really? 'I don't feel it.' His attempt at returning her smile failed; he felt too wiped out for anything.

'You will. As soon as you're up.'

'Up?' he asked, his mind unclear and circling around the idea. Get up? Getting up ranked right along with scaling Everest at the moment.

'Yes, it's always the way. Once you get out of bed, have

277

a shower, you'll feel a million times better. You can't give in to it. Do you want me to give you a hand to start packing?'

Packing? She had to be kidding.

'Sorry, Tara, but I really can't go. I feel like sh . . . I feel terrible.'

'Well, I've been talking to Cory and we don't think you're infectious. That awful girl was just making it up.'

Awful girl? Who? Maddie?

'It's just something you ate. It's probably that girl's cooking. I bet she never washes her hands.'

Tara had advanced into the room like a tiger stalking prey and threw open his wardrobe doors.

'Let me see . . . What do you want to take?'

'Tara –' he hauled himself upright, his arms shaking with the effort '– I'm sorry but I can't go.'

'But you must. Don't you understand?'

'No.' The blunt honesty was an error.

'How,' said Tara, outraged, 'is it going to look if I turn up on my own?' She flung her arms out wide.

Nick shrugged helplessly.

'I'll look like some kind of loser, that's what. Someone who can't get a boyfriend. It's bad enough that Cory's got Douglas; he might not be very good-looking but at least he's rich.' She sighed heavily. 'Don't be difficult, Nicky,' she wheedled, her voice changing, her eyes luminous and soft in a sharp change of tack. 'I really, really need you to come with me. It's not as if you'll have to do anything; you can lie around on sunbeds looking gorgeous. I've got some foundation; we can make you look a bit less peaky.'

She started rifling through the hangers in his wardrobe. 'Where's your new linen shirt?'

'I . . .' He lifted his hands. He had a vague recollection of Maddie unbuttoning it.

'Honestly, Nick. I suppose this one will do; we can go shopping in Hvar again. The villa's only a short walk into town.'

She turned round. 'Come on, Nick. You need to get up and dressed. Ivan says we'll be arriving in Stari Grad in the next hour. The taxis are booked to pick us up from the harbour. Dinner's at seven tonight.'

An involuntary groan escaped at the mere thought of eating. Sweat broke out on his forehead at the very prospect of getting in a taxi, bundled up against other people. Even staying in a new strange place seemed too complicated to comprehend. His stomach cramped, nausea swirling again. This cabin wasn't home, but he knew how many steps there were to the bathroom. He knew if he got out of the bed at the wrong point he'd bang his knee on the bedside cabinet. He knew the feel of the short pile carpet under his feet.

'I'm not coming, Tara.' A sense of relief settled as he lay back against the pillows and closed his eyes. It was, he realised, the first time that he'd said no to her in their relationship.

'Can't or won't?' she spat. 'I can't believe you're prepared to let me down like this.'

He forced his eyes open.

With her eyes flashing as she threw her magnificent mane of hair over one shoulder she seemed like a phoenix or a dragon, shimmering in fury and just as much a fantasy, as out of reach, as she'd ever been.

'I don't normally do ultimatums but . . . if you don't come with me, it's over.' With that she tossed her head in the air and marched out, her nose higher than her forehead.

Wearily he shook his head, the scene reminiscent of Nina, at eight, stomping out of the kitchen when he refused to let her play with his Nerf gun.

But then his stomach cramped with a vicious pinch. A hot flush. Then a cold sweat. His system bucked. He fought it. Fought it hard. To no avail. He grabbed the bucket just in time and stopped fighting, giving in to misery as he heaved and retched.

Chapter 22

The gulet slipped into the quiet, pretty little port of Stari Grad just after one o'clock. Within minutes the noise and chatter of frenetic activity, like monkeys in a jungle, suddenly cut dead as one by one Douglas and co trooped down the gangplank with their cases and bags to the waiting taxis.

Maddie waved them off.

'I hope Nick's OK,' said Siri, the last to leave.

'So do I,' said Maddie, a touch uneasy that he'd thrown up again this morning.

'I guess now you're in a port you can always call a doctor,' she said with cheery dismissal.

'I guess *I* can,' said Maddie, her voice a little tart. Siri gave her a guilty look, hefted her bag in her hand.

It wasn't that she minded looking after Nick, she really didn't, but she was outraged on his behalf with the casual, heartless assumption among all of them that it wasn't their problem, as if he wasn't really one of them. And, as for Tara, she wasn't even going to go there.

'We'll be back in a few days.' The conciliatory note in Siri's voice irritated Maddie, even though she was the only one who had even given Nick a second thought.

'Have a nice time,' said Maddie, her face carefully blank. If Siri expected Maddie to give her some kind of blessing and lessen any guilt, she could forget it.

Siri's nervous, apologetic smile gave Maddie some satisfaction, but not much.

She watched as they loaded everything into the two cars, with Ivan striding away down the promenade to register the necessary paperwork with the local officials, and then the two cars slowly pulled away. Despite having acquired sole responsibility for Nick, she heaved a huge sigh of relief – five whole days to herself.

'They all gone?'

She nodded, handing over a fresh bottle of water. 'How are you feeling?'

'Funnily enough, despite being sick again, I feel a bit better. Sleeping helped. Thanks for cleaning up after me.'

She laughed. 'It is my job.'

'Yeah, but . . .' he wrinkled his nose '. . . I'm sure that's not quite what you signed up for.'

'I've got used to it.' She weighed it up for a second and then decided against telling him about Tara's problem. 'You sound a lot better.'

'Thanks, my stomach is a bit sore but I don't feel nauseous any more, just yukky.'

'Why don't you have a shower?'

'Trying to tell me something?'

'No.' She laughed at his worried look. 'It'll give me chance to change the sheets on your bed. I don't know about you but fresh sheets always make me feel better and a shower might make you feel a bit more human.'

'As opposed to one of the walking dead.'

'Ah, I see you've looked in the mirror this morning.'

With a reluctant laugh, he said, 'Tell me how it is, why don't you?'

'Shower.' She pointed to the bathroom. 'I'll help you but give me a minute to get my stuff. This room could do with . . . airing.'

'You mean it stinks in here.'

'Mmm, wouldn't go that far, but . . . You could move cabins if you wanted to.'

'No, I don't think I've got the energy. Just contemplating the walk to the bathroom is enough.'

'Like I said, I'll be back in a minute. Give me two ticks.'

Of course, being a man, he knew best and by the time she'd returned with her cleaning bucket, mop and fresh sheets, his bed was empty and the bathroom door was closed.

She stripped the bed quickly and changed the sheets, giving all the surfaces a wipe down with the anti-bac wipes which were part of her cleaning kit.

She'd just posted the heavy feather pillows back into pillowcases when she heard a bang, followed by a crash and a yell from the bathroom. The shower was still running but there was no other sound.

She darted across the room. 'Nick! Are you OK?' she called through the bathroom door.

'Yeah, I er . . .' There was a long silence followed by a diffident, 'Erm . . . no. I think I'm going to need some help.'

'Can I come in?' she asked. 'Are you decent?'

Another long silence.

'No, but I'm sort of stuck.'

'I'll close my eyes.'

It was difficult to push open the door as the shower door was in the way and she could see Nick's legs sprawled in front of her, half in and half out of the shower. She wriggled through, grateful to see that he was face down on the floor. That spared some embarrassment. Grabbing one of the big white towels from the back of the door, she dropped it over his naked backside, although not before noticing that it was a very fine naked backside. Her insides clenched a little.

'What . . . er . . . happened?' Despite her best intentions, her words emerged a little unsteady and wobbly. Stop thinking about his thighs. Had she no shame? He was a sick man at her mercy and she should know better than to ogle the poor guy.

He lifted his head and looked over his shoulder at her. Half of his body was wedged under the toilet bowl and, in the tight space, it was obvious that trying to get any purchase to lift himself up was almost impossible.

'I slipped, went down, grabbed the shower head and the whole thing came down with me and . . .' he dropped his head to the floor '. . . I haven't got the energy to get back up.'

'Are you hurt?'

'No. Just my masculine pride which, to be honest, is a shadow of its former self after today.'

'How about I promise not to mention this again?' suggested Maddie, forcing herself to be matter-of-fact and businesslike as she switched off the shower and bent to help him.

'I'm not sure at this moment I care.'

'You need to wriggle back a bit and then I can help you up to your knees. Then grab the basin and between us we can get you up.'

There was only so much wriggling and tugging a towel could take and still protect one's modesty. When she pulled Nick up to his knees, the towel gave up the ghost. As he rose to his feet, hanging onto the basin with one hand, Maddie, still on her knees, got an eye-level view of flat stomach, dark blond hairs arrowing down and a brief glimpse of dark blond curls and other things that she wished she really hadn't seen. Although that didn't stop the sudden fascination about what would happen if she stroked her hands up those lovely thighs or caressed the masculine dip of muscle running across his hips.

She stood up, grabbing the towel, and clumsily shoved it at his crotch, which made things worse as she had to hold it there, waiting for him to take it from her. If only she could have been blasé and pretended it was no big deal. Now they were both standing here looking at each other, her cheeks flaming and his only a shade lighter.

'Awkward,' she said, focusing on not looking down. In the mirror she could see his bottom, still delicious. Nick Hadley had a very nice body. Had she noted that already a few times?

He swallowed. 'Sorry.' He clung to the sink with one hand, holding the towel with his other. The blush on his face deepened.

'Here, let me.' Now she felt awful, knowing that on a normal day Nick probably would have laughed this off, made a huge joke out of it. His blushing apology emphasised how lost and defenceless he was feeling. Keeping her eyes on his jawline, she took the towel and wrapped it around his waist, her movements brisk as her hands grazed his cool, damp skin. Heavy silence buzzed between them and the intimate touch, taking care of him, made her heart flip. She focused on the golden sand grains of stubble breaking out on his chin, heard him inhale sharply as her fingers slid across his firm stomach to tuck the ends in and felt her insides tingle at the soft bristles of hair below his navel.

'There.' She pulled her hands away and shoved them down by her sides, standing ramrod-straight like an obedient toy soldier. 'All done. Think you can make it back to bed? I'll . . . er . . . tidy up in here.'

His boxer shorts were on the floor, the shower head dangling downwards, the hose poised like a silver snake to strike and a large slick of water across the floor.

'Mmm,' he said, moving his grip from the basin to the door, taking a few careful steps on the wet floor. Like an old man, he shuffled back to the bed, drips of water from his wet hair running down his back.

'Wait.' He turned as he was lowering himself onto the bed. She hurried over with a fresh towel. 'You're still soaking. If you get the sheets damp, you won't feel the benefit.' Without waiting, she gently blotted up the lines of water inching their way down his back, warmth bursting in her chest at the sight of the towel against his skin, his muscles moving as he shifted to accommodate her touch. She worked her way from his tapered waist up to his broad shoulders, soaking up the drops in her path, towards his neck, where smooth, dead straight spikes of blond hair fringed the nape like a comb. He smelled of the supplied expensive lemon verbena shampoo as she buried his head in the towel and rubbed his wet hair, trying to make it brusque and impersonal while her heart hammered away in her chest so hard she could feel her ribcage vibrating. Like a child he let her, after making a half-hearted muffled protest.

When she finished it was still damp and she gave it a critical scowl. 'I'm not having you go down with pneumonia or something from sleeping in damp sheets. Let me dry it for you.'

Obedient as ever, he sat there, his shoulders drooping with weary patience as she made him wait while she plugged in the hairdryer in the bedside lamp plug.

'This won't take a minute and then I'll leave you in peace.'

'Good,' he muttered with a sigh and a look of longing at the bed.

As soon as she started fluffing his hair through her fingers, rough drying it under the blast of the hairdryer, she regretted it. What was she doing? Where had this determined impulse to look after him come from? Her fingertips massaged his scalp, tingles shooting up her arm as his hair touched her sensitive inner wrist, but she couldn't seem to stop herself, even though it was just asking for trouble and extending an open invitation to her hormones, which seemed to have woken up from a very long hibernation and were stretching and uncurling like hedgehogs scenting spring.

'Mmm, that's nice.' Nick's hoarse voice was full of sleep and sex . . . no, not sex. Definitely not sex. Those damn hormones had far too much spring fever in their step. Just sleep. Tiredness. Probably sore from all that throwing up.

'I think you're done now.' She almost yanked the plug out of the wall. 'Do you want a clean T-shirt or anything?'

Nick's eyes clouded as if he were confused by her sudden brusqueness. 'Yes. The second drawer down. And would you mind . . . boxers in the top.'

Yes, because she really wanted to go rifling through his underwear drawer. A soft blue T-shirt lay neatly folded in the drawer. 'This do?' He nodded and she dipped her hand into the top drawer without looking and pulled out a pair of navy jersey boxers.

'Thanks, Maddie.' He pulled the T-shirt over his head and she watched as the muscles in his back under his shoulder blades flexed and bulged.

'Can I get you anything else?' she asked, already at the door. It was too hot in here. She needed to get out fast and give herself a severe talking-to.

'No . . . erm . . . I'm fine.' Then she felt guilty at abandoning him; his eyes looked a little bleak and there was a defeated air about him. 'Where are you going?'

'Some of us are still working.'

He winced. 'And I've just made extra work for you.' Now she felt a touch mean.

'*You're* no problem.' She thought of the stack of towels that Tara had got through. 'But now we're in port I need to do boring things like get some laundry done and stock up on groceries and other bits and bobs.' And get away from him for a while before she had any more unseemly thoughts.

Laundry, think laundry. Washing. Towels. Not wrapping a towel around Nick's tanned flat stomach.

'I need to go. Do chores.' She wrenched open the door with a touch of desperation.

'Will you be long?' He let out a self-deprecating huff.

'Sorry, I sound like a needy four-year-old. Go. I'm a big boy.' In that quick denial she saw that he felt his own vulnerability and was embarrassed by it.

She softened her smile. Who'd have thought that big, strong Nick could be this cute? 'I'll be as quick as I can. Laundry drop-off, pop to a supermarket and come back. Is there anything you want?'

He gave her a shy hopeful look. 'I've got a craving for Lucozade. My mum always used to give it to us when we were kids and sick.'

Safer territory; this she could deal with. 'Mine too. She swore by it. I've no idea if they sell it here, but I'll have a look for you.'

'Thanks, Maddie. I . . . I do really appreciate you doing all this for me. It's not exactly part of your job description, is it?'

'No problem.' Her stomach grumbled with a loud whine that she couldn't hide from and which had him looking contrite.

'And you haven't eaten, have you? Or slept?'

'It's been a bit of a day.' She raised her eyebrows. She hadn't eaten since breakfast and then it had been a quick slice of toast because everything had been so chaotic.

Nick smiled back at her, a shy smile which lit her up inside. 'And I haven't helped. Go eat something. Can't have both of us fainting all over the place from lack of food.'

'Do you think you might want to try eating anything?'

'Not sure,' and as he said it he yawned, eyes blinking.

Despite the clean hair and a little more colour in his face, his eyes were smudged purple with fatigue.

'Why don't you rest for a while and then maybe, if you're feeling better later, come and watch a Netflix movie on the screen in the salon?'

He brightened, sitting straighter for a second as if he'd been offered a huge treat. 'That would be great.'

She gave him a sudden grin. 'You might not say that when you find out what I've chosen to watch.'

'I'll survive.' There was a flash of his usual humour as his mouth curved in a half-smile. 'You don't strike me as the sappy, weepy film type.'

'You'll have to find out.' With that cheery quip she left the room, grateful that she didn't have to watch him shim-mying into his boxers under that towel.

Slinging the heavier of the two laundry bags over her shoulder, Maddie headed confidently towards the gang-plank and out into the sun, grateful once again for the handy manual with its map and clear directions.

Her feet touched the solid stone promenade and imme-diately she felt a little unsteady on her feet. Funny how quickly she'd got used to the incessant motion of the boat. They were moored opposite a small hotel with a wrought iron edged terrace on the first floor, with greenery climbing around the railings. A couple at a table watched with avid interest, looking over the boat. She laughed quietly to herself; it probably looked terribly glamorous until she struggled off with her load, putting things into perspective very quickly. The *Avanturista* was one of the biggest boats in the little harbour.

The bags were heavy so she didn't dawdle, but her brief impression of Stari Grad was that it was a quiet and rather beautiful old town, with grand stately buildings that were impressive for such a small place. Ivan had told her it was one of the oldest towns in Europe. There was a quiet, calm sense that not much had changed here for a long time. If Hvar was the equivalent of St Tropez then this was the quiet, rustic little sister but still charming. As she walked along the quiet promenade, there were lots of interesting side streets, silent and empty, bordered on each side by buildings standing like sentries guarding hundreds of years of secrets.

With everyone away from the boat this week she could afford to explore the town and check out some of the restaurants and little bars. It was definitely an unexpected holiday bonus.

Finding the laundry took no time and, even better, the washing would all be ready for collection the next morning. Having skirted a small market with a handful of stalls packed with fresh fruit and vegetables, she doubled back to stock up on a few bits of salad before heading to the one supermarket.

The bread looked nice. White. Toast for Nick. She hunted high and low for Lucozade, to no avail.

She phoned Ivan. He'd abandoned her so quickly, he could at least help.

'I don't know what this is,' he said, 'but there is a vitamin drink, Cedevita. We give it to the children. You can buy orange, lemon or grape. It's a powder you add water to. How is he?'

'Better than he was.'

'Call me if you need a doctor.'

'OK.'

'Overboard?' Nick raised an eyebrow.

'I thought it was rather apt. Given we're on a boat. It's a remake and I loved the original. Goldie Hawn and Kurt Russell. Did you ever see it?'

'Yes, it's one of my mum's favourites. She loves Goldie. Or maybe it was Jeff?' he mused.

She looked down at the remote controls in her lap. She was quite pleased she'd managed to find the Netflix app.

'It is rather dependent on whether I can get the television working.'

There were two screens in the salon area, one large central screen by the seating area and another smaller one to the right of the cabin served by a smaller loveseat. So far she'd only been able to get the smaller screen to work.

'Don't ask me, I leave all that to my brother Toby. He's the family electronics whizz. We had to wait months for him to come home to get rid of the subtitles on the TV after Mum pressed something on the remote control.'

Maddie laughed. 'Sounds like something my mum

Julie Caplin

would do too. The TV at home is bigger than a small car, has a gazillion functions and no one seems to know how to work it.'

She looked over at Nick, stretched out on the opposite leather sofa; he looked a little better after drinking half a glass of the Cedevita, which tasted pretty good. Thank goodness for Ivan. At least she felt she'd done something to aid his recovery.

'Are you sure you don't want anything to eat?' She looked over at her empty plate, having eaten a chicken salad, feeling a little guilty for eating in front of him.

'I'm not that brave yet. This is going down well.' He raised his drink in toast. 'The Croatian cure.'

'Do you want anything else?'

'Maddie, can we make an agreement?' He looked over at her, his blue eyes serious and intent, which made her heart flutter just a little. 'If I wasn't here, you would be doing whatever you wanted. Why don't you pretend that I'm not a guest and just another person on board?'

'OK,' she said brightly, avoiding looking at his face. Another person. She could do that. All she had to do was forget the images of his naked body in the bathroom or the soft, sleepy smile he'd given her this morning when she'd woken up next to him.

'I don't want you waiting on me hand and foot. You've done enough already.'

She shrugged. 'OK,' she said, not entirely convinced that was the right thing to do.

With an impatient sigh, he said, 'Do you see any sign of Ivan worrying about abandoning a guest?'

She laughed. 'I suspect there's someone in the town who holds a much greater attraction, judging by the speed with which he shot off.'

'Exactly, so he's not exactly feeling guilty or obliged to stay.'

'True, but it just feels . . . I'm here to work.'

'I won't tell if you don't.' His blue eyes twinkled and, despite his pallor, her stupid stomach did that loop the loop thing. What would Nina say if Maddie told her she'd got a massive crush on her brother? That's what this was. A stupid crush. Yes, he was good-looking and he made her laugh and they had a ton of stuff in common and he made her hormones sit up and beg, BUT he was with Tara. And, let's face it, who was going to trade down from someone like her to someone like Maddie? Three times the size of a diminutive size six model, from a council estate in Birmingham, with no proper job.

Almost as if he'd read her mind he said, 'But this is just temporary, isn't it?'

Maddie wondered how much Nina had told him. 'Yes, I was free after I'd finished my degree and Douglas was desperate; otherwise I don't think I'd have got this job with no experience.'

'You seem to be pretty good at it.'

'Ha! You think. From your wide yachting experience?'

To her surprise, he flinched and looked away. 'Shall we watch this film then?'

295

His mouth had tightened and it seemed as if he was refusing to look her way.

'What's wrong?' she asked, genuinely puzzled by the sudden shut-down.

'Nothing,' he said. 'Are we going to watch the film or not?'

She frowned, trying to analyse her words. 'I was joking, you know.'

He didn't say anything but pointedly looked at the big blank screen, waiting for it to come on. She let out an impatient huff and flicked the remote at the television, muttering, 'Suit yourself,' under her breath.

He sighed and looked up. 'Sorry. I'm being an arse. And you don't deserve it. You sounded a bit like Simon for a second. He never misses an opportunity to remind me I didn't go to the right school, I don't work in London.'

'If you think I'm like Simon, you are being an arse,' retorted Maddie.

With a reluctant laugh he turned to face her. 'Sorry, you're nothing like Simon. I *really* don't like him.' The cross expression in his eyes softened as they met hers and held her gaze for a few seconds.

The unspoken subtext – that he did like her – hovered between them before Nick turned away. 'Shall we watch the film?'

'Good idea,' said Maddie, picking up the remote controls.

Unfortunately, after a few minutes pressing buttons with the odd suggestion from Nick, she finally admitted defeat.

'We could be here all night. I'm afraid it's the small screen or nothing.'

Nick rose, lifting his shoulders, and crossed to sit next to her without saying anything.

It wasn't called a loveseat for nothing, although Maddie did her best to squidge up into the corner to give him more room, but every hormone in her system was on high alert, horribly aware of the warm, living, breathing body next to her.

Ten minutes into the film, the irony of the story – the conflict between a super-rich, self-entitled hard-partying, super-dickish bachelor yacht owner who was thoughtless and boorish in his treatment of the super-poor, hard-working disadvantaged mother-of-three working two jobs while trying to study for her nursing degree – was not lost on Maddie.

She sneaked yet another sidelong look at Nick, who was steadfastly watching the screen with an iron cast to his jaw. Once again her gaze was drawn to the sandy golden bristles breaking out through his skin. Stop it, Maddie, she told herself. She wriggled in her seat, antsy and uncomfortable. Could he feel her looking at him? With her hand hidden under her thigh, she crossed her fingers and prayed that he couldn't sense how she was feeling.

Was he enjoying the film? It was difficult to tell; he was keeping himself ramrod straight and upright. Clearly he was avoiding touching her and keeping everything under control.

Then she caught his mouth twitch.

'Funny, isn't it?' she said, nudging him, unable to help herself.

'What, the film? Or the subject matter?' Nick's focus on the screen didn't waver.

'Both.' Maddie was beginning to think that this had been a bad idea; maybe she should leave him to it and head for bed.

'He's a caricature; he's not real. No one is that rude, or that self-entitled.'

Maddie raised an eyebrow before drawling, 'We are hot, the boat has been paid for and we'd like to sit down somewhere cool and wait for the rest of our party.'

Nick flushed and turned to face her, his blue eyes holding a touch of chagrin. 'OK, I admit I was a bit off that day. But . . .'

'But what?' Maddie lifted her head in challenge, her mouth quirking in memory of the imperious words. She wasn't going to let him off the hook, even if she'd long since forgiven him. 'You were above the rules? More important than anyone else?'

He closed his eyes for a second, his mouth twisting before he gave her a rueful smile. 'I was being a dickhead. Trying too hard to impress Tara. Be something I wasn't.' He reached out and touched her forearm. 'I apologise for being an arse.'

She forced herself not to react to his touch. Oh, shit, she wanted him to touch her again, to stroke her skin with those warm hands. She was turning into a nutcase.

'Apology accepted,' she said primly.

Nick rolled his eyes before asking with a quick dimpled grin, 'And you weren't being a tad passive-aggressive and deliberately difficult at all?'

'Of course not,' she said, folding her arms, all innocence, charmed by the mischief in his voice. But his words gave her pause for thought; if she were honest she had been deliberately antagonistic. 'OK, perhaps I could have handled it a bit better. I did have a bit of a chip on my shoulder. I thought you were some rich posh bloke, throwing your weight around.'

'Truce?' suggested Nick and this time he nudged her, leaving his forearm next to her, his body relaxing into the space so that they were now thigh to thigh.

'Truce,' agreed Maddie, swallowing, all too aware of the hair on his thighs teasing the nerve endings of her skin. She needed to focus on the film. Forget he was here.

She woke, her cheek pressed against something soft and warm and a buzzing noise coming from the television speakers. Slowly she lifted her head from Nick's chest. His ribcage rose and fell with the slow, even, rhythmic breaths of deep sleep. A small sigh eased from her. It was tempting to snuggle back in and enjoy the fantasy. For a moment she held her breath, conscious of the weight of his arm across her shoulders, not wanting to wake him.

Outside, the reflected lights twinkled in the ink-black sea and she could hear the sound of low-level chatter of people on one of the other boats, their laughter bouncing across the water. She looked at her watch; it was one o'clock in the morning and around the harbour most of the bars and restaurants were closed.

With his head tilted back against the sofa, Nick looked so much better and so peaceful, compared to the fitful sleep he'd had last night; she was loath to wake him. Perhaps she should just find a blanket and cover him.

Those long eyelashes fluttered on his cheeks and he stirred slightly.

His eyes opened, blue and confused for a minute, and then he gave her a sweet, sleepy smile at complete odds with sharp planes of his masculine face. 'Hey, Maddie,' he said, his voice raspy and low.

Her heart went clunk and her mouth dry. Oh, lord, she was in so much trouble. She'd been fighting this ever since she'd met him but . . . in that moment, she wanted to kiss Nick Hadley. She wanted him to kiss her back. This was bad news. Her eyes widened and his expression softened. 'You OK?'

'Er . . . um . . . er . . . yeah.' She couldn't even string a sentence together and he was looking at her with such gentleness in his eyes. He closed them and with the arm around her shoulders pulled her back into him with a sigh.

Maddie closed her eyes. He was obviously still half asleep. Carefully, she disengaged herself with a pang when his hold momentarily tightened.

Then his eyes opened and refocused as he pushed his hand through his hair. 'What time is it? I must have dozed off.'

'It's one o'clock. I fell asleep too.'

'Wow, I guess we both missed the end of the film then.'

'Yes,' said Maddie, trying to sound casual, as if waking up in his arms was nothing to write home about, despite the fact that her limbs all seemed soft and pliable.

'I'm not surprised; you must be shattered.' He touched her cheek. 'Thanks for staying with me last night.'

'That's OK.' Maddie tried to brush his words off but he picked up her hand.

Surely he could hear the galloping of her heart, thudding away in the silence of the salon.

'No, seriously, it was really kind of you. I don't think I said thank you properly. You didn't have to and . . . when I was feeling really wretched in the middle of the night – I hate being sick – it was so reassuring to have someone there.'

'Well, I'm glad I helped.' She wanted to snatch her hand out of his grasp in case she betrayed herself by doing something stupid like squeezing it back. Like she was doing right now.

'You more than helped.' His fingers rubbed over hers and she glanced down at where their fingers were linked and then back at his face. The moment took on a life of its own as they stared at each other, neither of them able to look away. She could hear buzzing in her ears as his eyes darkened, a slight frown creasing his forehead.

'Uh, it's late. We should get some sleep.' Maddie pulled her hand away.

'Yeah, right,' said Nick, rising slowly and a little clumsily to his feet. She put a hand out to steady him and he turned and grasped it to pull her to her feet. 'Bedtime.'

'Yes. What time do you think you'll be up?'

'Why?'

She lifted her shoulders.

'I can get my own coffee.'

'I know, but . . .'

He shook his head and squeezed her hand. 'You are not on duty for the next few days. Let's just enjoy the peace and quiet. If you're good I might show you the secret of how to make the perfect bacon butty!'

'There's a secret?'

'There is and if you're good I'll make them for you for breakfast.'

Maddie shook her head. 'It doesn't feel right.'

He lifted one eyebrow.

She sighed. 'All right.'

Nick smiled. 'Most people would be grateful for a lie-in.'

'I just feel . . . I'm taking advantage.'

'If it weren't for me, you'd have the boat to yourself.'

'There is that,' Maddie conceded, although she wasn't quite so sure that she wanted the boat all to herself any more.

Chapter 23

Sipping at her coffee, Maddie watched as a bird skimmed the water beside the boat, dipping its wings before arcing back up into the sky. The boat next door was preparing to leave and bustled with activity, the engine churning up the water and the captain at the helm, while two of the crew unwound the lines from the mooring posts. They gave her a friendly wave as they jumped on board and the boat puttered away, out along the channel towards the open sea.

Maddie tipped her neck back and looked up at the sky, her eyes tracking the distant, almost translucent puffball clouds that contrasted with the pure blue backdrop. Another glorious day, the sort that made you glad to be alive. Across the street, the sun warmed the pale stone of the buildings opposite, making them glow with a golden hue. As she stood on the boat, her feet square against the rocking motion with the swell of the departing boat, she smiled to herself. Life didn't get much better than this. Her eyes scanned the building opposite, committing the details to memory: the tall square windows with battered green wooden shutters, the heavy stone lintels and the vine tracing its way up to the balconies. Each of these were filled with a profusion of different-sized pots bursting with vivid scarlet geraniums, which were also peeping their way through the wrought iron railings fencing the flight of steps that led up to a pair of doors flanked by a pair of olive trees in enormous terracotta pots.

A steady stream of people carrying beach bags and mats walked past in colourful T-shirts and shorts, ambling with that all-the-time-in-the-world holiday gait: couples hand in hand, small family groups pushing buggies bursting to the gunnels with water wings, Lilos and parasols, all heading out of the little town, clearly ready for a day of swimming and sunshine. Maddie breathed in; the air here felt so clean and fresh, with the tang of the sea in the air along with the scent of pine.

She turned, hearing Nick's footsteps coming along the deck, ignoring the sudden lift of her heart.

'Morning. What a beautiful day.' He came to stand beside her, looking at the view.

'It is. And you look so much better.'

'I feel better, completely human. Ready for coffee. That smells good.' He pointed to the mug in her hand and laughed, stretching his arms up and making his T-shirt ride up. 'And I wouldn't have said that yesterday.'

Maddie averted her eyes. 'I . . . . I'll get you some.'

He turned to look at her, his blue eyes full of teasing reproach. 'I thought we'd agreed last night. You're not waiting on me.'

'It's just coffee.' She shifted on the spot and took another sip of her drink.

He tsked. 'If you were here on your own today, what would you be doing? What plans would you have?'

She waited a moment before answering. What would he say if she told him she'd like to spend the day with him?

'I'd take a couple of slices of toast up to the top deck with my coffee.'

'And?'

'I'd sit on the top deck and . . .'

'And what?'

'Paint,' she said.

'Paint?' He smiled. 'Well, you've certainly got plenty of inspiration. It is beautiful here.' He looked at her. 'What sort of painting do you do?'

'Er . . . watercolours and sketching, although I use watercolour pencils, easier when you're travelling.'

He nodded and then frowned. 'I feel I should have known you paint. Those sketches you did for Bill were fantastic.'

'Why?'

'Through my sister. She's talked about you.' And then she saw the light bulb moment. 'You did the mural in her patisserie.'

Maddie smiled at the memory of the glorious wall

305

painting in Paris. 'I helped restore it. Touched up would be more accurate.'

'So you can paint.'

'It's all in the eye of the beholder. Now, I'm going to make breakfast . . . and I'm making myself a poached egg on toast, which would be good for your stomach. It's probably still a bit tender and you need to go steady.'

He didn't looked terribly thrilled by the idea and she laughed at the sight of the pout on his face. It should have looked ridiculous on a grown man; instead it looked rather endearing.

With just the two of them on board, life was so much simpler. Chatting to Maddie was easy; there were no uncomfortable silences. Although he couldn't seem to quash the desire to touch her all the time. He came from a huggy, touchy sort of family; maybe that was it. He just felt comfortable with her. As soon as they finished breakfast, the poached eggs tasting far better than he could have imagined, but perhaps because he was absolutely starving, having eaten nothing for thirty-six hours, he and Maddie took the plates down to the galley and she washed up and he dried with the radio on in the background.

She was up on the top deck painting and she'd been up there for a couple of hours while he'd been having a WhatsApp exchange with the family on the Hadley Massive group, sharing a series of photos of the view from the boat.

'Fancy a drink?' he asked as he reached the top of the

steps, carrying a tray with two tall glasses filled with ice, a slice of lemon and Coca Cola. It was the best excuse he could find to come up and see her. For the last hour his book had failed to keep his attention and he'd wanted to . . . he'd wanted to be with her.

Maddie looked round, a pencil in her mouth, a second one in her hand. With her curls piled on top of her head, secured with a colourful scarf, wearing a postbox-red bikini which accentuated her white freckled skin and a sarong wrapped around her waist, she looked every inch the bohemian artist. Her eyes sparkled with delight as she took the pencil out of her mouth and she said, 'Oh, you star. I'd love one.'

Her body hid the painting, which was propped up against the sun lounger next to her, but as he stepped closer she pulled the painting towards her like a mother shielding her baby from the sun.

He put the tray down and handed her a drink.

'Tell me if I'm interrupting,' he said, trying to work out the expression on her face – not defensive but something, perhaps a touch wary. Was he interrupting? Would she rather he buggered off? And since when had he turned into this needy, wanting-her-approval, bloody idiot? That sickness bug, food poisoning thing had a lot to answer for.

'No, I was ready for a break.'

'Got much done?' he asked, deliberately casual. OK, he was being nosy; he was dying to see the picture but he didn't want to make her uncomfortable.

The sudden beam on her face took his breath away. One minute he was fine, the next someone had punched him in the heart. And suddenly all the weird emotions started to make sense.

He swallowed. 'May I see?'

Her white teeth nibbled at her lip. 'They're nothing special.' Shyness and diffidence coloured her low tones and he felt bad for pushing her.

'If they put that look on your face, they must be,' he said in a low urgent voice, reaching out and touching her forearm in reassurance. 'But if you really don't want to show me, you don't have to. I'm just being nosy. They're private.'

She laughed, the sound sparkling and lively in the still quiet midday air, and then sobered, shaking her head and looking at him with an expression of gratitude.

'What?' he asked, puzzled but also feeling like he'd won a prize.

'You've just shown me a huge truth. I've always told myself I'm not a real painter. It's not something people like me do. But . . .' she gave him another dazzling grin that made his pulse kick '. . . if they're private, then how will I ever know if I could even be a painter?'

'A very good point,' said Nick, trying to keep his expression bland when inside fireworks were going off and he was experiencing a bit of a hallelujah moment. Then he said with more urgency, 'Why shouldn't a person like you be a painter?'

'Because of where I come from.'

'Another planet?'

'No, I grew up in a council house in Birmingham. People like me don't paint, not unless they're painters and decorators. The people who do are super-gifted.'

'You studied History of Art. Surely you know plenty of artists that have come from less privileged backgrounds.' He folded his arms and regarded her with a fierce stare to hide everything that was churning inside him. Somehow it felt as if he'd not really seen her before. How had he missed the way she crackled with light and life or how her glossy curls, threaded with chestnut streaks, glowed in the sunlight? How had he not seen the freckles on her creamy skin, dotting her nose and cheeks, or her wide, mobile mouth that smiled more often than not? He realised he was staring, adding up all her features as if trying to calculate a complicated sum. Luckily she was frowning down at her picture and not paying too much attention to him.

She didn't say anything and it hurt that she didn't believe in herself.

He spoke again. 'Like I said last night. You can be anything you want, but sometimes you have to make compromises along the way. I'd say compromising on the private would be a step in the right direction, wouldn't you?'

With a quick smile she lifted her brown eyes, twinkling as usual, and shook her head. 'You're very persuasive, Nick Hadley.'

'I know.' Their eyes met and for a moment there it was again, that quick fizz of something. He lowered his voice, being gentle with her. 'Are you going to show me?'

'OK,' she said, lifting her chin in the air like a warrior steeling themself for battle. 'But you have to promise to be honest.' She levelled a serious gaze at him. 'I trust you.'

Her solemn declaration made his heart hitch.

'If you don't like them or think they're crap you have to say so; otherwise there's no point showing them to you.'

Nick swallowed. 'That's a tough call. A lot of responsibility. It's all subjective and I'm no expert.' He paused for a moment, now nervous. 'Are you pleased with them?'

'I think any artist always thinks they can do better. I suppose I need to take a risk and shove one out of the nest. They're like little baby birds. Once they're done they'll fly or die.'

'OK then, let's see your fledglings.'

Leaning forward, she whipped one of the paintings out of the stack of cartridge sheets lying face down on the sunbed, handing it to him as if entrusting him with something that could be easily broken. Trust.

As soon as he looked at it he took a sharp, sure intake of breath. It wasn't what he was expecting at all. He laughed out loud.

'Oh my God. This is fantastic. I love that –' he pointed to the angular dog splashing a chubby baby in the turquoise shallows '– and he's hilarious.' He leaned closer to study the older man, the sunlight bouncing off the sunglasses perched on his bald head. The picture encompassed several vignettes, stories in themselves on a pebbled beach with the islands beyond. The more he looked at it, the more the picture drew him in. A broad smile broke out over his face, part relief and part genuine pleasure. My goodness, she had talent in spades. She'd brought the people to life with such simple strokes.

'Who's this?' He raised an eyebrow as he pointed to a lone figure on the edge of the promenade. An Adonis-like figure with sunglasses perched on his blond head, complete with tiny salmon-pink shorts, stood just left of centre-stage, three teenage girls gazing at him.

Maddie's mouth dropped open into a little 'O' of horror, her eyes widening in an 'eek' kind of way as a red flush raced up her neck and flooded her face. She slapped a hand over her mouth.

'I can't decide whether to be flattered or offended,' said Nick, folding his arms, giving her a mock glare.

Maddie's mouth quivered. 'You should be grateful they're girls ogling you.'

Nick burst out laughing. 'I love that you always know how to keep me in my place.'

With a shrug she ducked her head, but he could see her shoulders shaking.

'I could step right onto that beach . . . Oh, I'm already there.' He shot her a mischievous wink when she looked up. 'These people. They're all so real. That's my granny, my sister, my cousin's toddler. You can almost smell the ice cream, the trees and the sea.'

'That's the ground-up pine needles in the paint,' she quipped. 'Do you really like it?'

Her earnest face was tipped up towards him, her eyes wide and searching. She let out a breath as if she'd been holding onto it. His eyes dropped to her parted mouth, suddenly fascinated by her lips. There it was again, that little spark that flashed bright and brilliant between them. Don't kiss her. Don't kiss her. His brain fought hard against the impulse to put his mouth on hers.

'I really like . . . it,' he rasped, his voice husky. He really liked her. The realisation struck him hard, his diaphragm constricting in shock. He really did like her. Liked the way she teased him. Liked the way she didn't take any crap. Liked the way she embraced life. Liked everything about her.

He could feel himself leaning towards her. Stop. He dragged his eyes away from her face and down at the painting, feeling his body rebelling even as he pulled back.

What was wrong with him? He was here with Tara; what sort of dick changed his mind like this? She might have dumped him, but he was still on holiday with her. An all-expenses-paid holiday that she'd brought him on. He shouldn't do it.

'It's a great painting. Let's see the other one.'

A quick frown of confusion crossed Maddie's face. And

for a moment there was that awkward what-just-happened-here sort of atmosphere between them.

'Thanks,' she said, brusque and back to business, as if the moment had never happened. His heart sank; the last thing he wanted to do was hurt her.

'Maddie . . .'

'Yes?' Hope blossomed quick and sharp and he felt like an even bigger dick.

'You shouldn't doubt yourself.'

'Easy for you to say,' she said and he knew he'd just messed up. 'It's not like you're an expert. They're probably all right for a local craft exhibition. Amateur watercolours.' She busied herself, pulling the different pictures together.

'I'm not an expert but . . .' He grasped her forearm to make her look at him. 'These made me feel something. Really feel. Happiness. Joy. There's emotion here. To make another person feel; that's a special gift. Even, philistine as I am, I can see you've got talent.'

'Oh.' Maddie looked as if she might cry, her eyes luminous, shining with unshed tears.

And he might have resisted if one solitary tear hadn't slipped down her cheek.

'Hey.' He couldn't help himself; he swiped at the tear and pulled her into a hug. Her gauzy sarong wrapped around his legs as he put his arms around her broad, solid shoulders. She felt real and solid after the insubstantial feel of Tara, which had made him fearful of his own strength. Maddie felt like a match. An equal.

'Don't be sad.'

'I'm not sad,' came her muffled voice as he held her to his chest, savouring the forbidden feel of her, soft and strong. She lifted her head, blinking away the tears. 'Sorry.' She lifted a hand to wipe her wet cheeks. 'I'm glad, honest. Just a bit overcome. You're the first person to see these.'

'And I'd better not be the last.' He gave her a squeeze, reluctantly easing back from her warm body. 'You need to show these to people. I reckon you could easily sell them. Especially to people on holiday in Croatia. What a fabulous memory of this place.'

He put his hands on her shoulders, easing her away from him, trying not to look at her eyes, scared he might give himself away. He couldn't mess with her. It wouldn't be fair; he wasn't really going to be a free man until this trip was over. Which meant he was going to have to keep his distance, emotional distance at least, given that there were just two of them on the boat and he enjoyed her company. He wasn't a saint, after all.

Maddie took a long cool shower, the cold water refreshing on her heated skin. She needed to get a grip. She snatched a handful of shower gel, scrubbing her skin hard as if in penance. Oh God, how embarrassing! How to make a complete tit of yourself! But had she imagined those strange undercurrents between Nick and her up on the sundeck? She could have sworn his eyes had dropped to her lips. At one point she'd really thought he might kiss her. The point when her heart nearly burst out of her chest and she looked at his lips. Bugger, she had made an idiot of herself and she'd seen the moment when he'd slammed on the brakes. And it had made her cry. Nick didn't want her. He might be attracted to her . . . but he didn't want her. For some reason that hurt more. The ability to shut down. But then he'd hugged her and when he'd . . . even now her heart missed a beat at the memory of that gentle touch . . . when he'd wiped away her tear she'd felt his heart thudding hard in his chest. Although he'd quickly put some distance between them. And she had to remind herself he was here with Tara. And she should not be putting moves on him. He was spoken for. And he probably just thought of her as good old Maddie. A friend of his sister. Almost part of the Hadley family. And that was the way it should stay.

But that didn't stop her going out for lunch with him. Friendship was better than nothing. It was just physical attraction; perhaps spending more time with him would make her immune, like exposure to germs. She giggled as she stepped out of the shower to grab a towel, wondering what he'd think being compared to a germ. And how could she not have realised that she'd painted Nick into the picture? What a giveaway. It showed that he was never far from her thoughts.

Despite her determination to treat Nick as a friend, feminine pride made her pull out one of the dresses that Siri had loaned her. It was a soft rust-brown silk sleeveless dress which finished mid-thigh and set off her colouring, exactly as Siri had told her it would. It was difficult to believe what a difference a colour could make but, as she gave herself a quick departing inspection in the mirror, she could see that the dress complemented the russet lights in her hair. No wonder Simon favoured those blue shirts all the time.

Slipping her feet into tennis shoes, she rammed on the big straw hat that was about the only thing in her wardrobe that Siri hadn't condemned and grabbed her bag, leaving the cabin to meet Nick on the deck.

Ack! He'd changed into a clean white T-shirt which stretched nicely over his broad chest. Having seen the muscles underneath already, the T-shirt did little to stop her imagination going AWOL.

He grinned at her. 'You look nice.'

'Oh, this old thing,' she said in quick dismissal, her heart taking its time to settle as she brushed the silk, enjoying the luxurious feel of the fabric beneath her fingers.

'Very nice and the hat – very glam.'

'Actually, the dress is Siri's,' she confessed, unable to stop herself.

'Well, it suits you,' he said. 'Shall we?' He held out a hand, inviting her to go first.

They stepped off the gangplank into a group of tourists taking pictures of the boat, most of whom turned and stared, a few nudging and whispering to each other. Nick winked at her, pulled down his sunglasses and took her arm with a gracious nod at their audience and they sauntered off as if they were a pair of celebrities, disguised by their dark glasses and her floppy hat, that people just couldn't quite place.

'Anywhere you fancy?' he asked as they strolled along the broad path towards the centre of the town.

'Apart from the laundry to pick up the washing, no. Yesterday I didn't have time to have a proper look around. Remember those pesky chores and I was worried about my patient.'

'Well, worry no longer. I feel a million times better. Stomach's still a bit tender but I'm hungry again, so I'm hoping that's a good sign.'

'You need to go easy then,' she said.

'Yes, nurse.'

They wandered along, past an official-looking building flying a Croatian flag and several private houses that looked as if they'd been tastefully modernised into holiday accommodation, before coming to a left turn that opened out into a wide area with plenty of restaurants and bars as well as a small shop selling suntan lotion, hats and beach shoes.

'Where do you fancy?' asked Nick.

'That place looks pretty.' She pointed to a restaurant below an old stone building, with pots of flowers lodged on every available ledge, the shutters painted a bright blue and with small square wooden tables outside, each laid with yellow and blue checked napkins. Everything about the scene suggested someone really cared and had put a lot of thought into making it look as attractive and welcoming as possible.

'This looks good,' said Nick, nodding at the menu on the wall outside.

'OK,' said Maddie and as they turned to choose a table a young man came out of the door.

'Welcome, welcome. You'd like to eat today? We have the house speciality, gregada. Good fresh seafood. Home-made pasta.'

Maddie smiled at his earnest enthusiasm. 'Sounds good.'

'Yeah, can we have a table for two, please?' said Nick.

'Of course – would you like to sit in the sun or the shade?'

Nick looked at her freckled arms. 'Shade?' he asked.

'That would be great.' She beamed at him, grateful for his thoughtfulness. 'Much as I love the sun, I have to be careful; it doesn't love me. Hence the hat.' She scooped it off and plonked it on the spare seat next to her. 'I'm covered in suncream but I can only take so much.'

The waiter returned with a carafe of water and a bowl of small black and green olives to take their drinks orders.

After requesting a glass of white wine for herself and waiting until Nick had ordered a Coke, she asked about the special. Gregada, it turned out, was a fish and potato stew and sounded very similar to the one Tonka and Vesna had cooked on her first night in Croatia.

'Sounds lovely; I think I might have that.' She turned to Nick as the waiter disappeared. 'I think you should avoid fish and shellfish for a while.'

'Absolutely. I'm convinced it was the fish stew I had in the restaurant in Hvar. There were mussels in there. The pasta dish sounds good, Gregada. Funny, you can get pasta everywhere these days.'

'Ah, now I can tell you something about pasta here,' said Maddie, grateful as ever to Tonka and Vesna's cookery class. 'We're not that far from Italy. They have their own pasta-making tradition in Croatia. Fuzi is flat diamond-shaped pieces of pasta which are then rolled around a dowel to create a tube shape.'

'I'm impressed.'

'All part of the service,' she said with a smug grin as the waiter brought their drinks. 'And with my medical hat, I'd say pasta is a good choice for your stomach.'

'Is there no end to your talents? Cook, painter and nurse.'

'None,' said Maddie with a smug tilt of her head, lifting her glass in toast. 'Cheers.'

He laughed. 'Cheers.'

When their food arrived, Nick let out a heartfelt groan at the sight of the plate piled high with pale yellow pasta dotted with small pieces of chicken and herbs. 'Proper food. I am so hungry.'

Her gregada tasted every bit as delicious as it smelled, the light broth flavoured with herbs and white wine and the whole piece of fish perfectly cooked while the chunks of potato were firm and tasty, but she had definite food envy. Nick's dish looked amazing.

'Want to try some?' asked Nick.

'You don't mind sharing?' she asked with a teasing smile.

'Must have been the pitiful look on your face.'

'Huh, in our house, you so much as turn around and someone will have nicked one of your sausages.'

He laughed. 'It's the same in ours. Every man for himself. You can imagine, with three brothers.

'Here . . .' He lifted a couple of the tubes and held out his fork. Without thinking, she put her hand to wrap her fingers around his forearm to steady the fork and as soon as she touched his hair-roughened skin her hormones decided to play silly beggars again. Her eyes jerked to Nick's, wondering if he'd felt that flare of electricity, to find that he was watching her, his gaze steady as the tines of the fork teased her lips.

She opened her mouth, feeling a flush race along her cheeks as she took the pasta, a sensation of her heart, taking off without, her filling her chest. It felt like the sort of thing a couple would do. She had to stop with the eye-meets she told herself, saying, 'That's very nice,' so primly that Nick burst out laughing and thankfully the moment was broken.

'I was always told nice was a non-word and you should never use it,' he said.

'And it doesn't do this pasta justice; it is delicious. Now

I've got a pasta craving. That is seriously good pasta. Do you want to try mine?'

'Think I'll play it safe for the time being.'

'Probably a good idea.' If she had to nurse him again, who knew what might happen.

After lunch they wandered through small, narrow shady streets, where there were a few tiny shops that were little more than front rooms. In a gourmet delicatessen, Maddie sought out some interesting-looking pasta and bought a couple of packs, as well as some of the bread-sticks, some little hessian bags of herbs which smelled amazing, some truffle oil and a bag of shelled walnuts which were considerably cheaper than they were at home. She had an idea for a simple pasta dish that Sebastian had taught her and hopefully it would go down well with Nick.

As they headed to the laundry, Maddie spotted a familiar dark head seated at one of the pavement cafés. She nudged Nick. 'Look, it's Ivan.'

He was sitting with another attractive dark-haired young woman and they were both drinking glasses of wine.

'And another lady friend,' observed Nick. 'Guess it's true about sailors having a different love in every port.'

'Let's hope he doesn't see us.'

'Why? You've got nothing to be embarrassed about.'

'I'm not embarrassed; I'm just not sure I could hold my tongue. She's young enough to be his daughter.'

They ducked out of sight down a small side street and picked their way over the cobbles.

'Well, look at that,' said Nick, stopping outside a double-fronted building with big wide picture windows.

'Very nice,' said Maddie, studying the dramatic picture on display. Golds, reds and pinks tinted the clouds of a stylised sunset.

'We could pop in with your pictures. See if they're interested.'

'Don't be silly,' said Maddie.

'Why not?'

'Because . . .'

Nick left the silence to stretch out as, standing side by side, they looked at the picture. His arm brushed hers.

She winced. What did Nick know about art? But ordinary people bought pictures. 'You're the first person I've gone public with and now you're talking about me selling them.'

'Don't you want to?'

'Of course, I'd love to . . . Do you really think people would buy them? What if he says no?' She gestured to the man in the shop behind a counter.

'What if he does? What will happen? The sky will fall in. You're the art historian. Didn't all the experts hate Monet at first?'

'Very good.'

'And now look at him.'

'He is dead.'

'Dead but very famous.'

Maddie laughed. 'So alive and unfamous is a bonus.'

'Yes, and what if he said yes?'

'That would be . . . amazing.'

'See, there you have it. It's a win-win really.'

'I'm not sure how you figure that. But I guess I don't have anything to lose.' If he laughed in their faces they could hop back on the boat and sail away.

'But it's the thought of going bowling in and . . . selling myself.'

'I could do it for you,' he said, tipping his head to one side.

'I can't ask you to do that.'

'Why not? Tell you what, why don't you go to the laundry and I'll go back to the boat and get your portfolio case?'

'What, now?'

'Strike while the iron's hot. Come on, Maddie, what have you got to lose? Unless you want to keep them all?'

Flutters of excitement rose in her chest.

'OK,' she said, 'I'll do it.'

'Oh my God. Oh my God.' Maddie stopped dead in the middle of the pavement as soon as they rounded the corner away from the gallery. 'He's interested in my paintings.' She couldn't help herself doing a little dance. 'He likes my paintings. My paintings.'

Nick looked very smug. She punched his arm. 'Don't you dare say I told you so.' She did a little spin in the street just because she could, her heart bouncing with sheer joy.

'Well done,' he said and scooped her into a big hug, his handsome tanned face beaming at her, mere inches away. 'I told you so.'

'You did.' She beamed back at him, fizzing with excitement, clutching his forearms. 'Oh my God, Nick. Oh my God.' His blue eyes glowed with pride and his smile was nearly as wide as hers.

'See, you can paint.' He planted a big smacking kiss on her cheek and picked her up and twirled her around. 'Told you! I told you, you are amazing.'

She laughed down at him. 'Thank you. It's all down to you. Pushing me.'

As he went to put her down, he stumbled slightly on the uneven cobbles and had to adjust his hold on her. He clutched her tighter and her body slid bump by bump down against his, nerve endings jumping to life at the feel of his strong arms encircling her waist to steady her. She came to rest, hip to hip, against him, his warm breath fanning her face. A flare of heat whipped through her. The grin on his face stalled as they stared at each other, wide-eyed for a moment.

'Thanks, Nick,' she whispered, looking at his mouth. Oh God, was she being too blatant? She saw the dip of his Adam's apple.

With his arm still around her waist, he gave her a quick squeeze as he said gruffly, 'All part of the service.'

He took a step back. 'I think we should go and celebrate.'

She nodded, still trying to find her voice.

'And find someone who speaks Croatian who can look at the contract for you.' Nick gave a businesslike nod. The brief moment winked out of existence as he dredged up a smile which didn't meet his eyes. 'Come on, Picasso, I'll buy you a drink.'

Ivan was still sitting at the same table with the beautiful young Croatian woman but as he saw them approaching he hailed them with a cheerful wave and not a trace of embarrassment.

'Maddie, Nick.' He looked pleased to see them. 'How are you?'

'We're fine,' said Maddie and gave him a broad grin, the enormity of what had just happened hitting her and feeling real as she explained to Ivan. 'I need some help translating Croatian. Would you be able to help?'

Ivan immediately beamed, his white teeth gleaming against his dark beard, and said, 'Yes, of course,' before saying something in Croatian to the young woman, who gave him an affectionate smile.

'And then perhaps you'd like to join me and my daughter, Gordana.'

Maddie felt the subtle nudge of Nick's foot against hers as they avoided looking at each other.

'Gordana, this is Maddie and this is Nick.'

'Hi,' she said. 'Papa has been telling me all about you.

He says this is one of the best trips he's made.' Her dark eyes danced with amusement. 'Especially since most of the guests have gone away for nearly a week.'

Maddie laughed. 'It does make things easier.' She gave a sidelong look at Nick. 'Now I just need to get rid of the last one. What do you recommend? Toss him overboard?'

Gordana laughed.

Nick nudged her and she was relieved that they were back to their easy teasing. 'You might want to wait. I might prove useful if you sell a painting.'

'If I do, I'll consider a reprieve for you.'

They ordered drinks and Maddie showed Gordana and Ivan her pictures on her phone. She'd taken careful snaps of them before she'd handed them over to the gallery owner, Franjo. He was going to show them to his business partner before making a final decision but if she was interested Maddie needed to sign a contract and go back in a few days' time.

'They are very good paintings.' Gordana's crisp matter-of-fact words, with their indisputable quality, made Maddie pause. She really could paint. Someone was interested in her work. Bill had liked her sketches, but that had felt like work rather than art. She'd been able to use her talent to good effect. And he was desperate. She'd managed to do the job he needed. But this was a real step forward, one that she'd never dared to dream of before.

'Very good,' said Ivan with a teasing glance at his daughter as if he read Maddie's mind. 'Congratulations,

Maddie. We need to go and celebrate, although I hope this won't . . . how do they say it . . . make your head big. I still need someone to cook and clean for the rest of the trip.'

'Don't you worry, Ivan –' she paused and then looked at Nick, who frowned at the mischief on her face '– I'm sure I can find a replacement to step in. Nick tells me he's a dab hand with a frying pan and bacon.'

He swatted her hand away. 'And already she's too big for her boots.'

'Too big for her boots; I like that,' said Gordana.

'So what do you think?' asked Ivan, looking at Nick and her. They were sitting on the rather swish terrace of the Villa Apolon, which had once been the Croatian equivalent of a stately home. It overlooked the water and was only a few hundred metres along from where the *Avanturista* was currently moored, although it looked as if they were on the move again.

'I don't have a problem with it,' said Nick, 'but it's down to Maddie.'

Which was kind of him because, after all, he was the guest and she was still crew. She looked down towards the boat, gently bobbing by the quayside.

'If you want to move the boat, it's fine with me,' she said in response to Ivan's request following a mobile call he'd received five minutes before.

'My friend will be very grateful, thank you.'

The *Avanturista* was taking up one of the larger limited mooring spots and Ivan's friend hadn't got a mooring secured and wanted to bring a party of people into the harbour for a couple of nights. They could actually see the boat moored not that far away, rather reminiscent of a plane circling an airport waiting for a landing slot.

'I've already stocked up on supplies today,' said Maddie, indicating the bag of shopping. 'And we have clean towels.'

'That's good and –' Ivan paused '– as a thank you, I will take you to a very nice place to moor. A secret cove. Tajna bay. And then come back here in a few days.'

'It is very beautiful and so peaceful,' said Gordana. 'No one knows it is there. A very special secret place that few people know about. The water is magical, so clear and calm. You can tell how clean the water is by how many sea urchins there are. They like clean water. It is a very good spot for snorkelling and paddle-boarding. And very private, even at the busiest times. No one goes there.'

'How come?' asked Nick with a degree of scepticism.

'Because the charts are wrong,' said Ivan with a wicked glint in his eye. 'The water in some places is deeper than the chart tells you. And it's a well-kept secret among the local people. You have to know what you're doing . . . but I know these waters well. My father was a fisherman here before we moved to Trogir.'

'Sounds idyllic,' said Maddie, already keen to see it. 'And perfect timing. We don't need to be back at the gallery for a couple of days with the contract. Perhaps, being some-where so beautiful, I can paint and take my mind off what Franjo is going to say.'

The three of them all looked at her with matching expressions of exasperation. She held up her hands. 'I'm allowed to be nervous.'

'Nervous, yes. Anything else, no,' said Nick.

'Are you sure you aren't the eldest? You're very bossy all of a sudden.'

'Not bossy, realistic,' countered Nick, leaning back in his chair and resting his arm along the back of her chair. Tingles crept along her skin where his fingers brushed – by accident, she was sure – her bare shoulder.

Maddie gulped as his T-shirt rose with the casual move-ment to reveal that fascinating tanned midriff with that smattering of masculine hair above the waistband of his shorts. Oh, Lord, Nick and her on their own for a couple of days. Talk about being caught between the devil and the deep blue sea, but she could hardly say no. Nick was a guest. Ivan was the captain; she'd been outvoted. Besides, Ivan was already on the phone, standing up and going to the terrace edge, where he hailed the nearing boat with a wide-armed wave.

'That's all sorted,' said Ivan. 'As soon as we've finished our drinks, I'll take you out there. If you don't mind I will spend some time with Gordana.' He turned to his daughter. 'You could borrow the Preseckis' boat and bring me back to the harbour.'

'*Da. Da.*' She clapped her hands together. '*Hvala*, thank you. Mama is coming tomorrow, with Bartul. We can have a family party.'

'Sounds like a win-win for everyone,' said Nick, as Gordana hurried off to borrow her neighbour's boat so that she could bring Ivan back to port and allow them to have the launch.

Within half an hour the *Avanturista* was sliding out of her mooring, passing Ivan's friend's boat, towing a little boat hitched onto the launch, and an hour later Maddie and Nick were standing on the deck, waving goodbye to Gordana and Ivan as the little boat puttered away back to Stari Grad.

Chapter 24

'Alone at last,' teased Nick as the little boat, containing a gaily waving Gordana, inched its way out of sight. 'And they weren't kidding. This is absolutely idyllic. There's absolutely no sign of human habitation.'

They stood side by side, leaning on the gunwale in rapt silence. Apart from the sound of the water nudging the boat's hull, the faint clink of the lines above and the shrill mewling cry of a hawk wheeling high above their heads in a perfect blue sky, there was a quiet stillness to the bay.

Maddie had seen plenty of beautiful things: paintings, sculptures, many famous works of art. She'd seen the stunning buildings of Paris – Notre-Dame, the Musée d'Orsay, the Eiffel Tower at night – but, in this rare moment, she didn't think that anything had come close to the simple beauty of this small, perfect crescent-shaped cove. There'd been a few heart-stopping moments as Ivan had driven the boat through the narrow entrance to the bay, set at an awkward angle, which took some skilled manoeuvring to enter but meant that the little bay was obscured from the view of passing boats out on the open sea.

The shoreline was fringed with trees and a white-shingled border which opened out at the far end of the bay into a tiny deserted beach, enclosed by a rocky outcrop of the familiar stark white stone. The water lapped across the bay in rippling waves, twinkling in the sunshine, and was so clear she could see the rocks and stones on the bottom of the cove as well as the shadowed shapes of shoals of fish ploughing their way along.

A hawk hovered above the tree line and Maddie watched as it suddenly plummeted downwards, prey in sight.

'It is gorgeous,' said Maddie, ignoring the shiver of awareness at his words. Just Nick and her.

'Fancy a swim?' asked Nick. 'That water looks so inviting.'

'Yes,' said Maddie suddenly. 'Do you know what? I haven't been in the sea since that first day in Bol, which seems years ago now.' She paused before adding with a wry grin, 'Well, not voluntarily.'

They both raced off to their respective cabins to change. Of course Nick was in the water before her. Remembering the store cupboard down by the galley, she stopped en route to pull out a couple of snorkels and masks. She looked at the flippers and decided they looked too much like hard work before dashing down to the lower deck and the ladder at the stern of the boat.

'What kept you?' called Nick, flicking the water from his hair, the sunlight turning the drops into sparkling diamonds.

'These,' she yelled back, dangling the masks from one hand. She tossed one towards him, delighted with her aim when it landed with a gratifying splash right in front of him.

'Good shot,' he called and she gave him a smug look, to which he responded, 'Are you coming in or not?' She threw the second mask towards him and climbed down the ladder, flinching at the cold fingers of water creeping over her skin. Darn it, she didn't want to do the girly 'It's cold' thing in front of Nick, but it was bloody freezing and she'd only got mid-thigh.

Before she could make any further decision, a pair of cold hands grasped her waist.

'Arrgh,' she squealed and then felt herself being pulled backwards.

She broke the surface to find Nick grinning at her. After the initial shock, she realised the water was rather pleasant.

'You, you . . .' With a flick of her wrist she splashed water towards him and he began to swim away backwards as she gave chase. She grabbed one of his feet and dunked him, knowing she was playing with fire because he was the stronger swimmer.

He ducked under the surface and disappeared from sight. Uh oh. A little thrill of fear filled her as she scanned the clear water and then she spotted him but it was too late; he came up behind her, picked her up and tossed her back into the sea.

When she came back up, wiping away the hair that had plastered itself over her eyes, she glared at him, which was hard to do when he was still grinning like a loon, looking very pleased with himself.

'You're going to regret that, Nick Hadley.'

'I am?' he teased with a wicked glint in his eye.

'Yes,' she promised him. 'Just you wait. You'll be sleeping with one eye open.'

'Promises, promises.' He swam up to her and grabbed one of the snorkelling masks that was bobbing in the water next to them. 'Truce?'

She narrowed her eyes and scrunched up her face, studying him for a second. If ever someone looked up to no good . . . 'I'm not sure I trust you.'

He flashed her another naughty smile. 'Probably sensible. Fancy a go?' He held up the mask.

'I've never snorkelled before. It's such a lovely word.'

'Me neither. There's not a lot of call for it in the North Sea. Too cold to hang about,' said Nick. 'Bloody sight warmer here though, thank God.'

'There's not a lot of call for it on the Grand Union Canal,' she retorted. 'I think that's the closest body of water to me at home. This is heaven.'

Nick began to pull on his mask and jammed the mouthpiece of the snorkel into his mouth, waiting for a minute as she tugged the strap over the back of her hair, the rubber strap pulling out a few painful hairs.

'Ready?' asked Nick, treading water in front of her. 'Let's swim towards the beach.'

'OK.'

He watched as she fitted the mask and mouthpiece of the snorkel into place; it felt a little claustrophobic and she wasn't sure she liked it. As if reading her mind, Nick held out his hand and gave hers a reassuring squeeze as she lowered her face into the water.

Immediately she forgot the restricting feeling of the mask, entranced by the way the sun dappled the water, green, blue and silver. Below the surface it was crystal-clear. Although there weren't immediately any signs of fish, the way the light filtered through the surface sent sunbeams scattering across the rock formations and pebbles on the seabed.

There was something intimate and relaxing about swimming side by side; it felt gentle and timeless. Every now and then one of them would point to something new to see, like the small shoals of tiny silver fish that swam into view and then, with a sudden nervous start, veered away in the blink of an eye or the black spiny sea urchins that in some places spread like patches of carpet covering the rocks below. The colour, the refracted light, it was fascinating and Maddie could have happily stared down under the sea all afternoon, just her and Nick in silent communication.

They swam for a while, including a slow circuit of the shallows of the small beach, before heading back to the boat.

When Nick pointed downwards, she followed him catching sight of an octopus, surprisingly graceful, as it danced its way through the water, all of its tentacles undulating as one in a wave before each one wriggled at the very tip. Entranced by the sight, Maddie swam a little deeper. Only when she registered the tilt of the snorkel, she realised what she'd done a fraction too late. Salt water filled her mouth, hitting the back of her throat just as she went to inhale. Panicking, she automatically tried to suck in a breath through her nose, realising with even more panic that her nose was pinched tight into the mask. Up, up. She needed air.

Even as she broke the surface she began to choke on the water trying to go down the wrong way. Coughing and spluttering, tears streaming, she spat out the mouthpiece and the water. Treading water furiously, trying to keep her head up, her fingers fumbled as she tried to release the suction of the mask on her face. Finally, she ripped off the mask. All she could taste was salt and the burning at the back of her throat as she wheezed, trying to get the water out and breathe in through her nose.

'Are you OK?' asked Nick, swimming alongside.

Unable to speak, she just shook her head, still coughing and gasping, splashing about trying to get a proper breath and sinking as she tried to tread water.

Nick cupped her under one elbow, which steadied her. 'Relax. I've got you.' His steady hold, taking some of her weight, enabled her to concentrate on catching her breath without having to worry about sinking.

'It's OK. You're OK. You're fine. I've got you.' Nick's calming refrain as he stroked her arm gave her something to focus on and eventually she got her breathing back under control.

'Thanks. Sorry. Mouthful of water. Took me by surprise. I panicked. Stupid.'

'Not stupid at all.' Still holding her, helping her to float, he led her towards the steps of the boat. 'You're OK now. I've got you.' When they reached the bottom rung he leaned forward and helped her onto the metal ladder, his arms on either side of her, and dropped a gentle brotherly kiss on her forehead.

She stared up at him, aware of his arms enclosing her, their eyes meeting for another one of those intense stares, and then she watched, her heart sinking, as his eyes slid away. She'd had enough of this. Him and his bloody idle kisses.

Irritated beyond measure, she gave him a belligerent stare as he began talking, the great idiot.

'I think when you get water in your snorkel you're supposed to blow it out, but I'm not sure I'd think to do that. It's not something that comes naturally, is it?'

'No, it's not,' she said shortly and with a sharp shove pushed him backwards into the water, before turning around and hauling herself up the ladder.

'Hey!' shouted Nick as he surfaced, pushing the water out of his face. 'What was that for?'

She paused as she threw her leg over the side of the yacht and glared down at him.

'What? What have I done?'

Her traitorous bloody hormones did a little jump at the sight of his biceps flexing as he pulled himself up the ladder in no time and suddenly he was there right in front of her face.

Did the idiot *not* get the message?

'You keep kissing me,' she snapped as he far more gracefully than she'd managed swung his leg over the side of the boat and came to stand in front of her.

He held up his hands in apology. Sorry . . . I was just being . . .'

'As if I were your bloody sister.'

'Right,' said Nick with sudden wariness. About flipping time too. She could see the realisation dawning. Yes, mate, you've stepped slap bang into the middle of a minefield.

Then his eyes sharpened. OK, so perhaps he wasn't so stupid after all.

'You don't want me to kiss you?' There was a definite quirk to one side of his mouth as he asked the question and his head had definitely lowered towards hers.

She swallowed but held her ground.

His eyes gleamed and she knew she'd inadvertently issued a challenge. Her heart thudded so hard she could feel it in her throat.

A slow wicked smile lit Nick's face and he moved forward and dropped another kiss on her forehead, except this time his lips barely brushed her skin, which somehow was far more intimate.

She glared at him.

'How do you want me to kiss you?' he asked, his voice low and husky, that tugged at something low in her belly.

Maddie glared at him again and stepped forward, putting her hands on his shoulders. Enough was enough.

'Like this.' She yanked him towards her, gratified to see his eyes suddenly darken, hunger sharpening his gaze and not a single sign of objection.

Her lips collided with his without finesse. She could feel the coolness of his skin contrasting with their hot breath. Desire hit hard and fast. And yes, hallelujah, his mouth moved under hers with eager responsiveness. Yes. Thank God for that. She'd been worried he might push her away.

Relieved by his reaction, she pressed forward, her breasts pushing against his chest. With a murmur of approval, Nick responded, wrapping his arms around her and pulling her against the length of his damp body. A thrill ran through her when his mouth opened under hers and she felt the first tentative touch of his tongue.

Yes, yes and yes. At last. This was it. Everything clicking into place. Their bodies locked against each other. Sparks of pleasure darted like silverfish racing over her body as her hands roved over his muscled back, circling the smooth skin, her palms caressing every plane. Bone and muscle, she could feel them moving under her touch as he pulled her closer. Still they kissed. It was delicious and tantalising, as if she might never get enough of him and, rather wonderfully, he responded to every move of her mouth. Her knees wobbled, almost overcome with sheer lust when he wove one hand into her hair, his fingers teasing her scalp as if he couldn't get enough of her.

Someone moaned and she wasn't sure who.

Nick's mouth slid away from hers. No, no . . . The words echoed in her head with dismay. She tugged at his shoulders, only relenting when he began to press kisses along her jawline. She squirmed as he traced a path down her throat to brush along her collarbone. It was definitely her moaning now. This was . . . ahhh and she squeaked as his hand moved up along the curve of her waist, skirting her bikini top. Yes, yes. His hand palmed her breast as his mouth returned to hers, the rhythm of his kiss matching the fingers rubbing over her nipple. She could hear herself murmuring incoherent words as the ripples of sensation intensified.

'Mmm,' she whimpered.

'Am I going too fast?' Nick's hands stilled.

'God, no. What took you so long? I've been waiting for this . . .' she gave him a candid look '. . . for days.' She followed it with a wicked grin as she rubbed her fingers around the waistband of his swimming shorts.

'Days, you say?' He undid the bow tie back of her bikini with one quick tug, breaking his kiss to pull it over her head and tossing it to the floor. She squirmed against him, the teasing fingers against her nipple almost unbearable. Both of them were gasping, their breaths harsh rasps as still they kissed, breaking every now and then to haul a desperate breath in.

'But you're making up for lost time rather nicely.' Gripping his waist, her legs feeling as if they might give way at any moment, she dipped her hand below the ruched elastic to feel the hard, silk-soft skin.

And then she stopped thinking as his clever fingers tugged harder at her nipple and she almost collapsed against him. She was on fire. With one clumsy tug, she yanked down his shorts, feeling the length of him jump free with a hotter-than-hell eagerness. Her fingers touched, held and slid down, to a guttural moan.

His mouth moved towards her ear. 'You're killing me.'

'Good,' she whispered back against his cheek, sliding her fingers back again in a slow, slow pull that had him sighing again.

She began to tug him down onto the deck floor.

'No,' moaned Nick.

Insistently, she tugged again.

'Not here,' he gasped, kissing her neck. He pulled away, his eyes wild and a touch feverish, a hand cupping her face. 'The first time with you should be in a bed.'

The words and the gesture made something hot and hard bloom in her chest as he took her hand, his fingers interlacing with hers, and led her towards his cabin. When they reached the door, he lifted it to his mouth and kissed her palm, nipping at her fingers before looking into her eyes.

'Are you sure?' His whispered question made her frown. Wasn't he? She gave a silent nod.

'Because . . .' he kissed her again, his lips sliding down her neck, making her shiver involuntarily '. . . if I get you on this bed, I'm not sure I'll be able to stop.'

Her mouth lifted in a slow sexy smile at his huskily spoken words.

'I've never wanted anyone as much as I want you.' Hot breath whispered past her ear.

'Yes,' she said, never more certain of anything in her life.

He pushed open the door, easing her towards the bed. With her knees backed against the cool sheets, he led her into a low languorous kiss, before his mouth moved to cover one crested nipple.

She squeaked in sudden pleasure before succumbing to the mindless pleasure of his tongue swirling and tasting the sensitive skin. When she was about ready to die from the intense sensation, he moved to her other breast and began the sucking, teasing attack all over again. Cries broke from her mouth and she gripped his arms. Any minute now she was going to start begging.

When he paused, giving her an unholy grin of threat and promise, she sucked in a sharp breath. Oh lord, she was on fire. Then, with another one of those wicked,

wicked looks, he leaned down and took one nipple in his mouth again before sliding down to kiss her belly, gripping the sides of her bikini bottoms and inching them down as his mouth stroked the smooth skin around her navel.

With a whimper, she tried to pull him up, almost overcome by the throbbing insistent ache between her legs.

He looked up at her. 'Sure?' he asked again, those blue eyes burning into hers. With a gulp, unable to say a word, she nodded. He rose slowly to stand in front of her.

With slow languid ease, she wrapped her arms around him and pressed him back against the mattress. They fell together and then he twisted so that he was lying on top of her, his mouth on hers again. Lifting her hips, she rubbed against him, his chest hair teasing her tender breasts, which were now almost too sensitive for her to bear, that blurred line between pleasure and pain. Every bit of her was burning up and the welcome, heavy weight of him felt so right. She plunged her hands into his hair, trying to pull him closer as their mouths ground together.

'Want you,' she breathed against his mouth. 'Now.'

Still kissing her, he stretched one arm out towards the bedside cabinet, fumbling with the drawer. And fumbled and fumbled. At last, with a curse, he pulled away from her mouth and she giggled.

'Don't laugh. I'm trying to be smooth here,' he grumbled, although amusement danced in his eyes.

She bit lightly on one of his fingers which had strayed across her face as he reached into the drawer and felt him take a sharp breath.

At last he'd ripped the packet open and was now balanced above her, his blue eyes almost sapphire as their gazes met. In a wordless exchange he asked again if she was sure and she lifted her hips.

Nick had never believed in soulmates or the 'one'. What Nick wanted eventually in life was a marriage as solid, content and affectionate as his parents'. All that had been blown out of the water in the space of an hour.

He stared up at the ceiling, his body soft and sated, his brain buzzing. Disbelief danced with excitement while Maddie, oblivious to the explosive realisation, slept next to him, her head nestled into his neck, her hand splayed on his chest and her breathing deep and even. Idly, he stroked his fingers across the top of her bare shoulder.

Shifting carefully so as not to disturb her, he looked down at her profile and smiled at the memory of her first angry kiss. That was the moment he knew. The knowledge so sharp and clear it had knocked all those clichéd thunderbolt, struck by lightning descriptions out of the park. That angry honesty. That was what he liked about her so much. Forthright, frank. An equal partner. Being responsible for what she wanted. With a wry smile he dropped a barely-there whisper of a kiss on her forehead.

'Thought I'd told you about that,' mumbled Maddie,

her eyes opening, already her expression full of mischief and wickedness.

His smile widened. 'Just testing the waters.' Turning on his side, he lowered his mouth to hers to kiss her properly. No second invitation needed, her body stretched against his, eager, warm and generous. All his, he thought, gathering her and hugging her against him, affection rather than sex this time. She wound her arms around his neck, the tip of her nose against his, her smile sleepy and feline.

'Consider the waters well and truly tested,' she murmured. 'What time is it?'

He laughed. Definitely the one. 'Back to practicalities.'

She hoisted herself up, propping her head on her arm, her elbow bent, not the least bit worried about the sheet dropping to her waist. 'I'm all out of rose petals.'

'And . . .' he paused and swallowed '. . . I wouldn't have you any other way.'

She caught the nuance. 'You wouldn't?'

'No.' He lifted his fingers, tracing her lips with a gentle promise, his eyes never leaving hers.

He felt her still, as if the word had stopped her.

'Oh.' She said it so quietly.

'Corny, but I've never felt like this, with anyone.'

'Oh,' she said again, her eyes wide, searching his face.

'It's as if everything, every girl along the way, has added up to this point. To you.'

He was so aware of her, the slight hitch of her eyebrow, the wary indrawn breath and the guarded lift of her chin.

'I'm not imagining this?' she asked and it tugged at his heart to hear the slight vulnerability in her voice, but at the same time his heart leapt, relieved that he wasn't going out on a limb here.

'I didn't think you even liked me,' she added and he could almost see the metaphorical arms folding.

'I didn't think I did. But –' he grinned '– you had me at the shorts.'

'Shorts!' Her indignant cry made him laugh. 'That's not romantic at all, Nick.'

'I'm sorry but any girl who can pinch her brother's shorts and not give a damn. Yup, you had me at shorts. Although it took me a while to realise.'

Maddie laughed and kissed him on the mouth. 'Good things come to those who wait.' She waggled her eyebrows and wriggled her body against his. 'But, unfortunately, all that activity has made me hungry. I'm starving.' The latter was delivered with real feeling, which made him roll his eyes.

'Better feed you then,' he said with one last kiss, rolling to the other side of the bed and opening a drawer to pull on some clean pants. 'It's ten to six. Lunch seems a long time ago.'

'It feels like another lifetime,' said Maddie, sitting up, running a hand through her rumpled hair, her words echoing his thoughts exactly. In fact he couldn't imagine life ever being quite the same again. It was as if he'd crossed some threshold that changed everything.

His heart hitched at the sudden anxious look that flooded her eyes and the swallow before she spoke again. 'I'm not very good at this . . .' She waved a vague hand, the other pulling the sheet up over her chest. 'Never sure of the rules.'

Rounding the bed, he sat on the side, tugging at one of her hands. 'Just be yourself. Just be honest. Just be you.'

'Just be me? But . . .' That worried look framed her hazel-flecked eyes, little lines running from the corner of her mouth.

He waited, letting her find her way. She leaned over to him, planting her mouth on his with purpose, pressing up against him as if she needed their touch to remind her of their connection. She sighed as she pulled away from the kiss. 'The problem is you're just so darned gorgeous.' She ran her fingers down his spine, curving around to stroke over his ribs.

'And so are you,' he groaned as her fingers hit a sensitive spot. She withdrew her hand as if she'd touched a live wire.

'No! No, I'm not. That's just it. I'm big. Clumsy. Not like Tara.'

'No, nothing like Tara,' he agreed. 'Better.'

'Don't talk rubbish,' she said, turning away from him.

'I'm serious.' He tugged at her arm, desperate to tell her what he'd just realised. 'Look at me.'

Reluctantly she turned to face him, a deep frown creasing her forehead.

'I'd have thought you'd be the first to tell me I've been a complete idiot.'

'You *are* a complete idiot. You're way too good for her.'

'That's not quite what I meant. You are so much better. When I woke up the other night, feeling like death and so homesick I could die, I saw you sleeping on the floor.' He swallowed, remembering the bleakness of the hour. Maddie touched his hand as if sensing his distress. He leaned forward and placed a gentle, reverential kiss of thanks on her lips. 'It . . . it made such a difference. Like you were a beacon. A link with what was right. It made me feel so much better.

'You've reminded me what's important. Family, love, loyalty, friendship, honesty. Since the day I met you, you've never given me an inch. You've challenged me. But, at the same time, around all these people you've been totally true to yourself.'

'So what happens now, with . . . with Tara?'

He grinned a little too cheerfully. 'She dumped me yesterday.'

Maddie grinned back, although she slapped a hand over her mouth. 'I'm not supposed to look too pleased, am I? That would be catty and not very nice. But you sound pleased too.'

'Let's say I was coming to the conclusion that we perhaps weren't meant to be, but it's a bit difficult to finish things with someone when they've brought you on holiday. It would seem a bit ungrateful. So when she issued me a sickbed ultimatum – either go to the Ellinghams' or it's over – even if I had been feeling up to it, I wouldn't have gone.'

'So you're not going to join them, now you're feeling better?'

'I'd rather boil my own bollocks in hot fat, quite frankly.'

'That's a bit extreme,' Maddie giggled. 'I'd rather you didn't.'

Chapter 25

'Pull the board past the paddle rather than pulling the paddle through the water,' instructed Nick from the paddle-board beside her, making it look easy.

'You mean I can't just stand on it?' She shook her wet hair out of her eyes, laughing at him. It had taken her the last twenty minutes just to stand upright on the darned thing. A glamorous date this was not, but then she hadn't laughed quite so much on a date before. She'd fallen in the sea so many times that she'd lost count.

'Well, you could and I could just stand and admire you –' Nick gave her the sort of look that made her forget the slight chill of the breeze on her wet skin '– but the whole point is to move.'

She grasped the paddle, wary now that she was finally upright, feeling the board wobble slightly as she shifted her weight.

'That's right; keep the paddle vertical. It will help you go straight.'

'I'll be telling you how to keep things vertical if you're

not careful,' she called across to him cheerfully as she gripped the paddle and took a cautious stroke forward.

'Keep your knees slightly bent.' He moved alongside as she gradually got the hang of it. Before long she was paddling along, although not quite with the same Greek god ease as Nick.

'Want to do a circuit before lunch?' he asked, pointing to the far side of the bay.

'You go first,' she said, a naughty grin tugging at the corners of her mouth. Nick shot her a quick suspicious look but she met his gaze with an air of total innocence. It was another perfect day, their third in the secluded bay, and today a slight crosswind ruffled the surface of the sea, making the sun's rays sparkle and glitter as they bounced off the water. And the view was spectacular, the muscles in Nick's back working smoothly in tandem as he paddled ahead of her. Watching the smooth coordination of his body reminded her of last night, a symphony of sighs and pleasure that even now had her feeling hot and bothered. Waking up in his bed this morning for the second time had felt the most natural thing in the world and it bemused her to find that being with Nick seemed so easy.

The previous two evenings they'd cooked together in the galley, eating under the stars on the deck with a bottle of white wine, talking with the ease of friends who'd known each other forever, the sort of conversation where they finished each other's sentences, which they found hilarious, making them burst into uproarious laughter, or where they kept unearthing unexpected similarities; they both hated mushrooms, they'd never seen a *Star Wars* film and didn't intend to, not even the new ones, and neither had been ice-skating or skiing.

Then last night, watching the sunset, a sky filled with pink tendrils fading to deep blue and the shimmer of gold on the sea, the perfect finale for the day, they'd sat side by side on the deck with a bottle of wine and the remnants of bread, cheese, cured ham and olives. Maddie's whole system had fizzed with barely suppressed excitement and every time she'd looked at Nick she'd wanted to pinch herself. The really lovely thing was that every time he caught her sidelong glances he'd lean over and kiss her or take her hand and squeeze it.

'Is this really happening?' she'd asked, studying the skyline as the sun dipped lower, casting her face into shadow.

'Yes,' said Nick.

She turned to face him. 'This has never happened to me before.'

'Explain *this*.' Nick's eyes had danced with that familiar amusement that made her heart sing.

'Man I fancy appears to fancy me back as much.'

'Better get used to it then,' he said, his hand resting on her thigh, warm and comforting. 'I'm not going anywhere – well, at least not for a few days.'

And it was that simple. At first. Perhaps because that

first night she'd been drunk on euphoria, a post-coital haze breaking down her usual defences.

Nick looked over his shoulder back at her, bringing her right back to the moment. Here, now, under the midday sun which was warming her shoulders.

'Everything all right?' He narrowed his eyes and slowed, waiting for her to draw alongside.

'What?' she asked, mirth dancing in her eyes.

'You're up to something.'

'Not at all. I was just . . .' she paused and deliberately scanned his body '. . . admiring the view.'

He returned fire, turning the tables on her with a searing look that shot her internal thermostat up to danger levels, making her wish she'd been a bit more circumspect.

'It's not bad from where I'm standing,' he drawled in a dangerous voice that made her think of cool sheets and slick, hot bodies. He was so much better at this than she was. Just one look and he had her thinking of getting him back into bed. She didn't seem to be able to stop thinking about him, his body or that delicious sigh of release when he'd come this morning.

'Maddie?'

She realised she was blushing. Grabbing her paddle, she pushed the blade in with force, making her board wobble precariously as she pulled ahead of him. As she passed she heard his low laugh and then felt her board tilt.

'You . . . you . . .' she cried as he tipped up her board

354

with his paddle, before overbalancing and falling in. He jumped straight in as she surfaced, spluttering, and pulled her into his arms to kiss her.

'I thought you needed cooling down. Your face is too obvious and now I'm beginning to think that perhaps paddleboarding wasn't such a good idea,' he muttered against her lips a few minutes later.

'We couldn't stay in bed all day.' Maddie's reproving tone held a hint of mischief, even though they had spent most of the previous day in his cabin.

'Want to bet?'

'It's far too nice to stay inside.'

'Who said anything about staying inside?' He winked at her and she burst into a peal of laughter. 'Those sun loungers on the top deck are very comfortable, I seem to recall.'

'You're terrible.' She splashed water at him.

'And you weren't the one that dragged me up there?'

'Dragged? You poor man, putting up such a fearsome fight against me.'

'I can't seem to help myself. Against you, I'm defenceless.' He stole another kiss. 'You're irresistible.'

'Yes, and if you keep that up I might start believing it,' said Maddie with a roll of her eyes.

Nick's face softened. 'I'm serious.'

Her heart did that proper missing-a-beat thing and she stared at him.

'I think I might be in love with you.'

'Oh,' she said, waiting for her heart to catch up as the rest of the world receded and all she could see was his deep blue eyes looking straight at her as if he could see all the way through to her soul. 'Can you say that again?'

'I think I might be in love with you.' Yup, her heart did it again but then she frowned, a questioning gaze roving over his face.

'I know it sounds a bit quick, but . . .' he lifted his shoulders '. . . there you go.'

Maddie let out a long slow breath, letting the sudden fear show in her eyes. 'When you know for definite, will you let me know?'

This was going too quick for her. The change in Nick's expression was so slight, so infinitesimal that if she hadn't been watching him closely she would have missed that tiny giveaway of disappointment. She put a hand on his shoulder. 'I . . .' she paused with a reluctant laugh '. . . I don't want to get it wrong. People don't fall in love with people like me.' Most of her knowledge of men was coloured by her mum's experiences. She'd been left too many times by blokes who wandered into their lives and wandered out again just as quickly and easily. Her dad being a case in point. She didn't tell many people but her siblings were all halves. And that was stupid because they weren't half anything – they were her brothers and sisters but they all had a different father. No wonder they all had such completely disparate personalities. But it had meant that Maddie avoided letting anyone get too close, until now.

'I'm not people,' said Nick, his mouth firming.

'No, you're not.' Her voice gentled with the quiet admission. 'I'm scared.'

He kissed her, his lips so gentle as they traced the outline of her mouth. She forced the truth up and out, looking at him intently. 'It's like I've got into a washing machine, it's on full spin and any minute I could be thrown out.'

Nick's eyes were full of understanding but he smiled and said, 'You have such a romantic turn of phrase.'

'Basically, I'm scared shitless.'

Nick touched her face. 'And, for the first time in my life, I'm not.'

They hauled the boards back on the boat, Maddie's heart humming with Nick's heartfelt words. She wanted to snip that final thread, the last one on a fraying rope, the one that anchored her to the fear and inability to trust, but she'd had a lifetime of men who had cadged her mum's fags, helped themselves to the beer in the fridge and sometimes the rent money. None of them ever stuck around for very long or promised her mum much of a future. In her heart of hearts, she knew Nick wasn't like that but there was just something that stopped her crossing the line.

She took refuge in tidying up, trying to put some space between them, and was relieved when Nick respected it, taking himself off to have a shower and after lunch, when she announced she was going to do some painting, he didn't sulk or brood. Giving her an affectionate kiss as she gathered up her materials, he settled himself in the shade with his book and a bottle of beer and watched her as she went up the stairs.

It took her a while to settle into work, her mind going round and round in circles about Nick, but eventually she lost herself in the magic of the creative process.

She started when her mobile phone began to ring.

'Hey, Ivan.'

'Maddie. Douglas is on his way back to the boat. You need to meet him at the port to take him back to the boat.'

Maddie's heart sank. 'When?'

'He's leaving Hvar in an hour. The taxi takes twenty minutes.'

'OK. I'll meet him there. I was going back to see Franjo anyway, so perhaps I can persuade them to stay in the town for a drink before going back to the boat.'

Damn, if they were all coming back she'd have to get some food supplies in. Her holiday was over. She swallowed. Nick and she hadn't thought this far ahead.

She gathered up her painting things and walked down the stairs, feeling like a condemned woman. Nick looked up and she almost burst into tears.

'They're coming back.'

'When?'

'Now.'

Their eyes met. 'What do you want to do?' asked Nick.

She shrugged, deliberately looking down at her feet. 'Go and pick them up.'

'You know what I mean.'

He had to push, didn't he, when all she wanted to do was barricade the entrance to the bay and not let anyone in or out.

'Isn't that down to you?' she said.

'I don't like keeping secrets.' There was a pause. She had no intention of filling in the gaps. Everything in her chest felt tight and constricted.

'Maddie. I'm not ashamed of us. I want to tell everyone but . . .' There it was – the big shouty capitals BUT.

'I'm worried about the way Tara will behave and how she'll treat you. She can be a bit unkind.'

Maddie turned and raised a sarcastic eyebrow. That was the understatement of the century.

'I don't want to make you the target of her . . . you know, comments. Being crew, you're in an invidious position.'

'Big word,' she said, finally looking up at him and then feeling shit when she saw the regret on his face. He was the good guy here, trying to do the right thing. 'I guess you're right.'

'It's only for a few more days and then at the end of the holiday we can make plans.'

She knew he was right but still, she couldn't bear the thought of the others coming back on board, especially not here. This little cove was theirs.

*

Maddie was absolutely dreading having the boat filled with everyone again, so it was a delightful surprise when they moored the launch in the harbour to find that only Douglas and Siri were there.

'Maddie!' Siri raced towards her and gave her a big hug and a warm kiss on her cheek. 'It's so good to see you.' She took a step back, holding her forearms. 'You look amazing. Having a holiday suits you.'

Douglas was clapping Nick on the back and then turned to Maddie. 'Well, you look in fine form, young lady.'

Maddie let out a gurgle of laughter. 'Douglas, you're only a few years older than me.'

'He's always been a bit of a fuddy-duddy,' said Siri in a loud whisper, a dimple appearing in her cheek as she said it.

'I feel bloody ancient.' His shoulders drooped and there was a decided sad twist to his mouth. 'Anyone fancy a drink? That taxi was bloody hot and no air-con.'

'Douglas, sweetie –' Siri rolled her eyes, but patted him on the shoulder '– the journey only took twenty minutes.'

'Twenty minutes too long, to my mind.' Douglas's eyes didn't match his perfunctory smile. 'Nick, a cold beer? Where do you suggest?' He looked around the harbour. 'Didn't get much of a chance for a look round, seems a pretty little town.' His mouth compressed again with what looked like regret.

'Cold beer is always a plan,' replied Nick, giving Maddie an uneasy glance. 'The bar over there is good.' He pointed to the same bar where they'd had a drink with Ivan and Gordana.

Once they were seated with four tall glasses of golden beer in front of them Nick asked the obvious question. 'So where's everyone else?'

Siri and Douglas looked at each other and then Douglas stared down into his beer as if it might contain the answer.

'We left them there,' said Siri with a touch of defiance and Douglas lifted his head slowly, his kind eyes unusually hard, and exchanged a look with her. Then he picked up her hand and squeezed it. 'Now, now, Siri.'

She shook it off. 'I'd had enough anyway,' she said with a contemptuous toss of her head. 'No fun without you there, Nick.' She batted her lashes at Nick in a way that was obviously fake but Maddie noted with interest that Douglas went very still, as alert as a gun dog awaiting orders, before shaking himself and saying, 'Bloody relief to have some peace and quiet. Non-stop noise, fuss, excitement at the Ellinghams'.' The poor man looked absolutely shattered. 'And the squealing. I swear Evie had invited every model from last year's London Fashion Week –'

'Paris too,' interrupted Siri, a grim set to her jaw.

'And they were all trying to outdo each other to get noticed. You know what Cory and Tara are like – can you imagine an entire roomful of them?' He shuddered. 'Hideous.'

'And you're away from it now,' said Siri, her hand stroking Douglas's in a soothing manner, as if his nerves needed calming. Siri caught Maddie's eye and shook her head very slightly.

Douglas, who'd closed his eyes and tilted his head back, missed this but mumbled, 'Thank heavens.'

'So, it's just the two of you,' said Maddie carefully to fill the sudden silence, which had stretched to uncomfortable.

'Yup,' said Siri. Me and Douglas. Douglas and me.' She shot him a challenging look.

Douglas let out a long heavy sigh as if admitting a defeat he was reluctant to accept. 'I'd had enough of Cory.' Douglas squared his shoulders and sighed again. 'Behaved badly.'

'She behaved badly.' Like a snake striking, Siri slapped her hand on the table, her bracelets jangling like alarm bells ringing, making the glasses shake, sending the beer slopping over the edges.

Douglas stiffened and kept perfectly still, which was all the more telling, the sort of tense posture people adopted when they were too scared to move in case it hurt more.

'Left her there.' His words were tight and clipped. 'Didn't actually tell anyone we were leaving.'

'Like she's going to notice,' scoffed Siri with a little shake of her head, but Douglas ignored her and carried on.

'Place was an awful squeeze. Full of phonies, wannabes.' He paused and then added with a quick, sad flash of humour, 'And swarming with bloody handsome gits like you, Nick, physiques like Atlas. Strutting their stuff around the pool. Enough to make a man move to the Arctic and never take his clothes off.' His rueful laugh was tinged with something else.

Siri grabbed his hand. 'Don't be ridiculous, Douglas, they had as much personality as cold puddings and most of them as thick as bricks.'

Douglas shrugged and squeezed her hand back. 'Thanks, love, but I've not got much to recommend me but money.' The sadness in his words made Maddie wince.

With a suddenness that shocked them all, Siri turned around and slapped him across the face. Maddie started. The sharp clap echoed around the enclosed square. A red palm print scalded Douglas's astounded face. Siri's face flushed pink, strident bright stripes highlighting her cheekbones while her eyes glittered like an angry ice queen.

There was a stunned silence as everyone in the small square turned their way. Maddie and Nick exchanged a nervous look. Then Siri burst into tears.

'S-sorry, Douglas. Sorry. I'm so sorry . . .' she sobbed but then dashed her tears away with her fist before getting to her feet, ramming her hands on her hips and standing over him '. . . but I just hate it when you say things like that.' Her face contorted in a weird combination of sternness, loyalty and exasperation. 'You're the kindest, nicest man I know and . . . and . . . and . . .' Running out of steam, she swallowed and did exactly what Maddie probably would have done and leaned down and kissed him. Even as an observer, Maddie could see she poured all her passion, love and longing into that fierce kiss.

Maddie turned to Nick, pinching her lips at the sight of the 'I'm a man – there's too much drama for me to take' look on his face.

'We've got a couple of chores to do,' said Nick, rising to his feet, almost knocking over his chair as he gathered his phone and his wallet from the table. 'Why don't we leave you here for a while?'

Maddie mouthed 'coward' at him but jumped to her feet too. There was no answer because it appeared that Douglas had pulled Siri onto his lap and was kissing her back with equal fervour.

'Well, that's a shocker,' said Nick as soon as they were out of sight, grabbing her hand and pulling her close to him, as if he'd missed the contact. 'Poor Douglas, that was a hell of a belt.'

Maddie rubbed her cheek in sympathy. 'I think she's kissing it better.'

'I should hope so, which reminds me –' Nick stopped and pulled her to one side of the deserted narrow cobbled street, pressing her up against the cool stone wall '– I haven't kissed you for ages.'

'Nick . . .' Her quick laugh was cut off as he rectified the matter with considerable enthusiasm, making her knees a little wobbly and leaving her breathless. Looking into his intense blue eyes, she swallowed as she tried to steady herself, conscious of the familiar thudding of her heart.

'It's going to be difficult to pretend around everyone else,' she said, touching her still tingling lips.

'I know.' Nick frowned. 'I don't want to . . .'

As they'd had to come into the harbour, they'd agreed with Ivan that they would meet him and Gordana at the gallery with the contract and the lawyer's comments to find out what Franjo had planned.

Nick took her hand, with a quick glance at his watch, and they began making their way towards the gallery.

'No, I know. I'm sorry about earlier. The disappointment, I guess, of knowing that we'd had such a perfect few days and that they've been cut short. You're right, it's the sensible thing to do. Even if Tara doesn't want you any more, like you said, it's going to be awkward enough without adding us into the mix.'

Maddie widened her eyes as a thought struck her. 'What will happen when Cory comes back?'

'Shit. Fans. Hitting,' replied Nick. 'Or maybe they won't come back. Perhaps Douglas can encourage the three of them to stay with the Ellinghams to the end of the holiday. There's only another week.'

'You don't clean their cabins; you should see how much stuff Cory and Tara have.'

'I carried Tara's suitcases, remember,' said Nick dryly.

Maddie shuddered. 'There's no way I'm packing all that up. Besides, everyone's got to get back to Split to the airport at some point.'

'They could catch the ferry from Hvar.'

Maddie raised a supercilious eyebrow. 'What, with the plebs? I can't see either of them doing that. And Douglas is too kind to abandon them, whatever happens with Siri.'

Nick grinned and shook his head. 'Siri and Douglas, I didn't see that coming. I knew she liked him but . . . looks like he likes her too.'

Maddie rolled her eyes. 'Well, you weren't looking. It's obvious that she's crazy about him. Hopefully he's just woken up to it.'

Nick lifted her hand and kissed her knuckles. 'You have to bear with us poor sods; we take a while to catch onto a good thing but once we do . . .' he paused, giving her a direct look that punched straight into her heart '. . . we don't let go.'

Ivan and Gordana were outside the gallery, wreathed in smiles. Their lawyer friend had OKed the contract and they ushered Maddie into the cool bright room ahead of them, exchanging glances brimming with excitement.

As soon as he looked up from the marble counter, Franjo beamed at her. 'I have a surprise for you.'

Clearly Ivan and Gordana had already spoken with Franjo before she'd arrived because they crowded behind her like her very own entourage, following as Franjo led her to the wall opposite.

'Oh! That looks wonderful.' Maddie clasped her hands tight in front of her, fighting back sudden tears.

Nick slipped an arm around her shoulders and gave her a squeeze.

'Looks like a proper painting to me,' he whispered into her ear.

The picture had been framed and, looking at it now, positioned in the very centre of one pale wall, she couldn't quite believe that she had painted it. It looked so professional in the stunning thick-edged white wooden frame, simple but elegant, the plain border highlighting the clear, bright colours of her subjects,: the sea, the sky, the sun and the people.

For a dizzying moment she simply breathed and looked at the picture, a sense of peace and calm settling over her initial excitement. Her picture. In a gallery. It didn't seem possible. She raised her head and gave Nick a brilliant smile, tears welling up.

'I need to take a photo, for Nina,' she said, scrabbling in her bag for her phone.

Ivan nudged her and she looked up at him. He nodded towards the picture. She frowned at him and looked back at the painting and then back at him, realising he was trying to tell her something.

He nodded again.

Then she spotted it: the tiny red dot to the right of the

picture on the wall. She whirled around to Franjo. 'You've sold it.'

'Provisionally, yes. If you are happy with the terms. We'd like to sell all three for you and more when you have them. Why don't you come through to the office and we can discuss the contract?'

'Of course they might not sell any more,' said Maddie twenty minutes later when they emerged from the gallery, her face a little pale but wreathed in a shell-shocked smile.

'Of course they won't,' said Nick in an ultra-cheerful voice. 'Pure fluke. It just happened to sell the minute it went on the wall.'

'I don't think so,' interrupted Gordana with an earnest lift of her chin, glowering at Nick. 'That couple that just went in were very interested.'

'She's right,' said Ivan. 'And I asked around. Gordana's boyfriend tells me Franjo is a good businessman. The gallery is well established, been here for fifteen years and he has a good reputation.'

'Well, he's sold a picture for me already. Six and a half thousand kuna. That's crazy. Seven hundred and fifty pounds. For one of my paintings.'

Nick nudged her. 'Told you so.'

With her lips twitching, 'Feeling smug now. Do I have to pay you commission?'

Nick's eyes lit up. 'Only in kind.'

She laughed. 'Name your price.'

In high spirits they went back to the little square to find Douglas and Siri sitting side by side, their hands clasped on the table.

'I think we should rename the gulet *The Love Boat*,' declared Ivan with a knowing look at Maddie and Nick.

Maddie blushed but Nick took her hand. Siri gave them both a broad beam.

'I think this calls for a celebration,' said Douglas, standing up still holding Siri's hand.

'Well,' said Maddie, not quite puffing out her chest but very nearly. 'The champagne is on me. I've just sold a painting.'

'That's amazing. Oh, well done, Maddie.' Siri jumped up and gave her a big hug, whispering in her ear, 'And bagged a damn fine man, by the looks of things. You and me have got a lot to talk about.'

Maddie squeezed her back. 'We have.'

'Why don't we buy some champers and take it back to the *Avanturista*?' suggested Douglas. 'I don't know about you but I've missed the old girl and I'd quite like to get back on board.'

'And I need to go back to work, Papa,' said Gordana. 'And Mama will be wondering what your plan is. Do you need to go back?'

Ivan looked at Douglas. 'The boat is moored in a little bay not far from here. Do you want to come back to port? Or stay there?'

'It's gorgeous,' said Maddie. 'And so peaceful.'

'Peaceful settles it,' said Douglas. 'I've had enough excitement, thank you.'

Siri ruefully rubbed his cheek. 'I am sorry.'

He placed his hand over hers. 'That kind of excitement I'm not complaining about, although I'd rather you didn't do it again.'

'I promise,' said Siri with uncharacteristic submissiveness.

'Why don't you bring Zita and the family for lunch tomorrow?' said Maddie impulsively. 'I'd like to see her again and thank her for all her help. Without her inside information, I couldn't have managed. You don't mind, do you, Douglas?'

'No, not at all.'

'I could take you fishing,' suggested Ivan. 'Catch something for dinner.'

'I'm not sure about that,' said Maddie, holding up both hands in protest. She didn't have the first clue about scaling or gutting fish.

'It's all right, Zita can do that for you,' said Ivan, laughing at her horrified gesture.

And suddenly it was all decided – tomorrow there'd be nine for lunch and Maddie was looking forward to it.

Chapter 26

Siri cornered her in the galley not long after they returned to the boat. Douglas, with a masterful turn, had decided to move into one of the spare cabins rather than go back to the one he'd shared with Cory and had disappeared below deck to move his things. Nick, spotting Siri and her determined intent to get the full story, had snagged a beer from the fridge and kissed Maddie on the nose, preparing to take evasive action.

'Cute,' said Siri. 'So how long's this been going on?'

She hoisted herself up onto one of the counters with a gin and tonic in her hand as Maddie tried to look busy as she prepared dinner. She'd decided to cook the pasta she'd bought the other day and toss it in truffle oil and lightly toasted walnuts and serve it with a rocket and Parmesan salad. None of which took that much effort or concentration, so it was difficult to avoid Siri's forthright questioning.

'Three days,' said Maddie a little shortly. The truth was she was a little nervous as to what Siri might say. How

Julie Caplin

much loyalty did the other girl owe Tara? After all, they'd known each other a lot longer and came from the same sort of world.

'Maddie . . .' There was warmth in Siri's wheedling voice, which made her turn around from her diligent Parmesan-shaving.

'Yes,' she said, her expression guarded.

'You're not worried about what I think, are you?'

Maddie sighed and put down the cheese grater. 'Yes.'

'But why?'

'Because I'm . . . the hired help, you know, and not like you lot.'

'Oh, for fuck's sake,' exploded Siri. 'I'm surrounded by idiots. First Douglas. Now you. I think I've walked onto the set of fucking *Downton* bloody *Abbey*! He's gone all "gentlemanly" on me and you're pulling the below-stairs crap.'

Maddie turned round with a flash of temper. 'It's all right for you –you all went to posh private schools and have parents who are loaded. My mum works down the local factory and only just makes enough to cover the rent. We were the kids on free school meals. I'm the first to go to university, which my mum views with deep suspicion. The way she carries on, you'd think I'd taken up witchcraft. And now I've graduated and haven't got some amazing job, my brothers and sisters never miss the chance to rub it in that it was a huge waste of time and that's what you get for thinking you're better than everyone else.' The truth was she felt like she was in some limbo between two worlds.

'Yeah, and have you stopped to look at what a bunch of fuck-ups we are, despite having money? Douglas has been trying to keep up with the Joneses and bankrolling bloody Cory, making himself miserable for the last two years.' She tugged at the big beaded necklace around her neck, her thumb rubbing the biggest amber bead in the centre. 'We're nothing special, just got lucky with our birth. Douglas's granddad was a coal miner. Douglas's dad was an engineer who happened to invent some clever widget and, lucky for me, asked my dad to go into business with him. They made the money which gave us the chance to go to good schools.

'I'm a complete screw-up. Been pining for the stupid bastard and taking every job I could to get out of the country away from him. And you do know Simon comes from a council estate himself?'

'What? Simon?'

'Yeah. He doesn't have a pot to piss in. Douglas bails him out all the time. They were at school together because Simon got some amazing tennis scholarship, but he's got no money.'

'Simon?' That couldn't be right. He was as posh as posh came.

'I promise. You should hear how he speaks when he goes home to Dagenham.'

'But . . . but . . .'

'Cory's no better. She likes to say she went to school in Cheltenham, as if it were Cheltenham Ladies College; what she means is she went to the local secondary school there. In fact, I think Tara probably is the only one who is properly posh and, let's face it, she's the biggest fuck-up of us all. Neurotic, with absolutely no self-esteem.'

Maddie winced.

'Exactly. So, out of everyone, well, perhaps apart from Nick, who seems a genuinely nice guy from a nice family, I'd say you were the most decent person of all of us. And please –' she twisted her lips '– don't you think that going to university despite your background shows you really wanted to go, shows that you've got more guts and initiative than the rest of us put together? Douglas and I went to uni because we didn't have a clue what else to do and it was expected of us.'

Maddie almost grated her thumbnail, her mind digesting all that Siri had said.

'Now, lecture over. And if you say anything that bloody stupid again I might just slap you too.' Siri's mischievous grin robbed the words of any genuine threat, although, on past performance, Maddie wasn't sure she wouldn't.

'Now, what can I do to help?'

'You can lay the table,' said Maddie. 'And get the champagne flutes out. We're celebrating tonight.'

'Hmm, yes. We might need more than champers. I've got to work out how to get Douglas drunk enough to take me to bed.'

Maddie laughed. 'Can't you just seduce him?'

'Is that what you did with Nick? I mean, how much more sodding obvious do I have to be?'

'I kissed him and . . .' she lifted her shoulders, her face lit with a misty smile at the memory '. . . let's just say he got with the programme pretty quickly.'

'Hmph, lucky you. Stupid idiot's got some stupid idea that we need to wait so that we're sure this isn't just a holiday thing. Doesn't want to ruin our friendship.' She pulled a face so grumpy that Maddie had to turn round to hide her smile.

'Ah,' she said, trying to sound sympathetic.

'Thing is,' Siri huffed, 'I've been bloody waiting since I was sixteen.'

'Oh, that is a long time. And you've never changed your mind?'

'Nope. As soon as I knew he was the one, that was it. I think it's a family trait. My dad was the same. Fell in love with my mum and she was engaged to someone else. But he waited it out. Although Mum cut it fine, only called the wedding off two weeks before. I'm like Dad, I've been waiting even though I thought it was hopeless.'

'Right, I'm taking these glasses up. Anything else? Gosh, it reminds me of that first night when you brought up that tray of glasses. Seems ages ago. And now . . . everything's changed. You. Nick. Me. Douglas. And it's amazing about your paintings. When you're exhibiting at Tate Modern, I'll be able to say, I knew her before she was famous.'

Maddie snorted. 'We'll see.' But the sale of the first picture had fired up her desire to paint more. As well as the business card that Bill had insisted she keep. Maybe, just maybe, she might be able to earn some money from her drawing and painting. She already had some ideas for beach scenes with typical holidaymakers on the British coast; perhaps she could visit places and paint the landscape for local galleries and shops.

It turned into one of the nicest evenings of the whole trip and Maddie felt like she was one of four friends on holiday. Siri kept her company in the galley while she cooked, fetching and carrying, and the two men did the washing-up afterwards.

'Will you stop topping up my wine glass, Siri?' said Douglas after their fourth round of cards, as the tealights flickered on the table on the deck. 'I'm not stupid, you know.' He folded his arms, attempting to look implacable, which made Siri's lips twitch before she peered at him over the top of her hand of cards. 'I could have suggested strip poker.'

'You're incorrigible,' he said. 'What would your mother say?'

'Why don't you ring her and ask her? You do know that she and your mum will be choosing wedding hats, so we might as well get on with it.'

Both Nick and Maddie tried to hide their sniggers as he took her hand under the table.

'Get on with it?' Douglas narrowed his eyes. 'You're such a romantic, Siri.'

'Well, I'm just being practical.'

'And I'm trying to be a gentleman and you're making it very difficult,' said Douglas very grumpily.

'Good,' said Siri with decided relish, a triumphant tilt to her head. 'And a gentleman is the last thing I want you to be.' She shot him a look that suggested so many indecent things that Maddie choked on her wine.

Nick tugged at her hand and pulled her to her feet, grabbing his wine glass. 'I think we'll go and do some stargazing on the top deck for a while.'

As they mounted the steps to the sun deck, carefully carrying their glasses of wine, Maddie whispered with another snigger, 'I feel quite guilty leaving him unprotected.'

Nick laughed. 'So do I but I'm more scared of Siri. She's a woman on a mission.' He put his arm around her to lead her towards the bank of sunloungers.

'Want me to be a woman on a mission?' murmured Maddie against his neck as she grazed his skin with a quick kiss.

He pulled her tighter to him. 'That boat is already well and truly docked. It's not going anywhere for a while.'

They dragged two sunloungers to the edge of the deck to look out over the dark bay, lit by a half moon reflected in the water. Maddie could hear the gentle lap, lap of the water against the hull of the boat. The clear night sky revealed thousands upon thousands of stars. More than Maddie had ever imagined were in the sky. 'I've never seen anything like it,' she said.

'No light pollution,' said Nick, wrapping an arm around her. 'Reminds me of home.'

As her eyes adjusted to the light, she studied his profile. He looked thoughtful as he stared out at the moonlit bay full of shadows and secrets. 'I sometimes go up on the fell on a summer's night. It's beautiful. Just look up. Stare for ages.' He took her hand, carefully lacing his fingers through hers and clasping it with the other in a careful protective gesture that for some reason made her heart pinch. 'Looking up like this makes me feel homesick.' She saw him swallow and squeezed his fingers between hers. 'I don't think I could live anywhere else. This is nice. But it's not home.' He paused and without turning around he asked very quietly, 'Think you could live on a sheep farm in the middle of nowhere? Twenty miles from the nearest supermarket. Cut off in the winter.'

In the quietness of the night, she felt the import of the question and took her time before answering.

'I lived in Paris.' She stared at the oasis of light on the water cast by the moon, reflecting on the contrast. 'One of the most beautiful, cosmopolitan cities in the world. And I was the loneliest I'd ever been. Meeting your sister and the others at the patisserie made such a difference. It made me realise it doesn't matter where you live, it's the people you live with, or around you, that matter.' She paused, realising that Nick had gone very still next to her, and leaned against him, feeling his rock-solid shoulder next to hers. 'I'd . . . I think I'd be willing to give it a go. I'm guessing it's quite beautiful.'

'I think so, but I might be biased.'

'Would people buy paintings of the scenery?'

Nick turned and kissed her temple, his warm breath fanning her face. 'If they were painted by you, definitely.'

'This is all moving fast.' Maddie felt anxiety rub low in her belly. Nick seemed so sure and confident. She felt way out of her depth.

'Maddie . . .' he kissed her gently on the lips '. . . there's no pressure. Let's just take each day as it comes. Who knows what tomorrow will bring?'

Chapter 27

Siri emerged looking tousled and triumphant the next morning as Nick was down in the galley cooking breakfast, the tantalising smell of bacon drifting up to the deck.

'Morning,' said Maddie. 'You look like the cat that's drunk an entire vat of cream and then some.'

Siri raised her arms above her head and stretched with a lazy groan. 'And then some.'

'Douglas succumbed to your womanly wiles, then.'

Siri sniffed and settled herself into the seat opposite. 'Was there any doubt?'

Maddie giggled. 'You terrified the poor man into it.'

'He needed to know what he's been missing all these years . . .' her voice dropped with sex siren huskiness '. . . and I can tell you he's been sadly neglected.'

Nick, who'd appeared behind her bringing up a pot of coffee, raised his eyebrows at Maddie. 'I think I've been neglected.' He attempted puppy dog eyes, putting the cafetière down in front of the two women.

Maddie burst out laughing. 'Not recently you haven't, you cheeky sod.'

'Where is he?' asked Nick. 'Is the poor chap still alive? I'm about to dish up breakfast; who wants one of my famous bacon butties?'

'Me, please,' said Siri. 'I am starving. And Douglas –' her lips stretched in a smug feline smile '– he's going to need quite a few. Needs to get his strength back.'

'Siri! You are awful.'

'I know,' she replied with a delighted grin.

'I know how he feels,' said Nick with a mournful look that had Maddie throwing a napkin at him.

'You're more than man enough; stop complaining and go and get my breakfast.'

'See, henpecked too.' Nick wiped a weary hand across his brow that had both the women laughing again. 'Ah, here he is. Morning, Douglas.'

'Morning,' Douglas trilled, looking extremely chipper and nothing like the shadow of a man that Siri had insinuated. In fact, Maddie thought he glowed with happiness. In a gesture of tenderness that made her own heart miss a beat, he came up behind Siri and wrapped his arms around her shoulders, rubbing his cheek against hers. Siri turned and smiled up at him. Yes, Maddie's heart was pooling into a soggy mess on the floor.

Halfway through breakfast, as they were all chatting through their plans for the day, Douglas began to pat his top shirt pocket and pulled out his phone.

'Simon, hi.'

Around the table everyone stilled.

'Today?' Douglas looked at his watch.

And, with that, the atmosphere around the table dampened as each of them receded into their own thoughts at the unhappy realisation everything was about to change.

To his shame, Nick found himself checking his cabin to make sure that there was no clue that Maddie had spent the last three nights in his bed. He hated the thought of eradicating all sign of her but he was conscious of Tara's return and all the attendant histrionics that could follow. He knew Tara well enough to know that she was quite capable of throwing a scene and upscaling it into a three-act drama.

Maddie had gone to pick up Ivan from Stari Grad, refusing his offer to accompany her. His last view of her, standing tall at the controls of the launch, had sent a shiver of foreboding down his spine. This really was it. Everything was about to change. But, he reminded himself, only for a few more days. He'd change his flight so that he could travel back to the UK with Maddie and then they'd make plans for the rest of the summer.

Siri had retreated to her cabin and Douglas had busied himself catching up with his office and his emails. For the first time in a couple of days, Nick was back to that feeling of not having anything to do, hence wandering around his cabin, which was full of reminders of Maddie. He collected up a T-shirt she'd left on his chair, the toothbrush that had taken up residence in the glass by the sink and the floral shower gel that perfumed the bathroom. It wasn't much to show for four idyllic days.

When Ivan returned with Maddie, Nick helped her weigh anchor and together they stood at the rail.

'I'm going to miss this little cove,' said Maddie, putting a hand on top of Nick's gripping the metal.

'Me too.' He turned her towards him and kissed her on the mouth with gentle reverence, trying to convey how he felt about her. 'This isn't the end. It's just a . . .'

Maddie exhaled. 'I feel like the fairy tale is over. We're going back to real life and it won't ever be the same again.'

'It will, I promise you. We only have to pretend for a few days. I've been thinking, when we get a decent Wi-Fi connection back in Hvar, I'm going to change my flight so that I can fly back with you.'

'What, to Birmingham?'

'Why not? It makes no difference to me. Gatwick is hardly down the road for me. I've got a long journey home once I land, whatever I do.'

'OK.' Maddie lifted a hand to his face, stroking the stubble under her fingers. He turned his face to press a kiss into her palm. For a second she wanted to close her hand and hold onto it, like capturing a butterfly.

'And . . .' he paused, lifting a hand to cup her face, his blue eyes solemn '. . . then maybe you'd come up to the farm for a visit, for a month or something, see how you find it.'

384

Her heart expanded in her chest. 'I think I'd like that.'

Together they gazed out at the water as the engines began to throb and the boat slowly began to move towards the hidden mouth of the bay. Holding her gaze, Nick moved sideways so that he was shoulder to shoulder and hip to hip with her, as if he needed to make the most of all the contact he could with her before they arrived in Hvar. 'You could . . .' he wrinkled his nose '. . . you could still visit my cabin.'

With a shake of her head, she turned her head, looking out to the open sea. 'I don't want to skulk about.'

'I don't really blame you. You deserve better.'

'Yeah. I do.'

'But I don't want to upset Tara. We might have broken up but she doesn't deserve to have her nose rubbed in it. Even though she dumped me, I think she'd take rejection hard. She's not as self-confident as she appears, you know.'

'Which makes me like you all the more. Choosing not to be a bastard,' said Maddie, not as convinced as Nick that Tara was some fragile flower that needed to be protected. She certainly had some issues but there was a scrappiness about her that suggested Tara would fight like a cat to keep what she wanted and would do anything to stop being bettered by someone else.

Maddie was pretty sure that if Tara found out that he'd chosen a strapping, broad, common girl over her she would find it a huge insult and hell would have no fury.

And goodness only knew what was going to happen with the Cory, Douglas and Siri triangle.

As the boat neared the harbour of Hvar, where Ivan had managed to secure a mooring, Maddie noticed Siri pacing around the deck.

'You OK?' Just watching her walking towards the guard rail and then back again made Maddie feel jittery. Douglas had taken himself off to the bow of the boat and stood with his shoulders hunched up to his ears.

'Yes. No. Yes. No.' Siri glanced towards Douglas, her face strained and white. 'Yes. Terrified. I'm worried that Cory will do the sob story bit and Douglas will feel sorry for her. She's been texting him but I've no idea what she's said or how he's responded. How about you?'

Maddie twisted her mouth and sighed. 'As Tara dumped Nick, I'd like to say I'm not quite so worried but I feel . . .' She wrapped her arms around her stomach. 'I don't like it, but we've agreed that we'll keep this to ourselves. And I do . . . I do see the sense in it. No point rocking the boat.' Her words belied the uncomfortable knotted sensation in her stomach which seemed to tighten with each wave they crested on the way into the harbour.

'What about Nick?' asked Siri, looking around for him.

'He's on the top deck, reading.' And the last time she'd been up there he seemed to be on exactly the same page. He'd brushed his fingers against hers with a small tense smile.

As they neared the port the number of yachts and craft

increased, converging on the harbour. It felt like a loud, frantic juvenile party after the quiet serenity of Tajna bay, an insult adding to the injury of having to leave the quiet secret cove. Siri joined Maddie and Nick in putting the fenders out over the side of the boat, but none of them spoke, all working in careful silence.

Ivan backed the gulet into a slot between two much larger yachts to take up their prize mooring on the main promenade. Conscious of the interested eyes of the tourists, Maddie jumped off the stern, thankfully feeling almost like a pro as she tied off the lines around the heavy cast iron mooring posts. She almost had to push one interested holidaymaker out of the way as he tried to take a photo and he was quickly followed by a second, all keen to see how the other half lived. My goodness, it was crowded. After Stari Grad, Hvar's bustle and cosmopolitan buzz came as a shock to the senses. The contrast was stark. Everyone here seemed younger, shinier and more alert, their eyes constantly scanning for the next new thing, when they were able to tear their gazes from their phones. She wanted to blink to shut it all out. Colour, noise and busyness on all sides. This time they were right in the thick of it. Along the row of boats, enormous-hulled superyachts reared up from the waterfront like monolithic icebergs dominating the quayside, attracting the attention of crowds of tourists mooching along in swarm-like configurations while in search of the smartest restaurant.

*

387

As soon as they were berthed, Maddie decided to head to the supermarket to stock up on water and beer.

'I'll come with you,' said Nick. Neither acknowledged that it was a delaying tactic to avoid being on the boat when the others arrived.

As they walked through the crowds side by side, as close as they could without touching, his hand brushed Maddie's. He wanted to snatch it up and hang onto her, swamped by a sudden fear that she'd be separated from him in the busy throng of tourists. After the peace of the cove, Nick felt hemmed in, claustrophobic and more out of place than ever. Anyone would think he was mad but just now he longed for them both to be up on Starbridge Fell, Rex at his feet and even . . . he smiled at his contrariness . . . no, perhaps not in the pouring rain.

Out of the corner of his eye he caught a blur of filmy scarlet fabric teased by the sea breeze rising in the air as a small figure burst into action.

'Nick!' The shriek gave him the barest of warnings before Tara appeared in front of them, all tumbling hair, big eyes and bright red lipstick. He gave a quick sidelong glance at Maddie, his heart clenching at her suddenly impassive expression. The urge to grab her hand hit him again with a deepening sense of foreboding.

Tara dropped her case with a dramatic clatter. 'Oh, Nick, Nick.' Repeating his name like a fervent prayer, she clasped her hands in front of her with a look of adoration and relief, before launching herself at him with the determined aim of a tactical warhead. He tried to catch Maddie's eye but she looked past him, the distance between them opening up before his eyes.

For a moment he felt suffocated by the flimsy fabric floating up into his face as Tara rained kisses over his cheek and neck and he wanted to reach out to Maddie to save him.

'Nick, Nick! Oh, Nicky, darling.' She linked her thin arms behind his neck, one of her nails inadvertently scratching him. 'Oh, I've missed you so much, darling.'

Somehow she'd managed to drape her tiny body over him and was not going to be detached by any means, her legs wrapped around his waist like a small determined bushbaby clinging to a tree.

Over her shoulder he caught sight of Maddie's narrowed and suddenly expressionless eyes and sent her a what-the-hell-do-I-do? look. He did his best to disentangle Tara, pulling his head to an awkward angle in a bid to avoid her enthusiastic kisses as if dodging an overfriendly dog trying to lick him to death. Every time he unpeeled an arm or a leg, another part of her would clamp onto him. Maddie's expression was one of amusement at first but, the longer he battled to pull himself free, it changed to sour repulsion before finally settling into stone-faced as she folded her arms, the rest of her body stiff and awkward.

It fired up his resolve. 'Tara.' Using a firmer hand, he finally unstuck her and put her down on the pavement but, almost as soon as she had both feet on the ground, she immediately curled her arm around his with surprisingly vice-like strength and leaned against him.

'Darling. What's the matter?'

He looked over at Maddie, who was stiffer than ever now. Tara caught his gaze and whipped her head around. He felt the tension in her body as she turned around and said to Maddie, 'Did you want something?'

Maddie pressed her lips together, her eyes dark and fixed, her mouth clamped shut in a fixed line. She lifted her chin and looked at Nick. Like a complete idiot, he hesitated a second too long. Maddie gave him a disdainful look, wheeled around and marched off with quick, what he was well aware were, angry fuck-you strides. He caught his lip between his teeth as he watched her go, his heart heavy, almost expecting the sea of tourists in her path to part.

They'd talked about this but he hadn't quite appreciated how shit it would feel. Even telling himself that he'd told Maddie in so many different ways how much he cared for her wasn't any sort of consolation. He'd asked her to come to stay in Northumberland with him. She had to know how he felt about her. But suddenly he didn't feel very confident.

He looked down at Tara, who was looking up at him with that familiar adoring expression and immediately he felt a pang of guilt. Oh, double shit. He was in so much trouble. She was a complicated, troubled woman and he owed her common courtesy and kindness.

'Hey, Tara. How are you?' His attempt at nonchalance almost stuck in his throat. The words came out stilted and awkward.

'Oh, darling Nicky, I'm so much better for seeing you. I've missed you so much and I felt so bad that we argued. You didn't answer any of my texts. I've been so worried, thinking that you don't love me any more.'

The words stalled in his throat as she looked up at him, her huge eyes shimmering with tears.

Before he could say that he hadn't had any texts, she gripped at his arm. 'I wasn't very nice to you, was I?' Her chest heaved and she clutched at her throat, her beautiful face crumpling. The obvious drama of the scene was starting to draw the gaze of the tourists around them.

'You . . . you . . .' He had to say this. 'You made it pretty clear that things were over between us.'

'Don't be silly, darling. I was just upset. It felt like you didn't care any more. And I said things I didn't mean. It's been awful without you. I've never been so unhappy in my life.' Her voice rose and quite a few people stopped and turned their way.

This wasn't supposed to happen. Nick swallowed.

'I am never going to leave you like that again,' she declared in such a loud voice that he winced. A few people standing nearby smiled at her words.

'Nicky, darling.' She paused, her eyes fixed on his face, and then in front of everyone she dropped to her knees. 'I love you. Will you marry me?'

391

Chapter 28

'Oh, Tara.' Cory, standing behind her, clapped her hands together and jumped up and down on the spot next to Simon, whose startled scowl was quickly replaced with an amused smirk. 'That's so romantic.'

Around them the quayside erupted with cheers as some people nearby began clapping and others took photos on their phone.

Nick's brain was mush, his tongue stuck to the roof of his mouth and his feet rooted to the spot. A hot flush burst over him, the heat climbing steadily up his neck to his face.

Tara didn't move but stayed in place, looking up at him, her eyes shining.

He felt sick as voices in the crowd began to call out.

'Come on, man, say yes.'

'If you don't, I will.'

'Say yes.'

'Say yes.'

'Say yes.' The refrain was taken up, quickly becoming a chant.

'Get up,' he muttered out of the side of his mouth. 'This is embarrassing.'

Her smile sweetened. 'All you have to do is say yes.'

'Tara . . .'

The chant was growing stronger.

Nick didn't even dare look round; his heart was banging hard in his chest.

Her mouth quivered. 'Nick. Don't do this to me. You love me. You know you do. I love you.'

He couldn't embarrass her in front of all these people. Image was everything to Tara; he couldn't be that cruel. It could all be sorted out later when they were on the boat. But how did he avoid embarrassing her in front of all these people without lying or making a promise he had no intention of keeping?

He pulled her to her feet. He had to be honest with her. He had to tell her it was over.

But, before he could say anything, she wrapped her arms around him and mashed her lips against his, her hand clamping his head in position in an endless pastiche of a kiss. His teeth were forced into the soft flesh on the inside of his mouth as she ground her mouth against his in a show of surprising strength.

Another loud cheer went up around them as everyone assumed the answer was yes when he finally disentangled himself, too shocked to say anything.

'Congratulations,' screamed Cory and kissed Tara on each cheek. 'I have to be a bridesmaid.'

'Of course you will be,' said Tara with a little skip, linking her arm through Nick's, beaming around at the people still taking photos.

'Over here, Tara,' called a voice. Both he and Tara looked towards the voice, straight into the lens of a big black camera. Nick was grateful that his dark sunglasses hid his furious glare but Tara immediately stopped and threw out one hip in what he recalled was her model-being-papped pose. 'Congratulations.' The photographer took a succession of quick photos before, with a cheery wave, he disappeared into the crowd.

Dear God, could this get any worse? Nick tugged at Tara's arm, trying to get back to the boat as quickly as possible, his brain threatening to explode with all the ramifications, but she'd dropped his arm and was now gaily chatting to Cory, her hands waving vivaciously, and he caught fragments of the conversation.

'Summer wedding, although winter . . .'

'Velvet cloak. Midnight-blue.'

'Gorgeous with your colouring.'

'Flowers . . .'

Simon handed him the handle of Tara's pull-along case, saying in a flat voice, 'Congratulations.' The other man's knowing smirk and supercilious attitude had slipped.

Nick, too light-headed and sick to the stomach, gave him a curt nod; he couldn't bring himself to speak.

Anything he said before he could speak with Tara would be cementing the whole lie.

As Simon handed the cases onto the yacht, Tara darted past them, running lightly across the gangplank before Nick had chance to grab her and tell her they needed to talk.

'Siri, Siri,' she called, running up the stairs to the main deck. 'Guess what.'

Grimly he chased after her, but it was too late. Siri was standing looking shocked and horrified, her gaze swinging between Tara and him. Douglas, rising up from behind his laptop, came to stand behind Siri. 'Nick?' The disapproving frown made Nick raise his hands in defence.

'Maybe I should ask you to marry me,' said Cory, appearing on deck followed by Simon, going straight up to Douglas with a sly smile, flicking her waterfall of hair over one bare shoulder.

Siri stiffened and Douglas took a step closer, putting a hand on her forearm.

'Actually, Cory, perhaps we could have a little private chat.' Douglas's kind eyes looked a little sad, despite which, Nick envied him. He was going to make a clean breast of things and handle things properly.

'Why don't we go up to the sundeck?' Without waiting for an answer, Douglas turned and went towards the steps.

As Cory followed him, she glanced over her shoulder to Tara and flashed a triumphant smile, mouthing, 'Double wedding.'

Siri folded her arms and glared at Nick; he glared back. He didn't need her unsubtle reminder.

'Tara, we need to talk.'

'Not now, sweetie. I'm exhausted. Pulling my case in that hot sun. Honestly, why is there never a taxi when you need one? I need a cold drink. Where is that serving girl?'

'I'll get you one,' said Simon, jumping in quickly as if keen to escape the strange atmosphere.

'Anyone else?' he asked with a touch of desperation, looking Nick's way.

'No,' said Siri curtly, her eyes trained on the staircase.

Nick shook his head just as there was a scream of outrage from upstairs and a loud crash. Simon winced and made a hasty exit down towards the galley.

'You bastard,' Cory's voice wailed. 'You can't do this. You don't finish with me. You'll regret this.'

One of the small side tables sailed past the deck, bumping along the side of the boat, bouncing off the neighbouring boat before landing in the water with a loud splash.

Siri's lips pinched together. 'Oh, dear, someone's not happy.'

There was another crash from upstairs. More screeching and the sound of a scuffle.

'What's going on?' asked Tara in a way that struck Nick as just a little too innocent and wide-eyed.

Siri gave her a quelling look. 'Douglas is calling time.'

'No,' breathed Tara. 'Poor old Cory.' Her face softened in sympathy although there was the briefest flash of something in her eyes which anyone who didn't know her might have taken for malicious satisfaction.

'And what's this about an engagement?' asked Siri, suddenly arch and enquiring, her eyebrows raised at Nick.

'Oh, Siri, darling, it's so exciting.'

'And so sudden,' the other woman said dryly.

Nick closed his eyes. How could everything have gone so horribly wrong in such a short space of time? If only they could have stayed in their secret cove.

From upstairs the scuffling sounds were more heated.

'I'll go and give Douglas a hand.' Siri smiled grimly at Tara and Nick. 'Perhaps toss her overboard.'

'Tara,' said Nick as soon as Siri's foot touched the bottom step. 'We have to talk.'

'Yes, there's so much to discuss. Do you think we should put an announcement in *The Times*?'

'No, I don't. Tara . . .'

Her eyes were suddenly hard, dark and bright. 'Yes?' She raised a regal eyebrow.

'We can't get engaged.'

The brow sailed a touch higher. 'What do you mean?'

'Look, I'm sorry but . . .'

Her lower lip began to quiver. 'You mean you don't want to. But . . .' A sob escaped. 'But I love you, Nicky.'

'No, you don't.'

'But I do,' she wailed.

Nick felt the pinch of his fingernails in his palms. 'Tara, it's never going to work.'

'But . . . but . . .' Tears began to roll down her doll-like face.

He sat down beside her and took her hand. 'I'm really sorry.'

With a dainty sniff, she tried to control her tears. 'You . . . y-you m-mean y-you d-don't l-l-l . . .' She buried her face in her hands and began to sob. Reluctantly, he put an arm around her.

'Shh, Tara, don't cry. I'm sorry. Please don't cry.' He'd never felt so inadequate in his life. It was a shock to realise that she felt like this about him. Most of the time, he'd felt he was the one running after her and trying to keep up.

But Tara was in full flow, weeping with her hands over her face, sobbing incomprehensible sentences. 'You don't l-love m-me . . . W-what will I do without you? Can't b-bear it. P-please don't break up with me. W-we can carry on. P-pretend I never asked you. It w-was t-too soon.'

He held her in his arms, feeling the sobs rack her frail body, guilt gnawing a hole in his stomach. Stroking her hair, he tried to comfort her. 'Hey, it's all right. Shh.'

Finally she stopped crying and turned up to face him, her eyes full of sadness. 'I know I jumped the gun but . . . oh, everyone is going to know.' Her face crumpled again. 'Everyone will know.' She began to cry again. 'I'm going to look such a fool. Everyone is going to laugh at me.'

'No one needs to know,' he said, rubbing her back in what he hoped was a soothing way.

'Everyone is going to know. That paparazzi, Jack Flynn, he knows who I am. He'll have already filed that photo.'

Nick sighed. 'Maybe we can tell him it was a mistake.'

Tara shot him an angry stare. 'A mistake. And what sort of story would that make? You turning me down. The papers would love that. All those jealous people seeing me making a fool of myself.' She swallowed, lifting her face to his. Although it was hard to resist the terrible sadness filling her big soulful eyes, he had to tell her.

'Tara, I'm sorry. It's over.'

She burst into a fresh gale of tears and he patted her hand, feeling totally ineffectual.

'P-please don't do this to me, Nick. It will ruin my reputation. And once that picture goes public all the paps will want pictures of us. They'll be swarming around. P-lease. P-lease. I'm begging you, don't finish with me.'

Nick closed his eyes, swallowing hard, hating that he was the cause of her pain. She clutched his forearms, her hands like tiny talons gripping the bones.

He sighed, his stomach turning itself inside out.

'P-please.' Somehow she'd found her way onto his lap.

'Tara, I can't. I don't want to hurt you, but . . . we're too different.'

'Nooo!' she wailed, winding her arms around his neck, staring earnestly up into his face. 'You're perfect for me. Everyone says what a great couple we look.'

And that was it, the words that made him realise that they'd never stood a chance. Her distress had surprised him; he'd half expected her to treat him with icy reserve and snub him, this clinging desperation made him feel guilty and an absolute bastard. But Tara's affection for him was skin-deep; she didn't care about him in the way that he cared about Maddie. It was all about looks and appearance.

'No, Tara, it really is over,' he said gently, once again trying to peel her limbs from his and firmly putting her arms down by her sides.

'At least wait until we get home,' she pleaded, immediately putting her arms around his neck again. 'Pretend to be engaged to me until we go home. Then we can just allow things to fizzle out, as far as the press and social media are concerned. In a few weeks' time I can be heartbroken . . . but no one needs to know the details.'

He sighed. He could give her that much, if it meant helping her to save face, but he needed to speak to Maddie as soon as she got back to the boat. Explain things.

A creak made them both look up.

Too late.

Maddie was silhouetted by the sun behind her, the rays spreading out like a halo around her body. Nick couldn't see the expression on her face. He didn't need to. He had all the answers when she swung round and stomped off down to the galley.

'Honestly, that girl, she's like an elephant, so big and ungainly, crashing about all the time.'

Chapter 29

Maddie rammed bottle after bottle into the fridge, satisfying crash after satisfying crash. Bastard. She stuffed the lettuce into the salad drawer, heedless of the crushed leaves, imagining she was mashing Nick's head in there. Fifty-eight minutes. Fifty-eight pitiful minutes. That was all it had taken for him to go back to Tara. Not even a full freaking hour. She pushed her fists hard into her eye sockets. She. Was. Not. Going. To. Cry.

Oh, dammit, she was.

Why was she even surprised? Tiny Tara versus her. What had she been thinking? A handy rebound while Tara was away. God, she was so, so stupid. That was all it had been and she'd been so desperate for Nick to like her she'd fooled herself into thinking it could be more. What an idiot.

The sight of Tara curled up in his lap like a tiny fairy, her golden head on his shoulder and him stroking her long hair down her back made her feel as if she'd run full tilt into a brick wall.

'Hey, stranger, good to see you again.'

Maddie whirled round to find Simon standing on the threshold of the galley. For once he seemed subdued.

'Hi,' she said, ducking her head with an unladylike sniff. With the exception of Nick, he was one of the last people she wanted to see right now.

'You OK? I'm guessing that lettuce has upset you somehow.'

'I'm just busy,' she said with her back to him. Couldn't he see she just wanted to be left alone to mistreat salad?

'You don't want any company?' His question sounded a little on the plaintive side.

Maddie didn't bother hiding her exasperated sigh. 'I'm just sorting dinner. What's the matter?'

Why the hell didn't he get the message and bugger off?

'Everything has just gone tits-up. Did you know that Douglas was planning to dump Cory?' There was a touch of accusation in his voice as if he should have been part of the decision-making process.

'Not . . . specifically.' She was irritated with his lack of awareness. He was supposed to be Douglas's friend; surely he thought Cory had behaved badly. 'I guessed something was on the cards. What with him leaving her at the party and all that.'

Simon shook his head. 'I never thought he'd do it. I suppose she did behave abominably at the Ellinghams'.'

'You suppose.' Maddie whirled round to face him. What was wrong with these people?

Simon looked puzzled and lifted his shoulders in an indifferent shrug. 'She's very naughty, but even so I'm surprised he's called her bluff while we're still out here. Going to make things very uncomfortable.'

'She's a grown woman, not a toddler,' snapped Maddie. 'And what do you mean, called her bluff?'

'He'll take her back. She'll be nice to him for a few days, behave herself, and it will all be back on.'

'I wouldn't be so sure about that,' replied Maddie with a brief sense of satisfaction, thinking of the rumpled, rather shy figure of Douglas that had emerged this morning with a bubbly, very pleased Siri. Oh, yes, she'd looked like a woman who'd bagged her man.

Thinking of them also made her think of her own start to the day . . . Her heart pinched at the memories that flooded insensitively into her head. The early morning sun slanting across the pillow picking up the natural highlights in Nick's hair. Play-fighting over the shampoo in the shower. Him with a teasing smile, wrapping her up like a mummy in a towel and holding her fast while he kissed her.

'And have you heard the other news?'

'What other news?' Maddie pulled open the dishwasher and began to unload the plates, wishing he'd go away.

'The Neanderthal and Tara are engaged.'

'What?' A plate slipped out of her numb fingers, hitting the floor with a ching before rattling in reverberating circles on the floor and coming to a full stop halt.

405

Simon rolled his eyes and looked heavenward. 'Precisely. You'd have thought she has better taste.'

'Engaged?' Maddie repeated dully.

'Yeah, engaged.'

'When?' Maddie could barely choke the word out. Engaged. Engaged. Engaged. The word lost meaning as it rattled around inside her head. Engaged, like a toilet or as in otherwise occupied, or to be married?

'This afternoon. Surprised she hasn't dragged him off ring-shopping yet. I got the impression it was all very spontaneous.'

'Spontaneous?' she repeated, her words barely above a whisper.

'Yeah, overcome by passion. Down on one knee and everything.'

Nick had proposed. The pain in her chest bloomed hard and fast and kept growing bigger and bigger and bigger until she thought she might suffocate with it. She had to press her hand to her sternum to try and stop everything bursting out.

'Absence making the heart fonder, clearly.' Simon's mouth turned up into a sneer. 'I thought Tara would grow out of the novelty, but clearly not.'

Maddie turned her back on him, her vocal cords too tight to speak. The white plates in the dishwasher were blurry and out of focus. When she tried to pick up another, her finger and thumbs missed. Like her brain, they didn't seem to be working.

406

Simon was still talking.

Why wouldn't he just leave? Maddie grasped the cutlery tray, the rack shaking in her hand. The forks were tempting. She might stab him if he didn't shut up.

'Maddie . . . are you listening?' Simon's petulant voice pierced her thoughts.

'I'm a bit busy,' she snapped, grasping at anger in protection.

'Fine,' he said, as sulky as a toddler, and thankfully disappeared.

Maddie slumped against the counter; her stomach felt hollowed out, everything numb. How did you go from . . . from whatever she thought they'd had . . . to engaged? Was she really that gullible? Nick owed her an explanation but at the moment she couldn't bear the thought of speaking to him.

She took her time in the galley, putting all the plates away with determined, methodical precision, cleaning the range top even though it didn't really need doing. She rearranged a few shelves in the cupboard before emptying the fridge and giving it a thorough clean, putting everything back in careful order.

And still Nick didn't come. She curled her lips, glancing to the doorway. You'd have thought she deserved some explanation. Perhaps even an apology. An acknowledgement at least. *Sorry, I changed my mind.*

When she slipped out of the galley up the back stairs

to her cabin, she cast a quick glance towards the deck area. Tara was on Nick's lap, her arms wrapped around him like a limpet doused in superglue.

Up in her cabin, Maddie sat on the edge of the bed dry-eyed, gripping the sheets with both hands, still hoping that Nick would come and find her. Come and tell her that it was all a big mistake.

She waited for two hours.

Quite how she got through dinner, Maddie wasn't sure. Conversation at the dinner table seemed heavy and leaden. On one side of the table Cory and Simon kept up an exclusive low-voiced conversation between them, Cory every now and then throwing spiteful, narrowed-eyed glares at Douglas. Opposite them, Siri and Douglas chatted in their usual easy-old-friends way, although both of them kept slipping her apologetic guilty smiles. Maddie steadfastly refused to make eye contact with either of them. She couldn't bear to; it might loosen something inside her and it was taking everything she had to hang onto her dignity.

Every time she came back to the table with another dish: the salad, the grilled fish fillets, the basket of bread, she was horribly aware of Tara's lean yoga-bendy limbs staking their claim on Nick. One vine-like arm linked through his, while one of her legs draped indolently across his lap and her head leaned against his shoulder. She couldn't seem to leave him alone, one minute stroking his neck, the next playing with his hair. Maddie took a certain amount of satisfaction in seeing Nick squirm a little; he didn't look particularly happy with all the over-the-top PDA. Served him right. He'd got what he deserved, although she was aware of his pleading eyes on her.

Well, he could forget it. She absolutely refused to look his way. He wanted forgiveness, did he? Wanted her to make it easy on him?

As she brought up the coffee, grateful that in another few minutes she'd be off-duty, she allowed herself another quick glance towards the couple. The sight of Tara's smooth coffee skin side by side with Nick's golden tan punched at her gut, leaving a visceral sharp-edged pain that almost made her double over. Clearing the last of the plates from the table, she headed back down to the galley, determined to keep herself busy, but within half an hour she'd tidied everything away. Now what? She looked around the spotless kitchen and, unable to help herself, closed her eyes, blinking back threatening tears. She had to get out of here. Without stopping to grab a bag or purse, she stuffed her phone in her back pocket and walked as quickly as she could towards the stern, praying that none of the guests would hail her. If they asked for anything, she might just tell them where to go.

As soon as she stepped off the boat she felt something lift, not a weight but more the constriction around her chest. Not that she felt any better. The leaden numbness still encased her, along with heavy-hearted resignation, but the constraint of having to hide it had gone. She laughed, a mirthless bitter sound; now she was free to be totally miserable.

Grateful for the anonymity of the busy town, Maddie walked along the promenade, in and out of the dappled patches of light, through the throngs of people intent on their own happiness. Hvar, it seemed, was full of beautiful, happy people and everywhere she looked there were couples: arms linked, fingers interlaced, stealing sly kisses or hip to hip, perusing restaurant menus. She scowled. Like she'd been with Nick in Stari Grad.

She completed a couple of aimless circuits of the piazza before she found herself in the little park just by the harbour and sat down beneath one of the palm trees. Opposite her on another bench were two women with toddlers running back and forth along the path and on a nearby seat a backpacker, her rucksack propped against her legs, held a FaceTime conversation on her phone. Maddie had never felt so alone in her life. She picked up her phone. Nina. Her mum. Her sister. She couldn't phone any of them. Her fingers strayed to Instagram. Unable to help herself, she gave into morbid curiosity and searched for Tara's feed.

#Engagementjoy #Justgotengaged #Foundtheone

Maddie stared at the picture. Tara's shining eyes gazing up at Nick's, her mouth parted. It felt as if a hand was squeezing her heart. The pressure in her chest hurt so much it was hard to breathe.

Idiot. Idiot. Idiot. How on earth could she have possibly believed that Nick would choose her over Tara? Look at the woman, for God's sake. It was pitiful.

Needing the cold facts to drum some sense into her, she clicked on a link to one of the newspaper websites and another bigger picture of Tara and Nick.

Tara Lloyd-Jones, twenty-seven has bagged her very own man of mystery, Nick Hadley, who, it's rumoured, is in the running for the next Bond film. Tara commented, 'We're thrilled to announce our engagement. It's been a whirlwind romance but I knew straight away Nick was the man for me. I hope that people will leave us alone to enjoy the rest of our holiday cruising on the Dalmatian coast.'

Maddie looked around, goose bumps covering her arms. She'd lost track of how long she'd been here. The mums had scooped up the toddlers and were long gone and the FaceTime girl had shouldered up her backpack and trudged away towards the piazza, where the crowds had thinned and lights were beginning to wink out.

Wearily she rose to her feet, walking with slow reluctant steps along the front. She had nowhere else to go. The normally busy promenade was quiet now and there'd been a new arrival, a huge gin palace of a boat. As Maddie neared she saw the name. *Never Say Never Again.*

A small sad smile lifted her mouth. Bill was in town.

411

Cory and Tara would be besides themselves. She scanned the boat for signs of life but the yacht was closed down tight for the night. Not a single chink of light showed anywhere. Maybe they'd all decamped to some posh party somewhere or a private villa.

With relief she pushed open the door to her cabin, having made it back on board without seeing anyone.

As she walked in, someone stood up from where they'd been sitting on her bed.

'Holy shit!' She froze in the doorway but Nick stepped forward, pulled her in and shut the door behind her, his hands on her shoulders.

'What are you doing in here?' she snarled, wrenching herself free. Shit, she couldn't do this. If he touched her again she might break and she had her pride. She was not going to let him see what he'd done to her.

'Maddie –' his eyes were confused and so they damn well should be '– this is all a terrible mess and it's not what it seems at all.'

'Just go,' she said, terrified she was going to cry in front of him.

'I can't. I need to explain.'

He'd chosen Tara; what was there to explain? 'Don't worry. I get it and I really don't want to talk to you.'

He stepped towards her, putting out his hands.

She put her arms up so that he missed her. 'Don't touch me,' she ground out through her gritted teeth.

'Maddie, this is all a mistake. I can explain.' He raked

his fingers through his hair, which stuck up in tufts as if he'd been doing that non-stop, and she had to admit the purple shadows under each eye were back. But then guilt did that to a man.

'Oh, dear lord, have you any idea how clichéd that sounds,' she sniffed with contempt or what she hoped conveyed contempt, giving him the evil eye. 'Look, you don't have to explain. We had a few days' fun. You were on the rebound. We're consenting adults. You realised you'd made a mistake.'

'That's rubbish and you know it.' Nick's face flushed with dull anger.

'Oh, come on, Nick. You said yourself, you want to live a little. Experience life. You came back, saw her and realised that she's the better bet. Her or dull old Maddie? Not exactly a difficult choice.'

'What?' Nick's eyes flashed and he took a step back. A small part of her relished the feeling of scoring a direct hit. 'That's what you think of me? That I'm so shallow? Really? You think that I would sleep with one person one day and go off with another the next?'

'Er, hello,' she said with hollow triumph that tasted bitter on her tongue. 'Isn't that what you did? Bye-bye, Tara. Hello, Maddie.'

He flinched and she clenched her hands to stop the natural instinct to reach out towards him. Instead she let her anger and disappointment take hold, enjoying the rush of adrenaline pouring through, a welcome relief to the hollow emptiness. 'Didn't take much to move onto me when she left the boat, did it?

'So yeah. I think you're shallow. Pretty much.' She felt sick as she said the words, with the realisation that that was exactly how it had been. She'd been hoping she was wrong but . . . it was everything she'd feared. No sooner had Tara gone . . . he'd suddenly been interested in her. It hurt. Really hurt. More than she could have imagined it would. She threw up her head and with a sneering glare added, 'And, to be honest, it suited me. I fancied you. Fancied a shag. A holiday fling.' Tossing the words at him like vicious pebbles, she ran a contemptuous look down his body. 'You're quite hot.' She shrugged. 'Who wouldn't?'

A red flush darkened his cheekbones and she watched his Adam's apple bob several times.

'Is that really what you think of me?' he asked, his voice so low she had to strain to hear it.

The lump stuck in her throat was impossible to swallow. He deserved this. He'd hurt her; he deserved to hurt back. She nodded.

Nick's face was expressionless as he turned and walked out without saying another word.

She waited until the door closed behind him and burst into tears.

Chapter 30

Her gritty, swollen eyes were probably going to be an asset, thought Maddie as she approached the *Never Say Never Again*, her footsteps slow and heavy with reluctance. She hated asking for help but she couldn't think of another option. It was only six o'clock but she could already see signs of life. Her eyes might score an early morning sympathy vote and, let's face it, she didn't have much to lose.

She was exhausted. That was what not sleeping all night did for you. She'd tossed and turned until, at four-thirty, she'd officially declared insomnia the winner and packed some of her things.

Now, with the air of an abandoned orphan, she stood looking up at the top deck, her suitcase in one hand. Creeping nervously out of the *Avanturista*, she'd felt like a grubby thief but it had been a massive relief that no one had spotted her.

'Hey, Maddie, what are you doing up at this godforsaken hour?' Max, looking as handsome as ever, grinned at her, lurking down on the jetty.

'Hi. I don't suppose Bill is up yet?'

'You're in luck; he's on the top deck having breakfast.'

Maddie twisted her fingers together, taking in a hurried now-or-never breath. 'W-would you mind asking if I could . . . er . . . erm . . . speak to him for a minute?'

Max's gentle face stilled and he gave her a cautious smile. 'Come on board. Bring your case.'

He waited for her as she climbed the stairs to reach where he was standing and he pushed his mop aside. 'You in trouble or something?'

'Or something.' Maddie gave him a bleak look. It went against the grain asking for help but she didn't know where to turn. There wasn't a flight home for several days and this was a huge boat; there must be some work she could do. Perhaps give one of the other crew a bit of a break.

'I'm hoping Bill might give me a job for a couple of days.' She just needed a breathing space.

He shot her a sympathetic look as he led her up towards the top deck. A split second of déjà vu assailed Maddie, except this time there was no Nick to make her feel slightly less intimidated by the wealth on display. With him at her side she hadn't felt like Little Orphan Annie.

Maddie didn't have the courage to phone Ivan; instead she sent him a text, explaining that, due to personal circumstances, she needed a couple of days off but that she'd be back in time for them to take the boat back to Split. His response brought a watery smile before she flopped back onto the plush stateroom bed.

> Siri and Douglas have explained the situation. Take the time you need. See you on Wednesday. Want me to punch him for you? Just to let you know, we'll be leaving the mooring tomorrow. We'll be anchored ten minutes out at the Pakleni islands. Otok Jerolim. In the bay facing Hvar, any water taxi will find us. Ivan.

She stared around the luxurious room, deliberately blocking the memory of being here with Nick. Instead she replayed her conversation with Bill over breakfast earlier that day.

He'd been his usual blunt self, after insisting she had breakfast with him, and she had to admit she'd got quite a taste for Eggs Benedict, although after this week she might never have them again. Real life was looming.

'You can stay as long as you like. I'm getting free labour. I need more storyboards.'

'I only need a couple of days until my flight home. As I said, things got a bit uncomfortable on the boat and I need some breathing space.' When she'd asked if she might work for him for a few days, he'd calmly accepted her story that there'd been a personal dispute on board that was making it difficult for her to stay. If it had come to it, she would have explained that she'd fallen in love with a guest, but she was grateful that Bill had been more interested in acquiring her drawing skills than why she was there.

'Not a problem. You can have the cabin you had last time.'

'I don't suppose you've got anything smaller?' ventured Maddie. 'I don't want to be a guest.'

Bill roared with laughter. 'If I had Benson here, he'd be in a stateroom with champagne on tap and I'd be paying him. If you want to stay, you're a guest.' His eyes brightened. 'But don't worry; I'll work you hard. And we've got a party coming up; it'll be all hands to the deck that night. Glo's been detained on the mainland, she's shopping, so I'll need some help sorting the last-minute party stuff out. You can be my PA on that one.'

As she lay back on the plus bed in the stateroom, her tired eyes drooping, her phone beeped again.

You OK? Atmosphere here is toxic. If I didn't want to abandon Douglas, I'd ask to join you. Let me know you're safe. Not been press-ganged into the Croatian Navy or run off with a millionaire. Siri xxx

At least Siri knew that Douglas was hers. She bet that there was a fair amount of sneaking down the corridor to his new room after dark. Her stomach clenched, remembering Nick sitting waiting for her on her bed last night, and she pressed her fingertips onto her forehead, the harsh words she'd thrown at him haunting her. Why hadn't she let him explain? But what could he possibly say? He'd made a mistake and realised that Tara was the one for him, after all? The thought of him saying the words out loud made her wince. He was so stupid. Nearly as stupid as she was for falling in love with the great oaf. He was stupid for allowing himself to be manipulated by Tara and going back to her. Why couldn't he see that the only person Tara would ever love was herself?

And she was even more stupid for believing that he'd ever have chosen her over Tara.

Giving into the headache pressing at her temples, she closed her eyes and curled up in a ball, clutching her knees as if that might keep the rest of the world at bay.

'Bill, I'm supposed to be working for you,' protested Maddie several hours later, with a determined brave face.

'Aaron and Max work for me; they're coming too.'

'They are also related to you,' she pointed out.

Bill waved a hand as if he were swatting a bee. 'You have to eat; I'd be paying for it either way. Boys, you ready?'

Max and Aaron, in their matching polo shirts and chinos, grinned at Maddie.

'He always gets his way,' said Aaron, taking her arm. 'You might as well cave now. I'm starving and I don't want to be hanging around waiting for you dudes to duke it out.'

'Besides, it'll do my reputation no harm being seen with a beautiful young lady.'

Maddie snorted. 'You're scraping the barrel here, mate.' She pressed at the bags under her eyes and pushed her tangled curls away from her face.

Bill stared at her. 'Maddie, I see plenty of beautiful women on a daily basis. Hell, I'm surrounded by them, hounded by them, and I'm telling you, from a man who knows, you've got it all going on. Looks, brains and charm. All the assets you need.

'Now are we going or not?'

Maddie gave a shrug, grateful that she'd chosen to put on Siri's shift dress this morning, determined to leave with her head held high if she'd bumped into anyone, and fell into step alongside Aaron as Max and Bill walked ahead, stopping frequently to assess the other boats on the front. She looked fixedly forward, not looking around at anyone in case she spotted anyone from the *Avanturista,* and was grateful when they finally arrived at a restaurant tucked away in one of the side alleys.

Oh, dear God, no! Maddie bit back a groan as she smiled at the waitress taking her order. There at the entrance of the restaurant were Cory and Tara, nudging each other and whispering. She ducked her head. They'd recognised Bill, but thankfully hadn't spotted her – yet. The two of them began to talk with extra-loud voices, lots of animation and a considerable amount of posing.

And then, just at exactly the wrong moment, Maddie looked up. Cory stared before mouthing *Oh my God* and then frantically tugging at Tara's shirt. Their shocked faces were a classic cartoon moment as they looked from Bill to her and back to Bill. It took all of ten seconds for the two of them to capitalise on the heaven-sent opportunity.

Maddie might have found it amusing if she hadn't caught sight of Nick's grim face, his mouth one tight slash across his face. Her stomach tightened and she swallowed hard. His eyes bored into hers but she wasn't going to look at him. Instead she glanced at Douglas, who gave her a brief nod, a touch of concern obvious in his kind eyes, while Siri flashed her a broad smile, clearly amused by the two models' dilemma.

'Maddie,' gushed Tara, coming straight over to their table, ploughing through the other diners without a care. 'Aren't you going to introduce us to your friend?'

Knowing that Bill was more than able to handle himself, she allowed herself a small inward smile.

'Bill,' she said gravely, although her eyes danced with amusement, 'let me introduce you to Tara and Cory. They're models, you know.'

Bill's eyes twinkled as they met hers. 'I guessed that. And how do you know Maddie?' he asked, all joviality.

Tara tossed her beautiful hair over her shoulder, 'Well, she's been crewing for us but, to be honest . . . well, she's more of a friend. You know what it's like, living in close proximity on a yacht. You all get to know each other terribly well and all pitch in, don't you?'

Maddie turned her snort into a cough, catching Max's eye, and he had to turn away. He'd obviously recognised Tara's hair and knew exactly who she was.

'Well, that's just dandy. I'm really grateful that you've been able to spare Maddie while she works on a little project for me.'

Tara shot her a suspicious glance and Maddie amazed herself by managing to adopt a pleasant bland expression.

'Of course we can spare you,' Tara said as if dispensing great largesse, before adding, 'Perhaps you could do with some more help too.'

Cory let out a small outraged gasp and nudged Tara sharply in the ribs.

Bill knitted his brows together, as if giving it great thought, but Maddie could see he was amusing himself at Tara's expense.

'Hmm, thing is . . . well –' he turned his head left and right, as if checking for unseen spies '– I'm working on a new film.' He tapped his nose in a hackneyed gesture that almost had Maddie snorting again. 'Hush-hush. Maddie's one of my trusted circle.'

Tara's eyes almost popped out of her head.

'And . . . er . . . um, how do you know Maddie?'

Bill beamed and then, as if he hadn't seen Nick all along, suddenly turned his head. 'Nick. How are you?' Maddie winced, remembering that Nick had told Bill he was her boyfriend.

'Fine,' said Nick with a curt nod, not making any attempt

to butter up Bill. His eyes were still narrowed on Maddie, which of course Bill hadn't missed. Maddie knew she was going to have to do some explaining.

Tara's head whipped around to look at Nick so fast she could have given herself whiplash. 'You know him?' she snapped.

Nick shrugged.

Douglas stepped forward and held out a hand to Bill. 'I'm Douglas, I chartered the boat and Maddie's been a real asset.' He winked at her. 'She's worked jolly hard looking after us; she deserves some time off.'

Bill beamed at Douglas, clearly liking what he saw.

'Nice to meet you all.' There was an awkward, what-happens-next? moment as the group loitered and it was obvious that neither Tara nor Cory had any intention of moving. Bill, not the least bit fazed by it, gave a surreptitious wink to Aaron, Max and Maddie.

'I'm throwing a party; why don't you guys pop along? Cocktails on deck from six tomorrow evening. The *Never Say Never Again*. I'll get Maddie to add your names to the guest list.'

Maddie saw Tara clasp her hands together and Cory do a funny little shudder.

She watched as Bill said with deliberate mischievous casualness, 'I'm hoping Barbara will pop by.'

'Streisand?' asked Maddie, wide-eyed, much to Aaron's amusement. He let out an appreciative bark of laughter, while Cory let out a little Chihuahua-like yip.

'No, honey, Broccoli.' Bill winked again at her. 'And Daniel might call in, with Rachel.'

'Craig?' she asked with a questioning wince, hearing Tara gasp next to her.

Bill raised his hands in an I-couldn't-possibly-say gesture. 'You'll have to wait and find out.'

'Oh, we'd love to,' gushed Tara, right on cue. 'Absolutely love to.'

Chapter 31

Robinson Crusoe, eat your heart out. The colour of the sea here never got old. Nick would always remember this incredible turquoise. He eased the paddleboard onto the tiny strip of shingle beach and immediately slipped the drawstring bag from his shoulders, removing his flip-flops and his wallet, wrapped in two layers of ziplock plastic bags. Aside from a T-shirt and a bottle of water, he hadn't brought anything else with him. Not much of a running-away kit, but he hadn't been thinking of much beyond getting off the boat. His panicky state brought to mind the frightened baas of the sheep when they were penned for shearing and their mindless changes of direction, only to find bars at every turn.

Dumping the paddleboard, he sat down in the shade of the pines that tumbled across the rocky ground down to the shoreline, grateful for the peace and quiet. This morning, despite the complaints of Cory and Tara, Ivan had moved the yacht out to this tiny island just opposite the port of Hvar. Nick, for one, was grateful for the solitude and so, he suspected, were Siri and Douglas. The silence buzzed in his ears and he dropped his head in his hands, conscious of a curious light-headed numbness. All his life he'd known his next step: what to do, where to go. At this moment he had no clue.

Since he'd woken up yesterday and discovered Maddie had gone, things had been a nightmare and it had got even worse after they'd bumped into Bill. The ugly scene in the piazza after they'd left the restaurant came back to him, with all its unpleasantness.

'Well, you kept that one quiet,' hissed Tara, her whole body radiating indignant fury as she stalked along the cobbled street, her fingers pinching hard on his bicep. 'We've been waiting to spot William Randall for over a week and you . . . you had met him.' She'd stopped dead and jabbed him in the chest with a sharp index finger, her face ugly and vindictive. 'I can't believe that you would do that to me.'

'Do what?' he'd asked, genuinely bewildered. Contempt and derision marred her features and he took a step back. It was as if she were a different person.

'Let me down so badly. What were you thinking? *I'll keep this one up my sleeve. Keep her on her toes.* Was it your ace?' Her eyes had glittered with malice and spite.

'Ace?' He frowned.

'Yes. Thought you'd use it,' she crowed.

'Use it for what?'

'As a bargaining tool. Negotiation.' Her mouth curled.

426

'But for what?' he asked again.

'Oh, come on, Nick. It's what everyone does. Keep something in reserve so that you've got something to hold over me.'

'But why would I do that?' Seriously, she wasn't making any sense.

'Everyone wants something.' She tossed her head, her voice snappish and irritable as if she was having to explain something to a child. 'That's how the game is played. I scratch your back, you scratch mine.'

But he'd never wanted anything. This hadn't been a game to him. And in that moment it was as if all the colour in life had faded and he'd felt like that child, the one who was too stupid to realise how the real world worked. The country farmer who didn't fit in at all. It hit him with a dull thud of realisation that she'd assumed he was like her, that he wanted something.

'Tara, what is it you want from me?'

Her heavy disdainful sigh made him feel even more stupid as she looked him up and down. 'You were supposed to play the game. You're my foil. Look good beside me. You're good-looking enough to pass for someone famous. Enough that people give us a second glance and wonder who you are.'

'Huh! Well that's . . . that's put me in my place.'

'What? I've just paid you a compliment.' She rolled her eyes with impatience. 'Told you you could pass for someone famous. What more do you want?'

Sitting here on the beach, that awful sick feeling came back to him. Not at her words but at his own naïve stupidity, the pride and vanity that had let him believe Tara wanted him for himself. His head had been turned by her sophistication, glamour and worldly experience.

Now he winced at the memory of his response.

'Is that all you want? To be seen with the right person?'

'Oh, dear God. You're so wet behind the ears, aren't you, darling? Of course it's about being seen with the right person. Do you know how many followers I have on Instagram? You know our proposal has gone viral. My agent is delighted.'

'What about . . . love, a relationship, a partner?' He'd stared at her, unable to believe he'd got it so wrong.

'Don't tell me you thought you were in love with me? That's so sweet.'

His fingers clenched around a pebble, remembering the sudden surge of anger he'd felt when he realised she'd played him. Sobbed all over him. Cried because he didn't love her. Made him feel guilty.

'No, Tara,' he'd said, snapping his head up and looking directly in her eyes. 'I never thought I was in love with you. I cared about you. Because I'm a decent bloke. You might think sweet is weak and derisible, but you're missing out.' He'd laughed, harsh and mirthless, because he'd messed up so badly with the one person who should have counted. 'I know what love is.'

He held his hand up to his face, rubbing the smooth

428

sides of the pebble between finger and thumb, trying to slow his breathing. The panicky bird's wings beating in his chest. He loved Maddie. He had to see her, talk to her. Tell her what an idiot he'd been. Explain that he'd been too stupid to see through Tara's manipulation. He shook his head as her final words came back to him.

'*I know what love is*,' Tara had mimicked in a cruel, childish voice. 'Bully for you. In the meantime, we have a few more days to get through of this holiday. I expect you to play ball. Pay for the holiday. You breathe one word about our non-engagement, I will make sure the whole world knows what a love rat you are. Instagram, Twitter, the papers.' And with that she'd stalked off to link her arm through Cory's and moments later he'd heard her laughing along with the other model.

Nick hurled the pebble into the sea as hard and as far as he could. Like he cared about that.

At least no one in the family had heard anything about the engagement and he thanked God that his Dad was wedded to *The Times* and the rest of the family weren't that into Instagram. He wouldn't want his family dragged into the mess.

Maybe he should have given them the heads-up, but he was too embarrassed and ashamed. What an idiot, too big for his boots, thinking he was in the big league. Dan and Jonathon would never let him hear the end of it.

Nick rubbed a hand over his tired, gritty eyes, feeling the ache in his shoulder from paddling this far. The wind whispered through the feathery pine needles of the trees around him and from high above him birdsong echoed, clear and high, as he breathed in the sharp, clean air. There was a moral to this story. The nagging feeling that life was passing him by had been well and truly exorcised. Painful clarity brought with it the realisation that he missed the farm more than he could ever have imagined and he missed Maddie. He could picture her in the kitchen at home, taking the piss out of him with Dan and Jonathon. Telling them what an arse he'd been, recounting with great glee the 'We are hot, the boat has been paid for' story, describing the salmon-pink shorts as well as sending herself up and revealing she'd been wearing the same FatFace shorts as him.

No wonder Maddie had been so furious with him.

What a fucking idiot.

Douglas was the only one on deck, studying the screen of his laptop as usual, when Nick clambered aboard, hauling up the paddleboard.

'Good trip?'

'Yeah. Good to get some exercise.' Nick rolled his shoulders, feeling a welcome ache in the muscles.

'I'm missing my weekly game of squash,' said Douglas, patting his pudgy middle. 'Going to be hell getting back to it. You play?'

'I'm a five-a-side man,' said Nick. 'Never played squash.' He didn't even know where the nearest squash court was.

'You getting changed for this shindig?' Douglas grimaced. 'Everyone's getting very excited.'

Nick sighed. 'Who wouldn't want to catch a glimpse of James Bond?' It would be something to tell the family; they'd be impressed at that, if nothing else.

Douglas laughed. 'Probably won't turn up. It's all hype, although Cory and Tara are beside themselves with excitement.'

'I can imagine,' said Nick dryly. Tara had already given him strict instructions that he wasn't to leave her side.

'I'd best go change. Ivan will be driving the launch over to Hvar at five forty-five. I bet it's the first time ever that Cory and Tara will be ready and waiting bang on the button.'

Clothes had been selected and laid out for him on the bed, as if he were incapable of dressing himself. Clenching his jaw, he ignored them and stalked into the shower, slamming the bathroom door. The quick shower did nothing to quell the irritation he felt and he glared at himself in the mirror.

Stupid bastard.

He shrugged into the linen shirt that Maddie had had laundered for him and ignored those bloody poncey shorts. A wry smile crossed his face as he remembered Maddie's views on them and instead he pulled out his favourite cargo shorts; he'd had enough of trying to be something he wasn't. As he pulled on the worn comfortable fabric, he wondered what Maddie would be wearing.

Maddie. Maddie. Maddie. All his thoughts kept going back to her. He needed to talk to her.

When he emerged from his cabin, everyone else was already assembled on deck. Tara had never looked more stunning in a show-stopping white dress with a large solitary peacock feather running down one side. This was co-ordinated perfectly with exactly the right shade of royal-blue shoes with laces wrapped around slender ankles and calves. Her hair was bundled on top of her head and a few delicate, wispy tendrils escaped, curling about her beautiful face, artfully arranged in a way that he knew had probably taken an hour to achieve, while her eyes glittered with the hard edge of diamonds. She cut a striking figure, cold and detached with chilly hauteur. And he'd never disliked her more.

'Evening, Max,' said Maddie as she emerged from her temporary cabin and walked along the corridor to where he stood with a clipboard and guest list. He looked rather gorgeous and very young in his smart tuxedo.

'Evening, Maddie. You look sensational.' He kissed her on both cheeks.

'Thank you.' She gave him a smile. 'I'm so grateful that you've put me up. I feel I'm putting you to loads of trouble.'

'Maddie, you're kidding. Some of the divas we get on board . . .' He pulled a sour face. 'You're a piece of cake.'

'Cake is always good.' Her eyes twinkled. 'Chocolate or carrot?' she teased.

'Definitely carrot.' He winked at her. 'My favourite. I don't like stuff that's too rich; it never sits well.'

'You're such a charmer. I'm afraid the richer the better. I love chocolate cake.' She laughed. 'But thanks for looking after me. It's much appreciated, as being here yesterday and today has given me some breathing space.' She sighed and ran her hand over the fabric of Siri's borrowed dress.

'You look great,' he added.

'I'm a bit nervous about meeting Bill's wife for the first time.'

'Glo? You're kidding me. She's going to love you.'

'That's what Bill keeps saying.' Maddie left him to mount the stairs to the main deck, where the party was already in full swing.

'Good evening, madam.' Krish, the steward, stepped forward with a large glass of champagne flutes. 'What do you think?'

The deck area had been transformed into an exotic Bedouin tent with hundreds of strings of coloured paper lanterns and jewel-bright triangles of silk fabric suspended like sailcloths. All the furniture had been removed and replaced with long silk upholstered benches covered in tasselled bolsters and cushions. Although she'd been dashing around all afternoon helping out with last-minute calls, polishing glasses, she'd been sent to get ready before the finishing touches had been made.

'Wow. You've worked hard. This looks amazing,' she said. He nodded and turned to the next guest.

The deck hummed with the buzz and chatter of a good party and she drifted through the crowd with her glass of champagne to talk to Dr Cannon, who was standing on her own with an amused look on her face.

'Evening, Maddie. Enjoying the show?'

'I've only just come up. Bill wanted a few final changes to the storyboards.' Actually, she'd been delaying deliberately in her cabin, waiting for enough people to arrive so that she could hide in the crowd. Now, using Zoe as a shield, she scanned the crowd, spotting Tara on the other side of the busy deck.

'Yeah, he's a slave-driver,' said Zoe with an ironic grin. 'I haven't had a single patient since you. I'm hoping one of this lot will break a nail or something. Or maybe you've developed a blister from all that drawing.'

Maddie's eyes narrowed thoughtfully. 'Do you know much about eating disorders?'

Zoe's eyes shot to her face in surprise. 'Enough to know they're very bad for your health.'

'Not me, someone . . . someone I know.'

The doctor followed her gaze across the deck. 'Do they want help?'

'I think so.' Maddie winced. 'Although maybe it comes under crew confidentiality.'

'If it saves a life, there's no such thing,' said Zoe crisply. 'Eating disorders can seriously reduce life expectancy. It can cause so many other health issues, all of which worsen the longer it goes on.'

Maddie sucked in a breath. She might not like Tara but she couldn't not do anything. Quickly, before she could change her mind, she told Zoe about Tara's eating habits and the constant sickness.

'It's a tricky one,' said Zoe, 'but she needs help. I'm happy to try and speak to her this evening, perhaps see if she'll come see me tomorrow.'

'That would be wonderful,' breathed Maddie. 'I'd be so grateful. I think, when I spoke to her, she was worried.'

'OK. I'll see what I can do. Now, what about you?'

'Me?'

'Yes, you. You could do with a good night's sleep. Something bothering you?'

'Nothing that you can fix,' said Maddie with a wince.

'Ah, broken heart then,' said Zoe with alarming insight.

'Is it that obvious?' asked Maddie, realising that only candour would work with the insightful doctor.

'Doesn't take Sherlock Holmes to work it out. Boats are great until a relationship goes wrong and then everything's a bit too close for comfort. You fled in a hurry. And I did wonder if there was something with the "concerned friend" who came rushing to rescue you from Bill's evil clutches. Is he fully recovered from his food poisoning?'

'Yes, more's the pity,' snarled Maddie.

'Oh, dear. I don't wish to be interfering but . . . being a sensible middle-aged woman who's had a fair amount of experience, have you spoken to him?'

Maddie closed her mouth with truculent finality.

'I guessed as much. Honestly, you young people. Every communication tool under the sun and none of you seem able to talk to each other.' Zoe shook her head, lifting her champagne glass to take a long slow pull. 'How long after your row did you sneak off the boat and come here?'

With a roll of her eyes, Maddie turned to the doctor. 'I think you are bloody Sherlock Holmes. How did you know we had a row?'

'Because if you'd spoken nicely to each other and had a sensible conversation, you'd still be on board the boat. I'm not prying, dear, but you look unhappy. And –' Zoe nodded towards the other side of the deck '– so does he.'

Following her gaze, Maddie looked across the busy deck. Tara had positioned herself opposite Cory and Simon, and from here Maddie could see that both the two women were looking over each other's shoulders, their eyes constantly roving this way and that, seeking out the right people to speak to.

Beside her, Nick looked ill at ease, like a prisoner longing for escape, and although Tara never missed an opportunity to touch him or tug him to her side as if she wanted everyone to know that he was with her, he looked like a cardboard cut-out brought along as a prop. Maddie's lips pursed and she clutched her evening bag tightly to her side. Why did she even feel sorry for him? But she couldn't help it; he didn't look happy. There were hollows in his cheeks and his mouth . . . She shouldn't be looking at his mouth, but the corners seemed perpetually down-turned.

'It's his own fault,' she said shortly. He was the one that had proposed to Tara. 'Excuse me, I ought to go and find the rest of the party from my boat.'

Zoe just toasted her with her champagne flute, the ghost of a smile on her lips, which made Maddie feel rather churlish. The other woman was a doctor; wasn't it part of the Hippocratic Oath to try and help?

Siri's bright red hair was easy to spot and when Maddie joined her she introduced her to the small group of people that she and Douglas had got chatting to. Most of them were friends of friends or shared City contacts with Douglas and, although everyone was friendly enough, Maddie couldn't help feeling like a third wheel.

It was a relief, an hour later, when Bill hailed her in his booming voice. 'Maddie –' he grabbed her arm and propelled her over to one of the tables near the bar '– come meet Gloria.'

The small plump woman gave Maddie an unnerving once-over and didn't say a word.

'Maddie, this is Gloria. Glo, my love, this is Maddie the mermaid.'

'You don't look like a mermaid to me,' said Gloria with a narrow-eyed stare and a very gravelly voice with, rather surprisingly, a definite tone of the Midlands.

'And I didn't when they fished me out of the sea,' replied

Maddie, realising she was being judged and needed to prove herself. 'I looked a right state. More drowned rat territory and then I threw up all down the side of Bill's boat. I don't think mermaids do that.'

Gloria's face relaxed as she let out a delighted belly laugh. 'Now I know why he took to you. Where are you from?'

'Selly Oak.'

'Kidderminster.' Gloria pointed to herself. 'I knew I recognised that accent. What's a girl like you doing out here, swimming with sharks?'

'Learning to find the dolphins,' said Maddie with a grin, recognising a kindred spirit.

'Good. After a while you figure it all out. Every now and then Bill gets it wrong and I have to step in and rescue him. I thought you were one of those starstruck model types who latches onto him.'

'No, but I brought a couple with me,' said Maddie. 'They're mostly harmless, just a bit single-minded about what they want.'

'Mostly harmless, I like that. Like mosquitoes, mostly harmless but bloody irritating and I take great delight in swatting them, which if I were of a more charitable disposition I wouldn't. But they say charity starts at home and this definitely isn't home.' She gestured at the yacht.

Maddie smiled. 'It's quite intimidating.'

'It's a boat. If we were supposed to live on the sea, I'm sure the good Lord would have granted us flippers. I much prefer dry land . . . but then this gives us privacy which, away from home, can be a blessing.'

Before Maddie knew it, Glo and she were deep in conversation. She was one of the easiest people to talk to and, it turned out, the buyer of the art in the salon. Before long Glo was telling her about some of the pictures in her Florida home.

'You have a real Degas?' asked Maddie for the second time, still not quite believing it.

'Yes. Twenty-fifth wedding anniversary present. I tell you, if I'd known when I married him how well he was going to do, I might have run a mile.'

'Why?' asked Maddie.

'You think I've always been this comfortable around all this?' Glo waved her hand. 'It's taken a while to adjust. Mostly I stay home in Florida but Bill misses me terribly.' She grinned at Maddie. 'He gets awful lonely, bless him.' Then she lowered her voice. 'I think he just likes me to keep the hot totties at bay.'

Maddie burst out laughing.

'Now, tell me more about Paris. I've not been there for years. Where should I go and what was the best art you saw?'

Grateful for another distraction from Nick, who seemed to be constantly in her peripheral vision, Maddie gave Glo a detailed rundown of all her favourite pieces in Paris.

After sitting chatting for nearly half an hour, Glo pulled a rueful face. 'And now I'm going to be in trouble for monopolising you. It's been lovely talking to you and tomorrow we'll have another chinwag about art. I hear there's a really good museum in Hvar and none of this lot will come with me. Philistines, the lot of them. However, as this is a social occasion, I guess I'd better do the hostess thing.' Her comic grimace made Maddie laugh.

'It's a date.'

'Now, where are your mosquitoes? I'll go make them welcome,' she said, before adding with an evil grin, 'and squash their pretensions. Tell them Bill's already cast the film.'

'You'll break their hearts,' said Maddie, pointing out Cory and Tara on the other side of the deck as Glo bustled over with righteous wifely zeal.

Left on her own, she drifted to the side rail, sipping at her champagne, gazing up at the fort lit up for the night, guarding the town, content to eavesdrop on the conversations around her.

'Have you seen Daniel and Rachel yet?' a tall blonde woman in the tightest white jeans Maddie had ever seen asked a second woman in a breathy voice, no doubt because her circulation was about to be cut off.

'No, I bet they're not coming,' replied the second woman in a whiny disgruntled voice. 'Just hype, although I think I saw Katy Perry and Orlando Bloom.'

'Really?' asked the other woman, although it came out as *Rarely*. 'No way.'

'I swear it looked like her. He always looks so different.'

'Hmm,' came the disbelieving reply. 'The only person I've seen is that Instagram engagement girl. You know, the one that proposed to her boyfriend, right about there.' The woman almost creaked in her jeans as she carefully leaned over the rail and pointed to the promenade. 'Look, you can see the restaurant name in the picture. It was right there.'

'Gosh, I didn't realise that. And she's here on the boat?'

'Yes, with the guy.'

'I've heard he's Mr Hottie. Is he as gorgeous as everyone says? Where are they? What's she wearing tonight?'

'White dress. Big peacock feather on it. Designer, by the looks of things. You can't miss her.'

'Oh God, can you imagine the wedding pictures with those two?'

'Well, let's hope he looks a bit happier in them. He looks a bit miffed tonight. Did you see the video? Talk about stunned, but then I guess it's not every day your girlfriend proposes to you in front of an audience.'

'No, but good on her, girl power and all that. Why shouldn't she?'

'Hmm, not sure about that. I reckon he'd have got lynched by the crowd if he'd said no. And he didn't say yes. You can see it if you watch the video carefully.' Astonishingly, White Jeans worked a mobile phone out of her back pocket, which was a Herculean feat in its own right.

'Didn't he?'

'No, watch.'

Dropping all pretence of studying the view and the fort,

Maddie turned round. 'Excuse me,' she said. 'Could I see that?'

White Jeans shrugged and held out her phone.

The video, despite being shaky and out of focus for half of the time, was clear enough to show exactly what had happened. It was also enough to show Maddie that she'd totally misjudged Nick. All this time she'd assumed that he'd done the proposing. Watching his face, if the situation hadn't caused her so much pain it would have been laughable. Every horrified feeling was broadcast across his face before he managed to compose himself, fixing a bland expression of equanimity on his face. Perhaps because she knew him, she could see that, behind the mask, he was acutely uncomfortable.

Her stomach contracted, hard and fast, the champagne she'd drunk swirling uncomfortably. Jerking her head, she scanned the deck, her eyes tracking, looking for the blonde head of hair. She needed to find him. Now. Talk to him. In her head she could hear him asking in that low urgent voice, 'Is that really what you think of me?' She had to find him. Tell him she'd lied.

But as she searched through the crowds of people there was no sign of him. For once Tara was flying solo and talking to an older man with greying hair who looked slightly familiar. He was rather like lots of people Maddie had seen this evening, thinking that she'd met them some place before but couldn't think where and then realising she'd seen them on the telly.

'Maddie . . .' Bill grabbed her as she walked past the bar area near the entrance to the salon, hoping to see him in one of the corners of the yacht. 'I hear you met Glo and she loved you, I knew she would. Come and meet some people.' He nodded towards a group of people standing by the Sonia Delaunay painting, almost shielded from view by Aaron standing on what looked like guard duty. She recognised two of the faces and, in front of them, Glo beckoning her with a broad welcoming smile.

She hesitated for a minute but Bill was ushering her towards the salon. With one last hopeful scan of the crowd, she gave in. Confronting Nick at a party probably wasn't the best plan of action.

She looked at her watch. Theirs was a conversation that needed to be had without interruptions and distractions.

'Bill, can I ask another favour?'

'Sure.'

Bill had rolled his eyes, muttered something about young love, grumbled that Gloria would approve and agreed that Aaron or Max could run her back to the *Avanturista*. Until then, she guessed meeting James Bond was a small consolation.

Thank God for silver fox movie guy whom Tara had latched onto in the last half hour. Nick moved away from her and Cory, his eyes searching the deck for another glimpse of Maddie. He'd seen her quite a few times during the evening and each time she'd been chatting away to someone. The last time he'd seen her she was ensconced with a middle-aged woman, her graceful artist hands gesticulating with enthusiasm, but now there was no sign of her anywhere. Perhaps she'd gone to bed already. His stomach dipped in disappointment. He could hardly go banging on cabin doors.

It had been a long evening and Tara, although clingy at first, had been uncharacteristically subdued since a visit to the toilet early on. Now, she was back to her usual dazzling self, charming the older man, who was some movie producer. Nick was knackered and, having accepted Bill's hospitality for as long as he could bear, he slipped off the yacht and walked along the promenade, the music of the party bouncing off the water. The town was quietening down but there were still plenty of bars open. He skirted the harbour area, where Ivan was dozing in the front seat of the launch. Going for a beer felt like the better option, so that he didn't feel a total loser going back to the *Avanturista* before everyone else.

Two beers later, neither of which had eased the dull ache in his stomach, he got into a water taxi on the other side of the harbour. The little boat bounced over the dark waves and Nick watched as the bright lights of Hvar and the fort guarding over the town receded.

So much had changed since the first visit to Hvar. Siri and Douglas both looked so much happier, even though they'd yet to go public. Poor Cory still traded on the assumption that Douglas would change his mind. She, along with Tara and Simon, now clung together like some bitchy collective that made him wonder why he'd ever wanted to be part of all that. How he wished that he could turn back the clock, go back to Tajna cove. Just the four of them. Images of the clear water, the sun sparkling on the rippling waves and Maddie's mischievous smile filled his head and regret pinched hard.

The *Avanturista* was in complete darkness when he returned, only the moon guiding him along the deck. This evening it was almost full, glowing with mysterious beauty, throwing the nearby islands into a relief of silver and black. Grabbing another beer from the galley, feeling a sense of freedom that no one else was here, he took himself up to the top deck and lay on one of the sun loungers looking up at the star-laden sky. If he watched for long enough he'd see a shooting star. It was a game he'd played lots of times with his sister when they were younger, making wishes for their future, too scared to share because if you told anyone what you'd hoped for it wouldn't come true. With a fond smile he could hazard a guess at what Nina would have wished for; she'd been in love with his best friend Sebastian for ever. In those days his wishes had been as simple as winning the next weekend's rugby fixture.

With a heavy sigh he rested the beer bottle on his chest. Maddie seemed as out of reach as the moon and he kept going over their heated final conversation, as he'd done for the last two sleepless nights. His thoughts turned muzzy and, giving in to tiredness, he closed his eyes and listened to the water lap, lapping at the hull, the background hum of the cicadas on the island and the far distant sounds of Hvar's nightlife.

He woke with a start to the sound of furniture being dragged across the deck below and Tara's voice, slightly slurred.

'Shh,' said Cory in a loud whisper that carried in the still night air.

Nick strained to look at his watch. He must have been asleep for a couple of hours.

'Quiet,' said Simon as Tara giggled and Cory let out a little snort of laughter.

'I am quiet,' said Tara, indignation in her voice.

'Be quieter,' said Simon. 'You don't want to wake everyone up.'

'I don't care,' said Tara, sounding unusually aggressive. Nick sat up and carefully put the beer bottle down beside him so as not to make a noise, feeling something wasn't quite right.

'You don't want them to catch us.' Simon's voice was lower.

Tara laughed nastily in a way that had Nick tensing. 'Simon, darling. Douglas's little blue-eyed boy. Always sucking up to him, but I guess it's useful having rich friends.'

Nick frowned but then Simon spoke.

'You can be such a bitch, Tara. Douglas is my best friend

because we looked out for each other at school. Neither of us fitted in but Douglas didn't care and he took me under his wing. Yeah, I'm lucky because he's a very generous guy but he's the most loyal mate you could ask for. And he wouldn't like this.'

Tara snorted and then carried on in a mocking cold voice, 'It's a wrap of coke, sweetie. It's not like we're main-lining heroin. Besides, I really don't care.'

'Keep your voice down. I tell you, Douglas wouldn't like it. He's pretty tolerant of most things, but not drugs.'

'Stuff Douglas, he's a boring prude.' Tara's voice rang out a little too loudly.

'Rich boring prude, please, Tara,' said Cory.

'Yes,' agreed Tara. 'Shame that gravy train has departed.'

'Thanks Tar, jealous much. It's just temporary. He'll come running back, he always does.'

'I wouldn't be so sure this time,' said Simon, a distinct tone of disgust in his voice which Nick almost liked him for.

'What's that supposed to mean?'

'If I didn't know better, I'd think he'd found someone else. He seems happier.'

'Who?' Tara laughed with derision. 'There's only us on the boat. What, you think he's got the hots for that fat Maddie girl? Don't be ridiculous.'

'Well, Simon had the hots for her, didn't you?' Cory's voice was sly.

'She was a potential shag.'

Nick clenched his fingers into a fist – OK, he really didn't like Simon – and rose slowly to his feet, taking a few silent steps to the top of the flight of stairs.

'Dear God. Seriously, Simon,' drawled Tara in catty outrage, 'you'd want to poke that? I thought you had some taste. Or are you desperate?'

'Actually, no, I'm not desperate. She's a nice girl.' He gave a self-mocking laugh. 'I thought I was in love with you, actually, Tara, but do you know what, I'm not that desperate.'

Nick heard the other man's footsteps retreating.

'Arse,' said Tara. '*She's a nice girl*,' she mimicked. 'She's a fat lump, with a backside as big as Birmingham.' Then, in a quieter voice, she added, 'I'd hate to ever get that big.'

There was a silence before she said, 'Does it worry you, Cory?'

'I'd worry more about looking like a bag lady. Seriously, like, where does she get her clothes from?' interjected Cory.

Tara laughed unkindly. 'Third-hand rejects. It looks as if she dresses from the wardrobe Oxfam forgot.'

'Or Oxfam rejected,' hooted Cory.

Nick saw Tara shake her head as he came down the last of the stairs, his fingers clenched hard at his sides. He'd never been so furious in his life.

'And have you heard how she speaks?' Tara's voice had risen in gleeful spite as she continued with her derisive diatribe. 'Who would want to be seen in public with that?

Those shorts she wears. Have you ever seen anything like it?'

'I have,' said Nick quietly, stepping from the shadows onto the deck.

'Nick!' Tara clutched at her throat. 'I didn't see you there. What happened to you? I didn't see you leave the party.'

'You were otherwise occupied. To be honest –' he sighed, the anger ebbing away and feeling weary to his bones '– I got fed up with it all. You. The shallowness and the bitchiness. And I could have borne it for a few days more but –' his lip curled as he looked at her, for the first time seeing the malice twisting her face '– when you started on Maddie, that was the final straw.'

'Her? What's she got to do with anything?'

Nick laughed. Tara would never understand in this lifetime. 'She's everything. Compared to you she's the sun, the moon, the stars, the sea.' Even though the words sounded ridiculously cheesy and his brothers would rag him to death right there and then if they'd been here, but he meant them with every last fibre of his heart. He'd do anything to tell her how much she meant him.

'What?' Tara's face twisted in disbelief, her eyes small and mean like a snake, her mouth petulant and cruel. 'What are you talking about?' Her voice was full of derision.

'I'm talking about Maddie. She's so many things.' He smiled, just thinking about them. 'Things that you wouldn't even prize. Kind-hearted, thoughtful, caring, warm, talented

. . . The list is so long I could go on but it wouldn't mean anything to you because those things don't mean anything to you. And the sad thing is she doesn't even believe she's all those things – another reason why I love her.' He gave a self-deprecating laugh, his heart lightening at saying the words out loud. 'And I really need to tell her that.'

From the corner of the deck a small shadow detached itself from the sofa.

'I think you just did,' said a soft voice.

Nick's heart went thunk in his chest as Maddie moved towards him, walking with bold strides as Cory and Tara stepped back to let her pass.

She came right up to him and stood in front of him, her face lit up by the moonlight and the love shining in her eyes.

He lifted a hand to her face, brushing back the curls from her cheek. 'Hey, you. I've missed you.'

'I missed you too. And –' her smile was starlight and sunshine '– I forgot to tell you something. I love you too.'

His heart would surely burst at that. With a smile, his breath slightly unsteady, he leaned forward and kissed her. The touch of her lips was like coming home.

'Shall we get out of here?' he asked her when they both came up for breath.

When he took her hand, he was suddenly aware of two pairs of eyes staring with complete amazement.

'W-what?' spluttered Tara, while Cory huddled next to her. 'You can't do this to me. Choose her over me!'

'There is no contest. You don't even come close. Goodbye, Tara,' said Nick, lacing his fingers through Maddie's and squeezing her hand.

'But Nick . . .'

For some reason that he would never understand they broke into a run, hand in hand, and headed towards the stern.

'Come on,' said Maddie, jumping off the back of the boat into the launch, giving him no choice but to jump with her. 'Let's get out of here. Do you want to be Thelma or Louise?'

Nick laughed as he landed in the boat, his heart flipping when she threw her arms around him and kissed him. 'Forgive me?'

'For what?'

'For thinking that you really would propose to Tara.'

'You thought I'd proposed!' He almost choked. 'Seriously?'

Maddie bit her lip and looked up at him, her eyes anxious and apologetic. 'Sorry, but you were engaged. Me, even Siri and Douglas . . . we just assumed.'

Nick rolled his eyes. 'I don't believe it.'

She turned on the engine and threw him a saucy smile as she pushed forward the throttle and the boat roared away from the yacht. 'Where to?'

'Wherever you want to go, as long as it's with me.'

'That's a given,' said Maddie with a shy smile as the boat headed out of the shelter of the bay into the open sea.

Epilogue

'Champagne. There's posh,' said Jonathon, dumping his keys and phone on the dresser on the side, spotting the bottle sitting in the centre of the table next to a large white box.

'And cake,' said Nina proudly, tapping the box.

'What are we celebrating?' asked Dan, kissing Gail, already seated at the kitchen table shelling peas. He looked at Nina and Sebastian, who were standing next to the table.

Nina shook her head but took a quick peep at the engagement ring on her finger as Sebastian put his arm across her shoulders.

Maddie hid a smile; that was old news and she was as thrilled as the rest of the family that Sebastian had proposed earlier in the month.

Nick put his hands on her shoulders and she tensed slightly. Everyone had been so welcoming but she didn't like being the centre of attention or the thought that she was stealing the limelight. 'Maddie has got some news.'

Everyone instantly looked at Lynda Hadley, who smiled

and shook her head. 'No, I'm not going to be a grandmother. Now, sit down, I'm more than ready for a glass of fizz.' She looked at the clock. 'Just waiting for Dad to come in.'

'Phew,' said Jonathon, putting his arm around his wife's shoulder. 'I was worried that Nick had beaten us to it.' Cath nudged him and gave a long-suffering what-are-you-like sigh.

'God, you lot are so competitive,' said Maddie, rolling her eyes. 'Is it any wonder Nina lives in Paris? There's too much testosterone in this family, some of the present company excepted.'

Nina laughed and linked her arm through Maddie's. 'Exactly.'

'Don't worry, doll. We're glad to have you on the girls' team,' said Gail, getting up from her chair and pushing Nick out of the way, coming alongside Nina to give her a quick hug.

Maddie squeezed her hand. 'Thanks, Gail.'

'Hold on.' Cath jumped up from her seat. 'I'm not being left out of the girl team.' She came up behind Maddie's other shoulder and leaned forward to join in the group hug.

Maddie had been living with Nick on the farm for the last three months and felt as much a part of the family as her own family – actually, probably more. It was as if there'd been a Maddie-shaped hole waiting to be filled all this time. She adored Nick's mum and got on well with all of his brothers and their partners and had a very soft spot for Nick's dad, Ken, who was a man of few words but what he said always seemed to count. But it was always best when Nina and Sebastian came back for a weekend.

'So what's the news if no one is pregnant?' asked Jonathon.

Nick looked at her. She drew in a deep breath. 'I've been offered a . . .' Suddenly she was too choked up to carry on. Nick squeezed her hand. 'I . . .' Tears blurred the expectant faces around her.

'What she's trying to say,' said Nick, dropping a kiss on her temple, 'is that my amazing girlfriend has been offered her very first exhibition at a prestigious gallery in Newcastle.'

'Oh, Maddie, darling,' said Mrs Hadley. 'That's wonderful news. You clever, clever girl.'

'Ooh, will they include that picture you did with me in it – the one in the farm shop and all those OAPs from the tour bus?' asked Gail.

'Yes,' replied Maddie, 'and the one in The Queen's Head, as well as the one at the livestock market.' Maddie had found a wealth of inspiration within the warmth of the local community and this family. She'd worked in the local pub behind the bar at lunchtimes and several evenings a week to ensure she paid her way, but during the rest of the time she'd been working on her new style of paintings, which she'd entitled her 'Fellside Neighbours' series.

She'd developed her own distinctive style, which was definitely unique to her. A Maddie Wilcox Croatian beach neighbours picture had even graced the walls of a certain art establishment in London, although its sojourn in the sophisticated gallery had been remarkably brief. It had sold almost immediately, for over a thousand pounds.

'They've agreed to take everything,' Nick butted in proudly. 'Everything she's done since she's been here and the Croatia pictures.'

'Which reminds me . . .' Nina jumped forward and opened the box on the table. 'Ta-da!'

'Oh, my, that's brilliant,' said Maddie, looking down at the top of the cake. 'How did you do that?'

'Nick got me a photo of the picture and I got it made into an edible cake-topper.' Nina screwed up her face. 'But I did make the cake.'

'It looks fabulous,' said Gail. 'Is the colour of the sea really like that?'

'Oh, yes,' said Maddie, turning to smile at Nick.

'It definitely is,' he agreed, smiling back at her.

'We are so going there on holiday, aren't we, Dan?' Gail poked her husband in the ribs.

'Yes, my love.'

'Well,' said Nick, taking Maddie's hand, 'we can recommend the perfect place.'

She turned to him, her eyes shining. 'We certainly can . . . Tajna bay . . . our secret cove in Croatia.'

Acknowledgements

I've so enjoyed writing this book. If you haven't been to Croatia – go, go, go!

I adored the Dalmatian Islands I visited, sadly I really didn't spend as much time as I'd have liked there (a year would have done) but I really hope that I've managed to bring the gorgeous scenery, the amazing blue of the oh so clear sea and the stunning historic towns to life.

It's been so wonderful to hear from so many readers who've read the *Romantic Escapes* series and added some of the settings of my books to their travel wish lists – I'm sure Croatia will make the grade too. I am always grateful to everyone that takes the trouble to get in touch, leave a review or recommend me to a friend. Those things make a writer's day so much brighter, especially when we're sitting on our own staring at a laptop screen and listening to imaginary voices in our heads!

I owe a massive thank you to my former colleague Gordana. When I first mentioned I was going to visit her home country of Croatia and planned to set a book there, she couldn't have been more helpful. Where would I have been without her initial fifteen-page email with recommendations, ferry times, car hire contacts, details of vineyards, olive oil co-operatives, secret beaches and so much more! I've shamelessly picked her brains over the last year and then repaid her by pinching all the names of her family to feature in the book.

Last but not least; my dear friend Donna Ashcroft, who plies me with Prosecco and pep talks on a regular basis, I'm surprised she's not sick of me by now; my fabulous super agent, Broo, who should probably receive some kind of award, or a sainthood, for constant reassurance and support. I'm surprised she's not sick of me either; and to the gorgeous Charlotte Ledger, my editor and publisher who always makes my books shine. Thank you ladies, I couldn't do it without you.